CARAVAN
OF
DREAMS

BETH LAPIN

Fio

FOR MARTY

THE PENNY PRESS
MAY 29, 1896

HARTFORD – The body of a woman was discovered on the eastbound track of the New England Railroad in East Hartford yesterday. Soon after the body was identified as the remains of Mrs. Williams, widow of the late 'Prince' Williams, who lived at the old Farmers' hotel in the meadow.... Her husband was the king of the Gypsies in New England and was a well known horse trader. He received a gorgeous funeral about 18 months ago.

ONE

Victoria had ignored the warning but, to be fair, it didn't come in the form of a vision, which was the usual case with her portents. That morning, she had decided she could no longer put off her visit to the cemetery. Winter storms had stopped her earlier in the week, but she felt an intense need to visit the grave of her son on this fourth anniversary of his passing.

She wouldn't bother her husband. She knew he mourned the loss of Wash as much as she, but he showed it in different ways. No, she would go alone, right after breakfast. The subtle subconscious voice saying, "I don't think so," didn't register with Victoria when she mentally planned her day. She didn't know that it was the beginning of the end.

Victoria rose from her bed and dressed. Her room, chilled from the nighttime temperatures, certainly was warmer than their caravan accommodations. She had pushed for the purchase of East Hartford's old Farmer's Hotel, and, like most of her ideas, it had been a good decision. It was large enough that her children and their families could come and go as they pleased, and had an innkeeper quarters for their married son. She sat down at her mirror and, as every morning, she braided her long graying hair, coiled and pinned it to her head, and covered it with her turkey red silk *diklo*, which she knotted at the nape of her neck. Her dark eyes stared back at her briefly as she put on her gold earrings and bangles. She never left her bedroom without them, a habit she had acquired when her husband had shown his appreciation of them. As her final step, she pulled on and laced her boots.

She stood, somewhat reluctantly, as her achy bones reminded her that she was getting on in years and should brew some willow bark tea. She shook her shoulders, covered them with her silk brocade shawl, and opened the bedroom door. Descending the stairs, Victoria heard noises in the kitchen. Her youngest daughter, Daisy, standing at the stove, was frying eggs. Victoria was pleased someone had remembered to check the chickens. She smiled at Daisy and considered she was becoming a useful young woman.

"Good morning, Mammis. Do you want some?" Daisy asked.

"Yes, dear, thanks," said Victoria as she poured herself some strong coffee and sat at the table. She glanced around.

"Dadrus and the others have taken the work wagons on the ferry across the river to Hartford," commented Daisy in response to her mother's appraisal of the kitchen. Victoria wasn't sorry she had missed the commotion but, for a brief second, she ached for her husband's embrace.

She glanced out the window at the weak winter sunshine. Bare tree limbs, outlined against the blue and white of the sky, were still, although she was certain it would be cold even without wind.

Daisy, following her look, said, "The men said they are forecasting a snowy February."

"This century is going out with a bang," Victoria added, thinking it was all the more reason to go to the cemetery that day. "I don't think so," was the subtle refrain that wafted past her consciousness. Her daughter placed a plate of eggs and crispy bacon in front of her and Victoria nodded her thanks.

"Any news?" asked Victoria, knowing that her husband and sons always had lively breakfast discussions.

"There's talk of a run on gold. The banks don't have enough to back themselves up."

Victoria's hand reached to pat coins sewn into her dress, as she said, "We don't have to worry about that."

Daisy smiled. "No, and they say President Cleveland is taking care of the situation."

"Well, that's good. We want people to keep buying our horses." Victoria finished her breakfast, poured another cup of coffee, and considered her choices. She wanted to go on her mission without much fuss. Probably it would be best to walk. A horse and carriage would be too much. Even saddling up the horse would require a groom. No, she would walk. Ignoring the whispering in her head, she glanced out at the dirt street, rutted by wagon wheels, and was pleased to see that most of the previous storm's snow had melted. It might be a bit muddy, but that she could maneuver.

Daisy was busy washing dishes, which provided Victoria an opportunity to slip away. "I'm going out," she called over her shoulder as she left the room. "I'll be home shortly." She wrapped a brightly colored woolen scarf around her neck and over her head and then put on her heavy winter cloak. She quietly let herself out the front door and took herself the long way around, so she would pass through the business district.

When she reached Main Street, Victoria could feel her blood moving through her body. Her breath was in rhythm with her steps and she imagined that she made a sharp picture as she walked past various stores. All her life, people looked at her and, even at her age, men would watch and imagine. They were always respectful. Lord knows they didn't want to incur the legendary wrath of her husband. Even though the town folks treated them well, she knew that her family was seen as different and would always be the first suspects if something went wrong.

She glanced in the courtyard behind the dentist office but she didn't recognize any of the horses. She nodded at Mr. Gaines standing in front of his harness shop. She could feel his eyes following her as she continued up Main Street to the cemetery. Her skirts twirled enticingly around her boots as she walked. She couldn't help her natural hip movement. Even though every inch of her skin was covered, she could feel the old man seeing through, imagining exotic actions unavailable to his staid upbringing. And, with years of experience, she knew how to encourage that fantasy to the point that it was fun for everyone: Mr. Gaines, herself, and even her husband, the proud old peacock. Oh, how often they would laugh afterwards at the upright citizens and their eyes on her. It could whip both of them into a deep yearning that they waited only as long as necessary to satisfy.

As she continued northward, her thoughts returned to her mission and she slowed. Just a few more blocks and she would turn down the path toward the cemetery. She envisioned the monument, a tall and handsome stone, topped with a bronze cantering horse. A lovely tribute, she supposed, but her insides churned at the fact that her wonder-son, the one intended to be head of the clan after them, was already there. Their firstborn boy, pride and joy. Already gone. Victoria was contemplating her ensuing sons and an appropriate successor for Wash's place when her right foot slipped out from under her. She felt herself fall backwards, rapidly, and could find no purchase or handgrip. After that, everything went black.

Victoria became aware of the bright light even through her closed eyelids. Its sharpness seared her brain and caused her to grimace. As quickly as it came, the light was gone, along with the sound of a door closing. She felt movement near her, a hand on hers, and a voice, "Princess, I'm here." She tried to open her eyes but was paralyzed by a deep, sharp pain in the back of her head. She attempted to touch the spot but her hand didn't obey her request.

"Princess, don't leave me, like Wash. Princess, I'm here."

She heard the urgent pleading in her husband's voice and mustered all her energy to open her eyes. Oh, the joy! There he was, sitting on her bed in dim light, his moustache outlining his lips and white teeth, and she smiled before almost immediately closing her eyes. She loved that moustache from the day she first saw it almost forty years ago.

It was the day that the women had been washing their clothes downstream from camp in the eastern foothills of the Blue Ridge Mountains when she was seventeen. Her brother Richard's wife Margaret gathered up one of his shirts that she had been beating on a rock and tied it around her waist, with one sleeve dangling in front and the rest of it gathered between her legs. She started strutting around, taking steps with her legs wide apart. "Now, sir, I would only tell you the truth about this horse," she started.

Victoria giggled. Samuel's wife Jennie followed Margaret's example and draped a damp skirt over her shoulders and stuck her thumbs into two imaginary lapels. "Yes, indeed, this horse is one of the finest, straight from the south of these United States of America." Marching along the stream bank, the two women kept up the running banter of a horse dealer. Victoria loved the way each captured her husband's nuances and gestures. She was just about to play the role of the buyer, when Margaret started swinging the dangling shirt sleeve back and forth between her legs, while saying, "I do declare, if this horse isn't what I say it is, I'll—" By then, the women were hooting and hollering and Victoria reached over and tipped Margaret into the stream. Their laughter rang up and down the riverside.

Victoria loved being on the road, traveling with her family, moving when they got news of a good sale or saw signs of other traveling families. Days started at sun-up and ran through evening campfire and, although there were always chores to do, she had more fun than in the winter.

Her sisters-in-law returned to laying clean clothes out on the rocks to dry and then sat nearby to bask and chat. Having nothing to contribute when they started talking about children, Victoria glanced around.

"I'm going to walk about," she said. Margaret and Jennie nodded, knowing that Victoria had the eye for the flora and often foraged for foods or medicines.

Although slightly different than back home, the fiddleheads she discovered were probably edible. She inhaled the tight ferns and sensed the flavor they would add to the stew pot. Long, dark braids dangling as she bent, Victoria gathered them into a sack she always carried and continued her search. Up the bank, she thought she recognized another spring delicacy and stepped in that direction. Her foot trampled one of the green leaves and Victoria broke into a smile, as she smelled their telltale odor. Ramps had such a short season, but these plants had persisted in this cove with its cooler temperatures. She gathered a few dozen leaves, careful not to break them or pull their bulbs when she placed them in her sack. Mammis would be pleased to see these, she knew. As they had been moving south, they were reaching spring and these fresh, green plants would be a welcome change from winter's food.

Victoria sat for a few minutes, enjoying the moss-covered rocks and garlicky aroma coming from her bag. She heard some shouts from the river and realized Margaret and Jennie were returning to camp. She should go soon, too, but she was savoring the solitude. The sun dappled the trees that were freshly leafed out. In the shadows, to her left, she noticed small leaves emerging on a low plant and she edged closer. She tugged the plant gently from the soil and saw the two small taproots. "Man root," she breathed aloud and blushed. Although no one in her camp needed its benefits, she instinctively gathered it and placed it in her sack to add to her pharmaceutical supply.

Nearby, a cuckoo startled her with its call. She rose to her feet and started back to camp. She hurried, so she could add the greens to the stew in time for them to cook before dinner. Back at the laundry area, she found her clean skirt dried from the warmth of the rocks and pulled it on beneath her other skirts.

Walking upstream, she saw Jennie and Margaret's footprints, heavy in the mud as they carried clean clothes back to camp. Victoria continued upriver past camp a short distance, where she cleaned the fiddleheads and ramps in running water and carefully shook the moisture from them. She folded them within a cloth in her bag and headed inland. She could just about make out the wagons in a small clearing among the cottonwoods, when she heard the jingle of a harness.

Victoria stopped immediately. They were the only horse traders they had seen in days, yet the harness bells were unmistakable. She continued walking, her eyes intently peering between the trees, when she saw the horse, a man astride, enter their camp. He dismounted and she could hear him call, "*Sarisham!*" and her father respond. She thought briefly of the man root in her sack. The stranger was taller than her father, with dark hair and a luxurious moustache. He was smiling and gesturing and she could see the tension release from her father's stance. Victoria knew better than to interrupt such a conversation, so she skirted around the camp and entered from the other side. Nodding at Margaret and Jennie, she went directly to the cooking area. There, she pulled out her cloth bag, carefully leaving her man root inside the sack, and prepared the greens for the stew pot. Meanwhile, she hadn't taken her averted eyes off the stranger, who was still talking to her father and brothers.

She realized that her mother had spoken and she nodded, although she had no idea what had been said. She was straining to hear the men's conversation.

"I saw the bent twigs and followed them here," she heard the man say.

"We haven't seen any other horse dealers for some time," her father said.

"Well, I am looking for mules this trip," said the man. Victoria thought that was certainly different than horses. She didn't relish the idea of convincing a pack of mules to travel back north. Horses could be bad enough.

"Would you like a smoke?" asked her father. That was a sure sign that either business or a friendship was being established. Victoria let out her breath, which she hadn't realized she was holding. He would be here for a while, she was grateful to know.

"Princess, I said, could you help me here?" her mother yelled with exasperation.

"Sorry, Mammis," Victoria said, as she turned to face her mother and grab two ends of the eating tarp. They walked to a clearing near some stumps and laid it on the ground. She felt eyes on her but didn't dare turn around. All the while she was aware of her sack, folded in her skirt, filled with man root. Suddenly, she could see them, she and this man, riding together on a large gray mare. Holding her close, the man's moustache tickled the side of her cheek. Catching herself smiling, Victoria shook her head and her mother looked at her.

"What's wrong?"

"Nothing. It's fine."

Her mother held her glance but Victoria would say no more. She knew that her mother, familiar with her skill and respectful of her accuracy, sensed Victoria had seen something. But this was a personal vision she was unwilling to share. She walked back to the stew pot and stirred, smelling both the ramps and the vivid green of the fiddleheads. Her mouth was watering and she hoped there would be enough for everyone.

The men started their meal, with the women ladling out stew and cups of tea that were carried to the eating tarp. Her brother Richard gave a plate to the stranger and waited for Margaret to bring his own, while the women stayed near the cooking fire. Victoria could feel the stranger's eyes on her, assessing her long braids and deft handling of the fire.

"A very fine stew you serve," the stranger said to her father loud enough for her to hear.

"Thank you, *pal*, we are pleased to have something to share."

"The tangy taste is new to me. What is it?"

"It's probably something my daughter added. She has a way with plants." Her father nodded in her direction. The stranger's eyes glittered and she could sense his opinion of her growing. Suddenly, she shrank, her hopes diminished. There was no way that he could afford her. He just rode into camp with no animals, no wagon, nothing.

Victoria felt her insides contract and she was no longer hungry. It was her curse, to be part of this family, with the talent of visions and healing. She would never be able to marry. Not that she wanted to leave her mother or father. Or her brothers for that matter. But she wanted a husband. Almost everyone had one, and she shuddered to think of what people said when someone went unmarried. She felt her eyes filling but she would not cry here with everyone around. She stammered to her mother, "I need to put something in the bender," and she hurried to the tent's safe walls. As she collapsed on her comforter, she hid her head in her hands and silently sobbed. Oh, the shame and pain of it all, again. After several minutes, she fingered the man root and drew a deep breath. There was some reason she found this plant just as the stranger came to camp. She would discover it, in its time. She knew she had to return to the cook fire, so she dried her eyes and steadied herself to face whatever happened.

She needed not have worried; there was plenty of food for the women and children, whom she joined. Although it was still light, the men had moved to the stumps and Richard had brought out his fiddle and was tuning. Company was always a good excuse for a party, but Victoria wasn't sure she was up for it right now.

The fiddling lasted way into the night. The women danced with the children in the darkness behind the tents, while the men stayed around the fire. Sitting with her mother, Victoria enjoyed her brother's favorite tunes and the idea of sharing them with the stranger, despite her fear she could never marry him.

Margaret grabbed her arm to pull her up and twirled her to the music.

"You're awful quiet tonight," she whispered to Victoria. "Did anything happen in the woods?"

Victoria shook her head and smiled to throw Margaret off-track. In fact, she decided to envision the gray mare and the stranger and their future and started dancing with grace and wild abandon. Her braids flying, her skirts swirling, Victoria turned from person to person, giving each a swing and bump. Her nephews grew red and her mother started to laugh. Victoria wondered if their gleeful shouts could be heard at the fire.

Victoria's legs were sore when she stood up the next morning. She felt a bit embarrassed by her performance but knew she had persuaded her family that she was feeling herself. She went to the cooking area, found the water pail, and started to the river to refill it. She walked upstream, daydreaming about the stranger's moustache. Only after she returned with a full bucket did she notice the extra tent to the side of her family's. She hoped if he had bothered to put up a tent, he planned to stay awhile.

After putting the kettle on the fire, she took a basket and went to the portable chicken coop to gather eggs. Victoria counted as she went and was relieved that all the chickens were laying again. She wished she had time to get more ramps to put in the eggs, but she would have to satisfy herself by serving sponge mushrooms they had gathered a few days prior. If she coated them with flour and fried them, they would make a nice complement to the eggs and coffee.

After Victoria had completed most of the breakfast, she was joined by the other women, who added the final touches. They were drinking coffee, the only part of breakfast that they would start before the men had theirs, when her father and the others came back from looking after the horses. Victoria brought plates of eggs and morels to each man sitting on the tarp, while Jennie poured coffee.

"Would you like milk?" Jennie asked the stranger. He nodded and she added a generous finger of milk to his cup. Traveling with the cow had its problems but it made meals richer, and provided milk for the children, too, which kept them healthy while on the road. Victoria and Jennie tended the men, carefully keeping their respectful distance, especially to the stranger.

That night, Victoria could hear her parents talking in their comforter. Deep rumblings from her father were occasionally punctuated by her mother's soft chirps. She sensed a positive discussion. There were no long icy pauses while her mother whittled away at whatever her father had proposed and no gruff rejoinder from her father to counter some nonsense from her mother. Victoria wondered if maybe they would be moving on tomorrow. She didn't relish the idea of leaving the stranger. She liked the way he handled the horses, whispered in their ears, and cajoled them into doing just what he wanted them to do. Well, she knew moving was what they were all about. They had stayed here longer than most places and they had miles of horse dealing to cover in the next few months, before they herded the animals back north to their sale stables.

But they weren't traveling quite yet, she discovered. Her father called her to him early the next morning, while they were still in their tent. "Princess, I have some news for you." Victoria looked quickly at him, catching his eyes. She saw their piercing blackness filled with warm love for her, along with a firmness that meant this was a final decision, obviously one that her mother had supported. "You and Mr. Williams," he began, for that was the stranger's name, "are marrying tonight," he finished. Victoria inhaled sharply and touched her left chest. He continued, "You've already used up your refusal last year. So you must accept."

"Oh, Dadrus," cried Victoria, "thank you, I am so grateful."

Her father looked pleased with her response and huffed himself out of the tent, while Victoria sat, stunned. She was getting married, to the handsome stranger. Oh, how exciting. She caught her mother looking at her and she went over to her. "Mammis, I am pleased." But, as she was saying that, she realized the consequences and rushed into her mother's arms. "But, Mammis, I will miss you, where will I be going? When will I see you again?" She didn't voice the biggest fear of all: that his mother would be cruel and hard to obey. Victoria's family had a flow and respect that was unusual in a traveling family.

"Oh, Princess," her mother said, "that's the best part. He has no family here. And, since his mother was a distant relative, Dadrus has arranged for him to join us, become part of the Cooper clan, and work with us."

Victoria couldn't believe her luck. She would have a man and keep her family.

Her mother continued. "Up north, he has a camp near us. When we get back there, you will live in his town, but there will be no mother-in-law and you can run your own place. Now, let's get ready for the *abiav*."

Victoria knew that the ceremony would be informal but the partying would go on for days. No one questioned her brothers when they arrived at camp with a young pig they presented to the women for roasting. Margaret was cutting up potatoes and Jennie set a pot of oil on the fire for frying. Mammis called to Victoria, "Go find more ramps. We're going to make stuffed cabbage and it would be the perfect flavoring."

Appreciative of a reason, Victoria excused herself and went downstream to the women's laundry area and entered the forest along the river's edge. She followed some rivulets upstream and checked their banks for ferns and wild leeks. With her sack filling, Victoria relaxed into the day, her last as a single person. Although she had slept in the same tent as her parents all her life, and lord knows they had a number of children, Victoria had never seen a naked man. She patted the man root in her sack, closed her eyes, and asked for success that night.

Glancing at the sky, she realized it was getting late and she should head back to camp. On impulse, she pulled off her layers of clothing and took a quick dip in the stream. Somehow, it made her feel ready to make the break from her family.

Victoria could smell camp before she got there. Her heart quickened and her palms were sweaty as she approached. She had been to several weddings before but not with a stranger. Her brothers had all married within their *folki* to families they knew. But she reminded herself this is a new country, with new ways. And she trusted Dadrus to make a good arrangement.

As she entered the camp, Richard was returning from the main trail. "I put out some hemlock branches," he told Mammis. Victoria doubted that any other travelers would be passing by, but if they did, they would follow the signs and be welcomed to the festivities. The more, the merrier when it comes to happy times, she knew.

Her mother called to her, "Princess, come with me. We have some things to do." Victoria wasn't sure she liked the sound of that.

They entered their tent, which was still bright from ambient light. Her mother gestured to her comforter. "Sit down. I'll be right back."

When she returned, Mammis had a brush and a scarf. She took out Victoria's braids and worked the brush through the thick dark hair. When it was manageable, she rebraided it and pinned it to her head. "Here's how you knot your *diklo*," she instructed, as she wrapped it around Victoria's head and tied it in the back. Victoria was trembling with excitement, fear, and sadness. This was the last time she'd be able to swing her braids, free as a deer's tail. Soon, she would belong to Mr. Williams and she really didn't know what that would mean. She decided if he were half as nice to her as he was with the horses, she'd be in good hands.

Her mother removed the *diklo* and began to insert coins and jewelry into Victoria's braid. Mammis strung a chain of coins around her neck, through her blouse, and around her waist. Victoria could feel the weight of the gold coins as they chattered when she moved. She could see the pride in her mother's eyes and she felt tears that she pushed away.

"Now, a card," said Mammis. Victoria reached into her things and pulled out her grandmother's Tarot cards, which she unwrapped and shuffled a number of times.

"Just keep moving the cards, shuffling, and sorting, until you find the one. It might fall out, or you might just feel that you're done."

Victoria closed her eyes and kept the cards moving. One after the other they kept passing. Several minutes went by; she heard her mother shift her position on the comforter next to her, but she did not rush. Then suddenly, a card flew from the pile and landed on the blanket.

Victoria was afraid to look, but she heard Mammis pick it up and let out a deep breath. "The Lovers," she said. "You are crossing the threshold of the garden of your family and moving to a new place.

One with passion, romance, and bonding." She looked at Victoria. "A good card, indeed, for a wedding day."

Indeed, thought Victoria. Any hesitation was gone. She would start her new life proudly as Victoria Williams.

A sound outside the tent caught their attention. Averting his eyes, Dadrus came in to change for the ceremony. When he was done, he joined his wife and daughter.

"Ready?"

"Yes, Dadrus, I truly am."

"Then let's go." He took her hand and put his other arm around his wife and they emerged from the tent. At the sight of them, Richard started fiddling and the rest of the family clapped and sang along. Mr. Williams stood alone on the other side of the group.

Victoria felt herself grow tall as she walked with her parents towards her intended. She met his eyes and they smiled at each other. He reached out his hands and she left her parents forever to join him.

Victoria was exhausted from eating and dancing and singing when they finally headed towards his tent for their first night together. He pulled aside the tent flap and she crouched to enter. It was dark inside but she could see that her comforter had been added to his.

"Mr. Williams," she began.

He threw his head back, laughing. "My outside name is Thomas," he said. "But my people call me Prince."

Victoria looked at him astounded. She realized that her mouth was agape but she couldn't help it.

"My family called me that," he tried to explain, "because—"

Victoria placed her hand on his arm to interrupt. "I am known as Victoria." She paused. "But my people call me Princess."

It was Prince's turn to look amazed. "This is too fortunate," he whispered in her ear, as he tickled her cheek with his moustache.

She was still drowsy when she heard a commotion outside the tent flap. Margaret's shrill voice was insisting, "Show us the sheet." Victoria could see shadows on the tent as the first rays of daylight streamed through the trees.

"We want to see," Jennie was saying. Victoria opened her eyes again. Prince, smiling at her, reached under the comforter to remove the cloth. He threw it out the flap and the women cheered as they carried it off for the camp to see.

Victoria looked at this man on her first day as his wife. She blurted out, "I thought I'd never find you," and then hid her head under the covers, embarrassed by that confession.

"Princess, I'm here," she heard the deep voice of her new husband say. Prince lowered the covers, tenderly touched her face, and whispered, "Princess, I'm here."

Opening her eyes, she watched with fascination as his face morphed, aging ten, twenty, then thirty, forty years. We will grow old together, she thought, before shutting her eyes from the bright light.

TWO

The days passed, as Victoria and Prince traveled with her family through the southern states, he procuring mules and her father's family, horses. She was relieved there was no competition between them. As before, she spent her days with her mother and sisters-in-law, searching for fresh greens, preparing food, cleaning clothes and dishes, and keeping the family organized. The men slipped off during the days to search for livestock to purchase and the group gathered their belongings and moved when an area held no more promise. It was a lazy, peaceful time, responding to whims and environment.

At night, she and Prince slept in his small tent on the edge of the wagons just as he had pitched it that first night. The night darkness enveloped them, with its heat and humidity as the southern summer stretched out before them. Night after night, they formed their own world of magic. Prince's caresses, starting at her cheeks, covered her body and she arched for more. Victoria didn't know what it was like for other people, and she really didn't want to consider her parents' or even her brothers' physical pleasures, but sometimes during the day, she found herself remembering the previous night. She could feel his hand running up her leg or around her back or sense his weight on her. He seemed to know things about her body that she didn't and she was pleasantly surprised by this skill.

Coming out of the tent one morning, she noticed that the days were getting shorter, the sun rising over the crest of the trees just a bit later each day. The sky still turned pink and willowy clouds were tinged with magnificent hues, their undersides often gray and upper parts salmon or pink or orange, depending on the weather, but summer was definitely waning.

Victoria joined her mother, already at the kettle.

"Not quite as hot today, is it?"

"No," replied her mother, "The weather's turning."

The women worked seamlessly together, each anticipating the other's move, their division of labor well established during this summer's travel. Victoria envisioned their breakfast preparation as a type of dance, their steps flowing and skirts swaying slightly. To and from the fire, back and forth to the eating tarp, and, almost effortlessly, the meal was ready.

Jennie came back from the nearby stream, lugging two buckets of water and sighed, dropping them near the food. She dipped her fingers in one of them and wiped her face, using her outside skirt to dry herself. "Where's Margaret?"

"She started the men's washing."

"Oh," said Jennie. "It was cooler last night. I didn't want to get my feet wet when I filled the buckets."

"Yes, time to start back north," replied Mammis.

Victoria stopped cutting the potato in her hand and looked sharply at her mother. Up until now, she had avoided thinking about the inevitable change.

"We have plenty of horses to sell," said Jennie. "I heard Samuel talking to Dadrus last night."

"I expect we will start heading back home in a few days." Mammis looked at Victoria out of the corner of her eye, knowing that her home would be a different place than when they had left Somerville that previous spring.

Victoria's hand grasped the knife tightly. As much as she had enjoyed Prince thus far, the idea of leaving her family or spending whole days with him caused her to breathe quickly. She reminded herself that women did this all the time. She glanced at Jennie and then Margaret, who was returning from her laundry work. They managed to live with her family with no problem, she reminded herself. But it would be different alone with Prince. With no family, it would be just the two of them, and she had no idea how she would spend her time all day.

"Let's do a little work around here before we leave," suggested Mammis.

"Ooh, I'd love to spend some time in town," squealed Margaret. "The people here seem easy to surprise."

"Good," said Mammis. "I'll put together some baskets and brooms. Victoria can help me gather the osiers. We can sell them while you *dukker.*"

Victoria looked forward to the quiet weaving work and smiled when she thought of her sister-in-law's skills with the locals. Margaret was a fast talker and loved the sleight of hand. She could move things that only the very trained eye could catch.

"The timing will be perfect," said Jennie. "We'll get out of here just when they realize what you've done."

"Excuse me but I'm always above board," complained Margaret. "I can't help it if people keep coming back for more." With that, Jennie and Margaret left the cooking area to prepare.

The men returned from their horse check and sat down to breakfast. Victoria overheard their rumblings.

"We have enough horses for the winter sales."

"We might try just a few more. I heard of some about twenty miles from here."

"Which way?"

"West."

"Well, I for one think it's time for me and my mules to start home. They take longer to move along than the horses and I don't want to wait too long."

Victoria's heart lurched with her husband's words. She felt her father glance at her.

"Whatever works for you," Dadrus said to Prince. "We can travel together and take our time, if you want."

"No, I think we would get in the way. Mules travel differently than horses," he said knowingly.

"I can send one of our men with you if you wish."

Prince pondered that suggestion and nodded. "That would be helpful. I've always managed alone but had fewer animals."

Victoria's mind was racing, trying to figure out how she could possibly run a whole camp on her own.

"The man's wife will come also to help Princess," her father said firmly.

Letting out a sigh, Victoria relaxed and returned to cutting her potatoes. She felt her mother's eye on her.

"Let's find some osiers and make some brooms. I'd like to make a few baskets, too," said Mammis.

Victoria nodded and added the last of the cut potatoes to the kettle. She gathered her knife and cloth bag to join her mother. They took the well-trod trail to the river and then veered away into a swampier section. Tall silver maples kept the understory dark and cool and they soon reached an area where osiers grew.

"No one's been harvesting here for some time," commented her mother.

Victoria nodded, intent on gathering the smallest twigs, being more supple and easier to bend and weave. Trapping smaller particles, they made better brooms, too. It didn't take her long to gather enough material to make several baskets and a dozen brooms. She spotted some ash saplings nearby and chopped down enough to serve as handles.

"I'm going to rest here for awhile," said Mammis, nodding to a moss-covered section of the forest floor.

"I'll forage a bit, then," said Victoria and she left her mother to doze. The quiet of the woods calmed her. She remembered her grandmother used to say, "God is in the forest, not in the church." It certainly felt that way to her, as she wandered around large trunks and stepped on mossy cushions.

When she found a large spread of ferns, she decided to harvest some. She wasn't sure about the women in the nearby town, but usually their customers were willing to purchase them along with the brooms. Each time she inadvertently crushed even the smallest piece of frond, the sweet scent of hay filled the air. She hoped the locals, with their tightly sealed homes, might relish the idea of bringing their fresh scent indoors.

Spotting some mushrooms, Victoria sat down next to them and carefully examined their undersides and stems. Still learning the flora of this new country, she was convinced these were edible ones. She decided she would add only a few to the pot to be certain. She gathered them into her cloth bag, which she tucked into her skirt waist.

"Princess, it's time to go." She heard her mother's voice calling faintly from a distance.

"I'm coming, Mammis," she yelled and walked back to find her mother.

They gathered their materials and prepared to head back to camp. Looking at the mushrooms, her mother agreed to add them to the kettle.

"The ferns are lovely. It will be a nice touch," she added.

With the saplings, osiers, and ferns, each woman had her arms filled. They slowly made their way back through the forest. After they entered camp, they heard loud voices and laughing along the trail, and Victoria smiled. "Sounds as though they had a good time in town," she said, placing the branches they had cut in a bucket of water to soften.

Her mother rolled her eyes, just as Margaret appeared at the cooking fire.

"We're in luck," she exclaimed. "This town is ripe for the picking."

"We barely got into town, when people started running up to us and asking for their fortune," continued Jennie. "We found a little shed with a bench on the edge of town, too. No one seems to be using it and as soon as we sat down, there was a line waiting for us."

"I can't wait to go back tomorrow," added Margaret.

"But they talked so strange, these people," added Jennie.

Margaret agreed, "I had just gotten used to the way people speak over here in America and now this. It takes them forever to tell me what the problem is. I can hardly get done with each one in ten minutes."

"And you know how Margaret is," teased Jennie. "In and out, unless there is promise of a bigger catch."

After dinner, Victoria and her mother worked the osiers into sturdy brooms with ash handles. Then her mother sat to start her basket weaving.

"We'll have to make certain that Prince has a kettle," she said, while her fingers nimbly built the basket base and supporting sides.

Victoria started from her peaceful reverie to realize what her mother meant.

"We can split up the rest of the potatoes and onions, too. Dinah can cook for the men when it's that time of the month."

Victoria had wondered how they would handle that. "Will Prince eat what she cooks?" She knew that Dinah and some other wives cooked for the grooms, but she had never seen her father, or any of the family for that matter, eat what they had prepared.

"I guess you'll see," said Mammis. "He seems to have survived on his way down here somehow, so he'll make do."

"Oh, Mammis, I'm scared," she sobbed, suddenly overwhelmed by the thought of leaving her family.

"You're lucky, you know, so no tears." The sternness in her mother's voice was unmistakable and Victoria knew what she said was true. At her age, many of the girls had been married for five years and had numerous children to show for it. She wondered if her father had told Prince she was already seventeen. Well, she didn't know how old Prince was, either, and decided it could stay that way.

The next morning, the women packed their materials and went

into town, with Jennie and Margaret leading the way. Just as they had described, a group of people started gathering as soon as they headed down the main street. Margaret took them to the shed and Victoria and her mother set out a tarp under a nearby tree. They placed the brooms in rows, with the handles downward, such that the display resembled a miniature grove of trees resting on the tarp. Victoria added clusters of ferns tied with small scraps of brightly colored cloth. She and her mother then settled into position, their skirts splayed around them, the dappling of the trees in the mid-day sun making variegated patterns on their faces and adding to their mystique.

Mammis sat with her partially completed basket and wove while Victoria trimmed bark from some of the stems still soaking. A crowd gathered at the doorway of the shed but, as people waited, they purchased brooms and admired the basket.

Margaret was in her glory, dressed in brightly colored scarves and skirts, with bracelets jangling. Her dark eyes sparkled as she glanced at the crowd before entering the shed, recently transformed into her *ofisa*. Jennie, more subtly dressed, interviewed potential clients, all within earshot of Margaret, sitting behind a vibrantly colored curtain covering the shed's doorway. The girls had developed several codes to help Margaret with the *dukkering*.

"Have you smelled this?" asked Victoria as she held a fern cluster toward a waiting woman's face. After inhaling the sweet smell, the woman smiled but looked puzzled. Victoria added, "You can place it in your dressers or closets."

"Ah," she said and purchased two.

Several women placed basket orders and Mammis promised they would be ready within the next few days. She finished the first and started on a second, with one woman requesting specific handles and another asking for a fitted cover.

Towards the end of the afternoon, an older woman arrived at the shed. "Oh, hallo again," said Jennie, recognizing her from the day before. "Are you back for more?"

The woman glanced around and whispered, "Yes, I thought about what your sister said and I want her help."

Jennie said clearly, "My sister can help you, yes, indeed," and she scratched three times on the cloth divider.

"Looks like she's got one," whispered Victoria to her mother, who nodded and continued her weaving. With orders piling up and their plans to leave shortly, she had to focus on her basket making.

The woman was in the shed with Margaret for quite some time. Jennie came over to chat with Victoria. "This might take a few days," she said, pointing her head in the direction of the shed. "We may have to stall Dadrus." The women laughed and, shortly after, the local woman poked her head out from the curtain. Confirming that no one was watching, she quickly left the shed and headed back into town.

Margaret started taking down the curtain and gathering her supplies. She gleefully slapped her skirt pocket. "A good day," she said, "even without the potential of more to come." Her eyes flashed with excitement, especially as she glanced down the road at her final customer. Victoria and Jennie helped with the basketry supplies and they returned to camp.

That night, when Victoria went into their tent, Prince was already inside. His eyes soft and full of affection, he gathered her into his arms and nibbled her ears. Victoria started giggling and playing with his moustache, which was tickling her neck. Prince reached up to untie her *diklo*. Her long hair fell across her chest and Prince grasped some in his hands. Smiling at her, he took the strands and started caressing her face and body. Victoria gasped at the sensations and her response.

It seemed like only moments later that they lay, panting, on the comforter next to each other. In the ambient light, Victoria could see that Prince's eyes were open. He turned on his side, holding his head with his hand, elbow resting on the ground. He touched her face gently. "We're leaving tomorrow," he whispered. Victoria tried to keep her face immobile. "I know this will be hard for you," he added.

Victoria resisted the urge to agree. "I will be ready," she answered. Prince smiled, his white teeth visible, fell back to the comforter, and was asleep in seconds. Not so for Victoria.

"Over here, Joe," Prince was shouting.

The sturdy groom was leading some of the mules to form their caravan. "Yes, suh," he replied, wiping sweat from his face. Victoria knew Joe was confident with horses and hoped he would quickly gain skill with the mules. Dinah was packing their few belongings and taking stock of Prince's supplies.

After feeding the men, the women were finishing their breakfast. Margaret asked, "What will you do in New Haven?"

Victoria gulped, her own pestering thoughts being exposed so clearly to everyone. She looked desperately at her mother and two sisters-in-law. "I—I—"

"You'll have much to do taking care of camp," her mother said. "And your children," she added with a smile. Apparently night sounds from Prince's tent were not totally captured by its canvas walls.

"You should try *dukkering*," said Margaret. "With your visions and Tarot skill, you could make some actual predictions," she laughed, "and not make them up, like me!"

Victoria smiled but, knowing that she would be missing this type of banter, the joke caught in her throat and pulled at her heart.

Jennie looked at her, thoughtfully. "You know, that's a good idea. I don't know if anyone already claims New Haven. But it's a big town, so there's probably room for another anyway."

Victoria nodded but she was uncertain. She loved the countryside, foraging in the woods, and spending her days outdoors. She wasn't certain she'd enjoy camping so close to a large city, even though she knew it was critical for Prince's business. She hoped it wouldn't be much bigger than Somerville where the Coopers lived. But the idea of going into town every day to *dukker* and deal with the locals didn't appeal to her. In fact, the Others still frightened her, although she had enjoyed their interactions the previous day. Selling brooms and ferns felt comfortable. Spending time with the locals or, even worse, censoring when she saw their difficult future made her queasy. Being confined in a space with them, with their odd clothing and smells, certainly did not appeal. She would have to see what else she could do once she got there.

Noise from the forming caravan caught their attention. Her father and brothers were saying goodbye to Prince, who turned to look at Victoria. She rose unsteadily and walked toward her men.

Dadrus gathered her in his arms. "Goodbye, Princess," he said, snuggling her head under his chin. She could feel the bristles of his moustache poking through her *diklo* and thought she heard him sniffling. When she glanced up, his eyes were moist but he was smiling. "Goodbye, my daughter," he said, letting go.

Samuel hugged her next, looking deeply in her eyes, and Richard followed suit.

"I'll miss your fiddling," she whispered in his ear.

"I'll be playing at your first baby's birth," he chided her.

Victoria turned to her mother, Jennie, and Margaret, who stood waiting. First, Jennie gave her a hug and stood back. Margaret playfully lifted her off her feet. "Think about it," she said. "Let's see if you can out-*dukker* me," she challenged.

Despite everything, Victoria laughed. "There is no one who can do that," she said with true admiration.

Victoria turned to her mother and swallowed.

Mammis drew her close to her and whispered, "We will see you often, don't worry."

"God go with you," chimed one voice after the other.

With eyes brimming and a smile pasted, Victoria waved at her family and climbed into Prince's wagon. As hard as she tried not to, she turned as they rounded the corner to wave her last time.

THREE

It was only a few days out that she saw the spotting. "Dinah, will you take over the cooking and cleaning?" Victoria asked. Dinah, versed in her family's ways, nodded.

Victoria saw Prince walking her way with a smile on his face. He started to reach for her and she shied away. "I—It's—" Victoria stuttered, her hands over the front of her skirt.

"Ah," said Prince, "I see."

Victoria let out a sigh at his quick understanding. "Dinah will be cooking. I can sleep under the wagon," she added. Although it was a new country and a new man, she felt compelled to keep the old ways. They spent a short morning in camp and then packed their supplies and continued north. Careful to avoid touching it, Victoria walked alongside the wagon. She had been adjusting to being without her family, but today she missed the other women. There was no one to pass a knowing glance or exchange a grimace when a cramp hit her. And the weather didn't help. The sun never made it out all day and the moisture in the air clung to her skin and dampened her clothing. She trod along, listening to Prince and Joe.

"They sure don't like to keep movin', do they, suh?"

"No, Joe, they truly don't. But they are better than donkeys." After a long pause, Prince added, "These are solid mules. Bred from draught horse mares. They'll be good workers and sell well."

Victoria heard Joe grunt and add, "Yes, suh." She noticed a late crop of berries growing along the road and stopped to gather some. Even if she couldn't share them with the others, at least she could enjoy the sweet tartness of the sun-kissed fruits. When they stopped for lunch, she and Dinah exchanged glances and Victoria nodded.

While the men were eating, Dinah quietly edged off to the adjacent orchard where she garnered a supply of crisp apples.

After continuing a way, they stopped for the night. Dinah served a delightful apple compote alongside a bubbling stew she had made. Victoria was pleased, as she watched Prince eat Dinah's food, to know that he would be well fed during this time. But as the daylight softened and the sun disappeared behind the hills, Victoria felt her stomach cramping. She glanced at the wagon and the space underneath. She could add extra grass and cover herself with one of her skirts. She kept to the side of the fire as they sat there, Prince enjoying a smoke on his pipe. The mules rustled around, making noises as they found their nighttime spots and finally, it could be put off no longer. It was time for bed.

Grabbing a supply of freshly picked tall grass, Victoria headed to the wagon. Prince's tent was nearby, blocking the fire's glow. She slid under the wagon, arranged the grass, and removed her outside skirt to use as a blanket. She clumped some of the grass into a pillow and tried to get comfortable. She heard Joe and Dinah laughing on their way to their tent and the soft shuffle of Prince's feet entering his. And then it was quiet.

But not for long. Victoria had never slept alone before. She heard snorting and decided it was the mules. She heard rustling in the leaves and thought it was field mice. She heard digging by the fire and hoped it was raccoons or possum. She clutched her skirt draped over her and tried to keep her eyes closed. With every sound, they shot open and her breathing stopped, until she had reassured herself it was a familiar sound. She wondered if she would ever sleep.

Branches crackling overhead almost made her sit up, before she remembered she was under the wagon. She heard hooves galloping down the road and, when she heard coyotes howling, she let out a whimper. She covered her head with her skirt and thought she heard a gentle voice, "Princess, I'm here." She felt his face hovering over hers but knew that was impossible and finally dozed.

Counting off the days, Victoria knew it was finally time to interact with Prince again. Eager to start the day, she pulled herself from under the wagon, smiled radiantly at him, and hooked her arm through his. She was pleased to see longing fill his eyes, leading her to believe that he had missed their nights together as much as she.

They rode in the wagon now, moving more quickly. Victoria noticed that the leaves of the swamp maple were turning. Geese honked in V's and she sensed Prince's restless desire to be home. Home, she thought, his home and soon to be mine. A little tightness in her chest reminded her of the strangeness of it all. His touch to her shoulder convinced her it was all worthwhile and she smiled at him. His eyes were luminous, his pupils wide drinking her in, and he tickled her cheek with his moustache. "Tonight," he whispered and she nodded, happily.

The day passed with subtle touches and reminders. She felt her body responding and aching desperately for his caress. After lunch when she relieved herself in the bush and dried herself with a fern frond, its tickling left her momentarily breathless. She moaned quietly, aware it would be hours before dark.

Prince seemed to have a similar problem. She caught him making adjustments to his trousers several times. Once, she laughed aloud and he joined her, their laughter building as a type of release, while both Joe and Dinah looked on, puzzled.

"It's nothing," sputtered Prince.

"It reminds us of something," said Victoria. Which sent them both into chortles of laughter again. Oh, Victoria felt so good, to be able to laugh and touch again. Previously, she had enjoyed the respite from work provided by her time of the month. Maybe she would relish it again some day, but, right now, everything was different with Prince.

The sun had barely set when Prince rose from the fire and yawned, stretching his arms to the sky. "I'm tired," he said ceremoniously. "I'm ready for bed."

Victoria rinsed her mouth with a mint tea and quickly gathered the remaining cups and left them for Dinah to finish. Using a birch toothpick, she cleaned her teeth and smiled at their helpers. "Good night, Dinah," she said and nodded to Joe. She caught them sharing a knowing look as she entered Prince's tent.

"We're getting close to New York," said Prince a few days later. "I'd like to stop at camp there."

Victoria nodded, remembering it from her first voyage to America. "It'll be good to catch up on the news," she replied. She hoped there would be word of her family. Or, even better, perhaps they, leaving later but traveling faster, would already be there.

It was dusk when they arrived. Smoky campfires filled the air and they hurried to settle into a spot on the edge of camp. Caravans and tents populated the broad area along the banks of the tributary that ran into the sea. Victoria inhaled deeply, enjoying the smell of a large group of people again. She had missed the camaraderie of traveling with her family. Off to the side, she heard fiddle playing and wondered if her brother might be there. Without realizing it, her feet started tapping and she found herself anxious to get unpacked and down to the dance area.

Prince raised his eyebrow while looking towards her feet and smiled. Victoria covered her mouth with her hand and said, "Sorry." She meekly sat down and waited.

"No, no, go ahead and have a good time," he said. "It's overdue. I'll be down shortly."

Victoria tried to walk calmly in the direction of the music and not run. She passed rows of tents and wagons, filled with families calling to each other before she reached the dance area. The musicians were seated on a small platform. A quick glance confirmed that her brother was not playing but the music was good, just the same. She saw the area to the side where the women and children were congregating and made her way to join them. As she walked, she nodded at a young woman, long braids swinging.

"Hallo, I'm Theresa," the young woman called out. Her accent sounded as if she had just arrived and Victoria stopped to ask.

"Yes, we landed a few days ago, me and my family," she said, glancing to an older woman seated to the side. "We come from Somerset," she added.

"Wiltshire," responded Victoria.

"Married long?" she asked, eyes on her *diklo*.

"Just this summer."

"I hope to get married soon," admitted Theresa.

Hoping to stave off questions about married life, Victoria grabbed her new friend's arm, said, "Let's dance," and guided her into the dance area. The young women swayed with the music, stomped their feet, and swirled their skirts. The night coolness helped keep them comfortable and they moved among a throng of other women and children.

"Victoria Cooper, is that you?" cried a voice.

"Williams now," she replied turning to face the voice. "Sarah!" she shouted and they fell into each other's arms. Extracting herself, Victoria explained to Theresa, "We haven't seen each other in so long. We crossed to America together several years ago."

She and Sarah sat and caught up on the news, each updating the other about family. "My brother has married again," Victoria finally admitted.

Sarah cast her eyes aside. Her mother had left an ill-fitted match with Samuel and headed out on her own once they landed in America. "Well, I wish him the best," she finally said.

Victoria yawned and turned to Theresa. "You know you're getting old when you have to go to bed when the music is still playing," she laughed. "In fact, I hope I can find my tent," she said, her face clouding. Finding the music had been easy, but she wasn't sure she could backtrack to find hers among the hundreds of tents. "I'd better start looking."

She hugged Sarah and her new friend Theresa goodnight, exchanging God-go-with-yous, and retraced her steps. It was a different world now, dark spaces interspersed with campfires. With enough light to see the main path, she kept to the edge where they had pitched their tent. She was beginning to give up hope, when she felt a familiar arm around her.

"Going my way?" asked the teasing voice.

"Oh, Prince, thank goodness!"

"Did you have a good time?" he asked.

Victoria hesitated, not wanting to sound too satisfied on her own yet wanting to be truthful. "The music was wonderful," she started. "And I met a new friend and ran into an old one."

That seemed to satisfy him. "Here we are," he proclaimed and led her into their tent.

The next morning, they joined a few other couples tenting nearby. Victoria helped prepare a communal breakfast that the men sat eating. A new arrival entered camp and Prince called out to him. "Joshua, how are you?"

The man stopped and shook his head with surprise. "Prince, I didn't expect to see you here." He sat and joined the men, who offered him a smoke and food.

Talking resumed and Victoria was startled to hear her husband say, "No, I'm here with my new wife," with the emphasis on "new." Victoria couldn't turn to see Prince without being obvious, so she sat waiting, her ears open.

Joshua said quietly, "Mary Defiance is with child." And after a long pause, he added, "Did you know?"

"No," said Prince. "I haven't seen her since May." May, thought Victoria, she and Prince had been married in May. Suddenly, Prince's skill in lovemaking and understanding at her monthly time took a different perspective and she felt herself on the verge of retching.

"Excuse me," she said to the women and walked off behind the tents. Noticing her heaving, one of the women smiled. Victoria registered the woman's assumption but chose not to clarify the situation. She could not bear returning to the cooking area and decided to duck into their tent until she could decide what to do.

She was sitting on their comforter, hugging herself, when she heard a scratch on the canvas. Prince let himself in and sat next to her, touching her arm. "I was going to explain before we got to New Haven," he started. "I knew you'd need to know before we got there."

Victoria could not look at him. This man, whom she had trusted with everything, had hidden a vital piece of information. It rattled her core, shook her deeply.

Prince sighed. "I have two children already, a daughter and son." He was putting everything on the table. Ultimately there were no secrets in their small community where all the news passed from person to person. The truth would always come out at one point or another and he'd been wrong to keep this to himself so long.

Victoria willed herself to take a breath and ask, "And is she carrying your child?"

Prince was quiet and then said, "I don't know. It could be. We decided to separate just before you and I met. She stayed in Virginia and I kept heading south. I don't know." He touched her cheek. "I am here now." She could tell that he hoped that would be sufficient but it was not.

They were scheduled to spend another day in camp before continuing to New Haven. Victoria spent it quietly near their tent. She kept thinking about Prince's disclosure and remembered her grandmother saying, "You can count the apples on a tree but you can't count the trees from one apple."

Victoria vacillated back and forth. On one hand, she too had kept certain things from Prince and felt it made sense to wait until they were closer before sharing them. On the other hand, she was terrified because he had left Mary Defiance. Not knowing the reasons, she worried he might up and leave her also, when he tired of her or found someone else to fancy. She saw Prince heading toward her and missed the privacy of her monthly time to give her space to make a decision.

Prince said nothing but stooped to leave a bowl of food and cup of tea for her. He smiled tentatively at her but she didn't reciprocate, so he nodded and left. Victoria appreciated his efforts but didn't want to be swayed by a small act. She needed to know whether he was worthy of her trust for the long-term. As she nibbled on the stew, she watched the activities in camp. People flowed along the main path, greeting old friends, and transacting business. The sun began its descent into the western sky and still she sat.

She wished Mammis were there to help. But, she realized she had another resource. She pulled out her Tarot deck, fingered the black silk wrapping, and closed her eyes. She focused quietly on the issue, unwrapped the pack, and fanned the cards, cutting and shuffling, until one fell from the deck. She opened her eyes to see the Queen of Coins. She was not surprised to see a queen, but coins stopped her. Patience, the card suggested. She would have to wait then, wait for clarity. The more she thought about it, the more she knew that was true. In the long run, she could choose to leave but, right now, she had nowhere to go. Her family was still coming north and, until they passed through New Haven to visit, she had to stay with Prince. But she had lost the joy and safety in the relationship.

With that, Victoria sighed and looked around her. The sun had set and fiddle music was wafting across camp. She wondered if she would ever feel like dancing again. Slowly, she arose, washed herself, and got into the tent with Prince. He gathered her into his arms and held her throughout the night. She lay very still.

Fortunately, they were not far from New Haven, so she wouldn't need to pretend closeness to Prince for long. She noticed Dinah and Joe sneaking glances at her. They saw the difference, she realized. Obviously Prince did, too. He checked on her regularly, asking how she was, and offering to help with her chores. They had stopped for lunch and Dinah and Joe were off along a brook, making their own meal and watering the mules. Victoria didn't feel much like eating and Prince finally put down his pipe and touched her arm.

Before he had a chance to say a word, she blurted, "If you're going to leave me, like you did her, you may as well do it now, before we have children or I get too happy with you." She could barely spew out the words, as her dammed tears came gushing out. She was so disappointed she had almost made it back home without making a scene. She pounded her fist on her leg in frustration and pain. It was only when she heard a strangled noise that she looked up at Prince. His face was blanched, his eyes red, and he was struggling to compose himself to speak.

"It wasn't that way, Princess, I swear," he started. "I don't want to say anything about Mary Defiance," he added, "but she lives up to her

29

name." After a moment of silence, he added, "I am so happy with you and I hope we have many years and many children together."

Lips quivering, she asked, "Do you mean that?"

"Princess, I do."

Victoria looked into his eyes and the world disappeared and she saw Prince and another woman standing before a tent. Two young children were sleeping nearby and the couple was arguing.

"I'm not going any farther," the woman, who must have been Mary Defiance, said.

"We can't stay here," answered Prince.

Mary Defiance stomped her foot and raised her skirt, the hem covering his head. "Be gone," she shouted. Victoria still didn't know what caused the argument but she could see clearly that Mary Defiance had made the final decision and Prince had no choice but to leave.

"Princess, I'm here." Victoria's eyes focused again on her husband's face and saw in his heart that this was true. She sighed deeply and her heart reopened to him.

Joe and Dinah returned and they reloaded everything and continued into New Haven. It was almost dark when they skirted the western edge of the town and Prince led them to a farmer's field at the base of a large basalt cliff.

"West Rock," Victoria said, looking upward.

Prince looked at her sharply. "Have you been here?"

Immediately Victoria realized her mistake. She had seen a sign a short distance away indicating the massive cliffs. Trembling, Victoria decided to share one of her secrets to see the results. "No, I read the sign back there."

Silence. More silence. "You read the sign?" Prince finally asked.

"Yes, I can read. Not fancy words, but I can read." There, it was out there. She had never told anyone outside her family and, even within the family, they didn't talk about her anomaly.

He shook his head and then laughed aloud. "You amazing woman, you can read. Do you know what that means?"

Victoria shook her head. She didn't know what he was thinking, his response being so unexpected.

"None of us can read. But most of the locals do." He seemed absolutely delighted.

"You're not upset?" she asked.

"Upset? In the country of the blind, the man who can see out of one eye is king," Prince said. "We will have such an advantage over everyone else here."

Later, he practically carried her into their tent, set up in the same spot that he had left earlier that year with his former wife. As they lay on the comforter, Victoria wondered if the ghost of Mary Defiance still lingered. She tested the air, listened, and waited. No, Victoria felt confident she was of the past. She turned hungrily toward Prince.

Having initiated their New Haven home, they lay satisfied, her head resting on Prince's shoulder. She could feel the jut of his jaw and his moustache hairs pressed into her head. As he stroked her cheek, he whispered, "I am here, Princess, I am here."

FOUR

She would recognize the calloused hand stroking her face anywhere. Victoria heard murmuring of voices—her husband and other men—but could not open her eyes. She rested there, feeling his hand first on her face, then her arms and shoulders. He pulled the covers up to her chin and adjusted a pillow under her head. She felt a stabbing pain in her head. Her eyelids must have fluttered, because she heard a whisper in her ear, "Princess, I'm here."

She smiled at the phrase that often led to heated touches and kisses. She tried opening her eyes again and recognized one thing: she was not in camp in New Haven. He exhaled deeply onto her face. "Princess, stay with me."

Victoria tried to nod but the pain was great. She was able to whisper, "Yes" and wiggle her fingers that were tightly enclosed in his great hand. She could see tears welling in his eyes and she murmured, "I love you."

"Dearest, I love you, too," he said, his voice cracking.

As the room came into focus, she realized that she was at the old Farmer's Hotel. Someone else was in the room and she moved her eyes slightly past her husband. The shadowy shape resembled him and she thought it must be one of their sons, maybe Noah. She wasn't certain why she was so sore and tried to sit up. Her husband placed his hand behind her, but her head grew dizzy and she struggled back to reclining position, her eyes still on her husband's.

Prince stroked her face a few minutes. He then reached for a glass of water on the bedside table.

"Can you drink?" he asked.

He helped her sit up slightly and propped pillows behind her. This time, she was able to remain upright. Prince gently offered her a sip of water. When the glass was almost empty, she reached for it and was able to drink herself. Prince let out a breath that seemed to come from deep inside.

"What happened to me?" she asked, as she returned the empty glass.

"You must have slipped on the ice and hit your head."

"Where was I?"

Prince paused slightly, as he looked surprised and then concerned. "You were on Main Street, past the harness shop." He paused. "We think you hit your head on the hitching post. You have a nasty bump back there." As he was speaking, Victoria again tried to touch the sore spot and succeeded in fingering a large tender lump. Her son, whom she had forgotten about, reached over with an ice-filled cloth. Prince adjusted it behind her head and she indicated it was comfortable. The cooling permeated the cloth and reached her head in minutes and she felt the throbbing subside.

"Thank you," she smiled as her eyes closed.

"Where were you going?" Prince asked.

"Oh," said Victoria, trying to think. She couldn't remember. She didn't know if it was day or night, she could only feel the bed and warm covers and cooling cloth as she faded. Her last image was the tall, handsome monument with the cantering horse and she thought of Wash.

"Mammis, can you eat something?"

A voice reached her and she struggled back to the room. She opened her eyes to see Daisy standing with a small bowl. Victoria tried to sit up and she found, if she went slowly, her head would not spin. Her left elbow was sore, so she had to use her right to prop herself up. Daisy put the food on the table and placed a towel over her mother's front to protect her from spills. She then reached for the bowl and blew on a spoonful.

"It smells good," said her mother.

"Rabbit."

Victoria's mouth watered and her stomach grumbled and she wondered how long it had been since she had eaten. She took a spoonful, which was warm but not scalding, and savored the flavor. She didn't remember making this stew and thought perhaps Daisy or one of the other family members had. She looked around the room to confirm that she was still in the old Farmer's Hotel. She remembered one of her grandsons had been born there recently, maybe last year or the year before. Daisy gave her another spoonful and, before long, Victoria was holding the bowl and feeding herself.

Later that day, Prince came back to the bedroom to say goodbye before he went off on business. As she grew stronger, he often would stop by at noontime, if he wasn't working far away, and he always was the one to bring her dinner. But she most looked forward to their nights together.

"Princess, I'm here," he would say, as he slid under the covers, the warmth of his body quickly radiating to hers. He'd wrap his arms around her shoulders and pull her close, covering her face and neck with kisses. By the end of the week, she was able to respond, playing with his moustache and kissing the edges of his lips before their true kissing began. It felt good to be back to some semblance of health and she knew it was his loving that brought her there. Prince had been the one to console her when they lost their sons. Even though his grief was as intense, she could feel his strength and love carry her through. She couldn't imagine going through her troubles without him.

That thought made her shiver, causing Prince to prop his head on his hand while his elbow supported him and ask, "What's wrong, Princess?"

Victoria quieted herself and saw an image of them riding the gray mare together sometime soon. The vision's feeling was joyous and exhilarating, which she took to be a good sign. "Nothing, really. You just give me the chills," she smiled winningly at him.

"Oh, Princess," he sighed, as he proceeded to kiss and caress her. She pulled him to her.

"Are you sure you're ready?"

Victoria pulled him closer. Prince checked with her at each stage to be sure that her body was able. Together, they warmed the room.

After that night, Victoria was able to slide back into her normal routine. The next morning, she was sitting at the table, drinking her morning coffee, when she picked up the newspaper and looked at the date. At first she was startled, as the letters on the page were blurry and she had always been able to read without glasses. But, as she continued to stare at the page, the print started to settle down. February the first, she thought, no, it was the eleventh. For a few seconds, she couldn't tell which it was. The two numbers remained and she became certain it was February eleventh. But she felt a distinct visceral response to February first. Then it suddenly hit her. That was the date Wash died. And she finally remembered where she had been going before she fell.

She heard his steps before the front door opened and Prince came in, placing his cloak on the coat rack and his hat on the table by the door. He looked tired, as he stopped to catch his breath. She wondered if he was exerted just from walking up the front stairs. He wiped his brow and then turned to the kitchen to catch her watching him and stopped short. For a brief second, she could see the startled look on his face that quickly turned to pleasant surprise.

"Princess, you're up! I was just coming to check on you."

"Yes, good morning. I am young again," she replied with a sly smile.

Prince laughed, his eyes crinkling with delight. He sat down with her and shared a cup of coffee. "It's cold out there," he said. "The Connecticut River has frozen."

"I was reading in the paper," she said, lifting the document, "that the Potomac is frozen, too, and the mail trains couldn't get through."

"It's been a bad February," Prince agreed.

"Ah, yes," said Victoria. After a few moments, she added, "I remember where I was going when I fell." She fixed her dark eyes on Prince's handsome features.

Prince looked encouraging.

"It was the first of the month," she said. She could see in his mind the development of an image of the handsome monument and realized that he knew. With their eyes locked, he reached to stroke her hand still holding the newspaper.

"My dear Princess," he said softly, "I'm here."

They sat without moving until he said, "I had better get some work done," and he rose, touching her gently on the side of the head. "Will you be all right down here without me?"

"Certainly. Daisy is here," she said as their daughter came into the room to replenish her coffee.

With that, Prince donned his cloak and hat and slipped out the front door. Victoria smiled at Daisy and noticed that she truly was a grown woman. At sixteen already, she needed to marry. Victoria couldn't imagine how she had gotten that old so quickly.

Daisy helped her move into a pile of cushions in front of the fireplace. She covered Victoria with quilts and surrounded her with more pillows.

"How's that, Mammis?"

"Fine, daughter, thank you."

Victoria was quite comfortable and the warm fire and quiet house lulled her. Some time later, she awoke with a jerk and it took her a few minutes to recognize where she was sitting. As the room came back into focus, she noticed she felt hungry. She must have slept much of the day. She preferred it here to upstairs in bed and was glad to be up and about, even if she tired easily. She heard plates being handled in the other room and called out.

"Hallo?"

"Yes, Mammis?" said Daisy's voice from the kitchen.

"I'm hungry. Bring me something to eat."

"Yes, Mammis." Daisy's head peeked around the corner of the door before heading back to the kitchen.

A few minutes later, Daisy returned with a bowl from the kettle. Victoria, pleased to be eating upright again, blew on the food and ate quickly. After the first few bites, however, she stopped to savor the subtle seasonings.

"Garlic?"

Daisy nodded. "And some thyme."

"Lovely combination." She saw Daisy blush from the compliment. "You'll make someone a good wife," she added.

Daisy quickly turned away to hide her face.

Victoria wondered if she really were that shy or if something else was going on. Daisy was the last of the Williams brood, the only unmarried one. Something about that didn't ring true to Victoria but she couldn't put her finger on it. She felt certain that Daisy wasn't her last child but no one younger was around and the more she tried to figure it out, the more her head hurt, so she decided to focus instead on a solution to Daisy's dilemma.

Later that night, when she and Prince slid between their comforters, Victoria left the candle burning. Prince looked at it and then her with a puzzled expression.

"We need to talk."

He settled on his back and locked his hands under his head. "About what?"

"Daisy."

"Daisy?" he questioned, as he propped himself on his side and looked at his wife. "What's wrong with Daisy?"

"She's sixteen and not married, that's what's wrong. And we've been so distracted by—" Victoria couldn't name the previous events but Prince nodded knowingly.

"So," she ended with a flourish, "we need to reckon this out." She lay down and waited. It would work best if Prince figured it out himself and thought it was his idea, although she would push the solution in the right direction if she needed to do so.

"Well," he started, "we have Richard married to the Wells girl and Bessie to a Stanley." He paused. "Of course, there's Kitty with the Boston Coopers."

They both lay there, neither one mentioning Wash's wife or her lineage and instead thinking of various families in their *folki*.

"Are there any Lamberts left?"

"No, the boys are all married," she answered.

More silence as he thought. Victoria struggled to remain silent and let him reach the same conclusion she had earlier that afternoon.

"There's Emma and her Squires boy, but we've had our fill of that family." There was a long pause as they both recalled the circumstances surrounding that couple's union. A replay of that situation would not be desirable, which made Victoria, remembering Daisy's averted look from earlier in the day, even more certain that they needed to take action soon.

"Well, there's poor Richard, your brother Samuel's son. The one Emma was supposed to marry."

Victoria sighed, with both sadness of the memory of Emma's choice and relief that Prince had finally gotten to the right solution. "Yes. There's Richard." She paused deliberately. "You know, Prince, you have a good idea there, with Richard."

Prince looked surprised. "I do?"

"Yes, I think they would make a good couple and it would solidify our connection to my brother's family long after we're gone."

"You don't think he's too old for her?"

"Look who's talking," she chided him.

"But he's much older than her. I'm only a little older than you. And sometimes you made me feel much younger than you," he said with twinkling eyes, trying to pull her to him.

Victoria laughed but held him at a distance. "Well, I think she could use someone who is settled, like her Dadrus."

"All right then, it will be poor Richard."

"We'd better stop calling him that," she laughed. "Certainly he won't be poor Richard once he gets Daisy for a wife. She's a good girl."

Prince lay back down, looked at the ceiling, and smiled, obviously pleased at finding an answer to the problem. "It's a good choice, too," he added. "The Somerville business is solid."

"Oh," gasped Victoria, turning towards him, "do you think Daisy will have to move?"

"Now, Princess," he said, turning to stroke her hair, "you know that's the way it goes. Just because you stayed with your family—" He chucked her under the chin, being careful not to hurt her head.

She sighed. "I guess you're right. But maybe—"

"No maybes. She will go wherever Richard decides. And that's that." Prince kissed Victoria on the top of her head and rolled away from her. Within seconds, she could hear his snoring and smiled. Right, Richard would make the decisions, just like Prince. She was certain that they could find a place for him at the stables at the old Farmer's Hotel, and she drifted off to sleep.

FIVE

Later that week, Victoria was walking down the stairs when she heard Prince saying, "Do you think it's wise, after her outburst yesterday?" She couldn't hear the words of the response but it sounded like one of her sons. Curious, Victoria slowed her descent and walked on tiptoes down a few more stairs. "Maybe a short trip would be good for her," said Prince. Through the doorway, she caught a slice of him sitting at the table. She was shocked at how old he looked, hunched over with his face puffy and serious. He must have felt her glance because he looked in her direction and visibly composed his face and body to rise and greet her.

"Princess, you are up. How are you today?"

She smiled at him, happy to see his transformation, and noticed he was wearing his suit, which made him appear distinguished. "I'm well," she answered, as she continued down the stairs. All physical damage from her fall was gone and she almost forgot it had happened. But occasionally, her family questioned her about it, or her health, in a way that she thought was excessive.

When Victoria reached the doorway, she found their son Noah, who had been sitting with Prince, standing near the door. He held her elbow and pulled out a chair. "Sit, Mammis, and we'll get you some breakfast." Daisy appeared with coffee and Victoria sat and nursed a cup.

"I didn't mean to interrupt your conversation. Please continue," she added.

Prince and Noah both looked intently at their empty plates. Prince cleared his throat. "Oh, we were just talking shop." Silence followed, saved by Daisy bringing in Victoria's breakfast.

"Here, Mammis."

"Thank you, dear."

"So, on another subject," began Prince. "Remember that arrest in New Haven?"

"Yes," Victoria sputtered. "The one for 'camping on private property' at West Rock where we've been since—" she paused. "Well, you and I have camped there almost forty years and you were there longer."

"Right. The owner is finally back in town and has agreed to tell the judge that he had given me permission."

Victoria felt her anger growing. "It's just one of those schemes to keep us in our place. It happens everywhere. We can't roam, we can't camp, we can't—" She felt Noah's hand on her arm.

"Mammis, it's the new law. No camping on private property without permission. We just have to clear it up with the judge."

"If Richard hadn't had so many horses roaming, they wouldn't have complained," Victoria continued, as if Noah hadn't spoken. "Fifty horses roaming through the neighborhood, pshaw. What was that boy thinking?"

Noah and his father exchanged looks. They apparently had been through this discussion themselves, because Prince said, "Richard isn't going with me. They are handling our charges separately." Prince rubbed his eyes. "In fact, would you like to come with me today? I'd like some company and Noah and Belcher have work to do."

Noah was nodding. "Yes, Mammis, I can't go. Are you up for it?"

"Of course I can go. I am so tired of you all babying me. I'm healthy as a horse now." She smiled at her joke but the eyes around her seemed serious.

"The hearing is at eleven." Prince pulled out his watch. "We will be leaving in about a half hour to catch the train."

Victoria quickly chewed her last bite, put down her fork, and drained her coffee. "I'll be ready." She glanced outside to check out the weather and rose. Noah instantly stood to pull her chair and help her to the door. She slapped his hand away and walked defiantly from the room.

Upstairs, Victoria put on her bracelets and earrings and a new skirt over her others. Draping her grandmother's silk brocade shawl around her shoulders, she decided that she would impress the judge and make it clear that the Williams family belonged on that land. For good luck, she reached out to touch the shells on her dresser, first the cockle from Bristol, then the jingle from New York, and finally the angel wing from Philadelphia. Heading downstairs, she recalled other times when she had been able to convey her strength and evoke changes by using only her will and cleverness and was confident that she could do the same this time.

Downstairs, Prince was standing by the door. Victoria reached out to finger the inverted U of the diamond-studded horseshoe tie tack that he wore and smiled at him, whispering, "You'll have good luck today." Prince nodded, just as Noah came around the corner. He was headed to Hartford to check on some horses, so he offered to take his parents to the station. The men put on their hats and cloaks and Prince helped Victoria with hers. Outside, Noah had brought around the work wagon and made room for them on the front bench, while a pair of horses waited impatiently.

"This is not as comfortable as our chariot," grumbled Victoria.

"It's not far, Princess," soothed Prince. "Let me wrap you with this robe." He tucked her in and drew her next to him. "Isn't that just fine?" he asked.

"Hmm," she murmured. "But the people won't stop and admire us."

"I'm tired today, Princess. Let's just get to the train."

Victoria, surprised by this comment, remembered her first impression that morning and turned to look at her husband. He did look exhausted with his puffy face. In fact, he looked less ruddy than usual. "Are you feeling well?" she asked, making a mental note to prepare some ground ivy for his eyes when they got home.

"Oh, it's nothing," he answered, not looking at either her or Noah. "Just not enough sleep last night."

Victoria didn't remember him being awake but was distracted by their arrival at the bridge. Noah jumped down to walk the horses and their clomping and neighing precluded any further conversation. By the time they got to the Hartford side, she was sidetracked further by the clang of the fire engine racing up the hill. "Shall we follow them?"

Prince consulted his watch. "We don't have time. Maybe Noah can look after he drops us at the train."

Noah nodded. "You know, it's amazing. They can get the horses harnessed and the engine out of the station in thirty seconds."

"What? That can't be true," said Prince.

"Yes, the horses are bridled at all times. And when the alarm sounds, the doors of their stalls automatically open and the horses run to their spots, where the harness, which is hanging from the rafters, falls into place. The men snap on the collars, put the reins on the bits, and away they go."

"Maybe our grooms could learn something from that."

"But, Dadrus, we don't need to get ready so quickly."

"I guess you're right," said Prince.

But Victoria could see that he hated to be outdone, even if the logic was there. "Let's just sell them good horses," she suggested.

Prince nodded. "All right, but it is an ingenious system," he said.

Noah laughed. "True, but it has its flaws. You know they practice every noon and evening. The horses are trained within two weeks to go to their places when they hear the alarm."

Victoria added, "I've seen them do that."

"Well, they keep their horses as long as they can and they do treat them well," Noah added respectfully. "But when they have to give up an animal, it can be a problem for the new owner."

"Why's that?"

"When the noon whistle blows, the horse will run to the station if it's nearby," Noah laughed. His parents chuckled, envisioning a distraught driver trying to check the horse as it dashed for its previous place at the fire engine.

"It's hard for many of us old folks to learn new tricks," his father commented. As they passed through the Soldiers and Sailors Memorial, Noah had to rein the horses sharply to the right to avoid colliding with another carriage. The steady clopping of horses testified to the congestion in the area.

"Being the nation's wealthiest city has some drawbacks," said Prince. "The population has doubled in just twenty years."

"But just look at the buildings," said Victoria, glancing at the skyline. They passed the Hartford Fire Insurance Company and the State Bank, all testifying to the glory of the city. She was always amazed by the long row of brick and stone buildings lining the street. Some three or four stories tall, she found their boxy appearance a bit stifling. Occasionally, they passed a building with massive columns or one with a cupola or captain's walk. She read the signs—tailor, dentist, bank, millinery, and watch cleaner—when they slowed for traffic. She watched people bundled in hats and scarves walking the sidewalks, passing by quickly enough that they became a blur.

By then, they had arrived at the train station, where Noah helped his mother down. The station, only a few years old, stood massive on the city block. Its gabled roof provided a huge interior space, as if boasting of its importance and cost. She and Prince entered and she noticed a silence and respect that the station conferred, along with an aura of importance and business. It caused her to whisper to Prince and clasp his arm.

Prince purchased their tickets and they waited on carved wooden benches until their train was called, the speaker's voice reverberating in the large space until she wasn't certain of the words. Prince led her to the platform, a conductor helped her up the stairs, and shortly Victoria and Prince were secured in their car. Victoria ran her fingers over the red velvet upholstery and noted the wooden paneled walls. Prince released the latch on a small table that was secured to the wall and it unfolded to provide a writing or eating surface.

"Similar to ours," he noted.

"True, I wonder if they copied our caravans."

Prince shrugged. "I'm glad the strike is over."

"Yes, it makes for better traveling," Victoria agreed.

"I've heard rumors that some parts of the line will be going all electric soon."

"Really? What is this world coming to?" But Victoria was distracted by the sounding of the final whistle and the train pulling from the station. In all their years of traveling, she rarely had taken the train.

Looking from the window for the duration of their trip, Victoria pointed out the vicinity of their Yalesville camp, where she had given birth to one of their children, and the nearby Quinnipiac River banks. Rumbling through the marshlands, they spooked a flock of ducks wintering in the open water. Victoria pointed to the west, appreciating the view of East Rock.

"Look, you can see the monument on the top."

Prince leaned over to look out the window and caught a glimpse of the structure rising above the exposed cliffs. The train began to slow and, indicating their arrival in New Haven, she said, "It surely is a quick trip."

"Yes, much faster than caravan."

"Will the train ever replace horses?"

"Oh, no, not the iron horse," said Prince definitively. "Track is too expensive. Horses can go anywhere, anytime. The horse will rule forever." At that, the train pulled into the station and Prince helped Victoria from her seat and off the train.

Looping his arm through hers, Prince started in the direction of the courthouse. "Will this be too much for you?"

"Of course not. I can't wait to tell that judge what I think."

Puffing his pipe, he squeezed her arm. "Princess, I'm thinking, in this case, that it's not a good idea. The charge is just a formality at this point."

"But the law restricts us. We must make a statement." Her voice was rising and her steps were faster, stomping on the sidewalk. She could feel Prince holding her back and trying to calm her and she knew that he would not budge. She was not going to be able to rant at the judge, which made her wonder why she was even going to court. If she would have to hold her tongue, it would be frustrating.

Just then a voice called out in the mother tongue. Astonished, they both looked to see a distinguished-looking gentleman calling them from the other side of the street. Prince looked at Victoria, who whispered, "Why is he talking the language?"

Prince shrugged. "How does he know us?"

"Perhaps he is that Yale professor I have heard about, the one who knows much about our people."

"Maybe," said Prince and he took off his hat. "*Sarisham!*" he called to the man.

"I suppose you want us to come over," Victoria added.

"Yes, please," said the man. "Professor Knapp," he added, removing his hat.

"I am afraid I cannot. We are headed to the courthouse. I must plead a case," replied Prince.

"Perhaps the queen can come. I have heard about you both for many years and I would enjoy an opportunity to visit and share some of my collection. I have some very old material from your people."

Victoria turned to Prince. "Would that be possible? I know you don't want me speaking to the judge."

"You could go," said Prince, visibly relieved to have a way to prevent Victoria from disturbing the courtroom. "I'll come get you when I'm done."

"Thank you, I would like to talk to him, if you don't mind."

"Go, it's fine."

With barely a glance backward, Victoria crossed the street, her skirts swirling and her hips sashaying. She could feel Prince's eyes on her, along with Mr. Knapp's. She was in her element, alive and working. She felt good and smiled radiantly at Mr. Knapp.

He helped her up the curb, saying, "Don't you go *mashing* me."

Victoria laughed gaily, excited to be with an exotic man who understood her ways. His handsome moustache reminded her of Prince, although she found his massive beard distasteful.

"Come in and see my library," he continued. "I believe I have some items that may interest you."

He helped her up the front stairs and directed her into the library to a large armchair. Mr. Knapp's maid brought a tea tray and placed it on the table between Victoria and the man. Her nose caught the scent of bergamot and she smiled appreciatively. "It's good to get a whiff of the old country," she exclaimed.

"Only the best for you, my queen," he said with a nod and poured the brewed tea over pieces of fruit in glasses in silver holders.

Victoria sipped her tea, taking care to protect her fingers when the holders grew warm.

"Perhaps you will tell me my future," he suggested, holding out his palm. Toying with the idea, she put down the tea and took his hand, which felt warm and soft in hers. Looking into his eyes, she decided he was about her age and felt a shiver run through her. She forced herself to look at his line and tried to calm her heart so she could focus.

"I see you surrounded by dark-haired women speaking other languages," she began.

"Yes," he said leaning in toward her. "I will be moving to Europe soon."

She nodded. "The words, these foreign words, they will make you famous."

"And rich?" he asked jokingly.

Victoria dropped his hand. "I don't know." She didn't want to share the rest of what she saw, which ended in his next decade.

"Well, then," he continued. "I am very lucky to meet you today. I have been teaching in Chicago for a few years and I am here just briefly trying to decide what to do with my collection. Let me show you."

At that, Mr. Knapp leapt from his chair to procure one item after another either from his shelf or bookcase or pile of papers on his desk. He showed her a book written in 1597 by Bonaventura Vulcanius, but it was in Latin, which Victoria did not understand.

"You may be interested in this," said Professor Knapp of another volume. "It's a romantic tale of a Gypsy maid, written by a woman in 1837."

Victoria thumbed through it but there were many words and few drawings. Knapp's blue eyes sparkled like the ocean as he moved on to describe where he'd obtained each item. He seemed to want to share a lifetime's collection in the course of an hour or two.

"Why are you moving?" she finally was able to interject.

"I find America's provincialism confining."

She raised a questioning eyebrow at him.

"People here are not interested in those from other cultures or lands," he added. "They think your people, for example, are the same as Gypsies from other parts of the world, such as Romania."

Victoria had heard of Irish travelers, of course, but knew less about those from Eastern Europe. Professor Knapp, she knew, was versed in the history and culture of her people from England.

He sat on the edge of his chair with a pile of papers from his desk on his lap. He eagerly thrust his face near hers and, as her vision blurred, she became confused and thought it was Prince sitting there. Then, her head cleared and her eyes recognized and rested on Professor Knapp. She noticed that his lips were moving and he, oblivious to her confusion, was droning on about the lack of appreciation for the Spanish language and things Basque.

Victoria began to breathe normally again. Her eyes roving, she caught a glimpse of an old magazine in the pile on his lap and thought it might be a copy of *Once a Week*, which she had heard about but had never seen.

Professor Knapp saw her look. "Please excuse my ranting," he apologized. "I can get off into my own world." He pulled the old document from the pile. "From April 1862," he pointed out. "One of my treasures." He opened to the article written about the coronation of Queen Esther Faa Blyth of Yetholm.

Mr. Knapp read, as if he expected her to be unable to do so, and she did not correct him. "The Queen, mounted on her palfrey, proceeded to the Cross, where the ceremony of coronation was to be performed—the crown-bearer and the crowner following behind ... he now placed the crown—a tinsel one, alas—upon the head of Esther ... and proclaimed her Queen Esther Faa Blyth, challenge who dare."

Victoria leaned closer to look at the accompanying illustration. A regal-looking woman stared back at her. Her hair, hidden by a white linen cap, was covered by an underscarf, knotted in the front. Victoria knew that Esther's mother was the source of her claim to royalty, so perhaps her father's influence led to the nontraditional tying of her *diklo*. Esther's dark eyes seemed to pierce her and she tried to break away from the image.

Professor Knapp, noticing her interest, suggested, "You could crown yourself queen here in America."

Victoria shook her head. "Not I, I am not related to the royalty."

But Knapp persisted. "We would enjoy honoring you."

Victoria demurred, "I am not a queen."

"But I've heard about your chariot," he said. "It sounds fit for royalty."

Victoria smiled slightly, pleased that word of their new chariot had reached New Haven. But she held her position. "We don't need to be named royalty, please."

Knapp relented. "I'm sorry, madam, it just seems natural. But I will drop the subject. Please stay, I have more to share with you. In fact, you may wish to see these," he said as he took out some illustrations.

Just a glance at the drawings of old campsites in rural England transported Victoria back to her childhood.

"Who did these?" she asked breathlessly.

"Charles Leland, the folklorist." Knapp glanced sharply at her as she inhaled loudly. "Are you feeling well?"

"Oh, I'm fine," she answered. But she felt shaky inside. The Coopers in England had befriended Mr. Leland and these illustrations might be of her own family. Perhaps the one with the woman and children by the fire was her grandmother when she was young. Victoria was struck with homesickness.

"Shall I fetch you some water? You look pale," said Knapp.

Victoria's eyes filled as she recollected her childhood. "No, thank you. You have touched a hidden spot inside me, one I have not visited in many years," she told him.

"I did not intend to offend you," he said. "I am sorry—"

She cut him off. "It is a mixture of sadness and joy. I welcome these childhood memories." She touched the paper briefly. "My púridaia, I miss her so."

Knapp nodded. "My family is gone also. That's part of why I am going to Europe. I have no ties here any longer."

Victoria sipped her tea, which had grown cold.

"Let me warm the tea," said the professor, rising quickly. The papers on his lap fell in confusion and they bent to gather them up into a pile. They heard her husband's voice calling from the street, "Hallo, there, I am back."

"Oh, I will finish later," said Mr. Knapp. He turned and looked out the window to confirm it was Prince.

Victoria rose, adjusting her skirt. "Thank you, this was lovely."

"Thank you for stopping in. And for telling my fortune," he added. They walked to the front door. Prince, looking up towards the house, was standing on the sidewalk. Mr. Knapp walked Victoria down the stairs and passed her arm to her husband.

"Farewell," he said.

"God go with you."

Since Prince had not climbed up the stairs to the house, Victoria turned to him after they started walking. "Was there trouble?" She thought that perhaps a bad judgment had soured his mood.

"No," he said, looking quickly at her. "The hearing went well. The judge asked our 'landlord' to the stand and he indicated that we had camped on his land for many years and with his permission. Charges dismissed."

"Capital. What about Richard's?"

"Separate case, as I already told you. He will be dealt with later." And after a pause, "How was your visit?"

Victoria described the story of the queen. "He wanted to make me queen here," she said.

"These Americans, they miss the royalty they eliminated during the revolution."

"I told him 'no.' Even in this country, it doesn't seem like a good idea to stand apart too much."

Prince agreed. "We must always be careful, no matter how much freedom there is. Remember why I just went to court."

She nodded and added, "Professor Knapp had some interesting illustrations. One may have been my family in England."

"Really?"

She pulled the illustration from her skirt as they arrived at the train station. Prince glanced at it, saying, "Very nice of him to have given it to you."

"Yes, if he knew."

Prince looked at Victoria and chuckled. "You have the knack." He looked at the family and nodded. "It reminds me of my childhood, also."

Victoria replaced the illustration in her clothing and Prince checked the timetable. Although he was not a reader, he could decipher the word for "Hartford" and knew his numbers. "One is leaving in about twenty minutes," he decided, after glancing at his watch.

"Good," said Victoria, leaning on his arm. "This day has had much pleasure but was tiring."

"We can rest on the trip home." He placed his hand on hers and she noticed how rough it was compared to Mr. Knapp's. Prince was a worker and a doer, not a scholar. She could see the difference. But their moustaches were the same, she decided. She was stopped from any further comparisons by the whistle of the arriving train. A number of passengers alit and, after a few minutes, she and Prince were allowed to board.

They stopped at a pair of seats and Prince gestured for her to enter.

"No, you can have the window this time."

"But you enjoyed it so," Prince demurred.

"I wouldn't be surprised if I nap on the way back. Please, you enjoy the view."

So Prince sidled into the row and sat down, with Victoria taking the aisle seat.

"Do you want anything to eat or drink? I heard there is a food car now."

"No," yawned Victoria, "I am fine. I had tea with Mr. Knapp."

The whistle blew and the train started to move. Prince pointed out someone on the tracks who was walking, and then running alongside the train, waving frantically at a young woman in their car. "I'm glad you're not leaving me," he said, squeezing her arm.

"I'm not leaving you," she said. "Where would I go, anyway?" They passed East Rock again and the snow on the fields glistened in the sun.

Victoria pulled her grandmother's brocade shawl around her shoulders. The seat gently rocked as the train gathered momentum. She rubbed the shawl between her fingers and remembered sitting as a child, holding those very tassels.

SIX

It was one of her favorite times of the day, just the womenfolk together. As a young child, she would pick up a pillow and place it on the floor, as she nestled between her *púridaia*'s bony knees. The lamp was low and exaggerated shadows moved across the bender's walls as Mammis sat across from them and did her work.

"A good day today," commented Mammis.

"Aye, a good one," her grandmother answered. "We sold almost all our brooms and baskets."

Victoria felt Púridaia's coarse skirt across her cheek as she sat between her grandmother's ankles. Her arms moved in a steady rhythm as she bundled osier stems they had picked earlier that day. Mammis was weaving a large basket and the quiet pulsed in Victoria's ears as she sat there, contented. Sometimes she had to help with the work, tying for Púridaia or stripping bark so Mammis could use a piece of willow. But right now, she could settle back into the folds of Púridaia's skirt.

Victoria could envision her grandmother behind her, sitting upright on her pillow, covered by a shawl, her face drawn and wrinkled, exaggerating her protruding nose. Victoria loved that old face and the comforting woman behind it. She had a certain smell, a mixture of wrinkled old skin and fresh bark. Victoria sighed and Púridaia reached down to caress her head.

"Princess, you be tired?"

"No, Púridaia, I'm fine," she replied, not wanting to be sent off to bed yet.

"Aye, Princess, of course you're fine. Sitting here with us, what could be better?" and she tugged lightly on Victoria's long, dark braid

50

before stroking her head.

Victoria nodded under Púridaia's hand. As much as she loved all her brothers and father, it was a special time when it was just the three of them, especially now that her older sister had married the Stanley boy and moved out. "Tell me a story," she pleaded. "The one about me."

Púridaia resumed her work as she began. "Back in the old days, there was a wicked Queen who was vain and jealous. One night, the Queen had a strange dream where she saw the full moon fall to the Earth. She summoned the old Gypsy Crone to tell her what it meant. The Crone said, 'Today is born a beautiful child who will someday be Queen.' The Queen was outraged and had soldiers cover the countryside to find this child and bring her to the castle.

"Some time later, the soldiers returned with a beautiful, kind young girl, born on that day, who lived among the Gypsies. When the Queen saw her, she became enraged and uttered a curse to change the girl into a small golden fish. She commanded her soldiers to place the fish in a wooden box and bury it in the castle garden." Púridaia stopped her story to reach for more osier stalks. She handed the completed bundle to Victoria who deftly finished the broom with an ash handle and Púridaia continued.

"The old Gypsy Crone watched all this and, that night, she unburied the wooden box and set the fish free in the garden pond. For sixteen years, the Crone watched and protected the golden fish in the pond. By then, the curse of the Queen was fading and the golden fish turned back into the Gypsy girl at midnight each night, when she walked the garden path and sat on the bench until she again became the golden fish at daybreak."

Mammis interrupted to ask Victoria for a piece of willow. They spent a few minutes matching the width of the strands that Mammis had been using, before Púridaia resumed her story.

"The Queen had a son, a very nice boy, who was an excellent student. When he turned sixteen and it was time for him to marry, he began to interview girls but none pleased him. One night, the prince had a dream that the full moon fell to the Earth and he went to the Crone to ask her what it meant. She said to him, 'Come meet me in the garden at midnight tonight and you will see what it means.' So, at midnight, the prince went to the garden and the beautiful Gypsy girl was sitting on the bench by the pond. The prince fell in love with her and met her at midnight every night for two weeks."

This was the part that Victoria loved, and she imagined, many times over, the point at which a handsome young prince would claim her. She caressed Púridaia's shawl hanging nearby and wrapped its tassels around her fingers.

Púridaia continued, "The prince went to the Queen and told her he had found his wife and a date was set for the wedding. When everyone gathered in the garden, the prince could not find his bride. The Crone pointed to the golden fish in the pond and said, 'Here is your bride.' The prince was surprised but he had grown to trust the Crone and agreed to marry the golden fish. The Queen was outraged and everyone at the wedding was laughing quietly at the prince. But as soon as the prince married her, the golden fish was released from its curse and became the beautiful Gypsy girl."

Púridaia reached down to touch Victoria's cheek as she finished the story. "When the Queen saw what happened, she realized that the prophecy had come true and she ran off into the woods and was never seen again. The prince and Gypsy girl lived happily together and had many children. And there was peace in the land and Gypsies were welcome throughout the kingdom."

Victoria sighed and closed her eyes. She must have drifted off to sleep, as the next thing she knew, she felt her mother carrying her to bed. Mammis covered her gently with her down-filled comforter and said, "Goodnight, Princess," as Victoria nestled in its folds. She heard Púridaia's words swimming through her head and could envision the beautiful Gypsy girl and her prince standing by the castle pond. She wondered when that would happen to her. She was certain that it would be her story. After all, Púridaia said so, and her predictions came true, like the one about her birth.

"When you have your next daughter, name her after the Queen of England," Púridaia had said to her parents some years ago.

"But I'm not expecting," said Mammis, "and maybe I won't have another daughter."

"And we are under a king here," added Dadrus, "King William."

"Yes, but not for long," Púridaia had replied. "Victoria will be Queen and your child will be named for the Queen of England. Certainly they won't harm us if we name her for the Queen."

Neither was terribly surprised when, a few months later, Victoria became the Queen of England and, shortly thereafter, Mammis had a daughter whom they named after her. And some day, she would be queen of her people, too, thought Victoria, as she fell asleep.

Victoria was several years older, when, one cold morning, she emerged from the bender and saw her brother Samuel shoveling ash and soot from their fire.

"You have a job?" she asked.

"Yes, over in Warminster." He continued his work without speaking.

"Can I come with you, please?"

Samuel looked up briefly. "No."

"Please." Victoria swung her long braids with excitement.

"You don't realize how much work it is to catch rats."

"I have small hands, I can help."

"Victoria, I don't use my hands. I use traps and I don't need your help." Samuel finished filling his bag with soot and started over to the cooking area to clean up.

"Please, I'll be quiet, I won't scare them."

Samuel sighed. "Little sister, come sit." And they both walked to the stumps near the fire and Samuel sat while Victoria stood, first on one foot and then the other.

"I have already prepared the site for several days. Now I have to go back and stay at the dark storehouse from dusk until midnight without sleeping. You wouldn't want to do that, would you?"

"Oh, yes," cried Victoria. "I hate to sleep at night. I can stay awake."

"Oh, really," said Samuel, raising an eyebrow. "Then I have to check the traps again at sunrise. I know you like getting up early, too," he said with a smirk.

Victoria hesitated before saying, "I can get up early if I have to." Her voice was a bit less enthusiastic.

Catching her braid as she stood there, Samuel continued, "I have to trap for three nights, which means I'm away for four days. You don't want to be away from camp that long, do you?"

By then, Victoria was doubting the wisdom of going with Samuel but she didn't say anything.

"And if you get bit, you can get all kinds of diseases and blood poisoning and—"

"All right, all right, I'll stay home," she pouted, hugging herself to keep warm.

Their grandmother joined them. "Do we have any milk? I can't seem to find any."

"I think you gave me the last of it in my tea last night," Victoria reminded her.

"Oh, dear, I suppose I'll have to go pay a visit to Farmer Scott," she said, took the milk jug, and headed off in that direction, almost bumping into Victoria's mother.

"Where are you going?" asked Mammis as she came to fix some coffee.

"Milk," replied the grandmother, with a smile and a nod towards the Scott's farm.

Mammis smiled back and Samuel said, "I'm off to Warminster. Eight shillings a night."

"God go with you and don't get bit," she answered. "And, Princess, what about you?"

Now that she wasn't going rat catching, Victoria had no plans, but she wanted to be as useful as everyone else. "I could look for buds and willow bark," she said, stomping her feet to keep the circulation going.

"That would be good," said her mother, pushing the girl off in the direction of the path.

A few hours later, Victoria returned to camp. She hadn't meant to surprise her parents, but she didn't realize that she was walking softly and was out of view, when she overheard their conversation.

"I just heard news from Ireland. There's nothing to eat there and people are starving. Many are heading to America, although I heard the story from one who came here instead."

"What's happened?"

"Potato blight." Her father paused. "The same thing could happen to us."

"Surely there would always be something to eat in England," protested her mother.

"Perhaps, but what I heard, it's pitiful. People falling dead, pregnant women losing their babies, and landlords evicting tenants. The man who came here was skin and bones."

"What do you think we should do?"

"Well, we really can't leave here. Your mother couldn't travel that far."

Victoria let out a sigh, cheered that they were not leaving, and especially relieved that she would not be separated from her grandmother.

The sigh must have been loud, because her parents stopped talking. "Did you hear that?" asked her mother.

Victoria adjusted her face to reflect innocence and, swinging her foraging bag, casually sauntered around the corner. "Hallo," she said jauntily.

Her parents looked at each other out of the corners of their eyes and resumed their normal affect. Nothing more was said of potatoes or famine or moving to America.

Several years passed and Victoria grew taller and stronger, while her *púridaia* grew weaker and thinner. But she still was able to tie up a strong broom and Victoria was not so large that she couldn't still nestle between her knees. They were sitting in the tent one night when her father burst in, his eyes wild.

Her mother jumped up to greet him. "What happened?" she asked, putting her hand on his arm to try to calm him.

Her father was shaking and his eyes were as black as Victoria had ever seen them. She scooted deeper into Púridaia's skirt, hoping to become invisible.

"They did it again, they passed another of those enclosure acts," he spit. "There is no place left."

Her mother's face dropped and then was set firmly into place. "We will find something."

"No, I tell you, year after year, they have taken away and taken away. Someone is paying the commissioner well." Her father was too distraught to sit down and the bender was too small to pace. Finally, he opened the flap and walked outside.

Her mother followed him and Victoria heard her soft voice talking him down. She could tell that they finally settled around the fire and began to talk. They must not have realized that their words traveled clearly into the tent.

"What will we do? Is there another site nearby?"

"Nothing. It's happening all over England. They want us to leave the countryside and go work in the city." Her father snorted. "Can you imagine me, sitting at a machine all day?"

"No, I can't. And I would never expect you to do that," said her mother calmly.

"In America, there is so much land. Miles and miles, acres and acres. Owned by no one, available for traveling."

There was a long pause. Feeling her shift behind her, Victoria grabbed on tightly to her grandmother's leg. "We won't leave you," she whispered fiercely and they strained to hear the rest of the conversation.

Finally her father spoke. "I know. We aren't going anywhere right now. But this makes it very difficult for us."

"We will sell more baskets and find other ways to get food. We have each other and that is what's important."

Her father grunted. After a few minutes, her mother added, "Thank you." Victoria understood, as did Púridaia, who wiped her eyes on her sleeve.

Not long after that, Victoria noticed that Púridaia wasn't eating much.

"Here, have some of mine," she offered her grandmother. "I've had enough."

Púridaia just smiled and shook her head. Victoria caught her sleeping much of the day and her bony knees grew knobbier. The days grew longer and vegetation turned green again. One summer day, Victoria decided to walk to the river, a distance away, to search for plants she needed.

"Púridaia, you need anything before I go?" she asked.

Her grandmother was propped up under a tree and covered with blankets. "No, Princess, I'm fine."

"I'll be back at sunset." She took her grandmother's hand in hers. "You're cold," she said, surprised.

"I'm fine."

"You're wearing your new dress," said Victoria, now that she could see the sleeve from under the blanket. "It looks nice."

Her grandmother smiled at her.

"I'll bring back some willow bark to make fresh tea," Victoria added. She knew it helped her grandmother's arthritis.

"Thank you."

"God go with you."

"And you. You never know what tomorrow brings."

With that, Victoria headed to the river. It was a long walk and she kept off the road to avoid questions or running into the Others who often threatened her people. It was cooler that way, also, as the sun rose brightly in the sky. She skirted cornrows and pastures of sheep and watched the silhouette of trees lining the river grow larger and larger as she neared.

When she finally reached the riverside, she stopped and pulled out a baked potato from the previous day's meal. She sipped fresh water and glanced around. With birds calling and water gushing along rocks, she felt at peace.

She spent the next few hours gathering plants. In one area, she found a cluster of mushrooms that were perfectly ripe—gills still closed shut and bodies full and taut. She remembered to cut a large piece of willow bark from one of the low branches of the tree lining the river.

Her tranquility was shattered by an ear-piercing scream and Victoria stood rooted in place until she caught a glimpse of a large barn owl entering the trees from the nearby open fields with something dangling from its beak. Willing herself to ignore its negative portent and trying to be practical, Victoria decided the owl must have been nesting if it were foraging during the day. Victoria glanced at the sun and realized it was later than she thought. She shook her head to dispel memories of the last owl she had seen, the one that flew through camp the day her uncle broke his leg, and gathered everything into her foraging bag to take one last look around before heading home.

She heard the keening before she reached camp and started running, her bag banging against her leg. She was almost certain that it came from their bender and, covering the uneven ground, she struggled to breathe. As she burst into the opening, the wailing grew louder and she stopped, mesmerized by what she saw. Her *púridaia* was still propped up under the tree but her mother was prostrate before her, gasping and banging the ground with her fists.

Victoria dropped on the ground near her mother, just as her father and oldest brother Richard arrived. She glanced up at her grandmother and confirmed that her bony chest was no longer rising and falling, before beginning her own lament.

Wails from the group brought other families from nearby camps. Initially, Victoria noticed their arrival but then she lost all external focus and was drawn into her mourning. She recalled her grandmother's final words and her sobbing grew out of control. Her grandmother had been trying to say farewell and she had been too interested in foraging to realize it. She wailed and moaned and thrashed herself on the ground.

"Princess, come here," her mother called.

For a week, everything had stopped and other camps brought bowls of fruit and vegetables, rice and potatoes. Mammis and Victoria had sat, rooted, near the cooking fire and frequently sobbed or tore their hair. But now they could bathe and cook again, although sadness still clutched at Victoria when she looked in the corner of the tent where her grandmother had slept.

Her mother patted the spot next to her and Victoria scooted over to her mother's comforter.

"I hope this isn't too painful," her mother began. Concerned, Victoria looked at her. She wasn't sure she could handle any more. "You know that we burned all of Púridaia's things." Victoria nodded. Of course they had; that was the way it was done.

"She gave me something her last day to be passed down."

Victoria, surprised, said, "I didn't know."

Her mother nodded. "Púridaia said you were the person to have this." As she spoke, she pulled out the silk brocade shawl.

Tears started in Victoria's eyes, as she reached to take the bundle. "It's heavy," she commented.

"There is something inside," her mother said quietly.

Victoria unfolded the shawl to reveal a small parcel covered in black silk.

Victoria gasped. "Her cards."

"Yes. They are yours now. I know I don't need to tell you how carefully to treat them or how much to treasure them."

Victoria nodded through her tears. Her grandmother's use of the Tarot had been private. In fact, when she pulled out her deck, the family knew to leave her alone in the tent. Victoria made no move to take the cards.

"Here," said her mother, with her arm stretched toward her.

With a shaking hand, Victoria took the parcel. "But why me?"

Her mother smiled a sad smile. "And why not."

Thirty days had passed since her grandmother's death and the family was marking the date with a feast. Richard had brought home hedgehogs and the women were cooking for the extended family. They had covered the animals in clay and then placed them in the open fire where they roasted, along with potatoes. Fresh berries, greens, and milk were ready to be served.

Group by group, the extended family and close friends arrived. People were talking at once and bringing dishes to share. Her mother greeted each person and handed the food to Victoria, who placed the items on the eating tarp.

Her father banged on the stump and removed his hat and everyone hushed.

"We are here to close the formal mourning period for a woman we all loved and cherished." He sprinkled some wine drops from his cup on the ground. "I was delighted to take her in when her son's family disappeared. As they say, you cannot walk straight when the

58

road bends."

People mumbled among themselves. Although they knew that the arrangement had been unusual, they had not known the details and their respect for Victoria's father increased.

Her mother took up the narration. "I thank you all for coming to honor her. And I thank my husband for allowing us to share her last decade together."

"Amen," called one of the family.

Others joined and then her father started the meal.

Her sister Betsey, who had come with her husband from their camp, pulled Victoria aside. "Where's Samuel?" she whispered. Victoria glanced around and spotted her other brothers. With all the relatives and members of her *folki*, she hadn't noticed Samuel's absence. Apparently her mother hadn't either or she wouldn't have allowed the feast to begin. Victoria shrugged and the two said nothing as they rejoined the women and children.

A short while later, there was a commotion by their bender and Victoria saw Samuel's back as he ducked inside. Several minutes passed and he came out and whispered something to their mother, who looked at him askance, while he took off his hat, ran his hand through his hair, and kept talking. Victoria saw their mother glance at the tent and shake her head. Samuel shrugged and walked to the eating tarp. He piled the remainder of the food into a large bowl, which he took into the bender.

Many hours passed, with the men smoking by the fire and the women talking near the cooking fire. Family and friends eventually said their God-go-with-yous and went back to their camps, leaving the Cooper clan alone. Samuel had stood guard at the tent and deterred anyone from entering, but it was late now and Victoria wanted to sleep. And she was curious about who or what was inside.

"What did you bring home this time?" she asked when she got near her brother.

She had expected Samuel to laugh, but he didn't.

"Another rat? Or maybe a ferret?"

A noise, coming from the tent, sounded suspiciously like a woman crying and Victoria raised a questioning eyebrow at her brother. He opened the flap and they entered. When her eyes acclimated, Victoria saw a dark-eyed Gypsy woman and two children huddled on a comforter in the corner of the bender that had been used by her *púridaia*. The woman was sobbing quietly and the children lay, wide-eyed, looking at Victoria.

Victoria touched her chest and then forehead. "What happened? Who are they?" she whispered to Samuel. Samuel put his finger to his lips.

"I'm already whispering," she hissed.

The woman stuffed her fist into her mouth to keep from making any sounds. Victoria pulled Samuel from the tent to find her mother and father standing outside. The three of them looked expectantly at him.

"Let's go over by the fire," he said. The family sat down and Samuel began.

"I was in town, checking one of my buildings that I had cleared of rats. I knew I needed to be back for Púridaia's ceremony, so I started back after noon. Not far from the edge of town, I saw a pile of three rocks on the edge of the road, so I veered my wagon into the brush." He took a sip of water before he continued.

"There I found a woman and her two children, all wild-eyed and distraught. The woman kept clinging to me, babbling. Finally, I pieced together the story."

"What happened?" asked his father, whose pipe was clenched between his teeth.

"She, her husband, and the children were walking along the road with their horse and wagon, when a brash young man came charging down the hill on his horse." Samuel looked around and said quietly, "I believe it was a young man of substance in town."

Victoria began to ask, "Henr—?"

"Shh," said her mother. "Let's not mention any names. Samuel, please continue."

"The earl spooked the man's horse, which ran out of control. It knocked down the husband and ran him over with the wagon. Killed him outright."

"Chut, chut," said his mother. "But why is the family" and she turned her head towards the tent and then back to the group "here? Why didn't they go to their *folki?*"

Samuel continued, "The young man fled the scene but not before he said, 'You are the only witnesses. I will erase you from the record.'"

"He's right, no one would know if the family disappeared," said Victoria.

"Yes, and even if the case went to court, with his connections—"

Samuel continued, "The woman is terrified. If she is seen again, he will snuff her out, along with her children."

Their father took a puff on his pipe and looked back and forth among them. "We have no choice but to keep the family."

Samuel nodded. "I will marry her and adopt Sarah and John. The family can come with us to America."

Victoria gasped but her father nodded. "That is wise. We will have to leave sooner than we planned. We can hide them here until we can secure passage."

Although in retrospect, it made sense now that her grandmother was gone, Victoria knew nothing about the family's plans to leave England. She couldn't help saying, "America?"

"We knew things were bad for us here, but this confirms it," said their father.

Her mother turned to her. "Before Púridaia died, she gave me her inner skirt." Her mother glanced around, checking that their voices didn't carry to the tent. "Her gold coins will be sufficient to get us all to America."

"You can close your mouth," Samuel nudged her. Victoria followed his suggestion, but her mind was racing. Leaving England and going to America. Having new cousins and a sister-in-law. All on top of the loss of her grandmother. It was all too much for her. She burst into tears and hid her head in her hands. She heard a voice urgently saying, "Princess, it's all right."

SEVEN

"Sarah, Victoria, you under there?" The two girls glanced at each other and then slid out from under the lifeboats. Victoria felt the swaying of the ship as it maneuvered the ocean swells and she easily matched its rhythm.

One of the Stanley women sighed as the girls came to stand beside her. "I need your help with the little ones," she said. "They are tired of being onboard already."

Victoria fell in step with her, while Sarah, with apparent disinterest, trailed behind. Victoria decided it was because she was older and, in a few years, she would be having children of her own. They reached their family cluster and Victoria lifted one of the girls high in the air and swung her around. John scrambled over, shouting, "Me, too, my turn."

Victoria laughed and gave John a swing. The Stanley woman handed a chunky baby to Sarah. They had left Bristol only ten days ago and already Sarah's skin had turned a chestnut brown. In fact, all the children were darker than when they left England. Wearing long skirts, Victoria could feel the piercing sun on the deck. She missed the respite that the lifeboats had provided, but she knew her responsibility was to entertain the young ones.

"Hey, let me tell you your fortune," she suggested to John. He quickly sat down and held out his hand. Leaning against a wooden box that provided a small amount of shade, Victoria folded her legs beneath her and settled on the deck. John looked at her, expectantly. Sarah rolled her eyes, but John, serious, said, "Victoria, tell me, what will happen to me in America?"

His mother, standing nearby, gave Victoria a warning glance, silently reminding her to be gentle, considering their recent trauma. "You will have many horses and children," Victoria began, looking earnestly at his palm.

John squirmed with delight. "Will I play the fiddle, too, like Uncle Richard?"

Victoria peered deeper at his hand. A troubling vision came to her but she brushed it aside. This was for entertainment, not a true fortune, she reminded herself.

"No, the tambourine," she told him.

The little Stanley girl was clamoring for her story, so Victoria gave John a small shove aside, as he pouted, "I want to play the fiddle," and reluctantly made room for his friend.

"John, come help me peel the potatoes," his mother called and he left to join the women who were making dinner.

Victoria sat with the little girl on her lap and felt the Others watching. Her family and the Stanleys made up about half the passengers; the rest were *gadje*. In these confined quarters, Victoria was physically closer to them than she had ever been. She trusted her brothers to protect her but wished her father were on the *Josephine* with them, too. But Victoria's mother had said it was best that they travel on different ships in case of accidents. They had heard stories about ships going missing or wrecking along the way. Plus, her father thought that Samuel's new family would pass undetected if they split the group.

The little girl squirmed off her lap, which returned Victoria's attention to Sarah bouncing the crying baby on her lap. He started pulling her long, dark braids and Sarah tickled him on the face with their wispy tips until he broke into peals of laughter and tried to toddle off. On the port side of the ship, a *gadje* baby was swaddled in clothes and protected from the sun. On the starboard side, their unconfined baby was taking small steps with help from the older children. The baby's mother came over, took him, and said, "Dinner is just about ready. Come help us."

The four adult women quickly served up food, while the children handed out plates. The men—Victoria's two brothers Richard and Samuel and two Stanley brothers—talked while eating.

"I hear that horses are wild in America," said Richard, chewing some re-hydrated meat.

"Only out West," replied one of the Stanley men, stabbing some potatoes. "There are good working horses in the South and Canada," he said with his mouth full.

"Did you hear the American man talk?" said Samuel, nodding his head to one of the *gadje.*

"I couldn't understand what he was saying."

"I can't even imagine what it will be like there," said the other Stanley brother.

While the women ate at the wooden box that had served as a table, Victoria hoped the good weather and their water supply lasted. She saw the ship-supplied water that the *gadje* were drinking and it turned her stomach.

After eating, Victoria watched the sky wash oranges and pinks over the ocean, as they sailed along. The up and down movement didn't bother her family, although Victoria heard some of the Others moaning. It was a bit like riding a horse, she decided. She turned her head to catch the cooler wind and watched as stars and planets rose along the horizon and filled the sky. Her families were sitting around, telling stories and smoking. Except for the missing family members and fire, it was much like camp.

May Stanley bent down to speak to her. "Help me bring the children to bed."

"Of course," said Victoria. She knew what was expected of her.

With a cargo of railroad iron, the passenger list on this voyage of the *Josephine* was short, only two dozen, compared with other manifests that were five or ten times that size. Victoria knew they were lucky to have less bickering for space and food and more time in the galley to cook their food. All the *gadje* slept below 'tween decks, as did the children in Victoria's family, while her brother and the other adults found sufficient room topside.

She rounded up the children, went down to their berths below, and sorted out who would sleep in which blankets tonight. The air was just cool enough to need some type of cover. Victoria saved a space for herself and Sarah. "Oh," said May, as she walked by, "I'll be sleeping with you for the next few days, too." Victoria nodded, understanding her monthly situation, and enlarged the space next to the children.

Shortly, Victoria heard the soft, plaintive sounds of a fiddle and headed up to join the adults on the deck. Her brother had started a very sad, keening song that sounded like a farewell to England. She herself wasn't sorry to leave, now that her grandmother was gone and she had not yet found a husband and knew that her time was running out. She was already twelve and no one had claimed her yet.

She knew her bride price would be high, but that wasn't the issue. She glanced around to confirm; her *folki* didn't include any boys her age. Maybe some of the families in America would have a partner for her. After awhile, she went below with the children and fell asleep listening to her family's music.

The next morning, Victoria hurried up the ladder to the galley to start breakfast preparations. With May Stanley unable to help, Victoria filled a critical role. The other women, already boiling water when Victoria arrived, gave her a small smile. Soon they were ready to serve the men and then the rest of the family.

"Just in time," one of them muttered, as a *gadje* woman started to enter the galley.

After everyone ate and they had finished the dishes, Victoria watched Sarah playing with the children and wandered off by herself. She tucked herself into a corner on deck and watched the crew nimbly climbing masts and adjusting sails. The ship was a beauty, she thought, rubbing the polished wood of the cleat post near her foot. She thought she blended into the shadows but one of the sailors cast eyes on her, so she huddled closer to the wooden beams. She had heard rumors about the packet rats, mangy men of dubious backgrounds that crewed these ships.

The foremast loomed above and she watched the tiny figures climbing aloft to adjust rigging. She imagined what they could see from up there, perhaps views behind of Ireland and endless ocean to the front. Maybe they felt like birds, flying in the sky. She longed for that freedom of movement.

The rocking of the ship lulled her to sleep and she dreamed of a new land filled with savages, or so she had heard. Their sweaty smell entered her dream and her heart beat faster as she imagined their marked faces. She felt one grab her arm and she struggled, awakening to realize, to her horror, that one of the sailors had slipped into her crevice and was pinning her down. His stench was unbearable and the stubble of his beard rasped across her face as he leaned into her. She had opened her mouth to scream but his other hand quickly covered it. Victoria tried to wrestle her way out of the man's grasp and was forced to use methods that her brothers had taught her. The man grunted as her knee reached his groin, but his hold was firm. She was just about to bite his hand when she felt his body slacken and his head roll to the side. The welcoming face of Samuel came into view and Victoria sobbed with relief as he rolled the sailor from her and gathered her up.

"Are you all right?" he asked, his eyes sparking with wrath.

"Yes, he just found me," said Victoria breathlessly.

Samuel looked at her clothing and seemed assured that all was intact. Their confrontation brought the first mate, his assessing glance taking in the situation. Samuel started to berate him but Victoria touched his arm and he toned down his complaints. They couldn't afford to get on the officer's bad side and he seemed likely to support his crew, the tawdry example of which was beginning to regain his awareness.

"Keep your men from our women," Samuel said, gritting his teeth.

"Keep your women in their place," retorted the first mate.

Samuel took Victoria's arm to return to their family on the deck closer to the mainmast. "Let's keep this to ourselves," whispered Samuel.

Victoria nodded, knowing that just being touched by *gadje* could be enough to lower her value. Recovering from her fright, she was starting to feel angry about the limitations she would now endure. And this was only the beginning of at least a month at sea.

The following day, Victoria heard loud yells coming from the poop deck. She spotted a sailor—she thought it was the one from the previous day, but they all looked the same to her—his left arm dangled useless by his side. Her eyes widened and then she caught a slight smirk on Samuel's face, as the first mate towered over the sailor, screaming, "You bloody well better use this arm. You're no good with only one. We won't need you if you can't work and it will be over the side for you."

With the children demanding constant attention and one woman or another unable to help with the cooking, there was plenty to keep Victoria busy. Occasionally, she and Sarah had a few minutes to themselves and they watched the horizon with increasing excitement.

"Land ho," shouted one of the crew up the mast a few days later. All heads turned to the direction he was pointing. Far off, Victoria could see a slightly darker section of the sky that eventually was discernible as land. Newfoundland, the rumor started. She had no reason to doubt that guess and, over the next few days, the crew confirmed their location. The *Josephine* continued, keeping the shore in view, day after day.

Rumbling from the *gadje* suggested they were near Boston, the area Victoria and her family would be settling. But they had to wait patiently as the ship continued past Cape Cod, along the shore of

Long Island and finally to the Sandy Hook Lightship.

"Why are we stopping?" asked Sarah.

Samuel looked at his brother, who shrugged. Suddenly, the captain sent up a signal flare and the children, who had been playing, ran to their mothers for safety.

"Is something wrong?" asked Victoria breathlessly. They had managed to cross the ocean without mishap and now things seemed awry.

The first mate, shouting through a speaking trumpet from the poop deck, ordered the men to lower the topgallant yard and sail. "Harbor pilot in sight," he added.

Richard spoke first. "Perhaps we need to be guided into the harbor."

Samuel added, "I see a skiff coming towards us. Maybe that's the pilot."

Sure enough, the skiff reached the ship's ladder and a man climbed in and shook the captain's hand as they headed to the wheelhouse. Within minutes, the first mate shouted more orders and the ship began its slow passage to the East River.

Entering the harbor, Victoria and Sarah crowded the railing.

"It looks like Bristol," whispered Victoria in shock.

"Sailboats and paddle boats, just like at home," agreed Sarah.

Rows of buildings several stories tall lined the harbor. As they got closer, Victoria could see people on ships in the harbor and they all looked like people she knew. "Where are the savages?"

Richard, overhearing her comments, laughed. "There are a half a million people living here and they are mainly from Europe. We won't see savages until we get out into the country."

Victoria could hardly hide her disappointment. What was the point of traveling all this way to come to cities just like what they left?

Richard caught her look and added, "America is a vast land and we will be able to roam here across unclaimed territory. We will be able to forage and camp unaccosted. You'll see. It'll be easier here."

Victoria nodded slowly, uncertain if she believed her brother. Reflecting on his previous comment, she blurted out, "How will we find Mammis and Dadrus, then, if there are so many people here?"

Richard put his arm about her, saying, "Princess, we have a plan. Dadrus and I worked it out before we left. There is a camp near the city and the first of us to arrive will settle there. Dadrus, if he gets here first, or I will spend the day in the city at the wharf checking the ships that arrive. We will find each other that way and all join together at camp." He gave her a squeeze. "Did you think we would be lost our first day here?"

Victoria managed a smile.

Just then, another skiff sidled up to their boat and a man climbed aboard.

"Health inspector," he shouted and set up his headquarters. Fortunately, with such a small passenger list, his survey was brief.

"All clear," he said to the captain, signing some papers. With his departure, the ship began moving again.

"What day is today?" Victoria asked Richard.

"September twenty-sixth, I think. We probably won't unload until tomorrow. Which is Saturday, if I'm not mistaken. That's good, because they don't process on Sundays. I'd hate to sit on this boat one day longer, if I don't have to."

Agreeing with her brother, Victoria watched as their boat eased into a slip at the pier. Crew both on board and at the dock scrambled to warp the ship and Victoria gasped as the bowsprit loomed across the mainland and seemed to graze the storefronts that lined the wharfs.

She scanned the waiting people for her father but saw no one resembling him, and her heart sank.

"We got here late today," remarked her sister Betsey. "Maybe Dadrus already headed back to camp. Let's hope for tomorrow morning."

Victoria nodded and watched the sun set over the busy harbor. At six o'clock a loud bell tolled from a tall tower, while people, carts, and cargo produced a background rumble that reached the ship. She could catch glimpses of the streets, arranged in square rows and columns, like windowpanes.

"Are you sure these people will accept our ways?" she asked. "Look how organized their city is."

Betsey shook her head. "I don't know, but we heard that there is much space here and most of it is open, not owned by anyone, and available for traveling. Maybe we will see once we get past the port."

Richard had joined them. "I'm sure camp doesn't look like this," he said.

Victoria nodded.

"Time to put the little ones to bed," Betsey said and she and Victoria went below with the young children in tow. Victoria lay with them but was restless, turning from side to side. She tried to envision where her parents were, what the camp looked like, and when they would meet up. But all she could see was the swell of waves that they had been watching for days and days. Even though the boat was still, she still felt herself swaying from side to side until she eventually fell asleep.

The following day, many hours later, after much commotion and paperwork, Victoria and her families stood clustered around bags and boxes near the wharf. The waterfront was crowded with wheelbarrows, chests, casks, barrels, horses, and people all trying to move in every direction. With no sign of her father, Richard said, "I'll scout out the area and come back soon. Everyone wait here."

Fortunately it was a sunny, warm fall day and, in the distance, Victoria could see masses of orange and red vegetation. The children ran circles around them and Victoria tried to rein them in.

"Don't trip that woman," she shouted to John, who was chasing pigeons. She, too, felt the desire to explore and celebrate the expanse of space, after so many days at sea. But she was also anxious to rejoin her parents and other brothers.

Richard returned to the group and they gathered around him. "I've met the runners from camp and they will lead us there." He paused and finally answered the question in Victoria's eyes, "No news of Mammis or Dadrus yet." And he added, "There will be no ships processed tomorrow because it's Sunday, so let's get settled at camp and wait until Monday."

With that, he grabbed a bag and loaded it onto a waiting wagon that the runner had arranged for them. Taking a final look at the ship that had been their home, Victoria thought it looked naked with its sails furled. With that, she fell into step with the rest of her *folki.*

"Look out for the horse cart," someone yelled and Victoria yanked John's arm as he narrowly escaped being struck by its wheels. Glancing up to the top of brick buildings, she could see the Stars and Stripes fluttering in the breeze, but any sense of peace was broken by the ruckus of merchants, ship owners, and workers moving quickly from street to wharf, yelling at each other and calling to colleagues at the counting house entrance.

As her family continued their passage, the throng thinned and moving was easier. Some hours later, Victoria could smell the smoke that suggested camp and shortly the clusters of tents and the vibrant red, green, and yellow wagons came into view.

"Pretty much like any other camp," said Betsey, remembering Victoria's fears about America.

Victoria smiled back, her heart feeling more joyous about their arrival. Children were running along the paths and people were calling out, *"Sarisham!"* Richard led them to a spot along the edge where they quickly put up their tents and established their fires. May hung the kettle and, in just a few hours, the place was home. A few families added generously to their dwindling food supply and Victoria and Sarah headed out with the water buckets.

Located on the edge of a marsh, the camp boasted two distinct water sources. A neighboring woman told them which was the drinking stream and where the various stations were along it and they were on their way.

"Doesn't it feel as though we are still on the ship, rocking with the waves?" Victoria asked.

Sarah shrugged, chewing on an apple that a neighbor had given her. They filled the buckets and returned to camp.

Later that night, Richard was tapped to fiddle at the dancing area. Victoria and Sarah joined the group and sat on the edge to watch the women and listen to the music. Except for the screech owls heard in the background, they could have been in England.

When Victoria went to bed and lay on her comforter, she felt the heartache of missing her parents. Quietly, she got up and found a small leather pouch that her mother had given her in Bristol before they left. From it, she removed a pink shell. Victoria had been walking along mudflats near the wharf, found the small ribbed bivalve, and showed her mother. "Cockle," Mammis had said. And then she had smiled and separated the shell into its two mirror images and handed one half to Victoria. "Hold on to this and I will keep the other half. We will be reunited on the other shore." Now there, Victoria fingered the shell and hoped it would be true.

On Monday, Richard returned to the harbor and Victoria waited all day for his return.

"We have to wash some clothes," Betsey pointed out. Grudgingly, Victoria left camp and walked upstream with her sister to the men's clothes washing area. She feared that she would miss her parents' arrival at camp while doing the laundry. She rushed through some of the washing until Betsey placed her arm around her.

"Remember how long it took us to get processed and disembark?" Victoria nodded.

"They won't be here before dinner, I'm sure."

Victoria sighed and went to work on the laundry. While it was drying on the rocks, she glanced around but decided she didn't want to forage. Without her parents, she felt lost. And here she was, almost a grown woman. She shook her head and decided she had to move past this childish behavior. After all, her sister and two brothers were here; it wasn't as if she were thrust by herself into a new land. By then, the clothes had dried in the late summer sun and they gathered them up and returned to camp.

By nightfall, Richard returned alone. Victoria almost lost her new composure but lifted her chin and said, "Maybe tomorrow."

September turned to October and the nights were frosty. Victoria snuggled gratefully into her down comforter, as she listened to the night sounds of the camp.

The days passed slowly. Victoria foraged and found a spot with a good growth of osiers to harvest for her mother when she arrived. By Saturday, she started looking for an opportunity to talk to Richard. That evening, she found him tuning his fiddle and she sat down near him. He focused on his strings, saying, "It's humid today; I can't stay in tune."

"Richard, I'm worried."

He looked over at her. "Anything in particular?"

"No, I haven't had any visions, except swells on the ocean. Nothing violent or disturbing."

"Well, then?"

"It's just taking them so long," she complained. "Why aren't they here yet?"

"Who knows," he said, as he finished tuning. "I'm headed to the dance area now. Are you coming?"

Victoria, sighing, nodded and the siblings walked together, Richard nestling his fiddle under his chin. Victoria joined the group of women and children and tucked herself on the ground. The music started and the rhythm was infectious. Victoria found herself tapping her feet and shaking her hands in time with the tambourine that someone was playing.

Suddenly a woman nearby fell to the ground, clutching her chest. Victoria ran to her side and found her huddled over her toddler whose eyes were bulging from a blue face. "Oh, my baby, my baby," the woman screamed, although her cries were lost in the sound of the music.

Victoria quickly opened the child's mouth and ran her fingers around his cheeks and as far down the throat as she could reach. With the sparkle in the boy's eyes dimming, she draped the child over her shoulder and hit him between his scapulas. She rapped hard, once, twice, three times, and suddenly she felt her back become damp as the child dislodged a chicken bone and lost the rest of his meal. Victoria swung the child back into her lap as she sat on the ground and checked him. He had started breathing and a faint tint of pink was returning to his cheeks. His mother, still wailing and pawing at her, opened her eyes and stopped mid-scream. The child coughed and slowly opened his eyes.

"You've saved him," the woman shouted. "You saved my baby." She pulled on Victoria's skirt. "My baby," she sobbed.

The boy sat calmly on Victoria's lap and looked at her. As their eyes locked, she saw where he had been and she shivered. He had been that close to leaving them. She cradled the boy nestled in her arms and rocked back and forth for a few minutes. She then looked again at him and said to his mother, "He's all right now. Here."

The woman hugged the child so tightly that he started to struggle. "Oh, my darling," she said and relaxed. Victoria patted the woman on the shoulder and returned to her previous seat.

Murmurs among the women grew louder as the news of her actions traveled. She felt endless pairs of eyes on her until she could stand it no longer and had to leave. She knew they were filled with gratitude but being different felt uncomfortable.

Early the next day, she was in the tent when there was a scratching at the flap. Victoria opened it to find a woman holding the hand of a small child. When the child looked at Victoria with glazed eyes, she could see her face was marred by a fresh burn mark that ran across her cheek, barely missing her eye. There was silence until Victoria said, "Please sit over on the stump and I'll be right out." She went back for her supply bag and then returned to sit down next to the child. She pulled out a container filled with one of her prized concoctions, a salve of bear grease mixed with cotton wool ash, which she spread generously over the burned area. The child's brow, which had been drawn together in pain, began to relax almost immediately. Her mother, seeing this, sighed. "I haven't slept since she tripped yesterday and fell into the kettle."

Victoria nodded and continued to rub the little girl's cheek. "You'll be fine now," Victoria smiled. "You may not even have a scar," she added.

"Thank you so much," said the mother, as Victoria gathered her supplies, rose, and returned to the tent.

After breakfast, there was another woman, alone this time. She sat near Victoria, who raised a questioning eyebrow to ask about her ailment. The woman moved her eyes toward the tent and Victoria led her inside. In the privacy there, the woman raised her skirts to expose a putrid gash on her shin. Victoria spread out the necessary materials to cleanse and purify the area.

It went on like that all day. Just before dinner, the woman from the previous night arrived with her toddler, who was in fine form. Shyly, the woman offered a small parcel wrapped in layers of cloth.

"For me?" asked Victoria, surprised.

"I cannot thank you enough," said the woman, "for my son's life."

Victoria unwrapped the cloth to reveal a very fragile circle of a shell. Almost transparent, its pinkish-orange tint reminded her of a sunset.

"It's beautiful," she gasped, looking up. The woman and child were already out of sight. Victoria re-wrapped the shell and placed it in the leather pouch that held her cockleshell in her supply bag.

After dinner, Victoria was exhausted and sat next to the fire. Betsey, sitting next to her, said, "Princess, I didn't know you had such skill." Between her exhaustion and the use of her nickname, Victoria burst into tears. Betsey put her arm around her and they sat together until it was time for bed.

The next day, and all those after that, there was a constant, steady stream of patients at Victoria's tent.

"We haven't had a healer for awhile," said the man who came for help with his ulcers. She brewed him a tea of honeysuckle flowers that she had dried earlier that spring and brought with her. Victoria was grateful to contribute to the camp, even though she fell exhausted into her comforter each night.

It was almost dinnertime and she had just finished treating someone in the privacy of the tent when she heard another scratch at the flap. She squelched a brief moment of irritation at facing yet another patient. She pulled back the flap and her irritation turned to absolute joy as she caught sight of her mother and father standing outside.

"Mammis, Dadrus," she cried, "You are finally here!" She ran out and grabbed them both and they were enveloped in a hug. "What took you so long?"

Dadrus said, "We were stuck at Sandy Hook for a week."

"Better than storms," added her mother.

"I suppose," said Victoria. "Am I glad to see you!"

Their conversation was interrupted by shouting from Samuel's tent, as his wife stormed off into the camp.

"Oh, dear," said Mammis. "Are they having problems?"

Victoria shook her head. "I don't know. I've been so busy with healing that I lost track of everyone else."

Samuel poked his head sheepishly from his tent. "What a fine welcome," he said.

His father shook his extended hand, as Samuel joined them, and said to his son, "Never buy a handkerchief or choose a wife by candlelight."

Samuel smiled grimly. "You could have reminded me earlier."

"And would you have listened?"

"Probably not," said Samuel as he turned to hug his mother.

The next morning, Samuel was sitting at the fire when Victoria left the tent. She made a cup of coffee and brought it to him. His dark eyes were surrounded by deep circles, suggesting that he hadn't slept all night.

After a few moments of silence, he said, "She's gone. She took Sarah, John, and their things."

Unsurprised, Victoria nodded. She had seen it in John's hand.

"I guess now I can find someone my own age," he added, trying to find the positive side.

"You did a good thing by bringing her here. And that was all it was. You're right; now you can find your true wife."

Samuel sighed and then stood. "I'm sure you're right." He looked at her. "Will you tell Mammis and Dadrus when they get up? I'm going to check about work around here."

"Of course," she replied and she busied herself with breakfast preparations. She hoped that she would have better luck in finding a husband.

EIGHT

This trip, Victoria barely watched the shore of England subside as they left Liverpool. She didn't notice the white dome or columns of the stately buildings lining the harbor. She hardly felt the excitement of riding the new steamship whose passage was twice as costly as her first voyage. She barely celebrated the presence of her parents traveling with her and her brothers this time. She stood gripping the rail of the main deck, gazing at the horizon but noticing nothing.

She felt her father's presence before she saw him out of the corner of her eye, as he joined her. Silence loomed, punctuated by calls from the sailors as they hoisted sails and adjusted rigging. The other women in the family were establishing their place in the ladies' cabin but she couldn't bear to be confined yet. And she wasn't sure if she would ever be able to face their reactions, if they included stares or silence.

Her father cleared his throat but, before he could speak, words flew from her mouth. "I just couldn't do it, Dadrus." She wanted her father to understand and support her but she wasn't sure where he stood. He had been silent since her decision. She knew that the way he handled her would set the tone for the rest of the family, their entire *folki,* although the Stanleys might apply their own standards.

Finally he spoke. "The age difference wouldn't have mattered after a while."

Victoria held her tongue. Her parents had started to subtract a few years from her age, as she remained unmarried, but she knew, as did her father, that she was actually sixteen. And Paul Stanley, her junior by five years, was a mere boy, not a potential husband. She shuddered, thinking about both the idea of marrying him and the likely consequences of her refusal.

"There will be no *kris*," he added. "The men agreed with me that you could refuse your first offer." Her father paused. "Only the first," he said significantly. Relieved, Victoria nodded and her father moved to join the family seated on the nearby deck. Only then did she glance around *The City of Manchester*. The men had extolled its virtues, including an iron hull and screw propeller, and downplayed the loss of two ships from the Inman line earlier that year. In fact, the last wreck occurred just before their departure. Perhaps it was the ship's larger size or absence of Samuel's run-away family, but her parents were content to travel all together this time back to America. They were bringing a large group of Coopers to settle in the Philadelphia area. At the last minute, the Stanleys had decided to avoid the embarrassment of traveling with them.

Their vessel entered the open sea and the swells immediately started it rolling. Victoria adjusted to the motion, rocking on her feet slightly with each wave. Up on the crest, down in the trough, she followed, smelling salt on the wind. They expected to arrive in just over two weeks, a vast improvement from their first voyage. Victoria worried about her future once they arrived, though. Her refusal had caused a glitch in the family's continuing plans to unite their *folki* through marriage. A lurch, as the ship floundered briefly in a cross wave, caused her to grab firmly to the railing. As much as she valued her family, she just couldn't do it. Paul's voice hadn't even changed. She felt as though she were talking to a younger sister. She just couldn't do it.

"Victoria," a voice called sharply from the direction of her family. Wondering if she would become their beloved princess ever again, Victoria ran to her mother. As she arrived, she noticed that the women were gathered around a small bundle on the deck and realized they were calling her in panic, not anger. Little Elizabeth, barely a year old, lay still in the covers.

"The wave surprised me and I dropped her," sobbed Betsey. "She hit her head on the deck. Oh, Elizabeth, breathe."

Kneeling down beside the baby, Victoria had only just unwrapped the child when Elizabeth gasped and her eyes fluttered open. While Victoria raised the baby and gently stroked her back, the women all started talking at once.

"I thought she was dead," gulped Betsey, wringing her hands.

"All she did was pick her up," added another.

"And the baby is fine. Amazing," whispered a third, shaking her head.

Victoria rose with Elizabeth in her arms. "I'm going to get my medicine supply. She has a nasty bump on her head." She handed the baby to Betsey, whose arms started shaking, but she sat down and cuddled her child.

Victoria turned to her mother and asked, "Mammis, can you get some hot water, so I can make some willow bark tea? I'll be right back."

After a few minutes, Victoria returned with supplies. She had diluted her arnica infusion for use on a small child and wrapped a moistened cloth strip around the baby's head. Elizabeth watched her quietly, until Victoria's cloth tightened on the sore spot. Her ensuing wails encouraged the women and Victoria gave her a sip of the fresh tea that she had doctored with some honey to hide its bitter taste. Shortly, the child struggled to her feet and started to walk around the group, holding on to various offered fingers for support. Mammis reached to hug Victoria and she knew that she would always have an important role in her family, married or not.

When her father approached the women, Victoria's discomfort returned. The women were forgiving, but she wasn't sure about the men. "Victoria," he called to her.

Victoria rose and went to her father. "Yes, Dadrus?"

"Go into the dining room and see if we can eat there. We need to know how their women handle food."

Victoria understood her father's concerns and walked down into the lower levels where the food was served. She saw men carrying platters from a room to the left and she positioned herself to glimpse the inside of the galley, as she supposed it was, when the servers passed through its open door. Victoria almost gasped aloud when she got a good look at the cooks preparing the meal. All men, she was certain. Who ever heard of this, men doing the women's work? But then again, they were carrying the food to the dining area, also. She peered at the contents of the platters and could identify mashed potatoes and the redness of beets. There was some type of meat, small slices arranged neatly on the plate. She thought she saw cheese and crackers on the tables and decided it was acceptable for their needs.

As Victoria was leaving the dining room, she almost bumped into a woman her age entering. Slender, with widened blue eyes, the young woman grabbed Victoria and gushed, "Oh, my, are you here by yourself? I am a Friend, Priscilla is my name, and I'm traveling alone.

This is my uncle's ship and I'm going to America to teach and it's so wonderful to see you here. Will you eat with me or have you just finished?"

Victoria deciphered the woman's words through her strong accent. She sounded Irish, Victoria realized, and must have meant she was a Quaker. "No, I'm not alone, I'm with my family. I came to look at the food before we came to eat."

Priscilla's face fell and then brightened. "But you can sit with me during the day and we can talk, then."

Victoria looked at her and was surprised to be able to see into her heart, which she found to be pure. Usually Victoria had trouble with the Blue-eyed Others; she was often road-blocked by some quality that prevented her access. She smiled uncertainly at Priscilla. Having a friend her age intrigued her, especially if her own family was lukewarm towards her right now. But having contact with *gadje* would taint her more. "I'll ask my father," she replied and escaped through the doors topside.

Victoria reported her galley survey results to her father. "Imagine, men cooking," he exclaimed. "Well, at least there will be no problems with women touching food during their time. We will go try it out. Let's go, men."

Soon after, Victoria led the women to the room. Priscilla, leaving as they entered, waved gaily to her.

"Who is that?" hissed Mammis. Victoria explained their brief encounter to her mother. "A teacher, you say?"

"That's what she said."

"She knows how to read and write?"

"I imagine, Mammis. Look at the beets," said Victoria, trying to steer the conversation to a safe topic. Her mother was not dissuaded.

"Chut, chut! A young woman going to America alone. Able to read and write, no less."

"Her uncle and his family live in Philadelphia and she will be with them once she arrives," defended Victoria. She could see her mother tuck this information away as the women tentatively ate the *gadje* food.

That night, she heard her parents speaking quietly in their comforter. She had begun to dread these conversations, as they usually meant something about her. The next morning, Victoria saw her father speaking to her brothers, while her mother talked earnestly to the women. She wondered what she had done now. She would soon find out, because her father stood and called her to him.

"Princess," he began. She decided it couldn't be terrible if he used her pet name. "We have decided, your mother and I, that you should talk with that Priscilla girl and have her teach you to read."

Victoria gasped, "Read, Dadrus?"

"Yes, and write. We think it will be good for someone in the family to know how."

Victoria's heart sank. They must have totally given up on marrying her off. She was already the unusual one, with vision and healing. Now she would be cursed with the ability to read and write.

"Princess," he continued, "You are the smartest one, the bravest, the most adventurous. You will do well. Go, now, and start," as he tilted his head in the direction of the deck where the *gadje* women gathered.

Victoria gathered her inner strength and walked slowly in that direction. She had never been alone in *gadje* territory before and she was shaking. Just then, Priscilla saw her and waved. "Hello, come sit here," she called, gesturing to an empty spot next to her. Victoria joined her and Priscilla started talking. "I saw your family, there are so many of them, and I think I know which men are yours and they are so handsome. I miss my brothers and I hope my uncle is good to me when I get to Philadelphia. Oh, excuse me, I haven't talked to anyone since we left Liverpool and I'm so nervous."

Together, the young women laughed. Priscilla handed Victoria some newspapers she had been reading. "What do you think?" she asked, pointing to the headlines.

Victoria knew it was the perfect opportunity to admit her lack of abilities and ask for help but she was tongue-tied. Maybe Priscilla wouldn't like her if she couldn't read. She looked again into her eyes and saw her pure heart. "I can't read," she whispered. "Maybe you can help me."

Priscilla's eyes opened wide.

"I never went to school; I know what my name, Victoria, starts with," she added, making her fingers into the shape of a "V."

Priscilla leaned into Victoria and whispered, "I've never taught anyone before. Here I am going to America to teach." She paused and added, "Maybe I can teach you to read and you can teach me to teach. That is, if you still want me to teach you, seeing as I have never done it before and maybe I don't know how to teach and maybe you'd like to ask someone else instead and—"

Victoria placed her hand on Priscilla's arm. "It's a perfect match," she smiled.

After that, the young women spent time together each morning and afternoon. "You're a quick learner," said Priscilla, as Victoria mastered the words in the primer. "I hope all my students are this good." Victoria smiled but she barely believed it. All those letters to remember and then to put them together into words where they didn't sound the same as they did alone. She wondered if she would ever catch on. Priscilla still corrected her but she was recognizing more words each day. Her father was right; she had a good mind and she was curious. Once the door was open, she could see the possibilities that reading and writing offered.

As they steamed offshore of Newfoundland and the Northern states, Victoria read simple stories aloud. "You're a good teacher," she told her friend.

"Do you think so?" asked Priscilla. "Do you think I'll be able to teach the children? What if they aren't as smart as you are? What if they act up and I can't handle them? What if—"

Victoria cut her off. "You'll be fine."

They were just outside Philadelphia and Victoria was trying to learn all she could before she and Priscilla parted ways.

"I don't have any more material," sighed Priscilla. "You've read everything I have with me."

Victoria sat back in her chair and surveyed the horizon. She could smell the land, confirmed by gulls circling overhead. She decided she could practice writing and sat with a small notebook to slowly start a letter on its lined paper. She began, "Dear Priscilla, I am happy that you" and was stumped on how to spell "taught." Well, she decided to be creative, as she continued, "showed me my letters. I will use them very much during the days to come. I hope that your students are good and your family is happy to see you. Your friend, Victoria." There, she thought, as she scrutinized the writing. She tore out the page, folded the paper, and handed it to Priscilla.

Priscilla's eyes filled with tears as she opened and read the short note. Then she looked up and said, "I am going to hear about you, Victoria. You will be famous somehow, somewhere. You are so smart and learn so quickly and I am so slow. It took me years to learn what you did in this short trip. And I hope my uncle is happy to see me and that there is heat in the school house and it's not too far from wherever I live and I wonder where that will be and I—" She was interrupted by Victoria's laughter. "Oh, dear, there I go again." At that, the two girls sat on the deck and viewed the sunset. Victoria was glad for the company and the skill that Priscilla shared with her.

Entering the Philadelphia harbor the following day, Victoria was surprised to see the low skyline of the town. "Compared to New York, Philadelphia seems like the countryside," she said.

"I've nothing to compare it with," said Priscilla, "but I think I'll enjoy a place with a bit less bustle."

"How will you recognize your uncle?" asked Victoria, thinking how strange it would be to come to a place where she knew no one.

"He said he would be waving a red kerchief." Priscilla added, "There certainly are many ships on the river here."

"Yes, that's true. Well, I probably need to help my family pack. We won't be on the ship much longer." Unspoken between them was that their conversations would be ending also.

"You could write me when you get settled," said Priscilla wistfully.

Victoria hesitated a second too long. "Yes, I could." But both of them knew that their friendship was one of convenience and would not continue. Their paths would lead to totally distinct and different worlds; no insult to each other, but they would not remain friends after the voyage.

Amidst the chaos of packing and moving, gathering family and children, they had no opportunity for further conversation on board. Victoria and her *folki* formed an appreciable group on the wharf once they and their belongings had landed. People were talking, the children were running, and it was a colorful but chaotic scene.

Victoria chanced to glance up at one point and noticed a man with a red handkerchief waving happily at someone behind her. She turned to see Priscilla moving slowly and precisely toward her uncle. Her heart filled with sympathy for Priscilla's situation, Victoria broke from her family to say goodbye.

"Priscilla!" she shouted.

The young woman looked at her, a smile spreading across her face. "Victoria, good bye and good luck."

"You, too. And thanks again for your gift."

"And you, too."

Her uncle, reaching the two, looked perplexed. As open as Quakers were, he didn't seem to expect his niece to be on familiar terms with someone looking like Victoria.

"Uncle, I am so glad to see you," said Priscilla, remembering her manners. "May I introduce you to Victoria Cooper, my literary companion during my trip?"

Victoria almost chuckled aloud but composed her face to greet the uncle properly. As she did, a terrifying image of him being crushed by a train flashed in her mind.

"I'm pleased, I am certain, that you kept Priscilla company during the voyage," he began. "I know these transports can be dangerous for single young women."

"Yes, of course, it was my pleasure," said Victoria, all the while troubled by the vision that kept pressing itself into her brain.

The uncle took Priscilla's arm and her bags and turned back toward the city. "I hope you have a pleasant visit in our town," he added. Just as the two were heading toward town, Victoria ran to the man and grabbed his arm.

"Please, sir, take care with the train crossing. I don't want you to get hurt." As soon as she said those words, Victoria felt ridiculous. This man would not know of her portents and she had no type of established relationship with him that would allow such familiarity.

However, the man stopped and looked carefully at her. "There is a crossing on our way back to my house."

"Is there another way?"

The man thought for a moment. "Not really." After a pause, he said, "But I will be very careful." He looked long and searching in her eyes. "You have the gift of vision," he stated and reached into his pocket. He pressed a coin into her hand. "Thank you. I feel that you have given me an important warning."

Victoria, stunned, stammered, "Tha—ank you."

"You befriended my niece and gave me advice. A small token of my appreciation." He tipped his hat to her, turned again toward the city, and said, "Priscilla, let's be on our way. Your aunt is awaiting."

Victoria watched as they left, until she heard someone calling for her. Her mother motioned for her to return to the family and, with slow steps and still watching Priscilla and her uncle until they disappeared in the crowds, Victoria joined them.

"Was that her uncle?" asked her father.

"Yes, Dadrus. And he gave me this." She thrust the coin into his hand.

He examined the gold piece and exclaimed, "Why, Princess, it is fitting," and returned it to her. On the face of the coin, she read, "United States of America" which was arched around the profile of an Indian Princess wearing a feathered headdress with letters. She spelled them out, "L-I-B-, oh, liberty," she said.

"A welcoming gift for a Princess," said her father, chuckling.

Victoria turned it over and gasped. "Three dollars," she exclaimed.

"That's quite a sum of money, isn't it?"

Her father nodded. "The first contribution for your skirt," he said.

"I will sew it in there tonight," she said, filled with warm thoughts of Priscilla and her uncle. She felt that he would heed her warning and be safe. "I hope I never need to use it," she said, grasping her coin tightly before securing it in her carrying bag.

By then, the ferry to Camden was ready for loading and the extended family moved their supplies onto the boat. When everyone and their things were aboard, the craft began its short journey across the Delaware River. Victoria could see the tents and wagons, along with welcoming smoke from fires just downriver from the ferry landing. Her heart soared at the sight and she realized that she would be glad to see new faces.

Now that newly arrived *folki* had found connections and headed off to their camps, Victoria's family was ready to return to their Somerville home.

"The train leaves in the morning," said Dadrus, when he returned from the station. "We can get to New York in the afternoon and then figure out how to get to Boston."

"I'm ready to get back," said Mammis. Victoria's brothers agreed. Victoria herself was silent on the subject. She had hoped to return to America ready to start a new life with a husband; she could almost hear her babies crying and feel them in her arms. But, without that on the horizon, she truly had no idea what she would do once they returned to Somerville. She tried not to think much about it as she packed her belongings in preparation for the train trip. But the uncertainty bothered her, so, when the sun was setting, she decided to walk along the shore to have some time to think alone.

She stepped along the river's edge, noticing plants and watching the lights of Philadelphia as they appeared across the way. One foot after the other, and, before she realized, she was near the ferry landing. She heard voices and passengers moving onto the boat, so she stopped and waited. As she did, she glanced down in the mud and saw something white glowing in the fading light. She reached to pick up the shell, for that's what it was, and saw that it rested on a midden of discarded shells including mussels and other ocean bivalves. Fingering it gently, Victoria saw that it opened into a pair of angel wings and she closed her eyes. Clutching the shell, she sensed a protecting presence; it reminded her of her grandmother and she felt secure. She rarely could see her own future but she was certain that it would have meaning. Releasing a sigh, she turned and headed back to camp, where she carefully added this shell to the others in her leather pouch.

The next morning, the family left camp and arrived at the train station. A short time later, they boarded and claimed one of the cars, filling it completely. Throughout the course of the day, Victoria helped distribute food and drinks they had carried with them. With many curves in the track, it was challenging to keep things from spilling and she was grateful that she had perfected the ability to stand in a rocking train, just as she had on the ocean voyage.

Finally, in late afternoon, after transferring to a ferry, they arrived in New York City.

"We could head to camp," suggested Dadrus, "and talk to the runners."

"Good idea," said Mammis, as she helped Betsey with baby Elizabeth and their belongings.

Victoria gazed around the pier, her eyes opened by the ability to now read the signs. At first, she was overwhelmed by the quantity and the terms. But slowly, she ciphered them out and recognized patterns in them, such as the ones for places to stay in the city and others for sightseeing. Suddenly one sign in particular grabbed her attention. "Steamboat to Boston," she read aloud. "The Fall River line, free dorms."

"What?" asked her father. "What are you talking about?"

Victoria pointed to the billboard. "The steamboat leaves from the North River at eight o'clock tonight and arrives in Boston in the morning."

Her father, at first confused, broke into a smile. "Princess, you can read that."

She smiled back. "Yes, Dadrus, I can."

By eight o'clock, the family had secured free passes and loaded onto the *Metropolis*. Victoria tried to sleep amidst the chattering and crying of the others in the women's dorm. Eventually, she drifted off to sleep.

Early in the morning, the steamer landed in Fall River and passengers were transferred to the Old Colony railroad.

"Yet another step," Betsey sighed. Elizabeth was teething and cried incessantly. Once they were settled on the train, Victoria rummaged through her bag of medicinal supplies and finally found some short myrtle stems that she wove together to form a necklace that she draped over the baby's head. She then moved a segment into

Elizabeth's mouth, and she began gumming it. Within minutes, the baby was asleep and Victoria gently removed the necklace from her open mouth.

Smiling at her, Betsey touched her arm. "Thanks."

Victoria nodded. She felt the swaying of the train, as it veered toward Boston. Its rocking, added to all the travel and transportation changes, lulled Victoria and she nodded off.

"It's time to get up." The voice sounded far away.

"Princess, we're home," she heard someone whispering in her ear as they shook her gently.

NINE

Victoria opened her eyes, momentarily confused as Prince's face materialized before her.

"You slept all the way from New Haven," he said gently. "We're home. Let's go."

Victoria felt the train jerk to a halt and she looked around her. The day's events came back to her and, still fingering her silk shawl, she sat up in her seat.

"Noah will be meeting us at the station." Prince paused. "Ready?"

Victoria nodded and rose to stand in the aisle, Prince just behind her. She walked to the door and noticed a fleeting look of pain cross his face as he stepped down the stairs to the platform after her. He put his arm through hers and they walked through the station. She too could feel she was getting old.

"Hallo," shouted Noah, walking toward them. "Let me get the wagon."

Prince clasped his shoulder. "Thanks, son." They walked out to the street, while Noah ran around the block and, within minutes, was driving toward them. "It's a wonder how quickly you can get around," remarked Prince, "now that the track is raised. We used to wait for a half hour, especially when the trains arrived, for the gate to go up before we could cross."

Victoria nodded, remembering those days. "And having such a beautiful station is a marvel," she added. "But what a commotion even at night," she added as carriage after carriage passed along the road, some stopping to gather passengers or unload them.

Noah stood by the wagon step and helped his mother onto the seat. Victoria turned to see Prince setting himself down gingerly next to her. She looked questioningly at him, but he just shrugged and moved over to let Noah sit between them to handle the reins.

The horses had just started to move into the roadway when they were startled by another carriage passing by. Noah managed to control theirs before there was any damage.

"Not even a glance in our direction," Prince growled. "Drivers these days are just so careless."

Noah nodded and then cautiously eased into the traffic in the road. They set out in the crisp evening toward the East Hartford bridge. Passing by the park, they could see people dressed in furs, strolling along the paths. Once they reached the outskirts of town, stars filled the sky and the horses' breath left puffs in the air.

"Any news?" Prince asked his son.

"There's a shipment of horses coming from Canada, probably next week."

Prince nodded, as he had been expecting them any day now.

"And we had a close call up in Springfield," Noah said with a laugh.

"What do you mean?"

"Uncle Richard's daughters were up there," he started.

"From Somerville?" Victoria asked, wondering why her brother's family would be there.

"Yes, they didn't want to be recognized and needed a good-sized town."

"Oh, I see. Go on."

"Well, apparently they decided they were 'women of the cloth' and started collecting for the church." He chuckled. "They were making out fairly well, until the local reverend heard of it."

"Oh, dear, what happened?" asked Victoria.

"I guess he chased them, robes and all, down the street until they ran into a carriage shop."

Victoria and Prince started laughing. "I can see them now, with robes tangled up in their feet," she gasped.

"Yes, over their skirts, what a sight!" added Prince.

"So, what happened?"

"Well, it's complicated. They ran up the incline for the carriages and ended up on the roof where they pulled off their robes and hid them behind the chimney. But while they were up there, the youngest, she stepped on an open skylight that had been covered with straw and fell partway through."

Victoria shouted with delight. "Can you see that? That silly girl dangling in the ceiling like that!"

"The carriage shop owner helped them down and the girls left, saying they were going to the hotel."

"Hotel? They were staying at a hotel?"

"No, of course not, but when the police showed up, the carriage owner told them where they were headed. When the police checked out the hotel, they found two young college women there and questioned them."

"Did the police arrest the college women?"

"No, they really couldn't. No evidence and the reverend didn't recognize them. Of course Richard's girls were far away by then."

"Oh, my, what those girls think of," said Victoria, still laughing. "They take after their mother, Margaret, don't they?"

"Yes, Mammis, they do."

Victoria paused and then sighed. "I truly miss my brothers."

Prince patted her hand. "I know, Princess, losing them was sad for all of us. We're getting old."

By then, they had reached the bridge, where the sound of the carriage crossing the wooden planks drowned out any further conversation. On the other side of the river, they passed through the shuttered streets and, aided by kerosene lamps on either side of their wagon, unloaded at the old Farmer's Hotel.

"Good to be back," said Prince.

"Thanks, Noah, for the ride," said Victoria. "We'll see you in the morning."

"Goodnight, Mammis. Dadrus."

"Goodnight, son."

Noah headed for the stable while Victoria and Prince walked up the stairs into the house. "Let me make you some tea before you go to bed," she said, going into the kitchen.

Prince sat at the table, while Victoria ferreted out a slip of yellow bark from her medicinal supplies and steeped it in boiling water. Adding enough honey to hide the bitter taste, she gave him the warm beverage, which he sipped. Warming his hands on the cup, Prince sighed.

"Tired?"

"Yes, I didn't sleep on the train like someone I know."

She chucked his arm playfully. "I wanted to be ready for whatever else might happen tonight."

"You crazy woman, you," he smiled and they went upstairs together.

"Daisy?" called Victoria, the next morning.

"Yes, Mammis?"

"Where are you?"

"The men's laundry."

Although they used two of the cast-iron troughs installed in the former hotel's suites as baths, they used the other two to separate the laundry.

"Let me know when you're done," called Victoria.

A half hour later, Daisy joined her mother in the kitchen as she dried her hands on an apron. Victoria had just finished cutting up a chicken and was putting it in the cooking pot.

"Noah found a chicken," she said, smiling.

Daisy nodded and rummaged for an onion and carrot in the pantry. She started chopping them but didn't say a word.

"Once the weather clears, I think Uncle Samuel's family is coming to visit," said Victoria. She thought it would be an opportunity to test out their plans for Daisy and Samuel's son Richard. But of course Daisy didn't know about this.

Victoria glanced at her and saw that her face was thoughtful. After a few minutes of silence, Daisy asked, "Do men ever bleed?"

Victoria hesitated, confused by the question, and Daisy continued, "I mean, like women."

"You mean each month?"

Daisy nodded.

"Of course not," retorted Victoria. "They have no monthly restrictions."

"Oh," Daisy said and continued chopping.

"Why?"

"Just wondering."

Just then, Belcher strode into the kitchen and Victoria forgot about the question until several weeks had passed, but by then it was too late.

"Hey, Mammis," said her son, placing his arm around her. "What's in the pot?"

Laughing, she pushed him aside. "We just started cooking. Come back at dinner time."

The following week, Victoria awoke to see the sun shining in the small window in their bedroom. She smiled, thinking of the previous night with Prince, and swung her legs to the side of the mattress.

With each day that passed, she felt more and more herself, although her memory of recent days seemed unclear at times. Wondering what Prince was doing, she got up, dressed, and headed downstairs.

She found him sitting at the kitchen table, nursing a cup of coffee. They exchanged smiles and he reached to pat her skirt as she passed by. Daisy poured her a cup and she sat across from him.

"You're looking good today, Princess."

"I'm feeling fine. It's all your nighttime attention," she laughed and Prince chuckled.

"Are you up for a ride today? Those horses from Canada are here and I wondered if you wanted to get out a bit." Prince was wearing his signature suit with the diamond horseshoe tie tack on the lapel.

Victoria beamed. "Can we go right away?"

"Absolutely not," he responded, knowing that they never started the day without a decent meal. Daisy came back from the kitchen holding two plates filled with eggs and bread and potatoes and she placed them in front of her parents.

"Anything else?" she asked them.

Both shook their heads.

"The newspaper boy says it will be sunny and a bit warmer today. You can sit in the chariot while I handle the horse unloading."

"That sounds lovely. I have been so cooped up here, I was starting to feel crazy."

Prince and Daisy exchanged glances, which gave Victoria a slight pause.

"Good, then," Prince finally said. "I told the groom we'd be ready to leave shortly."

Victoria nodded and went back upstairs to dress for the outdoors. She added her shawl and another skirt. Downstairs, she found her gloves by the front door and Prince helped her with her cloak. She noticed some mud caked on the hem but couldn't remember the last time she wore it or how the mud got there. She tried to focus but nothing came.

Just then, she heard the clip-clop of hooves as the chariot drew to the entrance of the old Farmer's Hotel. Looking out the window, Victoria caught her breath as the glint of silver buckles flashed in the sun. They'd had this chariot for only a short while and she continued to be stunned by its high half-coach, covered with gold paint and silver-plated decorations. What a change from those first wagons they used! This was truly a chariot fit for a prince and princess. Mirrors reflected the sunlight with such intense shimmering that she felt unsteady and wondered if it was her head or the chariot. She grabbed Prince's arm and he steadied her, while they walked out the front door and down the porch stairs.

"Good morning, Joe," she said, noticing, as he unfolded the mounting stairs and grasped the silver-plated horse head door handle, how his hair was stark white against his dark skin. She wondered how he had gotten so old but glanced at Prince and saw that his hair and moustache were streaked with gray also. She sighed, amazed by the quick passage of time, and she climbed the stairs, gently tracing the gold paint, striped on one side by green and the other by red, outlining the quarter panel. Prince helped her into the seat and she sank gratefully into the gold satin cushions, while he piled silk robes around her. He then added a buffalo robe and climbed down to make final arrangements.

Prince walked to his favorite horse, the gray mare Beatrix, and whispered to her. The horse's ears twitched as he spoke and she nuzzled against the man as far as her harness would allow. The movement caused a loud jingling and the second of the matched pair shook its head, starting a raucous, joyous sound. Prince patted the plump Percheron and turned back to the chariot. Victoria knew they had been fortunate to get the mare, which had belonged to a railroad tycoon who'd lost everything in the '93 panic.

Victoria felt the chariot shift as Prince climbed aboard. He settled next to her and tucked himself under the robes. He leaned back into the seat and let out a breath that was visible in the frosty air.

"All set, Joe," he yelled into the speaking tube, as the coachman set the horses in motion. The pair lifted their heavy feet in unison as they headed down Connecticut Avenue, tails and manes flying behind them. When they moved down the hill to the river, they strained backward, their custom-made backstrap successfully checking the chariot. Occasionally, Victoria caught a glimpse of the coach plumes of Prince's favorite colors—red, yellow, and green—streaming behind them. Reaching the bridge in short time, their dazzling sight and boisterous movement caught the attention of people milling near the electric cars and they all gaped at their finery as they passed by. The chariot stopped at the bridge entrance.

"Mrs. Williams, glad to see you up and about," a voice called. Victoria looked out the oval side window to see the harness maker, Mr. Gaines.

"Why, thank you very much," she replied, although she wasn't certain he could hear her through the glass. She noticed he was looking carefully at her and realized that he must have been the one to locate Prince when she had fallen on the ice. He nodded to her, as if approving her return to health, and returned to his wagon to take his turn crossing the river.

Joe alit and positioned the chariot in the line.

"No, you go ahead," waved several of the merchants.

Joe walked the horses into the darkness of the covered bridge. His voice, the horses' feet, and their bells echoed under its shed as they crossed the thousand-foot-long bridge. Small, high windows allowed some light to enter, which prevented the horses from spooking. Being early in the day, there was no traffic returning to East Hartford on the south side. Even though they moved slowly, their rumblings and janglings were heard at the Hartford end long before their arrival. When they emerged, Victoria saw that a small crowd had gathered to watch them pass.

Prince sat regally on his seat and waved at the throng, who cheered.

"Look at the silver horse heads," one young boy said, pointing to the chariot's sides.

"The inside shines like gold," gasped his mother.

Victoria smiled and snuggled up next to Prince as they moved along the streets. Prince pulled out his watch and said, "We are early. Do you mind if we stop at Smith-Worthington? I ordered something and want to see if it's ready."

Victoria enjoyed shopping at the saddlery and indicated so. Prince called to Joe, who turned in that direction. The chariot pulled up to the front of the building and Joe pulled down the leather steps, while Prince helped Victoria down.

"Remember when we'd bring the children here?" she asked.

"Yes, and how Bessie would try to ride the horse?" he said, as they walked past the old wooden horse used to display popular items. It currently sported russet reins and harnesses. Victoria toyed with them, but Prince shook his head.

"The harnesses will turn black in a few months."

"We could get new ones after that," she said wistfully, thinking they looked quite handsome.

"Wait until you see what I got," he said, cupping his hand under her elbow. "I hope it's in."

"Hello, Mr. Williams," called Mr. Roberts. "I'm glad you are here. Your rosettes arrived yesterday and I was going to send a messenger to you today. Let me get them."

Victoria looked at Prince, whose face was filled with joy and he could hardly stand still. Mr. Roberts returned with a small box about the size of a pound of butter. Inside, nestled in cotton, were two rosettes with the likeness of Beatrix protected by glass.

"Oh," Victoria inhaled, "they are lovely. A perfect image of her." She looked at her husband. "I am worried that perhaps you care for her more than you love me."

Prince looked at her sharply before seeing the glint in her dark eyes. "Just think of the commotion we will make," he exclaimed. "Will it be difficult to put these on her bridle?"

Mr. Roberts shook his head. "No, but I need a few days. You'll need to send it over here sometime when you're not using it." He paused. "Unless you want to put them on a new bridle," he added coyly.

Prince laughed. "With all my horses, I give you plenty of business. No, I'll wait and put them on the one I already have for her." He handled the rosettes. "But I'd like to take these home to enjoy until I can send back the bridle."

"Certainly," said Mr. Roberts and he wrapped the box in brown paper to secure it tightly. "You don't want to drop these, as the glass is fragile."

Walking them out, Mr. Roberts said, "Have you heard about Blacksmith Maher's son?"

They shook their heads "no."

"All of fourteen and he's racing horses! Whoever heard of such a thing?"

"Fourteen? How can he hold on?"

"We've been working on a special bit and reins. You wait and see, he'll go somewhere."

Shaking their heads, Prince and Victoria left the saddlery carrying their box and Joe steadied the horses while they climbed back into the coach.

"Bye," shouted Mr. Roberts as he stood in the shop doorway, with his arm around the wooden advertising horse.

Joe headed the chariot towards the horse lot and, after a few minutes, Prince said, "I hope this shipment sells well. It's a good mixture of work horses and some driving horses."

Victoria may have heard his voice droning in the background, but the gentle rocking had made her sleepy and she had nodded off. She started when Prince nudged her arm and asked, "Princess, are you well? Is this excursion too much for you?"

"Oh, Prince, hallo. I must have dozed."

She felt his glance assessing her. Apparently satisfied, he again asked, "Do you think business will continue to turn upward? This is a large shipment."

After a few moments of pondering, she replied, "Yes, things will continue improving."

Prince visibly sighed with relief at her pronouncement, flipped open the mahogany ashtray, and lit his pipe. Joe directed the chariot into the station and they could see that the horses were not yet unloaded. She could smell them, though, and a small smile played on her lips. She thought it was such a luscious odor, reminiscent of so much of her life. They were a constant, a life force, their income, and life style. Victoria couldn't imagine how people had ever gotten along without them.

"There's Richard," said Prince, puffing on his pipe, as he tilted his head toward the eldest of their remaining sons, who was standing near the horse cars.

"Is he talking with Mr. Kenyon?"

"Hmm," said Prince, as he peered at the man. "I think so."

"Isn't he the horse dealer on Albany Avenue near camp?"

Prince nodded, looking uncomfortable. He focused intently on tapping his pipe and relighting it.

"Doesn't he work with the racers in Springfield? Why is he meeting our train?"

"I'm not sure."

"Has he procured horses from Canada also?"

Victoria could see Prince squirming and she held his glance. Finally, he sighed and said, "I think Richard said something to him last month."

"What? What did he do?"

"I know, I know," said Prince, restraining Victoria as she struggled upright.

She glared at him. "What did Richard tell Mr. Kenyon? Why would he talk to another horse dealer? Especially one who is not one of us?"

"I'm sure Richard thought it was harmless, telling him about our source of horses in Canada."

"He told him that?" she asked incredulously. "What is wrong with that boy?"

Prince sighed. "Maybe Mr. Kenyon goaded him into it."

Victoria fixed her dark, piercing eyes on Prince. "And you didn't tell me about this?" She could hardly keep the venom from her voice.

Prince visibly recoiled from her words. "Princess, you've been ill. And besides, I wasn't sure it would amount to anything."

Victoria glared at him and then returned to looking at Richard and Mr. Kenyon. "So, does he have any horses in this load?"

"I guess we will see."

"We'll see? Why else would he be here meeting this train?"

"Maybe he's just trying to talk with Richard. This is where they conversed last time."

Victoria kept watch. The two men turned slightly. "Did you see that?"

"What?"

"It looked like Richard gave him something."

"I didn't see anything. But, what could he give him?"

Victoria shrugged, her mind searching for possibilities but she drew a blank. It really was unfortunate, thought Victoria. Richard was next in line, but he wasn't Wash and they all knew it. It was such a somber thought that her eyes filled with tears and Prince touched her arm under the robes.

"Princess, we'll figure something out. We need to let him find his way, even if he makes mistakes."

Victoria nodded, uncertainly. "Richard has always been different than the rest. But we can't afford many errors."

"True, but we have the advantage over other sellers because we guarantee our sales."

"Yes, that's true."

They watched silently as puffs of vapor came from Richard's and then Mr. Kenyon's mouth, as they carried on a conversation. Victoria's mind began to race with a new idea, as she traced a floral design in the plush velvet trim. "Belcher and Noah are close in age," she started, thinking of her other remaining sons.

"That Noah has a good head on his shoulders," said Prince.

Victoria nodded. "He and Belcher are close, too. They get along well."

"So, are you thinking they should take over? How can we do that to Richard?"

Victoria knew Richard couldn't handle the associated shame. "What if the three of them work together? Maybe we can figure out a way to divvy up the operations, so each one of them has a job and together they run the business."

Prince looked thoughtful and then smiled. "We don't really need to talk about this right now, do we? We're both here and healthy now."

Victoria nodded slowly. She knew this wasn't the time to point out how puffy his face was or that she had noticed him hobbling on bloated feet. Besides, her visualizations of riding together on the gray mare made her feel positive about their life continuing as is. She would put it on hold but knew she would keep thinking about it.

They heard men shouting and looked towards the yard. They were starting to unload the horses and could hear some frantic neighs.

"Time for me to get down there," said Prince. "I won't be too long," he said as he rose to alight. He turned to cover her with the robes. "Will you be warm enough? I could close the shutters," as he fingered them in the slot below the window.

Victoria gathered her grandmother's shawl and wrapped it around her head. The chariot was positioned such that she was bathed in sunlight. "I'll be fine as is."

"Maybe you could write up an advertisement for the newspaper about the shipment?"

"Yes, Prince, I can do that while I wait." Victoria leaned forward to get some paper, pen, and ink from a red velvet pocket hanging in the front of the coach and she began. Occasionally, she stared off in the distance as she absentmindedly toyed with the silk tassels of the window shade or rubbed the red velvet interior trim. Other times, she watched as the men worked the horse lot. Mr. Kenyon had already left, without any horses.

Traffic near the station began to pick up. Victoria noticed a man using the new-fangled safety bicycle and caught her breath as he bounced off its seat and landed on the ground. He hastily stood up and wiped off his pants before walking the contraption down the road until he was out of sight. How ridiculous, to try to ride on two wheels. She decided she'd stick with horses and returned to crafting her advertisement.

By the time Prince returned, she had a finished copy. Victoria read the text to him and ended with a flourish, "All horses sold on a written guarantee and at a reasonable price. If not as represented, money refunded."

"Thank you, Princess. Let's stop by the newspaper office on the way home."

"And Mr. Kenyon?"

"No horses this time," was all Prince would say.

"Did you talk to Richard?"

Prince straightened his suit, absent-mindedly fingering his diamond horseshoe pin. He sighed, patted her arm, and closed his eyes. Victoria was not satisfied with his response, but then they turned the corner to the newspaper office and, in the commotion of providing the advertisement and receiving flattery from the newspaper staff, she lost track of the issue.

The next day, Victoria was pleased to see her work in the paper. She thought it had more appeal than their competitors'. Apparently, others thought so also, because Prince was out in the sale barn all day with a steady stream of prospective customers.

TEN

Victoria didn't usually answer the door, but she was walking by when she heard steps coming up the stairs and a solid knock. Curious, she peered through the glass and saw an attractive man whom she guessed to be in his mid-forties. The man stomped his feet and rubbed his hands before looking at the window and seeing her.

Something about his face looked familiar but Victoria couldn't place it. She opened the door and gestured for him to enter, as cold air blasted into the house.

"May I help you?" she asked, wondering if perhaps he wanted to purchase horses.

"Is Mr. Williams home?"

She nodded. "He's around. Who is calling?"

"His son, William," said the man.

A bolt shot through Victoria as she registered the words. Victoria swallowed, trying to control the fear that had risen in her throat. For almost forty years, she had put aside thoughts of Mary Defiance until, at some point, she truly had forgotten about her and her children. "His son?" she asked, as she sensed Daisy, who had come from the kitchen, standing behind her.

"Yes, ma'am. From Ohio."

Victoria wished that she could shove William out the door into the cold, but he was already ensconced in the foyer and she supposed that would be rude and inappropriate. Instead, she invited him into the front room by the fire and sent Daisy out to the stable to find her father.

"Don't tell him who's here," Victoria whispered. She wasn't sure if Prince would come back to the house if he knew William was there and she certainly didn't want to entertain him alone for any length of time.

After Daisy left, she noted that William was glancing around the room, assessing different items. She made a mental note to check that everything was still there when he left, which she trusted would be soon.

"Was it a difficult trip?" she asked, hoping that it had been.

"Not much so," he replied. "Many of the rivers were frozen and, although there is much snow to the south, my route was unimpeded."

"Oh," she said, wondering what else to say. She couldn't help but look at the man and recognize his resemblance to her husband. She thought he was a bit shorter than her sons and wondered how tall Mary Defiance was. Or had been. She hadn't heard news of her passing, but she was at a loss to understand why Prince's other son would be at their door. Fortunately, she would soon find out, as she heard stomping at the back door and it wasn't long before she heard it close. She heard Daisy talking quietly to her father and Victoria could envision them sitting on the back bench, pulling off their boots. She heard Prince walk down the hall and turn into the front room where they were.

"Hallo, Princess," he began, "I hear we have company."

William, facing away from the door, turned toward his father. Victoria watched the blood drain from Prince's face, as he seemed to recognize the man standing before him.

"Father," started William, confirming Prince's suspicions.

"What—" he stuttered. "What are you doing here?"

William, glancing toward Victoria, gestured with his head that he wished her gone. Prince glared at him but then looked at Victoria, who excused herself from the room, and the men began speaking in deep, rumbling voices.

Victoria was livid about her dismissal but she would not be outdone. She stepped lightly up the stairs to the room above the men and sat quietly. Their voices carried through the fireplace vents and she could hear the conversation perfectly.

"—now that Wash is gone."

Prince retorted, "It doesn't matter. I have other sons and they will take over when I'm gone." He paused. "Not you."

"I am your eldest son."

Victoria waited, without breathing, to hear where Prince stood on this. It was true that the eldest son had priority, but wasn't the marriage to Mary Defiance over? Those many years ago, she had thrown her skirt over Prince and that was final, the end.

"Your mother dismissed me. I do not exist to her. And thus you do not exist to me."

There was silence below, as Victoria let out a sigh of relief. She was so grateful for his support of her sons and their future that she wanted to hug her husband.

"Or did she put you up to this?" Victoria heard the venom in Prince's voice.

After a slight pause, William responded without answering the question, "I understand that Richard has made some bad choices involving other horse dealers in town." William spit into the fire, or so Victoria thought that was what she heard. "*Gadje* in your family business," he hissed.

Victoria had to restrain herself from going back downstairs to slap the man. She didn't understand why Prince was tolerating this discussion.

"You and I could form a partnership," William continued. "I could come East and run the business here and my brother John, your other son, will run ours in Ohio. Together, we could control horse trading all the way to the Mississippi."

"Out," shouted Prince. "Out of my house."

Victoria heard the scrape of a chair and she couldn't tell if it was William moving on his own volition or being dragged by Prince. Terrified by another option of the younger man taking advantage of her husband, she started down the stairs, only to see William walking swiftly out the front door, with Prince right behind him.

"I don't want to see your face again," Prince yelled as he slammed the door and locked it.

Victoria reached the bottom of the stairs to join him, noticing that he was breathing heavily. Slowly calming, Prince looked at her, saying, "I don't know what got into him, after all these years." They both watched as William unhitched his horse and rode away, but not before he took one last look at the front door.

"I do hope that's the last of him," she started, trying to keep her voice level. "Do you think he'll take any action as the firstborn?"

"He certainly doesn't have a leg to stand on," Prince said vehemently.

Victoria looked sharply at him. "What do you mean?"

"Well, I, er—" Prince fumbled with his words. "I would think that my family—that this is my family and has been for years and years and certainly—," Prince's voice faded off.

Victoria could see his mind working through this and realizing that it wasn't as clear as he hoped. Maybe it was by Gypsy law and custom, and then again, maybe not. "Perhaps you should make up a will," she suggested.

"A will? That's a *gadje* thing."

"But we are living in a *gadje* world now. And our children certainly are."

Prince looked somewhat blankly at her. "I just can't deal with that right now."

Victoria took his arm and steered him towards a chair. "But now is when we have a problem. We don't know where William went after he left here. Maybe he knows something about the law that we don't." She paused strategically. "He certainly knew about Richard, didn't he?"

Prince winced. "Yes, that's true. But a will?"

"Well, we really do need to decide what to do about Richard," said Victoria.

Prince sighed and nodded. "But most of our assets are fluid. The jewelry," he said, fingering his diamond horseshoe pin, "and the gold," he added. "Plus, our sons can move the horses and wagons off to Willimantic or New Haven, if they need to."

"Yes, but will they fight over what we leave them?" Victoria sighed. There were several minutes of silence.

Prince started to say something, but, just then, the back door closed and they heard footsteps. Victoria, heart pounding, feared that William had returned. Her eyes wide, she looked at Prince. He started to rise from his chair and she could see him turn red and ball his fist, as he prepared to confront his firstborn.

But it was Richard who was walking towards them. Catching his father's face, he stopped short. "What? What did I do now?" he stormed. "You don't think I can do anything right, do you?"

He started to retreat to his lodging in the former innkeeper's quarters, when Prince yelled, "Richard, come back. This has nothing to do with you. We just sent off an unwanted guest."

"Yes," said Victoria. "We thought he was returning through the back door."

Richard stopped and turned to walk slowly towards his parents. Out of the corner of her eye, Victoria peeked at Prince. She wondered if he would confide in Richard about William's visit. She hoped he wouldn't. Right now, she didn't have confidence in Richard's common sense.

"Were you coming to talk to me?" asked Prince, facing his son. Realizing that Prince had no intention of saying any more to Richard about their visitor, Victoria was relieved. She would have felt differently if it had been Noah or Belcher, which saddened her.

"Yes, I was," Richard replied. "One of the horses is hurt and I want your opinion."

Prince rose from his seat and they walked out to the back door. Victoria could hear them talking as he put on his boots. "What did you notice?" she heard Prince ask before the door closed and they headed to the barn.

Victoria sat, trying to figure out what to do related to William. She was still stunned by his appearance at their home and it certainly complicated and accelerated their need to make a decision related to the continuation of their clan and business. Victoria pounded the arm of the chair and cursed that woman for reappearing in their life. After a few minutes, she calmed down and realized that the timing was perfect. They could figure out what to do now, when they just realized there was a problem, instead of waiting until it escalated. She could imagine several aspects of the work in which Noah or Belcher would excel, but she was stuck on Richard. It needed to be something that gave the appearance of control and importance and yet something that he could handle. Every one of her ideas hit a dead end; maybe she needed to relax until a vision appeared. As she settled into that idea, the back door slammed shut again and Prince came into the room and sat down with a heavy sigh.

"Richard's been racing," he said.

"In the snow and ice?"

"The sunny part of the field was mostly cleared."

"And the horse?"

"I think he'll heal. Nothing broken."

"He's always wanted to race. Sometimes he drives the wagons too fast for me."

"I know. He's reckless."

Prince sank deeper into the chair and shook his head. "I'm worried that he might be going to Springfield, too."

"To the track?"

Prince nodded. "And I've heard they are thinking of building one here in Hartford."

After a few minutes, Victoria blurted, "Mr. Kenyon. Doesn't he run the bets up to Springfield?"

Prince sat upright in his chair. "You're right. That's what they were doing at the train station." He paused before saying, "He can't run the business if he's involved with racing and betting. Too much chance that money will leave the family, for one thing."

Mirroring her thoughts, Victoria felt she needed to be positive. "We'll think of something for him," she said. "Meanwhile, when my brother Samuel's family comes to visit, we could ask Jennie if she knows someone who can write a will."

Prince nodded. "Yes, Princess, I think that is a good idea. And I'll consider what to do about our sons."

Victoria figured it would take time but she was certain that Prince would eventually agree with her plan to divide their responsibilities. At least she had gotten him to the next step. That, she decided, was progress.

It was later in the week that Victoria sat down to read the newspaper. Prince, Belcher, and Noah had left to do some business, Daisy, Richard, and his wife were off somewhere, and Victoria was finally alone. She relished the sense of peace, which didn't come often in their busy family home. She curled up in front of the fireplace and fussed with the pillows until she got comfortable, which wasn't as easy as it used to be. No, those creaky bones and a little extra weight made it harder to settle down. And she still felt a bit dizzy at times and had to lower herself gently into place and not hurry either the going down or the getting up. Actually, the getting up was harder. Sometimes she could feel blood rushing but see nothing, as if she had closed her eyes, although she didn't think she had. Well, she would worry about getting up later, she decided, and focused on the front page.

After a few minutes, she noticed a small column entitled "Trouble in Cuba." She had to think a minute but remembered it was an island, down near the equator, next to Florida. She read with interest that twenty-one men had been arrested for rebellious behavior. A rebellion in Cuba certainly would not be the kind that would be useful for horse-dealers. Not like the Great Rebellion thirty years earlier, she thought. That had been the war that had changed their lives, she recalled, as she leaned back and closed her eyes. Yes, indeed, it had been quite the time and she drifted back to those events.

"I just heard that Fort Sumter has fallen! The Confederates say they will march to Washington," Prince blurted breathlessly as he rode into camp and tossed down a newspaper.

Startled, Victoria's mouth opened but she made no sound. Two-year old Wash toddled from the tent when he heard Prince's voice. Victoria scooped him up and hugged the protesting boy close to her, as she reached for the paper.

Scanning the front page that was shaking slightly in her hands, Victoria read, "'At intervals of twenty minutes, the firing on Fort Sumter was kept up all night.'" She paused and read silently.

"What else does it say?" Prince prodded.

"'At nine o'clock, a dense smoke poured out from Sumter and the federal flag was displayed at half mast signaling distress.' It says that five men were slightly wounded." She continued to read and then swallowed and looked up at Prince, "I guess we won't be heading south, will we?" They had held off their departure for almost a month now, as rumors of potential war had been swirling around them.

Prince sat heavily on the stump near the fire. "No, I can't imagine we can buy horses to bring back north at this point." He looked deeply in the fire. Victoria ladled out stew from the kettle and placed it in front of him. She took a bowl she had set aside earlier and tasted a spoonful. Satisfied that it was cool enough for Wash, she sat him down with his bowl and went into the tent, only to return a few minutes later with Martha in tow. The curly-headed girl, almost three, sat with her younger brother and fed herself from her bowl Victoria provided.

Sighing, she said, "Do you think we can wait this out? Will it pass quickly?"

Prince shrugged. "I can't believe that the rebellion has the forces to beat the Union. But the Confederate States are growing."

They sat there silently, until Martha's cry, "My bowl, my bowl" interrupted them Wash, a sturdy growing tot, had finished his food and was continuing eagerly with his sister's, which was still half-full.

"There's plenty for everyone," said Victoria. "Wash, give that back. Share." She added a spoonful to his bowl and distracted him with it. "Here, here is yours." Wash settled back down to business.

"If we don't go south, where can we go? Can we get wild horses out west?"

Prince shook his head. "It's hard to say how far this rebellion will go. I heard that men from Pennsylvania and New York are standing behind the President. I don't know what will happen in Kentucky or farther west."

Victoria returned to the newspaper, as Prince ate. Startled, she read aloud, "There's a proclamation from the President for seventy-five thousand volunteers." A shiver ran through her as she considered the sheer number of soldiers. She glanced at Prince and she was momentarily incapacitated by the thought of losing him. "We have to figure out a way to go quietly about our business and avoid taking sides. Don't you think?"

"Maybe we could go north," said Prince.

"North?"

"Yes, up into Canada. They have horses there."

"Truly?"

"Yes. It might be cool for the summer. I know you don't really like all the southern heat and humidity anyway."

Victoria nodded. She never had adjusted to that climate where everything stuck to her and certain folds of her skin always felt damp, and for no good reason, except the weather.

"There are needle trees there, too," added Prince. Victoria was lost envisioning cool forests with deep blue lakes and plenty of horses grazing nearby. Maybe there were even mountains with cool, deep mists at dawn.

His voice startled her back to the campfire. "What do you say? Shall we head north?"

As pleasant as those images were, Victoria voiced a concern, "Perhaps we should wait to see what happens with the rebellion. After all, Canada is part of England."

"Yes, but they rule it from a distance. I understand that it is quite safe for us there."

Victoria raised an eyebrow, wondering how he knew this but decided it wasn't the time for questions. She already had more information to consider than she could address.

"We could wait a few weeks, maybe a month," Prince acquiesced. "There may still be ice or snow up north for a while."

"I can keep packing and then we can go either way, depending," she said.

"Sounds good," said Prince and he headed into the wagon.

A short time later, Victoria cleaned the children and brought them in with Prince for the evening. She sang quietly to them until they fell asleep. She and Prince tiptoed outside to the fire ring, which was a bed of glowing embers. They sat there together, Victoria tucked into his lap, her head resting on his shoulder. With Wash already two, she had been thinking about having another child. Maybe this summer, depending on how things went. Until then, she would continue her prevention tea. She felt herself becoming drowsy, as they listened to the peepers clamoring for their mates. Strident peep-peep-peep's brought images of the male frog's enlarged throat expanding and contracting rhythmically. Prince gently squeezed her arm in time to a nearby male's calling and he bent over and breathed into her ear. "Peep, peep, peep," he whispered. "Let's go to bed."

"Here are the comforters," yelled Prince, as he hoisted them up into the wagon. Victoria pulled them to the back and tucked them into place on the rear platform. Traveling with the wagon as home was an improvement over their previous tenting.

She stepped down from the wagon, just as Prince finished folding the tarp and packed it under the wagon. She glanced around at their vacant campsite. "Looks as though we are set."

Prince smothered the fire and nodded. "Up we go," he said. He hoisted Wash and then Martha up into the wagon and Victoria quickly followed to settle them into place. Prince released the horse, which had been hitched to a nearby tree, and climbed onto the front seat. "All set back there?"

"Yes, let's go." Victoria felt the excitement in her voice and the satisfying jolt as the wagon began to move. A few minutes later, she joined Prince on the bench and turned to see West Rock receding. She sighed and felt Prince's hand, holding the reins, touch hers.

"I'm here, Princess," and they smiled at each other.

The days ran together, as they crossed the marble hills of western Connecticut and reached the eastern edges of the Hudson River Valley. They seemed to be traveling at the same rate as spring and enjoyed her cascade of blooms that opened just as they arrived in each new location.

Cooped in the wagon, Wash was restless at times and Prince would take him and walk alongside as the horse continued its plodding. They switched out the horses during the day and rested both of them each night. It was an endless spring and the vibrant green of leafing trees filled their eyes each morning.

Northward they traveled, following the western foothills of the Berkshires and then the Green Mountains. They had reached Lake Champlain and decided to camp for a few days, while they stocked up on fish and other supplies. As the sun set, they settled into their site along the shore. Victoria suddenly pointed, "What is that?"

A brilliant white light swept across the water, aiming directly at them. Quickly, she gathered the children to her and they moved behind the wagon to wait. Within seconds, it came again, scanning the water and resting on their camp. And again. But there was no sound, no change, just the rhythmic sweep of light. Victoria and Prince exchanged glances, while she tried to quiet the children. After fifteen minutes, nothing had changed.

"Do you think—" she started.

"A lighthouse," said Prince.

"On a lake? Away from the sea?"

"Yes. Look."

Victoria peered but was blinded by the bright light.

"I think it's on that island that we saw earlier," Prince added. He walked back to their fire and sat down. "It's safe, I'm sure." When nothing happened to him, Victoria brought the children to join him. By the time they were ready to sleep, Prince couldn't help himself. "Quick, Princess, run. The lighthouse is coming to get you."

"Quiet, you—" she laughed.

"My lighthouse will come get you, just you wait," he gestured.

"Oh, Prince," she sighed happily. Maybe this would be a good time to start the next baby.

The next morning, Victoria could see the lighthouse standing tall on the island and laughed at her previous night's confusion. She stood at the fire, trying to decide if she should make her prevention tea or not. Prince returned with a string of fish that he had just caught. "Here's breakfast," he called.

Victoria smiled, the thought of fresh fish making her mouth water. She fried them up and the smell made her ravenous. The children were still sleeping and she and Prince shared a meal. As they sat there, enjoying the view and the lingering taste of delicate white fish meat, Prince stretched out his legs and lit his pipe.

Victoria pulled the meat off the remaining fish, making boneless piles for the children. "What will we do when we get to Canada?" she asked, glancing up at Prince.

Prince shifted awkwardly and looked to the side. "What do you mean?"

"How will we find horses?"

Prince cleared his throat and she looked closely at him, but he still wouldn't make eye contact. A few minutes passed before he finally spoke. "I wonder how hard it will be to find my brother."

"Your what?"

Prince looked sheepish, while nodding. "I have a brother up north. He trades horses also."

Victoria stood quickly, scattering the fish bones all over the eating tarp. She started to say something but held her tongue. Instead, she stomped to the fire and briskly stirred the kettle. Then she grabbed the water bucket and strode off in the direction of the creek.

Her mind swirling with wild thoughts, she could barely see the trail. Who was this man, her husband of six years, who had never told her about his brother? A brother, maybe with a wife and children, a few weeks' journey from their camp and she had never known? First Mary Defiance and now this. Secrets. Prince had a bucket full of them, she realized, as she reached the creek and started filling hers. She pulled it up, sloshing water all over her feet, and plopped it on the ground where she sank next to it. No, no more children with this man until she figured out if she wanted to stay. Oh, how she wished her mother could comfort her now and share some wise words. With that, she was washed in sadness and sat there, leaning on the water bucket and breathing raggedly. She wanted to scream or cry or do something, but she felt empty, as if someone had unplugged her and her insides had all drained out. Eventually, she felt anger rising in her and Victoria beat the ground with her fist and then hugged the bucket, just waiting. Softly at first, she could hear a whisper that sounded like her grandmother's voice. She could hear the hissing sounds of some of her words, "False truths, false truths." She remembered her *púridaia* saying to her when, as a child, she complained that her parents hadn't told her something, "There are such things as false truths and honest lies." Maybe that was the same thing with Prince, who told her his story without telling her the whole story. The more she thought about it, she realized that he tended to protect her from information she didn't need to know until it was time to reveal it.

Victoria heard Wash's shout ringing through the campsite and sighed. She pulled herself up, grabbed the full water bucket, and started back to camp. She would wait and see, when she met this brother. Meanwhile, she would brew some tea.

From Lake Champlain, they continued north, following the river valley as it wound across fertile plains. Spring was slower coming to this area but fresh green shoots poked through muddy shores and there were always fish to tease from the flowing waters.

Victoria was stirring the pot on the fire, making porridge for breakfast. She heard birds calling from the tops of nearby trees, each species starting its heralding at a certain point in the dawn chorus.

"Prince," she called. Sitting along the bank, smoking his pipe, he glanced back at her and nodded, both of them aware of the space still between them. He gradually rose and returned to the campsite. Victoria handed him a bowl and cup and he sat down to eat. With the children still sleeping, they passed a quiet moment together, as she sipped her coffee, watching him. Their eyes met and he smiled at her and she felt the warmth of spring flowing through her. It caused her to expand and feel hope. She saw his heart, knew he was a good man, and realized she was glad to be with him, regardless of the way he shared his stories.

A startled cry from the wagon brought Victoria to her feet, but she slowed when she realized it was just Martha's reaction to Wash's clambering on her while she slept. Victoria climbed up the stairs and found the little ones wide-awake and rolling on the comforter, tickling each other. Their joyous faces made her laugh. Oh, to be young again when life was simple! They both sat up when they saw her and she took them down to the fire.

"Let's get going," suggested Prince. "With such long days, we could make good progress, even if we need to rest a bit during the day when it gets warmer."

Victoria nodded and fed the children. Taking care of camp alone, especially with two young ones, was tiring and she was grateful that she could ride in the wagon while they traveled. She glanced up and saw the sun already rising above the trees across the river. It was time to start packing.

They moved along, with Prince generally walking alongside the horses. Although they tended to avoid the well-worn route, they were following it today.

"Do you think we are in Canada already?" Victoria asked.

"I hope so." After a short pause, he added, "Do you see how the river is broader? I wonder if we might be reaching its mouth."

They rounded a grove of trees and suddenly the area opened up before them. Cattle grazed in wide expanses and, in the distance, they could make out buildings along the river, behind which an escarpment led the eye up into the mountains beyond.

After a brief moment, they both turned when they heard someone behind them. A man, riding a horse, came up beside them.

"Hallo," shouted Prince.

The man muttered something that neither Prince nor Victoria

understood, but he did slow and smile.

"Are you from around here?" asked Prince.

The man's eyes looked friendly but he shrugged as if he didn't understand them.

"Are we near Sorel?"

Victoria looked startled and started to ask, "Sorel? What's—" but Prince hushed her.

The man nodded and pointed to the north.

"Do you know where we can find horses?" Prince continued.

The man raised an eyebrow and let out a flood of words that neither of them could catch.

Prince pointed to the man's horse. "Horses, do you know where we can find horses?" he asked, as he imitated animals galloping along.

"Ah, *le cheval Canadien*," said the man. He gestured to the mountains beyond town and said no more.

"Thank you," said Prince and the man nodded before galloping past them into town.

Victoria was again experiencing the frustration of learning that Prince had information that he hadn't shared. "Your brother lives in this town, this Sorel?"

"Hmm, no, nearby."

"You've known that? The name of his town?"

By now, Prince understood what made Victoria angry. He kept the wagon still and placed his hand on hers. "Princess, runners have told me about my brother, on and off, since he arrived in this country. The last I heard of him was a few years ago and he was near here. Dealing horses."

She held tight to her feelings and asked, "This brother, what is he called?"

"William."

Victoria was taken aback. William was the name of Prince's son with Mary Defiance.

"Yes, William after our father," said Prince.

So, there were three of them named William in his family. And Prince wasn't the eldest son.

Prince continued. "I believe he has a wife and maybe a child or two."

"Anything else?"

There was a long pause. Prince shifted in his seat and couldn't look directly at her. "The wife." He paused again. "The wife is not one of us."

"Oh," said Victoria, startled.

"It cost him his place in our family. He could no longer be its head."

"Oh," she said, as everything fell into place. Prince's reluctance to tell her about his brother was based on his shame of his brother marrying one of the Others. "I see," she said. She reached out to touch his arm, to let him know that she would support him. And she realized that, truly, there was no reason to know this sooner. She recognized that Prince's storing information until it was needed was not secrecy, even though it often felt that way to her, but selective sharing, those honest lies her grandmother mentioned.

"I believe we will be most likely to find both my brother and horses up in the mountains. Do you want to skirt the town or do we need to stop?" Prince asked Victoria.

"I'd like to get some milk for the children," she said, eying the nearby cows, "but nothing more."

When they got closer to town, they could see that the river joined a much bigger one and that the mountains with horses were on the other side of this larger river.

"We'll need to find a way to cross, so I guess we'll have to go through town anyway."

They eased themselves along the outer edge of the settlement. By then, it was close to evening and they could see people in their homes dining. They reached the docks and found a small boat that was willing to ferry them across.

While they waited, Victoria asked, "I wonder why there is a needle tree on their signs."

Prince shrugged and there was no response from the ferry pilot. They landed on the other side of the river and, by nightfall, they had started up a small valley heading toward the mountains. Even at this distance, they could hear the sounds of the town as boats ran the river and church bells rang.

ELEVEN

Needle trees replaced spring green as they headed north and some of the highest slopes in the distance still had remnant white patches. Tucked in protected areas between the rocks, spring flowers dotted the streamside.

"Who do you think uses the trails here?"

Prince grunted. "Trappers?"

"Maybe natives," Victoria suggested. She was bouncing Wash on her knee as she wiped part of dinner from his face and hands. The boy squirmed away when she finished and ran off to throw small stones into the babbling creek.

The following day, they entered a wide expanse of open grasslands with small stunted trees. They both gasped at the same time, as they spotted them, clusters of dark, compact horses grazing. They parked the wagon and Prince used the trailing horse to explore. Mounted, he knew he could get closer to the grazing animals before they spooked.

From the height of the wagon seat, Victoria watched as Prince's horse ambled among the others. She guessed there were a hundred animals spread out in the vicinity and felt a sense of relief that they had located a temporary home and source of animals.

"What beauties!" he exclaimed, when he returned to the wagon. "These animals will make good work horses."

"Do you think they belong to anyone?"

"Some of them have docked tails."

Victoria looked up. "Ah, so perhaps?"

"Or escaped?"

They pondered the options, enjoying the sight of the sunlight playing on the animals' backs. "We can stay here a few days and figure it out," decided Prince. Victoria glanced around, taking in the needle tree slopes that surrounded their basin.

Each day, Martha and Wash ran through the fields near camp after insects, while Prince observed the herd. He had learned to identify each group and their interactions and guessed which ones might be with foal. He had been able to approach them on foot and decided these horses were accustomed to people.

"I was able to ride one of the mares," said Prince returning that day. "She has a smooth gait and a strong body. She may not be tall but she's a good worker with a gentle disposition."

"Perfect! What will we—?"

The rest of Victoria's words were drowned by the sound of a galloping horse coming from behind them. They whipped around, Victoria instinctively grabbing Wash as he toddled by, and saw a dark-haired and black-eyed man rein his horse sharply as he arrived.

"*Sarisham, pal.*"

Surprised to hear the mother tongue, Prince paused before responding in the same manner. "*Sarisham*. Can I offer you a smoke?" he said to the man who was dismounting.

The man, hidden momentarily by the horse, answered, "Yes, thanks," and Victoria let out a sigh of relief. The man strode into their fire space and, as he approached, Prince's face changed from tense to questioning. The two men stood facing each other, before Prince whispered, "William?" and the man shouted, "Thomas!" and the two men raced to embrace.

Prince turned to introduce him to Victoria and their children. Victoria examined his face, similar to her husband's but with more lines and surrounded by more gray hair.

"How did you find us?" asked Prince, once they were seated by the fire and smoking their pipes.

"The trappers saw you days ago, when you crossed the river. They thought you might be one of us and sent a runner to me. I've been getting daily reports," he chortled. "You haven't exactly been subtle in your actions."

Prince laughed. "I didn't know anyone was watching. I am not familiar with the ways of this land, I suppose."

"I decided I had to take action when you rode my mare."

"These are your horses?"

"As much as anyone's. Mine at this point, yes."

"Tell me about these horses. They are good stock."

"Yes, let's see if they are still out," he said, and the men walked back to the basin. Victoria took a child in each hand and followed. The men were pointing to various horses and William was talking about their attributes. The children wandered among the plants and Victoria stood near the men, half listening and gazing.

As she stood there, she watched, astonished as each group of horses faded into the mist. She shook her head and the animals reappeared. She looked to see if the men had noticed anything, but they were still talking. As she stood there, breathing, her eyes partly closed, it happened again, until there were no more horses in the valley. She shook her head and they were there again.

"Prince," she called.

"Just a minute."

Time passed and Victoria saw the same scene, all the horses disappearing as she gazed at the fields. The silence was deafening and she felt herself getting wide-eyed. Prince's hand on her shoulder didn't change the view and she said, mesmerized by the image and not moving her eyes, "They are gone. The horses are all gone."

Prince looked where she was staring and saw at least four groups of horses peacefully grazing. "Princess, they are here."

"No," she said firmly. "They have left the valley. They are gone. Dead." She shivered with the clarity and finality of it.

Knowing better than to doubt her, Prince was glad that William was distant enough to not hear her words. He put his arm around her and said, "They are here now."

Slowly her focus returned and she could see first one, and then another, group of grazing horses. She looked, puzzled, at Prince. She felt weighed by a great sadness.

"We will leave enough that they can reproduce," he placated her. "It wouldn't make sense to destroy our source."

She shivered again and bent down to pick up Martha, tugging on her skirt. As she smoothed the girl's hair, William turned to her and she gave him a wan smile before they headed back to camp.

As they sat around the fire, William said, "My camp is nearby. You must come visit." William added, "I want you to meet my family."

"We'd like to do that. We can come tomorrow."

After giving Prince directions, William said his God-go-with-yous and headed out.

The following day, Victoria packed camp and they followed the signs that William had made and turned at the bent twig. They entered a clearing and saw a dark-haired girl rise from a small field and walk to a tent.

"It's not quite a bender," whispered Victoria, looking at the habitation.

"No," said Prince. "It's wider, unless they use quite long poles. No, I think perhaps it is made of several pole parts lashed together." They were trying not to stare at the inside of the tent to determine its construction.

A woman emerged and walked towards their wagon. She had a long, single braid down her back, not covered by any *diklo*, and wore a deer hide skirt. Her face, dark and angular, was lit by her smile. "*Sarisham*," she said. "My name Sonny. Welcome, brother of my husband."

Simultaneously, William emerged from nearby shrubs, followed by two boys. The families gathered around the fire and Sonny distributed bowls filled with venison stew. The conversation, awkward due to unfamiliarity and a language barrier, was eased by the food.

After they ate, William's daughter, Matilda, took Martha and Wash under her care and had them running and giggling near the tent. The men sat and smoked and talked horses while the boys listened and stared at Prince.

Sonny and Victoria were left to themselves. They cleaned up from the meal and, despite the language limitations, Victoria felt a bond with the woman who had used local plants in the meal to enhance the flavors. The women stood by the fire as Sonny stirred a pot of syrup that she was boiling down from sap collected earlier that year from local maple trees.

The families stayed together for the next few months. Victoria learned how Sonny grew squash beneath the corn stalks that were covered with climbing beans. The children spent their days together and Wash strutted with his older cousins when they fished or played hunting games. But most importantly, the men collected horses and figured out how they would transport them.

"We can take them by boat to Montreal," said William.

"From there, we can load them onto a train that will get them to Connecticut."

"But what happens then?"

"I'll meet them at the station."

"But it will take you longer to get back. I can take them to Montreal myself to give you more time."

Back and forth, they talked, detailing the trip and how they would divide responsibilities and earnings. And it wasn't long before it was time for Prince and his family to return home.

"I wonder what has happened with the rebellion," said Victoria, as they packed to leave.

"I'm sure we will hear once we are back in America," replied Prince. "Out here, there is not much discussion of it."

"I hope someone will need horses," she said. "If all the men are fighting, there'll be no one to farm and certainly little pleasure usage."

Prince was quiet. "I hadn't considered that. But I'm sure we will find customers."

"If the South is still rebelling, do you think we should return to America?" She remembered that newspaper headline requesting volunteer soldiers.

"Yes, we will meet the horses and try to sell them. And if there are any problems, we'll head right back up here before the first winter storms."

Victoria was satisfied by his answer. She was looking forward to seeing her parents and brothers again. Maybe it would be a good winter and they would stay there. And if not, they now had another choice.

"Here's a basket of vegetables," said Matilda, handing it to Victoria who was in the wagon door. Everything else was secure and she climbed down. She hugged both the young woman and Sonny, holding them close. Prince and William had their arms around each other and the boys had Wash on their shoulders to hoist him into the wagon. Matilda grabbed Martha and gave her a squeeze before placing her on the wagon bench.

"Next summer, we will be back," Prince assured them.

"If not sooner," added Victoria.

"Sonny!" Victoria cried, as she jumped down from the wagon, almost before Prince stopped the horse when they arrived the next summer. She ran towards the woman but stopped short. Sonny's face was smiling but her eyes were filled with deep sadness and she was gripping Matilda by the shoulder as if she couldn't let her go. Victoria slowed to a walk, reached her sister-in-law, and embraced her. She felt Sonny shudder and sob in her arms. She also could discern the smallest extension of her abdomen suggesting that she was with child. Meanwhile, Matilda had gathered Martha and Wash in her arms and they were tugging her hair and arms.

The women slowly broke apart just as William and his younger son Samuel came from the horse paddock.

"We heard your bells," William exclaimed, reaching to grab Prince. "*Sarisham!*"

Victoria noticed more lines in William's face. And then the absence of the older son. "Where's Edward?"

Sonny collapsed where she stood and William ran to support her. There was a long pause before William spoke. "We lost him this winter." His voice quavered and his eyes were on the ground. "I had taken him to Montreal to look at a possible sale barn. He—he caught the pox and never made it back home." Only the soft twittering of finches could be heard while his words sat on the air, waiting for everyone to absorb them. Victoria crouched down beside the couple and put a hand on each, before she uttered, "The world is a ladder, in which some go up and others go down." William nodded but Sonny only sobbed softly. They finally rose and helped Prince and Victoria settle into camp.

In the wagon later that night, as she and Prince lay in their comforter on their platform, Victoria could hear her children breathing in their bed below and was filled with sadness for Sonny and William. Prince pulled her close and wiped tears from her cheeks.

"Life is so fragile," she whispered.

"Maybe we need to add to our family."

"Not tonight," she said. "Sadness begets sadness."

Prince nodded and caressed her face. "Whenever you're ready, Princess."

The following day, William and Prince were sitting by the fire, deep in conversation.

"Did the horses sell well last year?"

"Did they ever!" said Prince, taking a cup of tea from Victoria. "This horrible war is continuing and the Union needs horses."

"Now, that's something we hadn't considered."

"True. In fact, they are offering a hundred and twenty dollars for each horse. I've never gotten that much for an ordinary animal."

William whistled. "A hundred and twenty! Why, that's a fortune in a small shipment."

"Yes." Prince puffed on his pipe. "Unfortunately, President Lincoln has also issued a tax on our income, anything more than eight hundred dollars."

William looked startled.

"Of course, we try to stay invisible, moving whenever an agent comes nearby."

"No taxes here. No war either," said William, shaking his head.

"Well, shall we go look at the horses? I'm anxious to see them," said Prince.

Although Victoria knew they were welcome at the camp, there was a heaviness in their first few weeks. The women were sitting near the fire one morning and Victoria's sense of knowing overtook her caution. "You'll be adding to the family before the end of the year."

Sonny looked quickly at her and nodded. "It started before—" but she couldn't finish her sentence.

"That's good," Victoria said. Noting Sonny's color, she knew that she wasn't eating well enough for the baby and started to devise ways to slip the necessary nutrients into their food. She felt even more pleased that they had gotten a cow and chicken back in Sorel before coming to camp this year. Although she originally had been thinking about the children, she now would add milk to some of their sauces and stews in order to get some into Sonny.

It was the longest day of the year and, when the men finally came back from the horses, Wash was just bursting. "Mammis, Mammis, I baby a horse, I baby a horse!"

Victoria suppressed a laugh and looked at Prince, who nodded. "Ask Wash."

"Let's sit down for dinner and, Wash, you can tell us what happened."

When all the bowls were filled and everyone was together, Wash started. "The horse, she was big and she hurt and she was bloody. And my hands," which he thrust out to the group to show them, "they are small and—I helped."

William continued, "The horse was partly breached and there wasn't much room. She just needed a little nudge to get that colt turned around."

"Wash was right in there the whole time, talking to her and coaxing her to calm down. We figured maybe his small hands would do the job."

"And I did it, I did it!"

His cousin Samuel doffed the young boy on the head. "Yes, you did."

"That boy has a way with the horses, I tell you," said Prince proudly.

"He was born into the right family, that's for sure."

Victoria felt herself swell with joy.

Later that night, she cuddled with Prince and tugged at his moustache. "A real horseman, our son."

"That is true."

"Maybe we need more like him," she whispered in his ear.

"Umm," said Prince. "Maybe a dozen or so."

And so the days passed, with the men working with the horses during the days while the women prepared food, washed, and did other camp duties.

Victoria had noticed that Sonny still was lacking the look of vitality of a woman with child. While pouring some milk for Martha, she tried to convince Sonny to drink some.

"No, I can't drink that. My stomach, it clutches when I have milk." Sonny had clenched her hand to form a fist to demonstrate.

Victoria pondered that information.

"I get sick, you know, here," continued Sonny, pointing to her intestines. "I am already that way now."

Victoria realized with a shock that her hidden milk had been harming Sonny. She rose, disgusted with herself for not being in touch with her healing powers, and thinking too much instead. Saying, "I'm going to look for some plants," over her shoulder as she left, she walked off into the surrounding bushes to visualize Sonny and what her body needed.

She wasn't by the small brook very long before she calmed herself. As she sat there, she envisioned a long table filled with foods, ones that clearly would be appropriate for Sonny: eggs, whole fish, and animal organs, along with nuts and her favored beans. Victoria saw that she should encourage her to eat all her normal foods, with extra servings of those. She rose, shaking her head at how blind she had been, and returned to camp.

After that, Victoria made it a daily practice to take some time to sit by the creek and clear her mind. Usually, nothing arose but she felt more open to any visions that might be floating around her.

During the heat of late July, Prince and Victoria were in their wagon getting things ready for the evening, when they first heard the sound.

"What was that?"

"Thunder?" asked Prince.

More rumblings careened up the ravines and across the hillsides. Prince and Victoria quickly climbed down from the wagon and joined the rest of the family calmly sitting at the fire. Within a few minutes, the sound rebounded through their canyon again. Prince looked questioningly at his brother. "What was that?"

"What?"

"That noise." Victoria edged closer to the children. It was sounding more like cannons.

"Ah, it's the boats heading from Montreal to Quebec City."

"They are announcing the beginning of the celebration for the Grandmother," Sonny added.

Victoria looked puzzled.

"Saint Anne, Mary's mother. There is a shrine downriver that houses a statue made from a huge piece of oak. It causes miracles," William clarified.

"And it's painted beautiful colors and she wears pearls and diamonds and rubies," added Sonny.

"Saint Anne," said Victoria thoughtfully.

"Ah, yes, she protects pregnant women and brings their child to safety," explained Sonny. After a minute, she added, "And she is the patron saint of women wanting a child also."

"And horse riders," added William.

They sat silently as they listened to the cannon. Prince put another stick on the fire and sat back down. "The sound reminds me of our rebellion back home," he said.

"We hear bits and pieces about it up here. We were all surprised when the Confederates kept winning battles," said William.

"Their spirit is strong. Did you know this winter they elected Jefferson Davis as president for six years?"

"No, truly?"

"And the Union government has forbidden the return of any slaves, completely canceling out the Fugitive Slave Law. The Southerners are strongly motivated to keep fighting now. Although when we left, the last news didn't sound good for them."

"Well, I hate to profit from war but I certainly am glad to have a market for these horses."

"Yes, as they always say, 'Gypsy gold does not chink and glitter, it gleams in the sun and neighs in the dark.'"

William laughed and then grew serious. "Do you think there are enough soldiers to keep the war going?" He paused thoughtfully before continuing, "Will you be needing to fight?"

Prince shrugged. "Similar to the taxes, I try to stay out of sight."

"Have you considered moving up here? We could find land nearby where you could set up your own camp."

Prince glanced at Victoria, who wanted to be near her family in Somerville at least part of the year. On the other hand, having a retreat in case things became unbearable might be a good idea and she gave a small nod of her head.

"I'll keep my eyes open for a good site," said William. "But now, it's getting late."

With that, everyone headed to his sleeping quarters. Victoria picked up a sleeping Wash and Prince put Martha on his shoulder and they placed the children in their bed.

Each day Matilda tended the garden and chased away crows trying to eat their crops. Walking by her one day, Victoria was startled by her appearance. She's growing into a young woman, she realized. When she sat down with Sonny, Victoria sighed. "Time goes so quickly."

Sonny shook her head. "Only the good times." After a few minutes, she raised her head to look at the clear, blue late summer sky. "Today is a good day to harvest sweet grass."

Martha, who was playing on the tarp with them, clapped her hands. "Look, she wants to harvest," laughed Sonny.

The women and the two girls gathered their sacks, baskets, and knives and started to the grassland area. Matilda carried Martha over the small creeks and, before long, they reached the open space.

Sonny bent to examine the plants. "Perfect. The blades are five, maybe six hands long." She used her knife to cut the grass about three inches from the base and laid the strands in a flat basket for drying. They moved along, with the women and Matilda cutting and four-year old Martha carrying the cut stems to the drying area.

"Look at her little legs," laughed Matilda. Martha turned and smiled joyously as she inhaled the grassy aroma and placed the material to dry.

By noon, Sonny stood up and said, "That's enough." She returned to the drying area, as she had been doing every half hour, and gave the blades a turn.

They ate a quick snack and then they laid all the dried grass onto a cloth that Sonny then rolled up. Matilda gathered the drying baskets and they started back to camp. Suddenly, a killdeer flew from the path ahead of them, loudly calling. It landed to the side and feigned a broken wing.

"She's trying to lure us away from her nest."

"Yes, look, there are her eggs."

Sure enough, Victoria saw four spotted eggs that looked very similar to the gravel on the path in a small depression just ahead of them. Watching for a moment, Sonny suddenly gasped, "The Grandmother, she is protecting us."

Victoria was puzzled.

"The nest, it's a sign of the Grandmother. A good sign. Let's go back to camp now," and Sonny almost started skipping down the path. Victoria raised her eyebrow but Sonny didn't notice.

Back at camp under the shade of the trees, they spread out the baskets again and filled them with the grass blades.

"Why didn't you leave them in the field?" asked Victoria.

"The full sun, it takes away the sacredness of it."

"Ah," said Victoria, as she handed a bowl of food to Sonny. They sat to eat lunch, and Victoria was pleased to see that Sonny finished her full bowl, which, unknown to her, Victoria had plied with extra pieces of liver and kidney.

At breakfast later that week, William suggested, "We should all go look at the horses. Wait 'til you see how well our son has been breaking them in." The women agreed and, after things had been cleaned up, the group headed to the fields.

Samuel had indeed done an excellent job with the horses. Generally of a gentle disposition, they took easily to the harness but needed reminders of civilized ways after spending the summer roaming.

Victoria watched as Samuel lunged several of the horses through their paces. Sensing a red, hot pain, she turned sharply to her left but saw nothing. She focused on Samuel again but the pain was in the same spot, forcing her to turn away from the group. Several horses were grazing a short distance away and they seemed to be glowing. Overcome by pain and fever, she stepped toward the horses and tried to understand what was happening.

The horses stood with their heads lowered, breathing, and sending sharp, pointed sensations to her. She came closer and the pain sent her to her knees. As she crouched there, she glanced on the ground and saw a mound of horse manure. It came into focus and she noticed it was coarse and filled with sand. Her brain tried to tease apart a reason for that, when it suddenly came to her. She rose with a start and headed back to camp.

Her departure caught Prince's attention. "Where are you going?" he shouted. But she was already running back for her medicinal bag. She dug out a large lump of beeswax and began to melt it over the fire. Once it was liquid, she added some softened oats to the mixture and rushed back to the horses.

Fortunately the day was warm and the mixture stayed fluid. Prince came to meet her and she gasped, "You have to help me. I need to get this into the horses," as she returned to the small group on the side.

Prince knew better than to question her. He held their heads as she encouraged the horses to consume large quantities of the paraffin. When she was finished, she looked around to see that the entire group was watching.

"Sand. They have been eating sand," she said, pointing to the dung. "It's clogging their bowels."

With a quaking voice, Samuel admitted, "This group was way down the canyon near the mouth of the river. I had to drive them back up here last week."

"We need to keep an eye on them and be sure the colic passes."

"I will do that," said the young man. Back at camp, he gathered some materials and then set up a tent near the horses to watch them for the next few days. When he returned to camp, he reported, "They are resting comfortably and run with the other horses."

Victoria smiled. "Now you know what to look for."

Samuel nodded.

Later that month Martha was on their tarp playing with strands of sweet grass that Sonny had piled nearby. Sonny settled near her and started to plait them into cords that she then would store for the winter. "I'll make baskets and—um, what do you call your hair?" she asked, pulling hers to the front.

"Braids?"

"Yes, braids when it's cold and I have much time."

"What do you do with the grass braids?"

"Ah, sacred. They smell good and help heal." She glanced at Martha, broke into a smile, and pointed. "Martha, she can braid!"

Indeed the young girl had made a coarse but recognizable braid.

"She takes after her grandmother and great grandmother," Victoria said, astonished. She didn't remember being so dexterous at that age. Martha smiled and continued her work.

"She can take hers home for the winter," suggested Sonny.

The women continued to work together, in the gentle quiet that comes with contentment. Victoria looked at Sonny and noticed her improved color. "You are feeling well," she said, somewhat as a question.

Sonny smiled. "Yes, I am growing stronger." She patted her belly. "And so is the baby, thanks to you." Victoria tried to look surprised, but Sonny smiled knowingly. "And you? When will you be adding to your family?" She smiled wider. "I can hear in the night, you know."

Victoria reddened but then looked directly at her. "I'm not sure." She had felt inside that her babies, or at least their potentials, were not catching. She wasn't sure why but she was certain that she would bleed again this month. She was glad that she and Prince had agreed to forgo the traditional separation during that time, although he wouldn't touch her. She enjoyed sleeping near him and it would have been close to impossible to run a camp alone if she couldn't touch the food or do laundry during those weeks. They had decided that they were in a new country with new customs and it was right to update their ways. For a brief moment, she wondered if they were being punished, by their babies not catching. She shook her head to dispel that thought and felt Sonny's hand on her arm.

"Your time will come when it is right. Remember the killdeer nest, the sign from the Grandmother."

Victoria nodded, hoping that she believed that.

The last things had been put on the wagon for the return trip. They had celebrated the passage of summer the previous night and it was only a matter of hitching up the horse and heading south.

"Goodbye, *pal*. We will have many horses headed south shortly."

"Yes, and all of them healthy thanks to Victoria," added William.

"All set?" Prince asked, looking at his family.

Wash and Martha did not want to leave their cousins and Victoria was struggling to say goodbye to Sonny.

"Next time we see you, we will have a new cousin," Victoria said with a nod to Sonny's waist.

"And next time we see you, you will be telling us the same thing," she whispered in Victoria's ear. Feeling hopeful, they loaded into the wagon and began their trip home.

TWELVE

Instead of Canada, the following summer found Prince's family in upstate New York, where they sold horses directly to Union agents. Having set up a small *ofisa,* Victoria knew, when she looked down the long dirt road, that the older woman trudging determinedly would be coming to see her. She wished she had closed shop already, but the woman had already caught sight of her sitting at her table. Sighing, Victoria promised herself that this would be the last customer. Under her skirts, she felt sweat covering her thighs and pooling under her belly.

The woman sat down, slightly breathless, and placed her coins on the table. "I want to know about my son," she said. "He's a soldier."

These were the visits that Victoria disliked the most. Her face always exposed the truth, which wasn't usually what the customer wanted to hear. "What is his name?"

"Jonathan MacComber, 8th New York Cavalry. Buffalo, now Rochester." The woman's face softened. "How he loves to ride and is he fast!"

Victoria closed her eyes and sat quietly. An image of a slim, redheaded young man rose to her mind and he was eating with a group of other soldiers. A few moments passed before Victoria was blasted with a cacophony of sounds: roars of cannons and shouts and bugles and thundering of horses and endless screams and smells of fear and death and panic. She felt herself collapsing under the weight of such dreadfulness and evil until she could bear it no longer.

Then suddenly, it was quiet, deathly still, not a peaceful quiet. No birds or wind, just still. She could see around her hundreds of bodies of men in gray and blue and horses of black and brown and white

125

followed by more bodies into the thousands and thousands and death hovered over the field and she could barely breathe.

She saw him there among the others, this Jonathan MacComber, and noted the irony that he had been riding one of their little Canadian horses, also lying motionless on the ground. The stench and the ugliness and the misery of that moment were captured in all of the cells of her body.

A sound from the waiting woman brought her very slowly back to her *ofisa*. Closed-eyed, Victoria struggled to compose her face. Eventually she opened her eyes and saw the frantic face of the boy's mother before her.

Victoria took a deep breath. "He will be honored greatly," she said slowly. "He will be decorated for his efforts."

The woman nodded and almost smiled. "So, he will live."

Victoria could say no more. She bent her head and closed her eyes. After a few minutes, she said, "You must go now."

Victoria heard the woman scrape back the chair and walk back down the dusty road. Victoria managed to reach over to draw her curtain closed. Images of the horror she had seen kept flashing through her mind, and her head sank on the table, as she leaned over as far as her full belly would allow. The baby kicked against the table pressing into her abdomen but she couldn't move back. Tears welled and then sobs came, deeper and deeper, until she could cry no more. Yet she still felt wretched by the weight of all that death and destruction.

When she heard the scratching at her curtain, she cautiously opened her eyes. An orange glow of the light coming underneath suggested it was getting late.

"Princess, are you in there?"

It took her a moment to be able to respond, "Yes, Prince, I am here."

He pulled open the curtain as she struggled to sit back up from the table. The golden light covered her face and highlighted the tracks on her tear-stained cheeks and the hollows of her eyes.

"What happened?" he asked, as he ran to help her sit up. "Are you well? Is it the baby?"

"We are fine," she said heavily. "It's the war. It's getting worse. I can't do this anymore. The visions are too painful, too awful, too terrific for me to bear. And it can't be good for the baby."

"Princess, I was thinking of moving you and the children away from here anyway. There's trouble brewing in Buffalo with this new draft. Come, let's go to the wagon and get some food."

He helped her up from the chair and they walked around the back of the shack to their camp where Martha and Wash were playing.

Their conversation lasted long into the night.

"I've explained already. It would be best for us to stay away from Canada right now. The French Canadians are sympathetic towards the Confederates."

"What about William and Sonny?"

"They live there and understand the politics. William thinks he can safely move horses to us here in Buffalo. But he said we shouldn't be there."

Victoria sighed with frustration. She wanted to see Sonny and their new baby who was already six months old. And she wanted Sonny to be with her when their child was born later in the summer.

"And I think it would be best for our child to be born in America right now," said Prince, anticipating the second part of her argument.

"Why?"

"Our children should be American citizens. This is where we will live and we must be part of this country. Not British."

Victoria sighed again. In her condition, she could not realistically do anything contrary to Prince and she was too hot and tired to argue.

"We can go up into the mountains where it'll be cooler." Prince always knew her soft spot, the way to win her over.

"I will do whatever you say. I just can't quarrel about it."

"The next shipment isn't due for several weeks. We can leave tomorrow."

They had retraced their steps to find a quiet, cool camp in the hills east of Buffalo. Prince settled the wagon into a pretty copse of deciduous trees mixed with the needle trees located near a small stream.

"Water, firewood, everything you need, right here," he exclaimed.

They had been there about a week when Prince sat down to talk to Victoria, who had collapsed her large bulk onto a cushion.

"I must return to Buffalo for the next shipment."

She nodded.

"I'll take Wash with me. You'll have one less mouth to worry about."

Victoria started to protest but realized that Prince was probably right. She was exhausted just moving herself around. The young boy, always into everything, would be more than she could handle. "You'll be very careful with him? Please don't take him anywhere dangerous."

"Princess," said Prince, cupping his hand under her chin. "That boy is our future. Would I risk that?"

Tears welled in her eyes. She knew Wash was the family jewel to Prince also. She had never missed a day of Wash's life and wasn't sure if she could bear it. But, again, reason won.

"All right."

"I'll be back by early August. Will that be soon enough?"

Victoria did some mental calculations. "It should be fine."

The pains started mid-morning, sooner than Victoria had expected. Despite accepting some new customs, she still felt that giving birth in the wagon would contaminate it. She spent the rest of the hot, sticky morning building a small shelter near the fire. Martha helped hang the tarp and together they gathered wood and then went to get water. Victoria sighed with relief as she soaked her swollen feet in the cool stream.

"Look, Mammis," pointed Martha. "The fish are back."

Indeed, a few small perch were weaving their way through the water flowing over the rocks.

"Shall I?" asked the girl.

Her mother nodded and Martha sat patiently on the edge with her hand dangling in the water. She wiggled her little fingers and, very slowly, she moved her hand closer to a fish, until she was able to swoop under its belly and throw it onto the stream bank. Before long, she had four small fish ready to cook.

Carrying them back to camp, Victoria gasped as a strong pain forced her to bend over for a few seconds until it passed. Martha looked questioningly at her, but she just shook her head and they kept walking, Martha toting the water jug.

Victoria began to clean the fish, pausing as the pains came more frequently. She thought she would gag at the smell but was able to complete the task and put the fish into the kettle to cook. She had no interest in food right now, but Martha would be able to serve herself later.

Wiping sweat from her forehead, she tried calculating how many days it had been since Prince left for Buffalo with Wash and when they would return, but she lost focus with the next searing pain. He wasn't there, that was all that mattered, and she couldn't tell when he might return.

"Martha, go into the wagon and get me some cloths from the storage next to the beds."

"Yes, Mammis."

Victoria was reaching up to take the cloths from the girl coming down the wagon stairs when she felt a warm gush flowing down her legs. She stood as a large puddle formed below her. Martha looked, surprised.

"My time has come," Victoria said simply. "My pains are close together and my waters have flowed. Come, let us sit in the shelter."

Victoria could barely feel the air move under the tarp but at least she was out of the direct sun. Martha had filled a bowl and, using one of the cloths, she wiped Victoria's face with the refreshing water and offered her sips to drink.

"Oh," Victoria said suddenly as she half sat up. "I'll need a knife. Can you find one?"

"Yes, Mammis, I'll go."

Victoria lay back on the makeshift bed and tried to breathe through the next pain. They were coming closer together and she was feeling a strong urge to push out this baby. She restrained herself, knowing that the time would be coming but was not yet. She clutched the damp cloth tightly in her fist as the next contraction pulsed through her.

She heard Martha return and place a knife near the bowl of water. Victoria tried to smile her thanks but another contraction turned her expression into a grimace.

"Mammis, are you all right?"

Victoria could hear the fear in her daughter's voice.

"This is the way it happens," she said as calmly as she could. "Things are going well. It's just—" Another contraction and she could stop herself from pushing no longer.

Victoria felt herself move away from her daughter in the shelter and into a place deep inside. She felt vapors swirling around and the presence of her *púridaia* who whispered soothing sounds into her ear. She vaguely felt the cool cloth on her face as Martha continued to wipe away the sweat, but she was transported somewhere quite distant from the shelter.

Sounds were echoing and muddled as if she were under water. Victoria felt her body buoyed and weightless, unlike the heavy bulk of the past few months. She could hear murmuring around her, some gentle, some dissenting. She felt that she had been in this spot some time before but she couldn't place it, and she couldn't muster enough mental energy to try. She relaxed into the sensations and felt the loving presence of essences hovering over her abdomen, soothing it and moving the baby along its passage to the outside world.

The peace was marred by a buzzing, a noise or vibration of irritation or anger. Victoria felt it near her shoulder and she could feel the other beings trying to shoo it away from her but to no avail. Like a wasp that kept coming for a taste of the stew, the noise persisted. It took the form of a cannon shot in battle, it changed into a young man shattered by bullets gasping for his final breath, and it transformed into the agony of his mother when she learned of his death.

Horrified by these images, Victoria tried to sit up and move away from the buzzing. Gentle beings soothed her back down and carefully gathered the buzz in their hands and carried it away. From behind her, Victoria could sense that there was resistance and struggle between the buzzing and the beings. A sense of chaos filled the air, as at the same time she felt a final push and the emptying of her womb. She felt herself sucked out of this distant place and returned to the shelter where Martha squatted beside her.

Victoria opened her eyes just as she heard the piercing cry of her newborn held in Martha's little arms. Victoria struggled to sit up to take the slippery baby and wrap it in a clean blanket. Handing the baby back to Martha, she slowly was able to raise herself into a kneeling position and then squat on her birthing blanket. Breathing deeply, closing her eyes, she used every ounce of her energy and courage to pull on the cord until the afterbirth passed through and she was completely empty. Victoria sank to her knees and reached for the knife. Reaching in the folds of the blanket, she cut the cord near the baby's belly and tied it off with a thread from the blanket. She then sank, exhausted, onto her bed.

She could hear Martha talking softly to the baby and washing the wax off its face. Suddenly she sat up, realizing that she hadn't noticed if it was a girl or boy. She turned and gestured to Martha who handed her the bundle.

Aware that she had been in a haze of subdued light until that point, Victoria felt her vision clear. She looked fully at the baby and almost dropped it when she saw its curly reddish hair, light skin, and blue eyes. Who was this child? She carefully unwrapped the baby and determined it was a son. Martha handed her a clean damp cloth and she wiped the child as she kept thinking, who was this child? Certainly he didn't have her dark hair, skin, or eyes. She couldn't recall anyone in her family looking so fair.

Martha interrupted her thoughts. "Mammis, he's so handsome. And quiet."

"That's true," Victoria agreed. The baby had been quiet since his initial shout and was gazing around. She rewrapped him in the blanket and brought him to her breast. He immediately latched on and sucked contentedly, even though no milk had started flowing.

Martha stepped out of the shelter and returned with some pillows to prop up Victoria.

"Thank you, that helps."

Martha smiled. "I'm glad you are well."

"Oh, you poor dear. I bet you are. Of course everything worked out." By now, it was getting dark. "Martha, dear, have some dinner. The fish is certainly cooked by now. Oh, and add a few sticks to the fire."

Martha nodded and served herself a meal. Victoria sank back gratefully on the pillows and drifted off to sleep, her new son in her arms.

Midmorning, the following day, they both heard the jingling of the harness and turned to smile at each other. Prince rode into camp, with Wash astride his saddle in front of him. It took Prince only a few seconds to assess the scene, with Victoria holding her bundle and Martha in the shelter.

"I'm a father again," he shouted with delight.

Victoria nodded.

"Martha, bring the child to me."

Victoria was pleasantly surprised that Prince was willing to see the child so soon after birth. However, she watched with concern as he took his first look at the child. Victoria saw his excited face change to surprise and then confusion.

"Princess," he said sternly. "Is this my child?"

"Yes, Prince. I couldn't have been more surprised myself to see him."

"He doesn't look like our other children," he whispered as he drew close to Victoria.

"I know." She shrugged. "I don't know any more than you." She didn't think it was worth sharing about the buzzing and beings and, besides, she wasn't sure if she could describe it adequately.

The baby opened his eyes and looked at Prince.

"He needs a name," Victoria commented.

"Yes, he does. I was thinking we would name him Richard after your brother."

"That would be lovely."

"Now, I'm not certain." Prince touched the baby's curly red hair.

"Let's call him Richard as you suggest," she said, wanting to reach a decision.

After only a brief pause, Prince agreed. "Richard it is. Welcome to our family."

The next few days passed quickly. Victoria was busy nursing and trying to get back into the family's routines.

"Princess?"

"Yes, Prince."

"Now that you are moving about, I want to talk with you about the last shipment."

"Was there a problem?" Victoria asked sharply. She realized that she had been so focused on the birth that she had forgotten about Prince's business.

"No, not at all, except this," said Prince, as he reached into his saddlebag and brought out a sack of gold coins. He poured them on the tarp between them as Victoria gasped.

"And I've already sent William's share back with a runner," said Prince, smiling.

"Oh, my!"

"The customs officer just waved us through. The quartermaster was so pleased to get horses for the Union Army."

"That's amazing."

"And the inspector was quite good," Prince continued. "He looked carefully at all the horses William sent down. You know, they are supposed to be between five to seven years old, and the inspector checked them all. No ridges on the incisors and all their teeth in place."

Victoria nodded, knowing that William prided himself of his ability to pick good horses. "And I'm sure they all had a good disposition and good feet. Those Canadians all do."

"Right. The hardest part is meeting the size requirement, fifteen to seventeen hands. Our little iron horses are on the small side and just make the five-foot mark."

"But, Prince," said Victoria, looking at all the coins. "We are rich."

"Yes," shouted Prince. "We are!"

"I can't possibly carry all that sewn into my skirt," she added. "I won't be able to walk."

Prince threw back his head and laughed. "You are quite right. I hadn't thought of that." He looked puzzled before asking, "Do you think you can carry them until we get back to New Haven?"

"Probably. Maybe we can figure out something then."

"What a problem to have! And we have one more shipment before it's time to head south."

Victoria fingered the coins piled on the tarp. "Maybe we could buy some land or a new wagon."

"Let's not spend it all yet," he chided her. "But those are good ideas." With sparkling eyes, he glanced at his new son. "And we'll figure out where this Richard belongs in the family, too, once we get home."

Victoria smiled at him. "What a summer!"

"Yes, indeed."

Prince rose and she heard his steps as he climbed the wagon stairs and closed the door behind him.

THIRTEEN

Victoria was startled to feel Prince's hand on her shoulder. She opened her eyes, trying to figure out how he had gotten back from the wagon without her noticing.

"Did you nap all morning?"

Victoria glanced around and saw that she was at the old Farmer's Hotel and in fact had slept away the first half of the day. Over what? Ah, yes, their life during the rebellion.

"I—I guess so, Prince."

"You must have been tired. We were too busy last night."

Victoria could see the warmth in his eyes but honestly couldn't recall any nighttime activities. Prince reached for her hand to help her up.

"Oh," she said, stretching her legs, "I'm sore."

"Let's have some lunch," he suggested, steering her to the table.

She sat down heavily in the chair and heard Prince calling to Daisy in the kitchen. She couldn't believe that she had wasted the whole morning.

"How are the sales going?" she asked when Prince sat down across from her. She could see deep bags under his eyes and thought he should have been napping with her. She wondered if the recent visit from his son from Ohio had upset him more than he let on.

"Briskly. Most of the stock is selling."

Daisy emerged carrying two steaming bowls that she placed before her parents. Victoria took some of the stew and blew briskly on her spoon, while she tried to be patient. Prince was already gulping down pieces of potato and then washing it down with water, as tears filled his eyes.

"Too hot," he gasped.

Victoria shook her head. If he hadn't figured this out at this point in his life, she knew he never would. They finished their meal in short time and Prince stretched back from the table and sighed.

"What is it?"

Prince shook his head and finally said, "Richard."

She raised an eyebrow at Prince to encourage him to continue.

"He's hiding a nicely matched pair."

"Hiding?"

"Well, he keeps moving them to the end of the barn. They're quite natty, actually. They would make a nice sale."

"But he's keeping them?"

"I'm not sure. Maybe he has someone in mind for them. But they were filthy the last time I looked at them. Mud all over their legs and bellies."

Victoria inhaled sharply. "He's racing them."

Startled, Prince jerked his head back and then, as realization flooded through him, he sank deeply in his chair. "You're right. That's exactly what he's doing."

"They were in the shipment?"

"Yes."

"The one with Mr. Kenyon?"

Prince nodded, unable to say more. Victoria rose from her chair to put her arm around him. She rested her head on his and stroked his hair. "We'll figure it out."

"I'd better head back to the barn," he said, as he patted her hand and rose from the chair.

It was a quiet afternoon, so Victoria headed up to her bedroom, reached into a satchel to pull out a black silk package, and settled onto the comforter. She sat in silence for some time, perhaps twenty minutes, before she felt clear enough to take the next step.

Gently removing the silk wrapping, Victoria began to handle her Tarot deck, thinking briefly of her *púridaia* who had bequeathed the cards to her. She tried to integrate her grandmother's strength and vision into her own and felt her spine straighten and her posterior sink solidly on the surface below her. She was finally ready, only thirty years after her son had been born, she laughed silently.

She brought images of Richard to her mind: his birth in the Buffalo hills, his marriage to Lottie, his conversation with Mr. Kenyon, his interaction with Wash during his final moments, and— At that thought, a card flew from the deck onto the comforter. Facing straight up at her, Victoria saw the ten of coins. Money. Certainly in the past few years, she had seen Richard blinded by wealth and greedy for more, always busy grabbing more riches. The reason for this was beyond her, but she knew it was true. She had seen it recently more and more, his almost frantic focus on money as if he had debts to pay or something he wanted that was out of reach. She clearly saw that Richard would not be the best person to manage the finances or administer the business. But again, she was stymied how to identify his strength. What would his mission be?

As Victoria settled into drawing the next card, she heard noise downstairs and the return of Prince, Richard, and others for dinner. Her concentration disrupted, she put the cards away for a later time.

That night, Victoria climbed into bed next to Prince, snuggled up to him, and pulled on his moustache. He smiled at her but he made no follow-up movements. Shortly, he turned on his side away from her. She put her arm on his shoulder and, after a few minutes she felt Prince's muscles relax and his breathing deepen. And, despite the fact that she had slept all morning, soon she had drifted into another place.

She found herself in a city and was surrounded by tall buildings. Carriages kept rolling past and horses were neighing, their breath steaming in the cold air. People were calling to each other and, although it was noisy and busy, there was pleasantness to the day. Suddenly, she felt a deep shadow pass over her as she heard loud rumblings along the snow-covered cobblestones. Her view was obstructed by something large and dark and she was filled with a sense of horror. She thought she saw one of her sons running by and she had images of him tumbling down the street, hanging onto the passing sleigh.

Victoria started to run, following the son, even though the dark shape of a sleigh hid him from her. She felt her breath get short and her legs tire but she sensed her son's panic and pain and kept going. People began to scream, several of them shouting, "Whoa, whoa!" Someone grabbed her arm, but she struggled to break free and continue. Arms gathered around her and held her tight and, as much as she twisted and turned, she couldn't get away.

She awoke in the morning, still disconcerted from her dream. Prince was already up, as she had expected. Slowly she rose, dressed, and started downstairs.

"She was a wild woman, Dadrus," she heard Richard shout.

Victoria stopped, imagining Richard's face as fiery as his hair, with his blue eyes flashing.

"Quiet, she's right above us," Prince said. Bewildered, Victoria realized they were talking about her.

"She was shouting, 'My son! I have to save him!'"

Victoria grabbed the banister to hold herself steady. How had Richard gotten inside her dream?

"I heard her," said Prince. "It woke me up. That's when I got up and found you two in the back yard, near the stables."

Victoria sank onto the stair. She had no idea what they were talking about.

"Do you think it's still her head injury?"

"I don't know, son. We'll have to watch her. I'll stay here until she's up."

Victoria heard a chair scraping, as Richard rose from the table. "I'll head out to the barns, then." Victoria tried but she couldn't force her body to do more than stand unsteadily on the stair.

Richard strode from the room and immediately caught sight of her. "Mammis, good morning. How are you?" He reached her side and escorted her down the stairs. Prince came from the room to take her from him and she walked, with Prince's arm around her, to the table where Richard's wife Lottie was finishing up.

They sat there in silence. Victoria looked at Prince, whose haggard face saddened her. But her head was so muddled. Daisy brought her some coffee which she drank, grateful for the hot liquid filling her. It convinced her that she was alive, even if she wasn't certain where she had spent the night. Lottie took her plate and headed to the kitchen and then the innkeeper's lodgings, where she and Richard lived.

Victoria felt Prince's worried eyes on her but she focused on the inside of her cup. Finally, she looked up and said, "It was a bad dream, I reckon."

Prince started to say something, paused, and then said simply, "I reckon."

"Poor Prince," she continued. "So much to worry about. Richard, the sales, and now me."

Prince muttered something that sounded like "better than me," but Victoria wasn't quite sure and she didn't know what that meant. She looked questioningly at him, but he just shrugged.

"If you are all right, I think I'll go keep an eye on Richard."

"I'm doing well, Prince. Please, go ahead."

Prince rose slowly from his chair, reached to touch Victoria on the arm, and went for his cloak and hat at the front door. He stayed out for most of the rest of the day.

Later that afternoon, Belcher burst into the house. "Noah's been hurt!" he cried. "He stopped a runaway sleigh in town."

All the blood drained from Victoria's face, as she looked, stricken, at Prince, who had just come in from the barn. She couldn't bear the idea of losing another son and felt the world closing in.

"Where is he?" Prince asked, gripping Belcher by the arm.

"They are bringing him here. The doctor bandaged him up. He's quite bloody and bruised. But he's conscious. Or at least he was. He kept insisting that he come home."

Just then, they heard the arrival of a sleigh and a second carriage with men yelling to each other. Belcher dashed outside to join them, leaving the front door wide open. Victoria started out with him, but Prince restrained her. She started to struggle but he turned her to face him.

"Princess, we'll need your help in here."

She opened her mouth to argue, but no sound came out.

The sleigh owner, wearing a fur hat and coat, stood next to his rig and kept wringing his hands. "Oh, dear, I do hope he is all right," he whined.

She turned to watch as the men maneuvered a makeshift stretcher from the carriage and carried it towards the house where she and Prince stood in the open doorway. Victoria stood on tiptoes to catch a glimpse of purple and blue marks on Noah's face and blood all over his hands. She gasped and turned back inside to follow. Images of her dream filled her head and her body shook with terror.

"I don't know what happened to the horse," the man continued behind her. "He just got away from me."

A short, serious man carrying a black bag followed the stretcher into the house. He shook hands with Prince and nodded graciously at Victoria. She felt herself drawn to the doctor's eyes and searched for and found his prognosis, a guarded sense of hope.

"Dr. Griswold, thank you for coming," said Prince.

Victoria let out a sigh, erased images of the runaway, and began to tap into her inner strength, as they followed the stretcher.

Belcher led the men into a sitting room to the left and they lifted Noah onto a sofa. Hearing the commotion from the stable, Richard came running to the house, quickly assessed the situation, and got the fire going, while Daisy arrived with a pitcher of water, cloths, and a glass of tea.

"Easy with him," said Dr. Griswold. He and Victoria made straight for Noah's head. "He has a nasty cut on the side here where the hoof caught him."

Victoria gathered Noah's head in her hands and his eyes fluttered open. "Mammis, I'm so glad to be home. I know you will fix me up." He winced, obviously feeling a sharp pain as the men shifted his legs, and closed his eyes.

"I've cleaned him up. He's got bruises all over and maybe a few broken ribs. But the bleeding has stopped. I don't think there is internal damage."

"We thank you very much," said Prince. Daisy handed the doctor a glass of steaming tea. He took it with a nod and sat on a chair near the fire and watched Victoria.

She tuned out all the other sounds and sights in the room and focused on Noah. She gently ran her hands over his face and head. "Only the one gash," she said quietly. Daisy stood beside her with a basin of warm water.

"I'll be right back," said Victoria and she returned in a few minutes with her pharmaceutical supplies. She added some warm water to a smaller bowl in which she had placed marigold petals and yarrow leaves.

"Make him some willow bark tea," she said quietly to Daisy, who left the room to do so. Victoria began to examine Noah, touching his arms and then chest until she elicited a response from him. Along his ribs, she could see deep purple starting to develop and she rubbed him with arnica ointment. Careful to keep him warm and covered as much as possible, Victoria picked up his hands and couldn't help but gasp. Pieces of skin were ripped from his fingers and his nails were torn. Using a cloth, she started a warm wash and Noah's eyes fluttered open.

"I had to stop him, Mammis. He was running wild."

She nodded, as his eyes grew large. "The sleigh was headed around the corner toward Main Street. It would have hurt many people." Breathless from the exertion of talking, he closed his eyes again.

"You did well, Noah."

One of the men standing nearby added, "I was on the sidewalk and heard the commotion. The sleigh, totally out of control, came tearing down the street. The owner, wide-eyed, was whipping the horse, yelling 'Whoa!' Total confusion. Amidst all this, I saw the body of a man hanging on to the side of the horse's bridle. He" and the man jerked his thumb towards Noah "was tumbling down the street, hanging on for dear life. I saw him manage to pull himself up on the horse, but not before the little beast kicked him in the head."

Focusing on her task and staunching the fear rising within her, Victoria checked the herbal infusion and decided it was ready. Removing the stained bandage, she dipped her cloth in the liquid and gently cleaned around Noah's head wound. Slowly, carefully, she teased out the grit and dead skin to clear out a nasty but clotted cut. Opening a bottle, she poured some witch hazel on her cloth and touched it up.

Victoria glanced up and saw Prince and Richard talking earnestly between themselves. They caught her looking at them and seemed embarrassed. She returned to her work with Noah.

"You're going to live," she said softly to Noah.

"I never had a doubt," he whispered back. "Not as long as I got home to you."

Dr. Griswold touched her shoulder. "I'm leaving now. I see he is in fine hands."

"Thank you, Doctor, for your help."

He nodded and joined Prince as he headed to the door. Victoria saw the doctor lean towards Prince and shake his head. She thought she saw the doctor slip a small packet to Prince and felt a pang of worry but didn't have time to address it. The men took their leave also and she focused on Noah's treatment, as she was almost finished with her task at hand.

Exhausted, Victoria sank into bed. Noah was resting comfortably downstairs and Daisy was staying with him for the night. Slowly getting under the covers next to his wife, Prince reached to stroke her face.

"Princess, we owe you an apology, Richard and I."

Victoria could barely keep her eyes open.

"We should have trusted you last night when you dreamed about this."

"Thank you," she murmured. She felt so drained that she sank almost immediately into a deep sleep.

When she awoke the next morning, Victoria sensed a deep hollow in her gut, the kind of feeling that told her something was wrong, even if she couldn't remember what it was. She sat up and it all came back. Noah had been hurt. She had seen him chasing after the sleigh. No, that wasn't right. She hadn't been there; she had only envisioned it. But she was certain he had been hurt and she had bandaged him and he was resting in the sitting room. Or was the whole thing a dream?

Victoria shook her head, trying to separate what had been real from the dream. Terrified, she didn't want to admit even to herself that she couldn't tell. She got up slowly and knew that she could at least confirm Noah's status by going downstairs.

She stood in the doorway of the sitting room, taking in the scene. Yes, Noah was resting on the sofa and Daisy was sleeping, sitting up in a nearby chair. Quietly, she sat down next to Noah and touched his shoulder.

His eyes fluttered open. "Morning, Mammis."

She nodded. "How do you feel?"

Noah gingerly raised an arm and then the other and managed to sit up. He took a deep breath. "Pretty good. You are quite a healer."

She shook her head. "No, I have good medicines. Arnica does wonders."

Noah smiled and then grimaced when he looked at his fingers that he had tried to wiggle. "They still hurt."

"I reckon they will for a while. Do you think you could get up?"

Together they stood, which woke Daisy. Noah sat back down. "That was enough for now."

"All right. We'll go get some food ready and bring you a bite."

"No rush," said Noah. "I'm not very hungry."

At breakfast, Prince joined Victoria and Daisy. "Dr. Griswold was paid well by the sleigh owner."

"Hmm, that's good," said Daisy between sips of her coffee.

"I wonder if he'll give Noah anything."

Victoria looked at Prince. "Why should he?"

"You recall that time in New Haven when I had to pay seventy-five dollars to that man who fell off his wagon and broke his arm because his horses shied at our clothes?"

"Right," said Victoria, somewhat disgustedly. "We had them drying on the bushes in broad daylight and the man was unable to control his horses."

"Yes, so, maybe the sleigh owner will pay Noah something."

"But Noah didn't break anything, I don't think."

"But he was quite hurt, in addition to the fact that he saved the man's horse from causing serious harm to others."

"The sleigh owner didn't seem to be the kind of person who cared much about that."

"Well, perhaps you can write him a note, making a suggestion?"

Victoria nodded. "All right, Prince, I will do that."

After setting up a breakfast tray for Noah, Daisy returned to her vigil in the sitting room.

"Noah, you need to take it easy today," reprimanded Victoria, poking her head into the room on her way by. "No running yet."

"Yes, Mammis."

Later in the day, Victoria returned to the sitting room. Noah was resting with his eyes closed.

"Daisy, take a break. I'll sit here for now."

"Are you certain, Mammis? I am happy to be here."

"I'm sure, daughter, that you have other things to do. Go."

Daisy left the room and Victoria settled into a seat near Noah. He was sleeping again, after spending the morning sitting up and talking with Daisy.

Victoria sat there quietly, looking at his bandaged face. The image of him hanging onto the horse and getting bounced along the street kept rising in her mind. Each time, she felt bile rise into her throat and she would chase it, and the vision, away. It kept returning with a vengeance and she finally gave in to it. She felt her fear of almost losing Noah course through her body as if it were her blood itself. She fought to retain mental clarity and remind herself that he was safe, but a gray mist rose within her and she was smothering. Air, she needed to breathe, and part of her brain helped ground her momentarily and she inhaled.

Now that she was certain that Noah would survive, Victoria allowed the reality of the situation to register. She started shaking, thinking about Noah's close call. Tears filled her eyes and her heart kept expanding, almost to a breaking point. She loved Noah with all her might and she couldn't stand the idea that she had almost lost him.

She stroked his hair and, in his sleep, his lips upturned into a small smile.

"Oh, Noah, no, I couldn't have stood it. No, no, no, not another son. I would have died," she sobbed into his ear. She tried to control herself but her body shook and her mind swirled, taking her back to that hot, humid day almost a decade earlier.

FOURTEEN

Sinking in the shade of the wolf tree along the field's edge, Victoria had sighed. Her daughter Bessie smiled and continued nursing her baby, less than a year old.

"I am glad I'm the grandmother now and you're having the children," said Victoria with a groan, as she wiped the sweat from her face.

Bessie laughed. "It wasn't long ago that you were nursing Morris," she teased.

It was true. Morris, that surprise child, was born almost five years earlier while they were in Canada when she was forty-three. Good lord, how had she managed that? And how had she grown so old, she wondered.

She glanced around, catching sight of her husband as he and the menfolk lounged by their *vardos*, the wagons arranged in a circle. Her men, she thought, pursing her lips and shaking her head, always acting as though they were the wheelers and dealers when everyone knew she was the brains behind it all. They hadn't listened to her and now here they were, camped in eastern Connecticut at the end of the summer when they should have been either north or south but buying horses somewhere.

Bessie, following her glance, said, "Maybe my husband can talk some sense into them."

Victoria nodded, saying, "I hope so. He's got the Stanley good sense that apparently the Williams men have lost. Your husband's a good man."

But she really didn't want to think about all that and was glad to be distracted by the grandbaby's noisy slurping. She glanced over at the field with rows of corn that weren't quite ripe, so they hadn't added any to the kettle that day. If they stayed here much longer, the children could pick some. Down the lane, she saw no movement from the farmhouse. The family had gone to church that morning and returned for a large meal. They would not be harvesting today, it being the day of rest for the farmer's family.

At least this trip meant they were able to visit with Bessie and her family. They had traveled up from Providence, where the Stanleys had a large horse stable business, and were enjoying the chance to relax and share news.

"Emma is well?" asked Bessie. Her sister, recently married, was expecting in the winter.

Victoria sighed. "Yes, she's fine. Another grandchild, I can't believe it."

"Oh, Mammis, you will always be young," said Bessie, chuckling.

Victoria looked at her, raised her eyebrow, and held out her palm. "You know there is an end somewhere. Just look at my line."

Bessie had heard this so many times that she just laughed. The women relaxed in silence, allowing the sound of the children playing in camp to echo across the fields. Victoria saw her two youngest chasing each other up and down rows of corn, followed by one of her grandchildren. What a brood, she smiled proudly. Many to continue the business and keep it growing. She started to think about her plans to expand, which led her right back to the annoying difficulties they were currently facing, and she stopped.

Her two, Daisy and Morris, came screaming down the corn towards their tranquil corner. Fortunately for the women, they turned and raced back up the next row. Trailing them, somewhat uncertain if it were appropriate for her age, was her granddaughter, Martha's oldest.

"Granddaughter," called Victoria, "come here a minute."

"Yes, Púridaia?"

"The kettle's empty. Wash it out, so we can make supper. Ask your brother if you need help."

"Yes, Púridaia," she said and walked, with her shoulders pulled back and her head tall, to the fire. She was just slightly older than Daisy but had already crossed the threshold into young adulthood. Victoria wondered if caring for all of Martha's younger children made her granddaughter so mature. Victoria watched as she and her brother Willie lugged the large kettle to the stream, finding an area just below the bathing section to wash the pot. As the oldest daughter of the oldest daughter, she would be the responsible one.

Daisy and Morris came, more slowly, down the cornrow and collapsed on the comforter.

"Mammis," said Morris, "I don't feel good."

"Me, neither," said Daisy.

Cuffing Morris on the head, Victoria teased, "All that running up and down on a hot day, no wonder." She turned to Daisy and sighed. She wasn't quite sure what to do with this daughter who refused to give up her place as the baby of the family. "Rest here a while and you'll feel fine," she said, wiping the girl's sweaty face.

Victoria hoisted herself up from the comforter and started to the campfire where Martha's children had returned with the kettle. As she walked, Victoria was struck with an ache in her stomach so strong that she had to stop to catch her breath. Doubled over, she felt the pain expand into her intestines and bile rose in her throat. The sensation passed as quickly as it came, and she straightened herself and continued to the fire. Watching her, her granddaughter looked worried, but Victoria shrugged it off. They started the kettle, adding wild onions and potatoes they had in their supplies. Willie came over and tugged on Victoria's skirt.

"Púridaia, I don't feel good."

She glanced down at him and saw that certain greenish tinge to his skin that preceded some unpleasant business. "Over here, Willie," she said, leading him to the edge of the camp. Just in time, she noted, as Willie ejected whatever had been in his stomach. Victoria cradled his head, as he squatted near his puddle. His skin was warm but not extremely hot. Suddenly Victoria felt a strong cramp and settled down next to Willie.

"Púridaia, I need the privy," he groaned.

Victoria glanced at his sister, who helped Willie to the area they had set aside for those activities. Again sensing a spasm, Victoria returned to the cook fire and sat for a minute. Something about her contractions was unusual and she wanted to think on it, let her inner wisdom have a chance to come to the forefront. She sat, closed her eyes, and waited. It didn't take long before it hit her; these cramps were sympathetic, similar to Willie's, not ones due to her own indigestion. But there was something else and she waited.

"Oh, my God," she shouted, jumping up and running back to the comforter where she had left Morris and Daisy. Her children's moans reached her just as she arrived and her scream woke up Bessie and the baby. Both of her children were covered with sweat, their eyes closed, and groaning. Morris had his hands clenched over his belly and was rocking side to side.

Victoria grabbed her son, gestured to Bessie to do the same with Daisy, and carried Morris quickly to the edge of the field. She stuck her fingers down his throat and he heaved in the bushes. He was doubled over and looked desperately at his mother. She glanced at Bessie, who was helping Daisy; she didn't look as bad as Morris and Victoria decided Bessie could take care of her. She returned her focus on Morris, wiping his mouth and caressing his face. She dug a small pit and helped him pull down his pants. The fetid smell only added to her panic, confirming the seriousness of the situation. She cleaned him as well as she could and cradled him in her arms and carried him back to the comforter where he curled into a fetal position. As he rocked back and forth, holding his stomach, Victoria held his hand, wiped his face, put her arms about his shoulders, and racked her brain for an explanation. Bessie, meanwhile, had Daisy on the blanket next to Morris. She seemed more stable, although when Victoria glanced quickly at her, she didn't look well. Victoria's frantic fear was preventing her visions from guiding her. She tried to calm herself but she watched her son's eyes sink deeper into his head and all she could do was scream.

The menfolk, occupied with Willie's situation, were startled to realize that problems were wider spread. Prince ran to the wolf tree, when he spotted Victoria huddled over his two youngest and heard her keening.

"What is it?" he shouted. "What's happening? Willie and now them?" He collapsed alongside Victoria, who raised her contorted face to him.

"We've lost him," she wailed. "We've lost Morris."

Prince frantically turned over his son and then looked at his wife. "But he's still breathing."

She shook her head. "He's gone. Maybe not yet, but he won't be coming back." She started screaming, startling Daisy, who opened her eyes. "My baby, he's gone," Victoria sobbed. She gathered the boy in her arms and rocked him back and forth, all the while wailing and lamenting and calling his name. Prince put his arm around her.

"Princess, are you sure?"

Victoria turned to him, but she couldn't see him. Her mouth was moving, saying strange words and incantations, and her eyes were focused on a vision of Morris, forever not quite five years old, riding a crimson wave of clouds. "Morris," she howled, "Morris, come back to us."

The camp was in an uproar. Three of their children were ailing from some unknown illness and Victoria, their source of knowledge and direction, was unable to help. Horses, upset by the commotion, started neighing and pulling on their ropes where they were grazing nearby. Victoria could hear shouting, as people bundled Willie and Daisy and placed them near the fire. Someone, she thought maybe Martha, was feeding them a broth that would help them heal if they could keep it down or pass whatever it was if they couldn't. Victoria remained cradling her son's body, which grew lighter and lighter. She again saw him riding, waving at her, his crooked smile teasing that she couldn't reach him. "Mammis," he yelled, "you can't catch me now." She watched, as his face grew luminous and turned into mist. Just at that moment, his body gave a last quiver and settled into her arms.

"Ay," she wailed, "Morris, come back." She keened and moaned and was joined by Bessie, hugging her baby who had begun to cry. Victoria scratched the ground and tore up clumps of grass. She heard a slam of the farmhouse door, as the farmer came running.

Prince met him partway up the lane. "Our children are sick," he yelled. "We must do something." A wave of fear passed over the farmer's face, as he imagined a contagious illness reaching his children, currently safe at home. He stopped briefly, hesitant to continue. "A doctor," Prince yelled, "Can you help us find a doctor?"

The farmer wavered no longer. "Dr. Stevens is down the road a piece," he offered, pointing to the south. Prince had already saddled his horse. Bessie's husband took the reins from his hand and said, "I'll go. They need you here." He got directions from the farmer and the horse galloped off in a cloud of dust.

Prince watched for a brief moment and turned to the farmer. "Stomach problems, it is." The farmer nodded before asking, "Anything else you need?"

His face lined with grief, Prince started to shake his head, but he heard Victoria calling him. "Wait, let me check with my wife," as he went to where she was sitting. "Princess, what is it?"

"Get some honey or sugar, if he can spare it."

Prince raised an eyebrow but relayed the message when he returned to the farmer.

"Yes, I have some fresh honey." He turned to hasten to the farm kitchen.

Victoria, meanwhile, had instructed Bessie to start the kettle boiling with fresh water. The two other stricken children, moaning but alert, were lying near the fire. When the farmer returned, Bessie followed her mother's instructions and made a concentrated honey drink and was helping Daisy swallow the beverage, when the doctor arrived.

Victoria took a quick look at Dr. Stevens and relaxed. He was a country man and appeared to approach them in the same manner as he would handle any patients. He took a look at Willie's eyes and throat and palpated his stomach.

"Ouch," Willie grunted, but the doctor continued his probe. He asked about the drink that was given and nodded approvingly upon hearing its contents. He took Daisy's temperature and pulse. He then moved to the wolf tree where Victoria was sitting with Morris.

"Too late," she whispered to him. She thought the other children might heal faster if they didn't know that they had lost Morris. The doctor, looking sadly at her, took a soft look at the young boy. "The others will be fine," he said, looking deeply into her dark eyes. She in her heart knew this was true and nodded. He rose to return to the rest of the family, leaving Victoria with her bundle and tears.

It was dawn when they broke camp and began the trip back to East Hartford. Victoria sat with her son's body and the other women in their *vardo*. Their sobs joined with the creaks from the wagon and the sound of the wooden wheels turning on the dirt roads. Prince rode his gray mare alongside the women and Victoria noted, between her sobs, that the horses were silent. Prince had removed the bells and other ornaments and their group was somber as it traveled the forty miles back home. Runners had been sent out to tell the other family members who would all converge at the old Farmer's Hotel.

Victoria felt herself drawn inward. She saw Morris again, riding on his cloud, which had toned down to pink instead of crimson. He was laughing and holding something in his hand, which she couldn't see. He finally raised his fist and opened it, gleefully showing her that he had found mushrooms.

"No, not those," she blurted, startling the women in the caravan. "No, Morris, not those." She tried to grab them from his hand, but he dissolved and she was left grasping at nothing.

After collapsing on the *vardo* floor, Victoria sobbed and pulled her hair. Her daughter gently kept her arm around her shoulder and they traveled on. At some point, Victoria raised her head, her eyes rimmed in red and her face drawn and pulled herself up to sit next to Bessie. She stared wordlessly out at the passing countryside and noticed, as they approached a cluster of buildings, that people lined the road. When they got closer, she saw that the men had taken off their hats and the women stood, quietly, some weeping. Victoria, her brow creased in confusion, looked at Bessie.

"It's been like this all day," said Bessie. "They must know. People have come out to pay their respects."

Victoria stared, shaking her head. These strangers, people who had probably only heard stories of her family, were trying to comfort her. Some of the small children held American flags and all were silent. One woman threw a bouquet of flowers into Victoria's *vardo* and she started wailing again. To think that poor Morris would never again see flowers or the sunshine was more than she could bear.

Eventually, the caravans reached the old Farmer's Hotel. Prince helped Victoria down and guided her up to her room, where he spread out their comforter and helped her lie down. She was afraid to sleep, terrified of visions that might come, but Prince's gentle stroking finally out-competed her fear. Even though her sleep was restless, her dreams stayed away.

When she awoke, the room was empty and, at first, she didn't remember why they were back at the Hotel. Quickly, the previous days came back to her and she began keening again. She heard footsteps and the door cracked open.

"Hallo, Mammis." It was Emma, quite large in the belly, with her luminous dark eyes filled with sadness.

"Oh, daughter," she gasped, pulling Emma to her. Emma helped her up from bed and provided an arm for support. "So sad, so sad," Victoria repeated.

"The minister is coming shortly," said Emma. "He wants to make arrangements."

Victoria felt dizzy and saw Morris, still on his cloud that had grown puffy and white, out of the corner of her eye. His face was peaceful and smiling. She sighed and got dressed, aided by Emma, and they went downstairs together.

Prince was in the kitchen and stood quickly when he saw her. "Princess, I'm here."

The familiar refrain caught in his throat and Victoria grasped his shirt, almost ripping it as she used it to cover her face. Her clenched hands turned white and he stroked her cheek. "Princess, we need to make some plans," he said quietly.

Victoria thought that the lamb, with its wooly fleece, resembled the cloud that Morris rode. "Yes, that will be right," she told the minister, "a lamb on the headstone."

"The innocence of the dear child," said the man.

She nodded, not needing to correct him.

Later that day, she pulled a recovered Daisy aside and asked her about the mushrooms. Her lips quivering, eyes filling with tears, Daisy nodded. "He added them to the kettle, Mammis. There wasn't much left in there, just enough for us children. He was so excited when he found them." She paused. "Is that what made us sick?"

Victoria nodded. Thinking that she heard Morris calling her, she tilted her head slightly to the side. Realizing it would never be again, Victoria turned away from Daisy and left the room before she lost her composure. She stepped into the sitting room and sank on a chair. Oh, she cried silently, she should have never showed Morris how to collect mushrooms. He would still be here with them.

She felt as though she herself had killed her son by giving him only partial knowledge. She wrapped her arms around herself, overwhelmed and filled with grief from her role in his death. Victoria sobbed from a spot deep within her, as she crumpled in the chair. "No, no, not my son," she wailed to no one in particular.

FIFTEEN

Victoria felt hands on her shoulders. "I am here, Mammis. I'm healing."

She felt herself twisting through time and opened her eyes. Her son, her other son, Noah, was standing over her.

"No, no, not my son," she whispered, her face wet with tears.

"No, I will not leave you," he said gently. He handed her a handkerchief and she wiped her face.

The previous days' events flooded through Victoria. "How are you?" she asked, taking note of his strength standing.

"Mammis, I am well. Look, even my hands are healing," he said, wiggling his fingers.

Struggling to leave her nightmare, she took his hands and examined them. "You are right. And your face?" She stood to scrutinize his cut. There was no redness along the edges and, when she touched it, Noah did not flinch. "I—I was thinking about little Morris."

Noah, nodding, put his arm around her. "Dear little Morris. But I am here, thanks to your healing." He kissed the top of her head. "I am feeling much better. In fact, I am ready to get back to work tomorrow."

"We shall see," she said. "What time is it?" she asked, glancing outside.

"Almost six o'clock."

"Have you eaten?"

Noah shook his head.

"Why don't you have some supper, then? I'm certain that Daisy has something ready."

"Yes, Mammis, and you'll see in the morning that I am ready to get out again."

As they walked together to the kitchen, Victoria called out, "Daisy, is there supper for Noah?"

"Hallo, Mammis, you are awake. And, Noah, how are you feeling?"

"Martha! I didn't know you were here," said Victoria. She looked and saw her daughter's three older children seated at the table and baby Richard, the one who was born here in the old Hotel, on a blanket in the corner. "The whole family, what a surprise!"

Martha hugged Victoria and gave Noah a squeeze. Daisy came from the kitchen loaded with plates that Martha quickly took and placed on the table. She followed Daisy back into the kitchen and, in a few minutes, they both returned with enough supper for everyone.

"We just got in from Lowell," Martha said between bites. "Aren't you eating, Mammis?"

"Actually, I am quite tired from this afternoon. I truly don't feel like eating. In fact, I'm heading upstairs. We can talk more in the morning."

She felt Martha's eyes assessing her. "All right, Mammis. Sleep well."

Victoria made her way slowly upstairs. She caught herself as she stumbled slightly on one of the stairs. Moving back and forth in her memories was exhausting and she was ready for bed. She turned into her room and saw that Prince was already sleeping. Quietly, she slid under the comforter and was asleep almost instantly.

When Victoria awoke, it was already light out but Prince was still by her side. She heard a gentle knock on the door and realized it was the same sound that awakened her a few minutes before.

Daisy poked her head around the corner of the door and Prince gestured towards the chamber pot. Daisy nodded and quietly came into the room and removed it.

"Prince, you are still in bed," said Victoria.

"Yes, I am taking it easy."

"Ah," she said and settled back down next to him. He took her hand and they lay together quietly. Victoria was remembering how they would often rest together that way when she was pregnant.

"Oh, Martha and her family came in last night."

"Nice," said Prince.

"The baby is quite charming. Remember Martha when she was a baby? All head, that girl."

Prince laughed. "Yes, I do. Our first child and we didn't know what to expect. Good thing we were traveling with your parents at the time. Out there in the hills of Pittsburgh in the heat of July."

Victoria added, "Who would have known what a help she would be all those years."

"The oldest always carries a burden, especially if it's a girl. No glory, just work."

"It was so sad when she lost her first husband. I wanted so much to comfort her, but how can you help someone in a situation like that?"

Prince looked over at her, but she said no more. "I like this one. He's a steady man."

Victoria nodded. "Martha is well situated now. But maybe we should get up to see them?" She looked questioningly at Prince.

"Why don't you head downstairs? I'm not sure if I'm able right now."

Victoria had never known Prince to stay in bed, but she didn't dwell on it. She instead thought about baby Richard. "I would like to see what the baby is doing. You know how I love the young ones."

"Yes, go on. I may be along."

So Victoria rose, put on her clothes and her gold hoop earrings, and left the room. Holding on to the banister, she walked carefully down the stairs.

She saw Noah, putting on his outer clothes, looking up at her.

"Good morning, Mammis. I was just coming to see you."

Victoria didn't think that was true, but she was glad to check Noah's condition before he headed out. She thought his color looked good.

"I'm ready to go to the barn."

"Yes, I see. Well, I know I can't stop you. Please, Noah, don't ride any horses or lift anything heavy."

"I won't, Mammis," and he kissed the side of her face as she reached the bottom step. He walked to the back door and started putting on his boots.

Hearing a ruckus in the dining room, she went towards the noise. Martha's three oldest, standing and reaching for food on the table, stopped when they saw her. "Good morning, Púridaia," they all chimed. Martha was crouched in the corner of the room attending to the baby.

"Good morning, children. You all look very well today." She paused only a second to realize that the older three were already teenagers. "Would you like to join your Uncle Noah in the barn?"

The two boys jumped from their chairs, while the girl rose more gracefully. "Thank you," she said. Then they all scrambled down the hall to join him.

"You look rested, Mammis," said Martha, looking relieved to have most of her brood out of her hair.

"Thank you, dear, I feel better than last night, it is true."

A few minutes later, Martha said, "I'm going upstairs to bring Dadrus something to eat."

"Good idea," said Victoria, distracted by the newspaper headlines about the sale of trotting stock. If Richard was keeping a pair of trotters, she was interested in their prices. They ranged from five hundred dollars to about two thousand, she saw. Horse racing might be a good source of potential customers. She certainly didn't want to see her family doing the racing. And as far as betting went, Victoria was certain that could come to no good. She glanced through the rest of the paper but nothing caught her interest.

That afternoon, Victoria was resting before the fire when she heard a commotion out front. It sounded like caravans arriving and many feet stomping up the porch stairs. When she heard the door open and several loud voices, she thought she should investigate. But she barely had a chance to rise from her seat when Emma burst into the room.

"Mammis, hallo," she said, giving her mother a strong hug. Her four children came right behind her, the two older boys carrying the two younger.

The youngest was squirming in her brother's arms and he finally set her down. She toddled over to Victoria and looked up at her. "We are here to see the old man."

"Charlotte!" reprimanded Emma.

But Victoria laughed. "Your grandfather will be glad to see you. Is your husband here, too?"

"Yes, he's out at the stable."

"How was the trip from New Haven?"

"Not bad. They say snow and cold will be coming, but our travels went well."

"I'm pleased to see you. Martha is here, too, did you know?"

Emma glanced at her somewhat oddly but Victoria moved on to hug all the grandchildren and welcome each one.

"Where is Dadrus?"

"Upstairs. Let me check in the kitchen to see what kind of refreshment we can gather."

"Thank you. Children, let's go upstairs and say 'hallo' before we have something to eat." And Emma marched the children upstairs, while Victoria went into the kitchen.

When they came back downstairs shortly, Victoria had set out tipsy cake, cookies, and tea on the table. The children came in and took some food and drink and sat on chairs. She wondered where Emma was and looked out into the hall. She saw her with Martha; they were holding each other tightly and Martha was patting Emma's back.

"Girls, are you joining us?"

Her daughters jerked apart, their eyes wide. "Um, sure, Mammis, shortly," said Martha. Victoria thought she saw Emma wiping her eyes, but at that moment one of the grandchildren started yelling and she returned to the dining room. By the time Emma and Martha joined her, they both looked composed.

In the evening, when Victoria went upstairs, Prince was propped up in bed. Several pillows backed him and Victoria thought he was pale.

"Prince, can I get you anything?"

"No, Princess, just come sit with me."

"Certainly, let me get undressed and I'll join you. Do you need more pillows?"

"No, this is enough. I couldn't seem to breathe lying flat."

"Oh, dear. Is this better?"

"Somewhat."

Victoria got under the covers with Prince and settled down. "I am so glad to see Emma," she said. "I think she looks well, don't you?"

"Yes, dear, I do," he said with weariness in his voice.

"Are you tired?"

"Not really."

"Isn't it nice that the girls are here? I love having the house filled."

Prince looked at her, started to say something, but didn't.

"That decision about the Squires boy has worked out well."

Prince nodded. "Yes, you were right about him."

Victoria felt her eyes getting heavy. "All those grandchildren wore me out," she laughed. She leaned back into her pillow. Yes, they had made the right choice about the Squires boy after all. Victoria closed her eyes. They certainly hadn't been sure about that at the time, she remembered. She hadn't been to the Yalesville camp recently, but she could easily envision it along the aqueduct, back ten years ago before all the sadness with Morris and Wash.

That night of the Squires boy, the campfire light had glimmered through the trees lining the river and sparks spiraled to the sky when someone added a log. Victoria loved this spot, where she and Prince had been camping on and off for years. In fact, she had given birth here to their daughter Daisy, now seven. What an easy one that had been, especially compared with Richard or Martha! Victoria shook her head in amazement of all that had passed during the thirty years that she and Prince had been married. To think that she was now forty-seven.

Her brother Richard's wife sat down to join her. Smiling, Margaret said, "It's good to be back. I love the traveling but I love seeing everyone again even more."

"Me, too." Victoria paused, looking around at the busy camp. With five kettles going and dozens of wagons and tents, the area was filled. "We certainly outgrew New Haven."

Margaret nodded.

"How was your *dukkering* this summer?"

Margaret laughed. "I had some good luck. I took one woman pretty badly. I sure hope they don't track me down." She patted her sides. "My skirts are heavy these days."

Victoria smiled, as her other sister-in-law Jennie joined them. The three sat and watched the children chase each other around the tents, while the men gathered near one of the fires.

"Mammis, Mammis, tell her to stop it!" Little Morris came rushing to her and she gathered him in her arms. Stroking his hair, Victoria murmured, "Poor Morris, what's wrong, little one?"

"Daisy's chasing me. She wants me to be the baby in her game. I don't want to." Morris' lower lip stuck out and Victoria couldn't help but laugh. Morris sat, cuddling in her lap for a few minutes, and then he squirmed out and, his chunky little legs flailing, ran back to where the other children were playing.

Victoria waved goodbye to him and Jennie stood up. "I need to check on the kettles."

Margaret rose, too. "I'll come along."

Victoria sat alone, enjoying the sounds of laughter and talking. Her brother Richard began fiddling and Victoria's feet started tapping to the music. She watched the young people dancing, their arms and skirts swinging in rhythm. She smiled, remembering the days when she would have been up there with them. Shortly, she saw her brother Samuel walking in her direction. He sat down with her and put his arm around her shoulder while she nestled into him.

"I wish our parents were here to see this," sighed Victoria.

Samuel nodded. "We all miss them. But we certainly are the harvest of the grain they put in the ground."

Victoria agreed. "Yes, I see that for me and Prince, too. Our brood is full and they are having children now, too."

"Speaking of which, I talked to my son Richard about your idea."

"And what does he think?"

"He was thrilled. He thinks Emma would make a lovely wife."

"She is lovely. But she's a handful, that girl. Strong-willed."

"Can't imagine where she gets that from," said her brother, poking her in the ribs.

"All right, all right." Victoria looked near the fire and saw young Richard, quietly standing by the menfolk. She looked around but couldn't spot Emma. That whirlwind of a girl was always up to something. "We will talk to Emma, then. Perhaps the wedding can be this fall."

"Sounds perfect. Well, I will go join the others."

Samuel stood and walked slowly back to the group of men. Victoria remembered how he had protected her so many years ago on that first passage to America. All this reminiscing, she must be getting old. After listening and watching some more, Victoria decided that indeed she was getting old and she definitely was tired. Slowly she got up and walked to their *vardo.* It was a beauty, all glittering and reflecting the nearby firelight. The glass and gilt cost a fortune but she felt happy every time she saw it. She didn't want to be too bold but, as she glanced around, she knew it was the loveliest one in the bunch.

Victoria climbed up the stairs and bent slightly through the door. She fingered the linen on the table as she walked to the sleeping platform. She pulled off the lace coverlet and got into bed. She fell asleep, smiling to the sound of Richard's fiddle.

It seemed like only minutes later that Prince burst into the wagon to wake her. "Princess, Princess, where is she?"

"Who? What's wrong?" she asked, seeing his red, angry face above her.

"Emma—she's gone."

"What do you mean? I saw her earlier this evening."

"We have looked all over and can't find her."

"But where would she go?"

"Someone said they saw her talking with that Squires boy."

Victoria looked puzzled.

"The one I had hired for awhile to work at our stable. He's not there any longer; he's working at Belle Dock now. But he was here this evening, hanging around."

Victoria vaguely remembered the man. "But he's older."

"Yes, and quite handsome. If she went off with him, I'll kill her."

Victoria sat up, realizing that this was serious. "Maybe she's just playing with us, hiding with one of the cousins. It's dark now. Can we wait until the morning to see if she truly is gone?"

"No. If she's gone off with him, I'm hoping we can catch them tonight. Before there's any damage done."

"Where would you look? How could you possibly find them?"

"I've already sent off some runners."

"Well, then. Let's wait to see what they tell us in the morning." Victoria lay back down. "Come to bed, Prince."

He ran his hands through his hair. "I can't possibly sleep. How could Emma do that?"

"We don't know if she did. But maybe we should hold her wedding with Richard this week, when we do find her. I talked to Samuel and they are happy about the match."

"Yes, a good idea. Since we are all here, they will wed as soon as we find her."

"Can you try to rest now?"

Prince shook his head. "I'm going to sit by the fire, in case one of the runners returns." He patted her on the arm. "I'll let you sleep."

Without Prince by her side, Victoria didn't think that was likely, but she finally dozed off.

The next morning, Victoria awoke to recall the wild scene with Prince the previous night. She hoped it had been a dream, but when she dressed and left the wagon, she saw him alone sitting dejectedly by the fire. She walked to join him.

"No news?"

He shook his head. "I will not have it, her marrying a *gadje*."

Victoria sat down next to him and stroked his arm. "Does this Squires boy come from a good family?"

Prince glared at her. "What difference does it make? He's *gadje*." Prince spat into the fire.

"Prince, remember Sonny," she said quietly.

"But it cost my brother his place in the family. I will not have that shame in ours."

"Is he part of the Squires family with the stables in New Haven?"

"Yes," grunted Prince. "But I don't see why that matters."

Victoria was quiet for a few minutes, thinking of business opportunities. She would have liked to link her family with her brother Samuel's, but the Squires' operation was a big one. In fact, they were competition. Maybe binding the two wouldn't be so bad. And she had quite liked Sonny and saw that William's marriage was utterly happy.

Victoria spotted Samuel walking towards them. "Have you told anyone?"

Prince shook his head.

"We must tell Samuel. Maybe he has some ideas. After all, she's his future daughter-in-law."

Samuel slowed as he saw their faces but Victoria gestured him to join them. "We have a problem."

Samuel raised an eyebrow.

"Emma's missing."

"Oh," he said, heavily sitting down next to them.

"We think she may have run off with the Squires boy."

"The one from the stables?"

Prince grunted. Suddenly he raised his head. "I'm going to offer a reward for her return. Let me get in touch with the papers. That should bring her home."

Victoria wanted to restrain him but knew it was of no use. Prince would do what he needed to, and she watched as he saddled his horse and rode off towards town.

Samuel patted her on the arm. She looked at him and spotted his son Richard, standing past them. "Poor Richard," she said quietly.

"Yes, poor Richard. And poor Prince," added Samuel.

Later that week, the couple, having been married by a justice of the peace, was located in Hartford. The runner brought the news back to Prince and Victoria.

"You are certain?"

The man nodded. Prince sighed and paid the man, who thanked him and left.

They sat there quietly for several minutes.

"Prince, Emma is an impulsive girl, but she is our daughter."

He grunted.

"I talked to some of our men. They say that the Squires boy was a hard worker. And he could handle the horses."

Prince grunted again, his eyes fixed on the ground.

"To connect with his family could be a good thing for business."

Prince whipped around to face her. "Is that all you think about? How it can help us financially?"

Victoria was taken aback. "No, not at all. Actually, my first thought was that Emma must have gone for a very good reason. She would know the implications and how we would react. She must have fallen in love. And I know how that feels, to fall in love with a handsome older man. Especially one with a charming moustache."

She smiled at Prince, but he didn't return the favor, although she felt his muscles relax slightly. She continued. "If Emma is willing to risk losing her family for him, her feelings must be very strong."

Prince nodded.

"Just imagine if my parents had said you were wrong for me. We would have fought them to the end."

Prince nodded again and put his arm around her.

"Prince, I think we should invite them back to the family."

He looked at her.

She saw the deep lines on his face and the sadness in his eyes. "You don't want to lose her either, do you?"

Tears welled in the corner of Prince's eyes. Victoria was surprised; she couldn't recall seeing Prince cry before. "Prince, dear, we must invite them back. Hire the Squires boy at the stable, make a big welcome, and keep them in our fold."

When Prince didn't reply, she added, "Think about it, sleep on it. You'll see it is the best thing to do."

Two weeks after Emma had left, she and Bill Squires returned to the Yalesville camp. All their *folki* was waiting, with tin cans, flowers, and large kettles of food. The uproar of shouting and yelling when they arrived traveled up the river valley and filled the air with joy. Showered by petals and ears splitting from the noise of sticks on cans, the couple ducked through arches made by the welcoming crowd. They stopped at the end of the line, where they faced Prince and Victoria, who were waiting calmly to greet them.

"Our daughter, welcome home." Prince smiled broadly as he took her hand.

"Our son, our caravan is our family, and the world is our family," said Victoria, who took Bill Squire's hand. The four made a circle and Victoria continued, "We welcome you to our ways. Do you agree to keep them, along with our daughter?"

The silence was overwhelming, until Bill shouted, "I do!" People cheered and Richard started fiddling. The new couple danced wildly down through the arch again and then everyone joined in a fast and furious jig. The festivities lasted until late in the evening.

Victoria noticed, amidst the ruckus, that poor young Richard was not among those gathered.

"Poor Richard," she muttered.

"What?" asked Prince.

Victoria, opening her eyes, realized that she must have nodded off. "Oh, I was thinking about when Emma ran off with Bill and left poor Richard behind."

"But he's going to marry Daisy soon, right?"

"Yes," said Victoria, somewhat hesitantly. "Yes, that's right. Next time I see his mother, I will talk to her. We will set it all straight."

Prince moved slightly, trying to get comfortable.

"Can I fix your pillows?"

"Just raise them up a bit, so I am more upright."

"There."

"Thank you, Princess. I can breathe better now."

"Shall we go to sleep?"

"Yes, dear. Goodnight."

SIXTEEN

Victoria tiptoed from the bedroom after she dressed the next morning. Prince's sleeping face was haggard and Victoria decided she would add some barberry to his tea that morning. She went downstairs to fix it and then sat down at the table.

Daisy brought in the newspaper. "Here, Mammis."

"Thank you, dear. I made some tea for your father," she said, gesturing to the cup. "Please bring it to him when he awakes."

"Yes, Mammis."

Victoria read an article indicating that horse sales were down. She made a mental note to share that later with Prince. She read more articles, including one about a small pox outbreak in Arkansas. Recalling her nephew's death in Canada, she shuddered. There were so many things for a mother to worry about, things that can take away her children. Noah's accident was too recent for her comfort.

Hearing the train whistle as it reached the East Hartford crossing, Victoria started. Already ten o'clock and she had done nothing thus far. She started bustling in the kitchen, thinking about what to cook for all the visiting family. She heard a carriage rattle into their driveway and the pawing of impatient horses. She wiped her hands on her skirt and started for the front door, when it opened.

"Jennie, Margaret! My, how did you get here so early in the morning?"

The two women gathered Victoria in their arms and then stepped back.

"We took the train."

"The rest of the family is coming in the *vardos*. They should be here by tomorrow."

Victoria was surprised that they would be traveling when it was still winter, but she was so pleased to see her brothers' wives.

"Can I offer you tea? Breakfast?" She called her daughter's name loudly, "Daisy?"

Daisy descended gracefully down the stairs where she had been giving Prince his tea. "Yes, Mammis? Oh, hallo, Aunt Jennie and Aunt Margaret."

They hugged her and Victoria continued, "Can you get breakfast for them?"

Daisy nodded and went to the kitchen while they all sat at the table.

"I'm so glad you got here safely. I was reading in the paper," Victoria pointed to the document on the table, "that a train derailed in New Jersey." She sighed. "There is so much danger out there, potentially hurting our loved ones." Then she brightened. "But we are all here and safe." And she smiled at her sisters-in-law. She thought she noticed pain in their eyes and attributed it to her reference to lurking hazards. She realized that they probably didn't know about her son's recent episode. "Did you hear about Noah?"

"Noah? No, what?"

Victoria proceeded to tell them about his brush with the sleigh and speedy recovery.

"Well, that's a relief," said Jennie, as Daisy brought out the breakfast.

When they had finished eating, Margaret pushed back her chair. "I'd like to see Prince. Where is he?"

"Upstairs. Please, go say 'hallo.' I'm sure he's wondering about all the voices downstairs."

Jennie made to go upstairs also, but Victoria pulled her aside. "Can we speak alone first?" She guided her into the sitting room and they sat down. "It's about Daisy."

"Daisy?"

"Yes, Daisy and poor Richard, I mean, your son Richard." Seeing no recognition in Jennie's eyes, Victoria continued. "Daisy is sixteen. Ready to be married."

"Ah, so you are trying to pair her up."

"Yes, with your son, Richard."

"Princess, Richard is still recovering from Emma."

"Jennie, that was ten years ago. And Daisy's different. She's a good cook and can manage a house. She's obedient and caring and—"

"Are you certain that she doesn't have a suitor who will come riding by on a horse in the middle of the night and steal her away?"

"You still harbor anger over that."

"Everybody sees only his own dish. It was very difficult for Richard. As I said, he still hasn't gotten over it."

"I think Daisy will help him heal."

"And what does she think of this?" asked Jennie, hearing her footsteps coming down the stairs.

Victoria fidgeted slightly and took a breath. "Ah, well, she doesn't know about it. I wanted—Prince and I discussed it and we wanted to talk to you first."

"Very well, here's my position. I support it, as long as Daisy agrees on her own accord. Not being forced. She must choose Richard."

Victoria considered her statement. It seemed fair, particularly due to the previous disaster. She nodded. "I will ask her shortly and let you know what she says."

"Thank you. Now," she said, standing. "I'd like to visit your husband."

"Of course," she said, as they left the sitting room and Jennie climbed up the stairs to join Margaret.

Martha, Emma, and their families came in from the stables where they had been looking at horses with Richard, Belcher, and Noah.

"Good-looking stock," said Emma.

"Business is doing well," smiled her mother.

Her sisters-in-law, having been upstairs with Prince an hour, descended the stairs and joined the rest of the family. Victoria noticed that Jennie kept an eye on Daisy. A good sign, she thought.

At the end of the day, she climbed wearily up the stairs.

"Prince," she said, "I think the Hotel is full. We are a big lot." She looked in the mirror to see his response but she could not see the part of the sleeping area where he was. She looked down on the dresser, where she put her golden hoops, and noticed the old leather pouch that housed her special shells. Realizing that she hadn't looked at them in years, she gently stroked their outlines through the leather. Funny how she had forgotten to honor them.

She turned to Prince and saw he'd been watching her. When she climbed into bed, she said, "I told Jennie our idea about Daisy and Richard."

"Yes, she mentioned it when she came upstairs."

"She wants Daisy to pick Richard."

"Yes, she explained. Actually, considering everything, I agree with her."

"What do you think Daisy will say?"

"Hmm," said Prince, somewhat groggily. "I don't know."

"It's been a busy day. So much company."

"Yes, Princess, I am tired."

She blew out the candle and settled next to him. "Sleep well."

"You, too, dear."

Victoria could hear his breath deepen in only a few minutes. She realized she had forgotten to mention the decline in horse sales and would have to tell him tomorrow. She drifted off to sleep.

It was his rasping breath that woke her in the middle of the night. She could feel him sitting up and hear him gasping.

"Prince, what's wrong?"

"I can't breathe," he panted. "The air, it doesn't seem to fill my lungs."

She lit the candle and looked at him. He was grasping the sheets and had his mouth open as he inhaled. "I just can't get enough air."

"Shh. Lay back down and relax. Here's another pillow," she said, giving him hers. She stroked his head and he closed his eyes. A bit of color seemed to return to his cheeks and his breathing returned to normal as he fell asleep.

It must be all the excitement of the company, she decided, blowing out the candle. Perhaps she should keep everyone downstairs tomorrow. Or maybe some would be leaving. No, she remembered, Jennie and Margaret's families were still arriving.

It was Sunday morning, but Victoria felt no difference, except that there was no newspaper. Prince was sleeping almost sitting up, with his mouth agape, when she closed the door behind her and quietly went downstairs.

Below, there was a hubbub of noise and people. Adults and small children walked from table to sitting room to fireplace, with Daisy bringing out plates. Thank goodness, Richard's wife Lottie, Martha, and Emma were helping with the food. Victoria wasn't certain how she could contain this brood and keep them from tiring Prince.

She glanced out the window and could tell that a cold front had arrived. She saw etchings of frost on the window and trees coated with ice. Traveling during the night would have been brutal, but she thought she could see the sun trying to break through the gray clouds.

When Noah noticed her, he started upstairs. "Noah," she called.

He stopped mid-step.

"Where are you going?"

"To see Dadrus, of course."

"I think we should let him rest. He was up during the night. He couldn't breathe."

Noah's face drained but he kept hold of her eyes. "But someone needs to be with him."

"He needs to rest."

"I will be quiet, but someone should be with him." Noah walked resolutely up the rest of the stairs.

Victoria shook her head. These children of hers were so headstrong, doing what they thought was right regardless of what she said. Well, not usually, but certainly now.

She was bombarded with questions from Emma and Martha when she tried to sit at the table.

"How is Dadrus this morning?"

"Did he sleep well?

"How are you, Mammis?"

"My goodness, let me catch my breath." She took a sip of the coffee that someone had placed at her seat. "We are fine this morning." She felt skeptical eyes on her. "Your father was awake once during the night, so he is still resting." Victoria remembered her concern about too much company. "I think he had too many visitors yesterday. Noah is up there now. We need to let him regain his strength."

She saw Martha and Richard exchange looks, while Emma grasped the back of a chair until her knuckles turned white.

"I'll go up after Noah," said Belcher.

"I'm after that," each of her children chimed in. Apparently Prince would still have a steady stream of visitors, but at least only one at a time. Victoria sighed, but what could she do?

Later in the afternoon, when the front door opened again, Victoria felt a sweep of cold air. "Close the door, would you? We have all the fireplaces going and it's still not warm in this place." Victoria saw Richard head out to the wood shed to replenish the boxes.

She turned when she heard a voice call, "Mammis."

"Bessie, oh, my!" Victoria saw a stream of children behind her daughter, followed by her husband. "All the way from Providence, my goodness." She rushed to greet her daughter and was surprised to feel her round belly pressing into her. Victoria was momentarily confused. She thought Bessie had just had a baby. Maybe that was one of the other children. She shook her head to try to straighten out her mind. Just then little Ida, in Bessie's other arm, started squirming. "Another baby?" she whispered in her ear.

Bessie nodded.

"Ida's not much older than a year."

"I know. I was surprised."

"Dadrus will be so pleased."

Bessie looked at her, relieved to know the answer to her unspoken question. "How is he?"

"He's resting. Noah is with him. You can take the next turn."

It was chaotic while the newest arrivals said their 'hallos' to the rest of the family. Victoria bustled off to the kitchen to see how the supply of refreshments was holding up. She walked in to see Daisy sobbing hysterically while hanging on to Emma and Jennie. At first Victoria thought Daisy had burned herself or perhaps ruined a batch of bread. But she quickly glanced around, while the girls rearranged themselves and Daisy pulled herself together.

"What's wrong here?"

"Nothing, Mammis, everything's fine."

Jennie took her by the arm and led her to the sitting room, saying, "Come sit with me, it's too hot and noisy in the kitchen."

Victoria thought it was just as noisy in the sitting room, but Jennie had a strong grasp on her arm and she had no choice but to comply.

"Princess, you have a full house," said Jennie. "So we're going to set up a system to cover the food. We'll make sure there is enough for everyone to eat."

Victoria interrupted, "Tomorrow, send the men to the butcher to get some cuts of beef."

Jennie looked aghast, so Victoria continued, "We have an account, they need not worry about the cost."

"But, Princess, soon we won't be eating meat."

"Of course we will. How are the chickens?"

Jennie took a breath before answering. "Margaret is checking the henhouse for eggs and we will take care of everything. You can just sit here and relax. I'll be back later." Shaking her head, Jennie left the room.

Victoria felt a great fear start to nibble at her. She was terrified to just sit and relax, in case it allowed her to think about what was happening. No, she could not do that. "I'd like to look outside," she said aloud in case Jennie was still listening. She walked to the window that overlooked the back stables and was astonished. The yard was filled with the family's *vardos*, caravan after caravan, almost as if it were camp. Well, she reviewed, there were Jennie and Margaret's families, and then Bessie and Emma and Martha and— She glanced around, trying to count and attribute each to a member of her family. She was struck by an eerie sense of having seen this type of array of caravans somewhere before, but she couldn't place it. She feared her memory was going, which was disturbing.

The afternoon sun was strong and it accented the dark of the trees overhead. Many of the caravans seemed striped from the shadows of the branches alternating with the white of the *vardos*. Horses, browns and blacks and even a gray, were grazing nearby. It truly was quite a gathering of her clan.

When Martha called everyone for dinner, Victoria was impressed by the feast the girls had assembled and the quiet dignity with which everyone ate. Even the younger grandchildren sensed the need to focus on eating, not running around.

There weren't enough seats at the table for everyone to eat at once, so they went in shifts. Family groups sat together and Victoria noticed that Jennie seemed to be paying special attention to Daisy. Somehow Jennie managed to seat the two, Daisy and poor Richard, next to each other and kept a conversation going among them. Victoria would have to remember to tell Prince when she went upstairs that evening.

Thinking that, Victoria wondered if anyone was with Prince right now. She started to sneak away from the table to peak upstairs, but Noah grasped her elbow. "Mammis, how are you holding up?"

"Fine, son, how are you feeling? Are your ribs hurting at all?"

"No, Mammis, I've almost forgotten about that incident the other day."

"Do you know if anyone is upstairs with Dadrus? Has anyone brought him dinner?"

Noah fixed his gaze on her. Somehow she felt that she had said something out of the ordinary, but, when she went back over it, it all made sense to her.

Finally Noah spoke. "Bessie is up there right now. I think Emma will be going up after she finishes her turn eating."

"I'll be heading up there soon. It's been a tiring day."

"Just let me know, Mammis, and I'll walk up with you."

She patted him on the arm. "Thank you, son. It's really not necessary. I can walk up the stairs alone."

When families finished eating, some of them sat in front of the fireplace while others washed up their children's sticky hands and faces and changed them into their sleeping clothes. Bessie came downstairs and, when her family had finished and was ready, she and her husband gathered them together and went out to their caravan. Victoria could see smoke from its chimney and she envied their cozy quiet night out there, reminiscent of so many nights she had spent in the *vardo* with Prince and their family.

Realizing that she wasn't needed, Victoria decided to go to bed. She climbed the stairs slowly, hanging on to the banister with each step. She turned the corner and entered her bedroom, startling Emma. She was holding Prince's hand as he slept or rested, Victoria couldn't tell for certain.

"My turn," she said quietly to her daughter. "You can join your family now."

Emma stood and hugged Victoria. "Sleep well, Mammis. I think he's resting comfortably."

"Did you bring him anything to eat?"

Emma looked aside. "No, I think someone else took care of that." With that, she left the room and Victoria was alone with Prince. She closed the door, took off her jewelry, changed her clothes, and slipped under the covers. Prince didn't stir.

SEVENTEEN

When Victoria woke on Monday, she could see sunlight shining through the window and it made her feel better. Open-eyed, Prince was resting beside her and she smiled at him.

"Good morning, dear," she started. "Taking it easy again?"

Prince nodded. He licked his lips.

"Are you thirsty, dear? I'll send Daisy up with some water."

Victoria rose, dressed, and opened the door, which she closed behind her. Within seconds, Emma came from the next room and gently opened the door, to sit with Prince. Victoria started to say something, but was distracted when two of Emma's children grabbed her hands and started pulling her downstairs.

When she saw Daisy, she mentioned Prince's need for water and went to sit at the table. Two of Margaret's sons were deep in conversation that stopped abruptly when she entered.

"Go on, please."

"That's all right, it was just—uh—business."

She glanced at them, decided to let it pass, and picked up the paper. "Oh, they say we should expect snow today." She glanced outside. "Couldn't tell by looking."

The boys shared side-glances and their brows were furrowed.

"Is that a problem?" she asked.

"Uh —no, no, not at all."

"Good, then you can go to the butcher's this morning," she said, resuming her reading.

The two, looking at each other, shrugged. One of them started to protest, "But we can't eat meat after—" but the other tapped his shoulder and gestured to him to be still.

"In fact, perhaps we will get the horses ready," said one and Victoria nodded absently at them.

The two left Victoria to her paper. The sun shone on the table and she basked in its warmth. Daisy brought coffee and eggs and Victoria smiled at her. "Sit down, dear. Rest yourself in the sun for a moment. They say it will snow later."

Daisy sat, her leg crossed over her knee and her foot swinging. She clasped her hands in her lap but Victoria could see her thumbs playing games with each other. They heard the men leaving with a work wagon to carry the meat home from the butcher shop.

It hadn't been a half hour when they heard the wagon return. "That was quick," Victoria commented.

"I'll go help," said Daisy as she rose and rapidly left the room.

Victoria heard voices outside and was astonished when her daughter Kitty entered the room.

"Kitty? What are you doing here from Boston?" Victoria was visibly confused. "First Martha, then Emma, and now you. Does your mother-in-law know you are here?"

"Yes, Mammis, Aunt Jennie knew we were coming."

"Well, chut, chut, this is quite a turn of events."

"Is Dadrus—?"

"Emma is with him. Or maybe by now it's Martha or Belcher. I can't keep track. They insist that someone needs to stay with him, although I think it tires him out. He would be up on his feet by now, if all you children weren't here keeping him awake."

Kitty's brow wrinkled but she leaned to kiss her mother. "I'd like to go see him. I'll be back down shortly."

Victoria decided she might venture into the kitchen and get the kettle ready for the boys' return from the butcher. She found Daisy and Martha frying onions and garlic. "She doesn't seem to understand," she heard Daisy say.

Martha replied, "I think it's just protection," before catching a glimpse of Victoria. "Hi, Mammis, can we help you?"

"What kind of protection? From what?" she asked.

"Nothing important, Mammis. Did you see that Kitty is here?"

"Yes, having all my children here has flummoxed me. The Hotel is full of people."

"We have the cooking organized. Why don't you rest in the sitting room?'

Victoria, her head starting to swim with all the noise of her family, decided it was a good idea. She sat down on the sofa and shortly found herself napping. When she awoke, she saw that large flakes were falling and the sky was leaden. She rose to look outside and saw that the water melted by the sunshine was now freezing into icy sheets that covered the sidewalk. Someone should spread some sand, she thought.

Heading to suggest that to one of her sons, Victoria caught sight of yet another *vardo* out front. She was absolutely astonished when her husband's brother William from Canada came walking briskly to the house. She quickly pulled open the door. "William, I can't believe—"

"Victoria, I was held up by the storm last night. Did I get here soon enough? Is Prince still alive?"

"Alive? Of course he is, he's just resting."

William, in the middle of hugging her, pulled away a bit, his arms still around her. "Resting?"

"Of course. He's just quite tired."

"I see," he said slowly. "Where is he?"

"Upstairs with a gaggle of guests. That's what is tiring him out, I do declare. How are Sonny and the children?"

William released his hold and held her eyes. "Fine. If you don't mind, I'd like to say 'hallo' to Prince."

"Certainly. Join the procession. I'll be down here when you want to talk."

Victoria watched as William quickly mounted the stairs and knocked on her bedroom door. She saw her son Richard register surprise at seeing his Canadian uncle and gesture for him to enter. A few minutes later, Richard left the two brothers alone and came downstairs.

Victoria returned to the sofa and heard Belcher lugging in wood from outside. She heard the boys unloading the meat and her son Richard directing them on its storage. There was clanging and banging from the kitchen, and shouts from outside where various family members were still in their caravans. She was a bit overwhelmed by it all, particularly Prince's brother's comments.

"Is he still alive?" she muttered. "What kind of question is that?"

She didn't know how long she sat there, but William's hand on her arm brought her to. "Oh," she said, "was Prince surprised to see you?"

"Actually, Princess, no, he was surprised I took so long to get here."

She startled.

"The runners were sent out several days ago—"

"Runners?"

"Princess, dear," he said, taking her hands, "It is a very sad time. Very difficult for everyone." He looked deep in her eyes and she held his look until she could not.

"Very difficult," she whispered.

"Prince is dying," he said gently. "He doesn't have much more time with us."

Victoria rose quickly from the sofa. "No, no, I will not have it."

William rose and put an arm around her. "It is very difficult."

Victoria felt her eyesight fail; the world was gray and formless. As hard as she stretched herself, she couldn't envision a world without Prince. She felt herself start to crumple, but William put his arm under hers.

"Let's go upstairs. It's time for you to be with him."

Very slowly, they climbed the stairs together. William opened the door and helped her inside. Prince, quite pale and gasping, lay, eyes-closed on their bed. Victoria collapsed onto the floor next to him, her arms resting on the bed. "Say it isn't true, Prince. You are just resting; you will be better and with us for many years to come. Say you will."

Wearily, Prince opened his eyes and looked at the love of his life. He could barely reach to caress her hair. "I will never leave you. Princess, I am here."

She rose and spun to address William. "See? He isn't dying, he will be better."

"Princess," she heard his weak voice call. "Come lie with me."

William quietly left the room and closed the door behind him, as Victoria walked to the other side of the bed, removed her shoes, and got under the covers with Prince.

Victoria lay, suspended in time. She thought it might be morning. She heard noises from below that indicated breakfast. But next to her, Prince's breathing was quiet and slow. He had turned on his side, like a baby, and didn't open his eyes any longer when she talked to him.

But talk to him, she did. "Prince," she started. "The family's all here. All our children except little Morris and Wash, of course. And your brother and my brothers' families. It's a full house. I am so glad that we bought this place. You should see the yard. It looks like camp, all the *vurdos* and the fires going." She checked but he wasn't responding.

She heard the door open and slowly turned her head. Martha glanced quickly at her father and then walked to her mother's side.

"Mammis, come, get up. It's morning."

"No, dear, I am staying here with your father."

"At least let me get you something to eat and drink. Come wash up."

"I don't need that. I am fine the way I am."

Martha started to argue but Victoria held up a hand.

"All right, Mammis. We'll be back later to see if you want something." The door closed quietly behind her and it was still again.

William's conversation kept nibbling at her consciousness but she pushed it aside. When it grew quite loud, she felt a rush, a flood of thoughts and feelings overwhelming her. She actually saw her mind go blank. Empty. Whitish-gray. Like life without Prince.

And then she returned to where she was, lying next to him and she talked some more. For some reason, she was reminded of their first son. "Remember when Wash was born? Out in the backwoods of Tennessee, it was. Oh, how happy you were to have a son. The wonder-boy. Of course, that's why we named him George Washington. Just as I am named after the Queen of England, we named our son after the first president of this amazing new country. We knew he was destined to become the head of our family from the very start. Oh, that boy." But then she was filled with an uncomfortable feeling that she couldn't place, but it hurt her heart.

Her mind flitted to another topic. "Daisy will be all right. I think she and poor Richard will be married soon." She turned to look at Prince but he was unresponsive. She reached to touch his face. "Oh, you are cold." She pulled up the covers to warm him. She moved her feet over to his. "Your feet are freezing, poor dear."

She must have dozed. Noah opened the door. "Mammis," he whispered. She heard and opened her eyes. "Mammis, you haven't eaten all day. Here is some tea and bread." He brought her a small tray, but she shook her head.

"I'm not hungry, son. But thank you." She looked at her son. "How are the fingers?"

"Fine, Mammis, thanks to you." His eyes shifted to Prince but only for a few seconds. "Mammis, it's dark in here. Come downstairs. Someone else will sit with Dadrus."

"I'm not leaving." She set her chin in a determined fashion that her family recognized as a firm decision that was not about to be changed.

Noah sighed. "All right, Mammis. But we will keep checking on you. You will want to come down to eat some time today."

Victoria wasn't certain that was true, but she knew better than to voice her ideas. They would leave her here if they thought she would eventually give up her vigil. No, they didn't need to know that she would not leave Prince's side.

Her thoughts wandered until they were disturbed by loud voices downstairs. It was an angry hum and she could hear Richard's voice above the others. The possibility of discord among her children catapulted her to action. She needed to go down there and stop whatever was happening. She sat up, her head swimming a bit from the sudden change in position. Slowly, she swung her legs to the ground.

"Prince," she said, "I am going downstairs to see what the commotion is all about. I will be back shortly."

She was just finished putting on her shoes when the door swung open and crashed into the side of the dresser. The brightness of the hallway momentarily blinded her and she automatically put her hand on her heart. As her eyes slowly adjusted, she saw an unknown young man standing there, with Richard right behind him.

"I tried to stop him, Mammis," Richard hissed. Someone else was trying to close the door, but the young man stood forcibly in its way.

"I am John Williams," he said clearly. He looked eagerly at Prince curled in the bed, but his face fell when he realized that Prince was beyond coherent. "I came as quickly as I could."

Victoria's mind was fuddled. Who was this man? A flicker of remembrance of the recent arrival of Prince's firstborn son from Ohio ran across her mind, but this wasn't the same man, this man named John.

John Williams stepped into Prince's bedroom and knelt before Prince. "Father, I am sorry I am too late to meet you." He bent his head and sobbed.

Victoria's head jerked. Another son? Who was this one? Would Prince's secrets never end?

Noah slid past Richard and touched the man on the shoulder. "Excuse me," he started, "but who are you?"

The gentle tone of his inquiry allowed John Williams to look around. "I am John Williams, son of Thomas Williams and Mary Defiance Burton."

Noah looked blankly at him, but Victoria grasped at her skirts with both hands. The man continued, "I have just arrived from Ohio." He glanced at Prince. "I wish I had gotten here sooner." He looked up at Noah. "I have never met my father. He left before I was born."

Apparently trying to decide whether to believe him, Noah and Richard both looked at Victoria. She nodded her head ever so slightly. He must have been the result of Mary Defiance's pregnancy that summer after Victoria and Prince had been married.

"My brother, William, was here recently. Afterwards, he went out West to purchase horses. When the runners arrived to tell us about" he gulped before continuing "—our father, we sent them after William, but he has not yet returned."

Victoria sat down heavily on the bed, her head filled with the disconcerted voices of her children.

"What do you mean, Mary Defiance? Who is she?"

"Ohio? We don't have family there."

"William is Dadrus' brother from Canada, not his son."

The cacophony of sound resonated through her, echoing around until she thought her head would burst. "Enough!" she shouted. Everyone looked appalled, as they glanced at Prince. "All of you, downstairs."

For several seconds, everyone was frozen, some with their mouths still open, others with their gestures stopped in still motion. Martha, from the back of the group in the hallway, turned people around and gently pushed them to the stairs. When she reached John, she grasped his arm and, closing the bedroom door behind her, escorted him out.

It was very still in the room, but Victoria could still hear all their voices. They bounced from wall to wall, filling her with dread. Back and forth, her eyes kept darting as if she could follow the words, until she felt so dizzy that she had to lie down.

"Oh, Prince, help me!" She closed her eyes and felt a whirlwind carrying her spiraling down.

When Victoria came to, it was quiet in the room. She viewed that as an improvement from the disturbing visit from this John person. But then she realized it was very quiet. So quiet that she couldn't hear Prince breathing. She turned to him and put her hand on his chest. It was still and he was cold.

EIGHTEEN

The shrill scream that filled the air hurt her ears. It was only when she put her hands to her face that she realized the noise was coming from her. Steps pounded up the stairs, dozens of them, and the door slammed open. Eyes filled with horror, Victoria frantically pawed at Prince's bedclothes and yelled to the dark bodies filling the doorway, "Someone help him. Call the doctor, he can't breathe. He's so cold." The screaming started again, but this time, there were others. Wails and howls of anguish filled the air. She thought of wolves howling; once one started, the others joined. She felt gentle arms gather her and remove her from the room, but she struggled.

"I'll go get someone to move the body," she heard someone say.

"I was surprised that she let him stay in the house this long," said another.

"She wouldn't have him outside in this weather. And it's a new era, a time to put aside some of the old ways."

"Well, I certainly hope his *muló* doesn't hang around."

Then she heard no more.

When she opened her eyes, bright light seared her brain and, when she closed them, she saw echoes of silhouetted figures on her eyelids. Her face was awash with tears and she thrashed on a bed where someone had placed her. She moaned and screamed until her throat was so dry that no sound escaped but she still tried to cry out. Someone covered her and kept an arm across her, so that she couldn't move far. She tried to think but her mind was empty. Totally blank. She felt cold and couldn't feel her heart beating, although she could hear moaning throughout the house. The cold dark filled her and she entered a void, a place of nothingness where there was no form and no feeling.

Time passed, she supposed. She opened her eyes. It was daylight. She wasn't in her room, she was disoriented, and then she remembered why, and she shrieked. She heard someone rushing to her, as she turned her head frantically from side to side, looking, and yelling, "Prince, you said you wouldn't leave. Where are you?" Exhaustion overtook her and she slept.

On this day after Prince's death, when she awoke later, the gray was only around the edges and Victoria made herself get up and go downstairs to the sitting room. She noticed her sons huddled together talking but, when she reached the doorway, they stopped the conversation. Then Noah looked at her.

She felt he was trying to assess her mental and emotional state. "What is it?" she asked drearily.

"Mammis, you have given us no instructions about how to destroy Dadrus's possessions."

For a moment, she felt the air get sucked from her chest. She willed herself to breathe and answer. "Take the caravans and horses to the other sale barns, in Willimantic and New Haven," she said. "They belong to everyone. They will not be destroyed."

"Even the chariot? Beatrix?"

Victoria's eyes misted over and she hesitated.

"Yes, of course," said her son Richard. "Beatrix and the chariot are no different."

Victoria started to contradict him, but she became confused. She knew there was something she wanted to remember about Richard but it wasn't coming to her. Maybe he was right, she decided and closed her mouth.

"What shall we do with his clothes?"

"Burn them." She was clear about that.

There was silence, as each of the sons waited for another to ask about what they really wanted to know. Finally, Richard ran out of patience. "And the horseshoe pin will be mine?"

He said it as a question but with such firmness that it sounded like a statement.

Victoria, lost in thought, jerked to. She observed her three sons, Richard, Noah, and Belcher, in front of her and saw clearly the need for them to work together. The pin would divide them, give one more power than the others. "No, that will go to Martha."

"Martha? You jest." Richard, outraged, stood suddenly.

"Martha is the eldest. To Martha."

Richard clenched his fist and set his jaw. He started to say more but decided against it and had to leave the room. He muttered over his shoulder, "His *muló* will not be happy about this."

"Mammis, are you certain about the pin?"

She looked at Noah and Belcher and nodded. The pain of Richard's anger merged with the terrible loss of Prince and she felt herself consumed by grief again and shut her eyes. She lowered herself into a chair and sensed the rest of them leave the room.

A short time later, Victoria was roused by someone calling her name. "What? Yes?"

"Mammis, the man from the newspaper is here and he has some questions." That was Noah's voice, she thought, and she opened her eyes to confirm that.

"I can't answer questions," she sighed.

"We covered most of them, about Dadrus and where he was born and such." She nodded. "But they want to know about the business, what is going to happen."

Victoria felt the gray disappear. "The three of you will run the business."

"Not Richard? The three of us?" squeaked Noah.

"Yes, Richard, Belcher, and yourself. Tell the reporter that."

"All right, Mammis, I will go tell him."

She knew that was the correct decision. She hoped that Richard wouldn't make much trouble when he heard about it. But the whole episode exhausted her and she returned upstairs to the extra bedroom.

"Mammis," Martha's voice said urgently, "it's been three days. You need to wash." Laggardly, Victoria began the cleansing protocol by being the first to wash herself. She noticed her nails needed cutting but knew that was not allowed until later. The rest of the family followed her example and cleaned themselves. Martha lit incense to purify the house, while Daisy sprinkled water around the rooms.

The days ticked slowly by. The family sat alone at the house, with mirrors covered, food restricted, no changing of clothes or grooming. Most of the time, Victoria was alone, even when others sat beside her.

Sometimes, in the extra bedroom upstairs, as she lay lost in the gray, she felt the rustling of skirts in the room with her. Downstairs she heard the murmur of soft voices, furniture shifting, doors opening and closing. She had no desire, no energy to contemplate more than that.

One day, she heard loud voices that brought her back. "No, we cannot wait," someone, Richard perhaps, said loudly.

"But he is the oldest son."

"No."

"I insist. Our father would have wished it."

"Your mother dismissed my father. He did not exist to her. And thus neither of you exists to us."

Victoria thought those words were echoes of ones she had heard before at some other time or place. She could almost recall the scene but it evaded her and when the voices continued no more, she sunk back into her blackness.

At some point, a voice called, "Mammis?" She turned toward the sound but didn't open her eyes. "Mammis, we need to get dressed now." She shook her head, but the arm of the voice lifted her to sitting position. There were other voices, whispering, "Do you need help?" "Where is her skirt?" and other words that didn't fall into place. She slowly opened her eyes.

Martha was next to her, holding her hand and touching her hair. Victoria reached up, noticing that her *diklo* was missing. "Oh," she gasped, "I must not be seen."

"Shh, shh," soothed Martha. "I will help you."

Victoria sat there helplessly as Martha brushed her hair, put on her earrings and bangles, and tied her scarf. She noticed that Martha herself was dressed in going-out clothes and saw her own clothes hanging from a hook. The wall mirror was covered with a cloth, a shocking sight that brought everything back to her and she began wailing again.

"Mammis, we must get dressed. Dadrus would want you to do that."

Victoria felt that she was hovering near the ceiling in the corner of the room as she watched her daughter dress her in mourning clothes.

"Come, swing your legs down and we'll put on your boots."

Victoria's body did as it was asked and, when she stood, she felt herself slip back inside. Victoria sensed something was missing and an image came to her. "Wait. A red ribbon for my wrist." A sob caught in Victoria's throat as she spoke.

Martha sniffed, trying to staunch the flow of tears as she went to the sewing basket and returned with a narrow yarn of red. Victoria held out her arm and Martha tied on Victoria's symbol of devotion to Prince.

Her feet felt very heavy and she almost lost her balance. Martha steadied her and she felt someone else on her other side, someone who had just come through the door. She felt him kiss the side of her face and knew it was Noah. His arm supported her and she walked, solemnly, down the stairs.

When she reached the front door, she noticed many others were standing in the hallway waiting quietly for her arrival. She saw their dark forms and their pale faces and felt their sorrow.

Victoria was wrapped in her cloak by some unseen hands and Martha and Noah steered her through the door. But her heart stopped her feet from moving any farther when she saw the hearse hitched with four of Prince's beautiful black horses. Her wailing began anew and it gave permission to her children and grandchildren to cry and scream. Voices filled the air, startling the horses as old Joe reined them in.

Prince's brother William joined them and led her to their chariot, the chariot that had been hers with Prince. She registered a long procession of *vardos* and carriages lined up behind her. William helped her into the chariot, drawn by the beautiful Beatrix, and Victoria sobbed again. She clutched the velvet strap inside the cab and felt her knuckles turn white. She struggled to accept what was happening.

She felt the chariot jerk as the wheels began to turn. Then all went silent as if her ears were filled with cotton. The gentle rocking carried her away and thankfully she didn't see the people of the town of East Hartford lining the streets as they rode to the church.

When she felt William nudging her, she looked around. She opened her mouth to ask where Prince was, but then she remembered, and all she could do was gasp. He patted her arm and opened the door. After stepping down, he reached for her.

Victoria stood on the step and glanced behind them. Hacks and carriages stretched for miles as far as she could see. Puffs of vapor came from the horses' mouths and they stamped their feet restlessly.

She did not remember passing the hearse or walking into the church. She found herself sitting in a pew and felt a hand on her shoulder. She lifted her head and Reverend McVey was looking into her eyes. "My dear," he said, "I am so sorry." She nodded, before her head sunk back to her chest. Mumblings filled the church, a dull drone, as row upon row was filled by family and friends. Sobs and the blowing of noses and then silence.

The silence continued and Victoria looked up. A massive oak casket was moving up the aisle, aided by six men wearing dark suits. When they stopped at the front of the church, Victoria yelled, "Prince, come back." Several of her daughters cried loudly and the drone grew to a chaotic din. Victoria felt herself slide back into the noise and, when it finally quieted, she stayed in the silence.

It was gray there in the silence and minutes passed without her seeing anything. When her eyesight returned, she was standing outside with many people in cold weather, her arms gripped around herself, trying to stay warm. Her feet were moving down a walk joining the momentum of the group and, when she glanced to the side, she saw tombstones. The cold pierced her heart just as the group stopped. She didn't have to look to know that she would see a tall white monument with a cantering horse atop, or a small stone with a lamb behind it to the right. Men were struggling with the large oak casket, carrying it to the gaping hole in front of the monument. Victoria considered flinging herself into the pit and might have done so, but she felt a strong grip on her left arm where Prince's brother William stood.

The Reverend began to speak and his words ricocheted off the monument and onto her ears. She heard moans and loud cries from those in the group and the sound of Prince's personal items being dropped into his grave. She opened her eyes and could make out his pipe, gold coins, and a spreading pool of red wine before she squeezed them shut again. As soon as she felt the pressure on her arm slacken, she looked to see that the casket was already in the ground and mostly covered with loose clods of dirt. In agony, she pulled out some of her hair and tried to reach the monument itself. She threw herself down, wishing to be absorbed into it, but her temple only grazed its corner. She felt blood gushing down her face at the same time that strong arms lifted her back to the path. Someone wiped her face and pressed a handkerchief against her wound and her world went gray again.

The old Farmer's Hotel came into focus and she realized they were almost home. Slowly she got down from the chariot and, flanked by William and her children, walked up the sidewalk. Victoria hesitated before climbing the porch stairs and turned to look at the family behind her. She caught a glimpse of John Williams.

"You," she hissed, pointing a finger at him. "You are banned. You may not enter our house to mourn with us." His pained look didn't change her mind. "Go. Away from here." She turned and walked into the house, pausing only slightly to say, "Richard, make certain that he does not join us." With that, Victoria felt herself regain her composure and remain lucid. Being defensive and protective of her own family gave her purpose again.

The following morning, there was a knock on the front door. "Mammis," Noah called, "I think we have trouble."

Victoria came around the corner and took a quick glance at the two men standing outside. "Oh, dear, you are quite right."

"Do we have to let them in?"

Victoria hesitated. With William and John Williams standing on the porch stomping their cold feet, waiting for them to open the door, she wanted to say, no, of course not. We can let them freeze out there if we want. But she felt a chill swirling around her shawl and pressure on her arm to reach toward the door. "We have always been hospitable and generous. Even if he sent William away, your father would not approve of rudeness. We must honor your father's memory and open the door."

By then Belcher had joined them and, hearing those words, he turned the doorknob.

"But we don't have to be pleasant," she added in a whisper.

"Good morning, thank you for letting us in."

They all stood uncomfortably in the foyer.

"I am so sorry that I missed the funeral. I was out West purchasing horses and the runners couldn't find me. I got here as soon as I could."

The conversation stalled as Victoria and her sons said nothing and offered no opportunity for the visitors to remove their coats or sit by the fire.

"We—uh, I am greatly upset that I was not able to see my father before he was placed in the grave."

Still no one else said a word.

"I would like to arrange for the grave to be exhumed and have an opportunity to see him."

With that image, Victoria felt the floor give way and she crumpled and would have fallen if Belcher hadn't caught her. Noah gave the two men a small shove back towards the door, which he opened. "You have greatly distressed my mother. You must go now."

Richard grabbed his hat and cloak. "I'll keep an eye on them," he said, hurrying to the back door to get his boots.

Victoria started to wail, the image of Prince so strong. "Bring back my Prince to me," she cried. She pulled her hair and banged her head on the nearby wall. Belcher struggled to contain her and the noise brought Lottie and Martha from the kitchen. They managed to get Victoria to the sofa in the sitting room.

All she could see was dirt, clods of earth and the heavy oak coffin and the looming white monument and a spiral of grief and loneliness. She sobbed until her heaves were dry and still she cried and wailed and moaned. It was like starting her mourning all over again. "Curse those boys," she shouted to the fireplace. "Send them back to Ohio where they belong."

NINETEEN

The days passed as they sat and mourned, and, at the end of the week, Martha and Daisy repeated their incense and water rituals. Then the family gathered in the dining room, where another table had been added to form a "T." An empty place was left for Prince, while his children sat around the remaining seats, grandchildren on eating tarps in the corners of the rooms. Daisy and Emma brought out bowls of grains, beans, and rice to Victoria who then passed them around. Martha poured tea into glasses filled with fruit that she carried to each person on a tray. When everyone's plate was full and all were seated, everyone looked expectantly at Victoria. But her face was vacant and, after a few awkward moments, Prince's brother William stood and raised a small cup of wine to say, "Thomas Williams, we are gathered here in your memory. We hope that you have found peace in your final resting place." With that, he sprinkled the wine on the tablecloth in front of Prince's place. He looked hopefully at Victoria, but she was still mute.

"We offer this humble food which, as the provider of your family, you supplied. We are grateful for all that you did for this family. May you rest in peace." At that, William sat down and Victoria picked up her fork. Others followed suit and the meal began. Victoria thought she heard Richard mutter, "May your *muló* be satisfied."

The following day, her sisters-in-law came to where she sat on the sofa. "Princess," said Jennie, "we must return home now." Victoria looked up at them and their faces swam into focus. Gray disappeared and she felt clear at that moment.

"Will you be all right?" asked Margaret.

Victoria nodded. "My children are here."

"We will check on you frequently."

She nodded again. "And, when it is appropriate, I will tell you what Daisy says about your son Richard," she said to Jennie.

Wearily she rose and clutched both of them.

"The children are already in the *vardos*," said Margaret.

"We didn't want to be too noisy," added Jennie.

"Thank you. Give them all hugs from me. And thank you for being here. I—" but Victoria could say no more. She just waved as they left and entered their caravans for their return to Somerville. She went back to her seat on the sofa. Her brothers' wives were managing to survive without their husbands. She wasn't sure she would be able to do the same.

She heard footsteps enter the room and she felt Prince's brother William sit down and put his arm around her. "I will be leaving also."

She nodded. She envisioned William heading back to Sonny and their family and she felt a pang of envy.

"I will keep an eye on the boys," he added, glancing at her sons who were outside saying goodbye to their cousins. "I am going to spend more time at my sale barn in Bridgeport now."

"Thank you," she sighed, knowing that she wasn't at all ready to think about the business.

However, that afternoon, as they sat near the fire, Victoria overheard one of her sons say, "But we must ask Mammis."

"She's in no condition to answer this."

She lifted her head and nodded. "Ask me what?"

The sons were silent at first and then Richard rose to come sit near her, with Belcher and Noah following. "Mammis," he began, "we need to do some paperwork. It's the American law. Dadrus left no will and—"

"I had warned him," she interrupted. "I told him we should work on a will. In fact, we planned to ask your Aunt Jennie for the name of a person to write one."

"But still he left no will."

Victoria sighed. "Yes, that is true."

"We have also heard," and Richard glanced at his brothers. They both nodded, so he continued, "that the other sons, William and John Williams, are still in town."

Victoria pulled herself up stiffly and spewed, "What do those men think? They have no right to be here."

Noah put his hand on her arm. "Mammis, we understand. But we are afraid that they might go to the courts and ask for something from Dadrus. And—"

Belcher continued, "And the court won't understand how Mary Defiance sent Dadrus on his way. The court might add John and William to the list of heirs."

Victoria stood quickly. "And there is also a sister in Ohio."

"Yes. Three of them all together," said Belcher.

She collapsed on the chair and put her head in her hands. "Oh, what can we do? I told your father we should take care of this."

Richard stood up and put his arm around Victoria. "I would like to go to the court and ask to be the administrator of the estate."

Victoria looked wearily from one son to the next.

"In order to do that, I will need your permission." Richard said.

Victoria didn't like something about the idea but she couldn't put her finger on it. They all were looking anxiously at her and she knew that she was in no condition to argue. "All right," she sighed. "I am certainly unable to administer this myself. But, remember," she added, looking fiercely at Richard, "all three of you are running the business."

Richard almost smiled. "I'll get started on the estate right away. When I get the papers, I'll bring them for you to sign." He left the house, a cold breeze entering the hallway as he opened the door. Victoria felt the chill and shivered.

In the days that followed, there were times when Victoria would come to, realizing that someone had spoken to her or some activity was happening around her. Other times, she disappeared into herself, too numb to participate in life. She began to notice a sense around her, a light or presence, a touch on her shoulder or a whisper in her ear that reminded her of Prince. She might turn her head sharply or look quickly but there was nothing there.

One night, Victoria was already asleep when she heard a dreadful racket outside. Peering out the window, she saw the headlight of the electric car stopped on its tracks down on the corner. In its light, she could see men gathered and she heard the front door close. She put on her robe and joined Emma and Bessie, who had gathered in the sitting room.

"I thought I heard someone scream," shivered Emma.

"I looked from the front porch and I could see lights on in the drugstore," added Bessie.

A half hour later, Belcher returned to the Hotel. He unbundled himself at the door before joining the women. He shook his head.

"Bad?" asked Victoria.

"Hard to say. They just took Mr. Gilroy to Hartford by ambulance."

"Oh, dear, what happened?"

"You know how wretched the streets and sidewalk are, with all the ice and snow."

Victoria nodded, recalling icy sidewalks in front of the Hotel.

"Apparently he was walking and slid into the tracks just as the electric car came by."

The women murmured words of distress.

"It didn't help that he had been drinking," added Noah who had joined them. "They found a bottle of liquor in his pocket. Funny how that didn't break in the accident."

"Chut, chut," said Bessie. "I guess we will know more in the morning." She yawned. "I'm glad it was nothing worse."

Emma agreed. "I think I'll go to bed now. Come, Mammis, let's go."

Victoria tried to stand, but her legs were shaking. She tried to smile. "I guess—I guess this upset me more than I knew."

"We don't even know the man, do we?"

"Only in passing." But Victoria trembled as she stood with assistance from Bessie. She felt a wave of fear passing through her. Almost hyperventilating, she tried very hard not to envision one of her sons under the electric car. She willed herself to take a deep breath and, after a few minutes, her shaking subsided. Bessie helped her up the stairs and they stopped on the landing to allow Victoria to catch her breath.

Down below they could hear Belcher saying, "It's not good when these things happen so close to home."

"No, Mammis is so sensitive."

"Hopefully, she'll forget about it in the morning."

"True. Maybe we should hide the newspaper. There will surely be a notice about it."

"I don't think we can do that. Mammis loves her paper."

"You're right. Well, we can only hope she feels differently in the morning."

Several days later, Victoria was looking absentmindedly out the back window when she spotted Richard walking with an unfamiliar man into the stable. She watched for a half hour, at which point, the two emerged, leading a beautifully matched pair of horses. The men shook hands and Richard returned to the stable, as the man led the team away.

Later that afternoon, Richard came into the house from the

innkeeper's quarters. He said nothing to Victoria and she gave him some time to do so. After a few hours, she called him to her.

"Yes, Mammis?"

"Anything new at the stables today?"

A fleeting shadow passed his face. "New? Nothing I can recall," he replied. He fumbled nervously with his pocket.

Portions of her conversation with Prince came back to her and she felt great distrust of this son in relation to money.

"No sales?"

"No," he sputtered.

"I thought I saw you come from the barn with a man leading away two horses."

Richard's face grew red, as he stuttered, "T—t—two horses? Oh," he said, "you must mean Mr. Chapman. He and Dadrus had already arranged the sale. He just came to retrieve the horses." She waited. "He already paid for them."

"I see."

Richard would not look at her directly, but he nodded. Just then, Daisy called them for dinner and Richard turned quickly. "Let me escort you to the meal."

Still feeling a great deal of unease about the conversation, Victoria walked with him. True, she had not seen any exchange of funds between the two men. But it had been almost three weeks since Prince had been able to conduct business. No, she did not like this and she promised herself she would take a look at the ledger sheets as soon as she could.

When she was reading the newspaper the following morning, she saw distressing news that Judge Fenn had not yet recovered from his icy fall in which he suffered a head injury. Previous articles had reminded her of her own incident, so eerily similar that she got chills whenever she read them. Her reaction to this article was no exception. In fact, she started to shake violently and Daisy insisted that she return to bed. Daisy helped her up the stairs and covered her with a comforter and placed a foot warmer underneath her.

"Thank you, dear. You don't have to stay."

"Oh, but I will, Mammis. I'll feel better."

Victoria tried to resist but her eyes closed and she slept. After a brief nap, Victoria woke refreshed.

"How are you feeling, Mammis?" asked Bessie, who was seated next to her.

"Fine. But I don't remember why I returned to bed. Was I ill?"

Bessie looked at her and opened her mouth. Then she said, "No, Mammis, just tired."

"Ah, well, I feel better now."

"Shall I help you up?"

"Yes, thank you. But why am I sleeping here? Why am I not in my bedroom? And where is Prince?"

"Oh, Mammis," said Bessie, hugging her. Victoria felt her sobbing and saw Martha over Bessie's shoulder.

"Why are you all here? Bessie? Martha?"

"Martha, help me," pleaded Bessie.

Martha gently took Victoria by the arm and brought her down to the sitting room. It was there that the memories of the past few weeks came flooding back and Victoria cried sadly into her hands as they sat on the sofa. She wondered if she would ever feel normal again. Although she knew it made sense to mourn the loss of Prince, she was terrified that she suffered from something more. A defect caused by her fall that impacted her ability to stay focused, just like Judge Fenn. Or maybe even worse. She shook her head, trying to dispel that thought and convince herself that she was fine. Just a bit more time to get over Prince. After all, it hadn't even been a month.

It was early April when Martha and her other daughters prepared another feast to honor their father. Again, they set a place for Prince and toasted his name in hopes that they satisfied his ghost.

"May your *muló* be happy," said Noah.

Richard fumbled a bit with his napkin.

Victoria felt a gentle breeze flowing through the room and it felt like a spring day and wildflowers. Maybe Prince was trying to remind her that the seasons would be changing, just as life did. She felt peaceful and smiled at each of her children before reminding them, "You have to dig deep to bury your daddy."

At those words, Richard started, but the other sons nodded their heads in agreement. Her daughters sniffled quietly, holding hands under the table. Victoria sprinkled drops of wine near Prince's place. Feeling her face caressed by the gentle breeze, she said, "We are all wanderers on this earth. Our hearts are full of wonder, and our souls are deep with dreams. Prince, may you wander in peace."

At that, they ate their remembrance meal in silence. Even the grandchildren on the eating tarps were unusually quiet. When the meal was over, everyone rose from the table.

"I'll take the leftovers to the river," offered Richard. Victoria thought he seemed rather anxious to escape but she let it pass. She was grateful that at least someone was willing to take care of that part of the ritual. Richard held out his hand to Lottie and, together, they left the house.

The following day, Victoria noticed there was much activity and movement going on in the kitchen. Emma came out with a basket filled with food. "Mammis," she began, "we're leaving now. We must return home."

Victoria realized that this would be the case for all of her daughters from other towns. Indeed, Bessie and Kitty emerged with similar baskets. Victoria sat down quickly, struck by this change. She would be here alone.

"Martha will be staying here, along with Daisy."

"And of course the boys."

Not exactly alone, but she would be responsible again for life in the Hotel. Thank goodness Martha would keep things ticking. Feeling a warmth around her shoulders, Victoria gathered her strength and smiled. "Thank you, daughters, for being here."

Hugs all around, the women sniffled and tried to smile. Victoria could see their spouses hitching up their horses to caravans and children running around in the yard.

"God go with you," she said. "Have safe journeys."

It took a few hours, but when they had all finally left, a silence descended on the Hotel. Victoria could hear whispers in many corners and she was drawn upstairs to her old bedroom. She had not been back in there since that last night with Prince. Now, she decided, she would return.

Slowly, she opened the door, with an expectation of something rushing from the room. But there were only more whispers, ones that called her inside. She walked to her dresser and removed the covering from the mirror. Tracing the outline of the shells in her leather pouch, Victoria felt at home. She glanced at the sleeping area and realized she would need her comforter and returned to the room she had been using.

Martha, hearing the noise, came upstairs. "Mammis, what are you doing?"

"I'm moving back into my room."

"But, Mammis, that is forbidden. It is bad enough that Dadrus died inside the Hotel. You can't go sleeping in the same room."

Victoria eyed her eldest. "Time is moving forward and there are new ways in this country. We have had babies born here, one of yours, I may remind you. Now someone has died here. We cannot leave the room empty and I am the only one who should be sleeping there."

Armed with her comforter, she walked in and closed the door. She settled the comforter in the sleeping area and got ready for bed. Although she felt a heavy weight in her heart, she sensed warmth again around her shoulders.

She smiled slightly. "You didn't leave me, did you?"

TWENTY

Prince's whispering presence accompanied her during the days that followed. Green leaves began to poke from brown buds and peepers began their nightly calling. Victoria felt a growing sense of him in her daily activities and the pain of his death lessened. She removed herself from many of the decisions of the family business as she slid into another world filled with vapors and essences from the other side.

In the sitting room one day, she found herself startled from her thoughts by her son's voices in the dining room.

"Richard, we should be packed and ready to leave by now."

"I have matters that I must attend to before we leave."

"What do you mean?" asked Noah.

"That is none of your business," retorted Richard.

"It's our business when it costs us money."

Victoria heard Belcher mutter something.

"If you ever say that in front of Mammis, I'll—" Richard stopped with the realization that she was in the other room.

"Don't worry. Your secrets are safe with us. Until you don't share the profits of your sideline."

Victoria heard a chair scrape and someone stomp from the room and leave out the back door. Noah and Belcher continued.

"He's got the roadster listed for Moore Park this weekend."

"He says it's good for business, that people see our stock doing their gaits."

"It's an interesting tactic, for sure."

"And he does look striking, all dressed in his silks and whatnot."

"But he—" and Belcher's voice dropped off.

"I know," sighed Noah. "I just hope we can get out of here and head south before he loses too much."

But, by then, Victoria had lost interest. She found that was true many days. She would be startled to find herself walking on Main Street with no recollection of how she got there. Or sometimes she would be out in the yard by the stable, without a coat, and realize that she must have been out there for some time, as she was chilled to the bone. But, try as she might, she had no memory of getting there, much to the consternation of her children. Often, she felt the whisper of Prince around her and she felt comfort.

Many of the trees were in full-leaf by the time they started packing the caravans. Victoria was gnawed by the inconsistency of Prince's presence. She couldn't tell when she would feel him the strongest and struggled to understand if there was a pattern or a sign related to it. She started to wonder if he were restricted to stay where he had passed and the idea panicked her. If she went south with the family, maybe Prince would be here still at the old Farmer's Hotel.

"I'm not going," Victoria announced at dinner one day.

Everyone turned to look at her. "Mammis, you can't stay here alone."

"Prince will be here with me," she smiled.

Noah and Daisy exchanged looks.

"Now, Mammis, you know he won't feed you. He never could cook," Noah jested.

Victoria, enjoying the exchange, responded, "Ah, but now he can do anything. No, I'm not leaving."

"Mammis," protested Martha, "I can't stay here with you any longer. My family needs me and I was planning on going to Hoosick Falls for the summer."

"Go," said Victoria. "I will be fine."

"I guess I could stay," said Daisy. "I can take care of us."

Richard raised his eyebrow. "Really? What will you do when you find her wander—" and he stopped short, silenced by a dark look from both Noah and Belcher.

"Let's leave it for now. We need to get those sale horses ready to go over to Willimantic."

Richard nodded and the sons rose and left the table.

Victoria wandered onto the front veranda. Mourning doves were busily picking gravel from the drive and she guessed they already had fledged their young. She sat down on a rocker and faced the direction of the river. Occasionally she could hear shouts, as wagons reached the end of the bridge or passengers disembarked from the electric trolley. She was glad for the longer days, with the sun setting long about seven o'clock. She did feel a bit restless, as if her body was urging her to move on, but she resisted because of Prince. She wished there were someone to ask about his *muló*, whether it would travel with them or not. She sighed, knowing she was the elder at this point and, if she didn't know, there was no one who would. Plus, she wasn't certain anyone else would encourage her to keep in touch with his spirit. She knew that most people wouldn't want to be haunted, but this was her Prince and she much preferred that to losing him completely. She was certain he was around because they hadn't destroyed all his things, and she also rathered that he hovered around her than her sons. Maybe she would check her Tarot cards to see if he could move with her, but the effort to go upstairs to get them was more than she could exert at this time.

She was rocking gently in the cooling air as the orange sun met the horizon, when she heard a shout and the galloping of horses.

"The bridge is burning!" shouted someone riding by.

Daisy came running out to the veranda. "What is it?"

Victoria struggled up from the rocker. "They say that the bridge is on fire. We should go see."

"Lottie," called Daisy. "Where is Richard? Maybe we could harness a *vardo* to go see."

Lottie called from inside, "I'll check with him."

As they waited, a steady stream of people walked, ran, and rode down to the river. Their excited conversations carried to the veranda.

"I wonder if they can save it."

"Do you think it was set?"

"Well, since we, on this side of the river, were supposed to pay for most of a new bridge, I wouldn't be surprised."

"Arson, you say?" asked another.

"Well, you never know."

Within a few minutes, Richard pulled his caravan to the front of the old Hotel and helped Victoria, Daisy, and Lottie up into it. By then, the streets were filled and it was slow going down to the river. Richard finally was able to drive close enough to the bank for a view. The murmuring of people hovered in the background and, across on the Hartford side, throngs lined the banks.

The clanging of the Hartford fire hose company traveled across the water. They could hear the rumble as the horse cart started across the bridge.

Every boat owner on the eastern shore was launching their craft and capitalizing on the opportunity to make some money along the way. Their offers filled the air. "I'm heading out in my boat. I'll take someone with me for a dollar. Come see the fireworks!"

"I'll take you for fifty cents but you have to help row," shouted another.

From their caravan, Victoria could see a mass of people, glowing in the light from the flames, huddled along the western bank, and a loud roar passed through the crowd on both sides as the bridge roof burst into flames. Smoke billowed downstream and the dark waters roiled as burning timbers dropped into their depths.

"The third span," someone shouted.

"That span was ready to fall down already," yelled another.

"It's going," a voice called. They watched as the section nearer to Hartford fell atop the second span. But the remainder of the third span hung suspended before finally teetering southerly into the river and floating, afire, downstream. There it blazed as the crowd cheered and whistled.

"Look at the framing, Mammis," gasped Daisy. Without a roof, the magnificent arches and crossbeams of the bridge were exposed and silhouetted against the sky. Sparks flashed into the river, steaming as soon as the water extinguished them. Suddenly, there was a loud roar as the spans closest to East Hartford collapsed. Loud hissing filled the air and the crowd on both sides of the river shrieked with pleasure and excitement.

As the crowd settled down, Victoria was pulled upright by screams that filled the air. She grasped Daisy's arm. "What is that?"

The screaming continued and it became obvious that the fire horses had gotten caught on the bridge. As their span collapsed, they —and the cart they were attached to—fell into the river to be covered by beams as the entire span fell. Flames reached into the dark sky, sparks showering down on the people standing near the shore. The hiss of sparks, crackle of the fire, smell of burning hair— all kaleidescoped in Victoria's consciousness and she blinked furiously, trying to peer into the darkened night. Panic overtook her, as she could only imagine what she couldn't see clearly.

"The children," cried Victoria. "Morris and Martha's baby are in the tent! We must reach them!"

"Mammis, it's all right. We are here along the river. It's the bridge burning. The tent fire, that was years ago. Morris and Samuel were fine. Remember that Dadrus pulled them out?"

Victoria was shaking and all she could see before her were the flames, and all she could hear were the screams, echoing in her ears. "I must go help. The babies." She started down from the caravan. Both Lottie and Daisy tried to hold her back, and the rocking alerted Richard to the activity within.

"What's going on?" he called to the back.

"I must save the babies," Victoria gasped.

"We must stop Mammis. She thinks it's that tent fire at camp in Yalesville."

Noah rode up just at that point and Richard called to him. "Help us with Mammis. You always know how to calm her down."

Victoria, her eyes wild and wide-open, struggled out the door and stumbled down the stairs.

Noah, who had dismounted, caught her at the bottom and held her steady. "Mammis, look at the bridge on fire. The bridge across the river to Hartford. It's almost gone."

Victoria tried to focus in the dark, with the sparks and flames shooting across the mile stretch. "The babies," she began.

"No babies. Those were horses. They must have been from the Hartford hose station. Look, the span is burning." They stood watching as the supports burned until they were unable to carry the weight of the span, which sank gracefully and gently into the river. "Only the span near Hartford is still standing."

Victoria squinted into the night.

"Look, Mammis, the beams floating by are still burning. They look like dragons spouting fire at the mouth."

She could see where he pointed and the surroundings began to register. She felt her feet steady a bit on the ground and she took a deep breath.

Noah patted her shoulder. "We are fine, Mammis. Do you need to go home?"

She slowly shook her head. The bridge to Hartford, their link to the capital, was gone. She leaned into Noah. Her world was changing and she wasn't sure where she fit into it any more. She knew she was no longer in charge.

They stood watching the fire, as boats maneuvered through the fiery debris, and people shouted back and forth.

Richard came over to join them. "We're ready to head home. It's already nine-thirty. We have to work tomorrow."

Victoria looked at the river and then at Richard. "How will you get across the river?" she asked.

"I don't know yet. We'll have to see. Ready?"

Noah took Victoria by the elbow and helped her up into the caravan. Wearily, she sank into the sleeping platform. Before they had covered the few blocks back to the Hotel, she was asleep.

When Victoria went down for breakfast the next morning, she spotted a newspaper on the table, its front page covering extensive stories about the fire. "How did they deliver the paper from Hartford?" she asked.

Belcher grunted. "There's ferry service across the river until they can rebuild the bridge. People were grabbing them out of the paperboy's hands."

"Truly? I hope he wasn't hurt." Victoria, reading the features, said, "It doesn't sound like arson." She pointed a finger at the article.

"Really? There was much discussion that suggested it was."

"Hmm, yes, but it seems that the last person who crossed the bridge noticed the fire in only a small section of one span." She looked up. "If it had been arson, I imagine there would have been some type of fuel added that would have burst into flames."

Daisy poured coffee and Victoria muttered, "I wonder if it says anything about the fire horses."

Noah looked startled and started to say something, but Victoria continued scanning until she found the appropriate section. "Yes, here." She read silently for a minute while her sons waited, Noah drumming his fingers on the table.

"Oh, dear," she said, but nothing more as she continued reading.

Richard and Lottie came into the dining room from the innkeeper's quarters. "Good morning," they said to the group clustered around the table.

Noah and Belcher nodded and Victoria started at the sound of their voices. "Oh, my, hallo. It's dreadful," she said, tipping her head towards the newspaper. "The horses were on the cart when the fire escalated. Their driver couldn't turn the cart around and he had no knife to cut the traces."

Victoria's voice trembled and Noah rested his hand on her arm that was holding the paper. "Mammis, you don't need to read about it."

She drew a long breath before continuing, "He had gotten one trace off and one horse was freed from the harness, but it became too dangerous." She was silent for a minute and then gasped as she continued the next paragraph. "Last night, a man rowed around the piers and found the cart and the horses and—" she faltered before completing, "only their ears were out of the water."

"Oh, dear," cried Lottie. "What a shame. A terrible loss."

Richard suggested, "Let's go down again to the river and see for ourselves."

Victoria began to shake her head but her natural curiosity overcame her tender feelings for the horses. The family assembled at the front of the Hotel and Richard again picked them up in his *vardo.*

Thick groups of people lined the shore and there was a buzzing sound similar to a moving hive.

"What's that noise?" asked Daisy, as they climbed down into the mob.

Victoria shook her head, just as Noah pointed across the river. A dark mass lined the river and the noise was coming from that direction. "It's all the people out there," he exclaimed.

"I hear there were twenty thousand last night," contributed someone standing near them.

"Watching?"

"Yes, indeed. Standing on box cars of the trains stranded near the warehouses."

Victoria looked across the river. Only cement stanchions that had held the wooden sheds still stood, one after another, like stepping stones for giants across the water. On the Hartford side, the entrance to the bridge was faintly visible on shore, as it gaped open into empty air. It reminded her of a cicada's shed covering, its head somewhat intact and its body split open and empty.

She shuddered from the sight, at the same time realizing that she hadn't felt Prince since the fire. And she knew that she couldn't stay here alone for the summer.

"How will we head south?" she asked her sons.

Noah and Belcher exhaled with relief and Noah said, "We will take the ferry across the river."

A few days later, Victoria stood as their caravans gathered at the ferry landing. The gold leaf was highlighted by the sunlight striking the inlays of Richard's *vardo* and the silver-plated fittings sparkled. Their horses milled around, snorting and pawing, perhaps sensing the recent death of their colleagues.

Richard's voice carried from the ferry's captain's quarters. "We need to all go together."

"I can't risk it. With twenty horses and three wagons, I cannot fit you all," said Captain Fuller. "The shifting sand bars out there and all the debris make it too dangerous."

"I'll take you all over," shouted Captain Taylor. He was standing on the poop deck of the *Gildersleeve.*

Richard quickly ran over to his ferry. "What's the fare?"

"Five cents for each foot passenger, twenty-five cents for your single team, fifty cents for a double."

"And the individual horses?"

"Ah, ten cents each."

Richard glanced at Noah and Belcher, each of whom nodded slightly. "All right, we will board you."

The sons each drove his caravan onto the ferry and then went to secure the horses. The rest of the family walked toward the ferry.

"Isn't she a bit unusual?" asked Daisy. "What's that on the port side?"

"I think it's the boiler," suggested Lottie. "And the engine is under the Captain's poop deck."

"Perhaps that balances the ship," Daisy suggested hopefully, as she guided Victoria onboard.

It took about a half hour to load the family and their possessions. By then, a group had gathered to watch. During the few days since the fire, people had been coming from all over the state to see the remaining bridge abutments. Some bystanders ventured on the remnants of one of the piers to pry melted iron or wood shards from fallen bridge spans.

Once everything was set, the Captain, windlass in hand, yelled, "Go ahead."

"Why isn't he using the bells or whistle?" asked Victoria. "His yelling is infuriating." She could see a string near the captain that went to a whistle over the boiler and two bell pulls that could communicate with the crew. But the yelling continued.

"Go ahead, I said," he yelled again and used the windlass to direct the ferry. At first, he headed it right across the river in a direct line to the Hartford ferry landing. But she had barely passed the other boats at the pier when the ferry started heading wildly downstream.

"Do you think this captain knows what he's doing?" asked Daisy, as she clung to Victoria's arm.

Captain Taylor, sweat breaking on his brow, was frantically working the windlass until he finally seemed to capture control and the boat again headed across river. He recentered his cap on his head and heaved a sigh.

"The river runs different here than down in Middletown," roared Captain Fuller, laughing as he passed the *Gildersleeve* floundering across the river.

"Go ahead, damn you," screamed Captain Taylor, as his boat again began to slide downstream. This time, his working of the windlass quickly regained control and they finally neared the Ferry Street landing in Hartford. A group of well-dressed people, some using parasols to protect themselves from the sun, stood dockside.

"Stop," he yelled. The momentum of the boat continued to push it rapidly toward the dock. "Back her, back her," he shouted.

Lottie, Victoria, and Daisy were clinging to each other as they watched the pier loom into view.

"Goodness, we are going to die," yelled Daisy.

Lottie closed her eyes and shrieked, while Victoria stood, wide-eyed, as the shore came closer. Her mouth opened and closed several times, but her throat was so dry and her terror so absolute that she couldn't say a thing.

The horses, seeing solid land coming quickly toward them, started in that direction, which made the bow of the boat dip into the water. Seeing the bow awash, Noah and Belcher ran fore and dragged several of the horses aft and watched as the ferry steadied itself. The captain, still screaming, "Back her," looked ready to abandon ship, but the boat finally pulled into a slip, banged from side to side against the restraining piers, and stopped just before ramming into the waiting crowd. With the engines cut, the Captain dropped the windlass and the throng broke into cheers.

"You should charge admission," shouted one young man.

"Quite a show," claimed another.

Captain Taylor, his face crimson, turned to face downstream until the jeering stopped. He pulled a handkerchief from his pocket to wipe his face and neck. Meanwhile, Noah and Belcher had led the horses to disembark and then Richard drove the caravans off the ferry. Once all this was complete, the women were free to leave the ferry and get into the caravans.

"We are on our way," shouted Noah, as they headed south.

TWENTY-ONE

Victoria was jarred from her thoughts, which had involved pleasant sensations of cuddling with Prince, when the *vardo* stopped and Daisy stirred from the seat near her.

"We're here, Mammis." Daisy passed through the door and the caravan swayed a bit as she jumped to the ground.

Victoria wasn't certain where they were and was hesitant to leave her imaginary world to join the real one. But shouting and hubbub outside kept disturbing her daydream and she rose wearily to look out the door. She tentatively stepped out to the bench and sat down, her breath draining from her as she looked up. Victoria felt her body fill with memories as she leaned back to take in the immense expanse of West Rock. New Haven, she identified, that first camp with her new husband. Her heart started beating as she remembered her fear when he discovered that she could read and his subsequent joy of it. She leaned back her head to laugh but caught herself. She was here now with her children and without Prince. Her anchor in time was loose and she fluctuated between feeling her age and reverting to her youth. Fortunately, no one seemed to notice her lack of grounding.

"I'll check up the stock we have here," shouted Richard to Noah and Belcher, "and deliver some of these horses."

They nodded, as they rounded their *vardos* along the field's edge and Richard rode to the sale stable. Victoria glanced around at the trees lining the stream, full from spring rains. The vibrant green buds set against the basalt rocks just made her heart ache for times when she felt that same pulsing of life through her. She doubted that feeling would ever come again, which filled her with sadness.

She woke the next morning with an uncertainty of where she was. Not exactly true, she knew she was in the sleeping platform of a *vardo*. But she had to sort through her thoughts and images to come up with the most recent memory, the one of sitting around a fire the previous night as the hoots of the owls, "Who cooks for you? Who cooks for you all?" echoed off West Rock.

But it was now the next morning, she was certain, as she saw sunlight flickering through the curtains. Victoria shook off the association of danger with the owl calls. A gnawing in her stomach convinced her to swing her legs over the edge and add some layers of clothing. The spring air was still cool at these early hours.

Shortly after breakfast, the family packed their cooking supplies and continued to Bridgeport, where they planned to stay with Prince's brother William and his family for a few days. Sonny came out to meet them, and Victoria, despite her own, was shocked by Sonny's wrinkles and gray hair.

"Hello, sister," greeted Sonny, giving Victoria a hug. But Victoria sensed her reserve. With Prince's passing, there seemed to be a wedge between them, something that identified Victoria as different and as a threat, a hint of their future. At some point, either Sonny or William would leave the other alone and they didn't want to confront it. Victoria could feel the chill and wanted to shout that she didn't like it either, but she knew it was something that could not be verbalized. She felt herself alone in a vast space, abandoned by Prince and Sonny, people she had loved and depended upon. Now her children were the only constants.

"We must leave now, Uncle William," said Noah, his arm around his uncle's shoulder a few days later. Victoria caught a tender glance pass between the two. It was good to have Prince's brother nearby to help her sons, she decided.

"Yes, I expect you must. Making all the usual stops on the way south?"

"I reckon we will," Noah nodded, "although it's up to Richard." William raised an eyebrow and Noah shrugged.

After they said their God-go-with-yous to Sonny and William, they formed a colorful procession of *vardos* that caught the attention of neighbors as they left town. Many people waved gaily at them, while some men stood silently, leering at the caravans.

"I don't understand why they do that," shuddered Lottie.

"They're harmless," said Victoria glibly. "Don't worry about them. We're safe here inside."

During a short stop to attend to some of the horses, Noah suggested, "Let's swing by the old camp near New York."

Victoria made no comment, while the other sons agreed and Daisy nodded vigorously. They traveled the back roads under clear skies. They encountered a few other wagons, passed men riding bicycles, but saw no *vardos* other than their own.

Suddenly, Victoria felt their caravan jerk to a halt and she heard yelling from her family's various *vardos*. She and Daisy moved to the door and peered out.

"What is it?"

"I can't see," said Daisy, as she started to climb down.

"Is it safe?" asked Victoria as she heard a loud noise.

"Ooh," Daisy squealed, Victoria right behind her. Coming toward them was an open wagon in which two men were seated. The vehicle, for that was what it was, had four large iron-rimmed wheels. One of the men grasped a round steering wheel and they were slowly careening from one side of the road to the other.

By then, the whole family was standing by the side of the road, watching.

"Can't you go in a straight line?" taunted Richard.

"Why, mules would get there faster," added Belcher.

"What happens when you run out of fuel?" asked Noah.

The engine backfired, sending Daisy behind her brother for protection.

"Look out, they're headed right for our *vardos*," yelled Victoria. The driver of the vehicle began honking a loud horn but there was no place to move their caravans from the side of the road where they waited.

"Move behind the *vardos*," yelled Richard. The women, Daisy and Lottie dragging Victoria, scrambled up a small embankment, with the thought that their caravans would shield them from the major impact.

"Be careful, Noah," cried Victoria when she noted that he was trying to unhitch the horses to move them to safety.

Fortunately, at the last minute, the steering engaged and the vehicle bounced down the center of the road for a bit.

"Watch where you're going," yelled Richard. "You could have killed us."

"It should be illegal for you to be on the roads in that," shouted Belcher.

The women gingerly climbed down from their small hill and

joined the rest of the family.

"Everyone all right?" asked Noah.

The women nodded and Belcher reported that the horses were calming down. One had snapped a strap while trying to escape from the oncoming danger, so Belcher made to replace the damaged leather.

"Guess that will never take the place of a dependable horse. Even the most stubborn of them is better than that contraption," laughed Noah.

A short time later, as they skirted the city, Victoria caught sight of the New York skyline filled with tall buildings. She could envision the busy streets thronging with horses and wagons, horse-drawn trolleys, and men hurrying along crowded sidewalks under the flagpoles of various offices. As her mind sank deeper into the image, along Broadway she could see the striped canopies that protected the pedestrians from inclement weather, and she continued to travel in the direction of the harbor. Her heart beat faster and faster as she saw the tall masts of the *Josephine* and its bowsprit hovering near the windows of the buildings lining the wharfs. A sudden jolt of the *vardo* brought her back to the present and she squinted at the distant view of the city. Nostalgically, she remembered her first view of New York and her visions of how life would be in America. Slightly embarrassed, she recalled her expectations of the savages in the new land and how it contrasted with her actual meeting of Sonny. Things weren't always as expected.

They pulled into the marshlands smoky from campfires and reeling with the sound of fiddles. Victoria felt herself swirled into a vortex of memories and sat still near their fire, while the others headed to the dance area or to the streams to gather water. She wondered if everything she did and everywhere she went would remind her of the past. If there was no more future, she wasn't certain she could bear it.

"Mammis," breathed Daisy, returning to the fire. "There are so many people dancing. Come with me to watch?"

Victoria shook her head. "No, go ahead back and enjoy yourself. I will go to sleep soon."

"Are you certain you don't want to watch?"

She smiled at her daughter. "I've had my share of the dance area." She thought back to her first trip here and the choking baby she had saved, the beginning of her work as a healer.

Daisy took her hand. "Are you certain, Mammis? If you don't want to come, I'll stay here with you."

"I need no company and you don't need to deprive yourself. Go ahead. I'll hear about it in the morning."

Daisy ran back to the music and Victoria sat alone, listening to the fiddle. She could feel the ground vibrating under the stamping feet of the dancers and allowed it to travel up her legs and spine as she sat. She tried to find its joy, the energy from the music, but it eluded her. This was where she and Prince had stopped on their trip north after their wedding, and it was where she had learned about Mary Defiance. She shook her head to banish that thought, but it stuck tight. No wonder she couldn't find the music inside her.

A few days later, they found themselves in camp outside of Philadelphia. Here she felt the presence of her parents when they had landed from their second trip from England. She sensed an arm around her now, protecting her and providing company. As much as she expected that from her parents, she also felt a tickling along her cheek, as if a moustache were rubbing alongside. She wondered if it were possible that Prince's *muló* might have found her. Her heart started to soar with the idea that he might accompany her on the rest of their summer journey.

Spring turned quickly into summer as they continued south. Victoria enjoyed the green of the countryside, the emerging vegetation, and flowering trees. She felt the tickle on her cheek and let her eyes lose their focus as they looked across the rolling green hills. Horse farm country, she knew, and a good source for their livelihood. Life had a new lease, a fresh breath, even if she felt as though she weren't truly part of it but was watching from a distance. Ah, she and Prince were fortunate to come to this country, and she sighed.

"Are you all right, Mammis?" asked Noah.

"Yes, dear."

"Are you certain? You haven't done any foraging or cooking so far."

She looked closely at her son. "Things have changed for me. I am letting you children take my place. In fact," she said, "I think it's about time you get married. And Belcher, too."

"Married, Mammis?"

"Yes. Richard has Lottie and you two need wives. How else can I teach them to make great tipsy cake or gather ferns?"

Noah opened his mouth and then apparently thought better of it.

She would pursue this idea once a year had passed after Prince's death, the appropriate mourning period before a happy occasion.

"In the spring," she said as she felt the tickling at her chin. Her eyes welled slightly with tears from Prince's confirmation of this plan. "Your father would approve."

Noah nodded and rose. She watched out of the corner of her eye as he tried to walk inconspicuously to Belcher and pull him aside. She giggled slightly as she imagined his reaction to her idea. Prince, she said to some vague sense of him in her head, we must keep the family going somehow. All our sons need children to work in the business.

After several weeks, they arrived on the outskirts of the nation's capital. The large white Capitol dome and Washington's obelisk monument, punctuated by an occasional church steeple, dominated its skyline. The combination of forest and fields that surrounded the city was pleasing to the eye and felt comfortable to Victoria and her family.

"Mammis, we're going to camp here near the river," announced Richard. "There are so many horse farms nearby and we'll do well here."

"And you can do some *dukkering*," added Belcher, providing her with a role and a potential return to normalcy.

Victoria nodded and they settled into their daily routine.

The day had started out just like many others. Victoria sat on her chair, wishing she were invisible or non-existent or somewhere else. Camp was virtually empty and there she was in her *ofisa* hoping that no one would come by. She knew that her *dukkering* income helped the family and it was the least she could do these days, but truly her heart wasn't in it. Even the fluttering whisper that reminded her of Prince was absent today and she just felt lonely.

She glanced at the sun. Only morning and many hours before the boys would return from their horse dealing. Daisy and Lottie had headed off to do the washing. Victoria mused that the weather was at least good for that: sunny and hot. Raising her skirts under the table to cool off, she resigned herself to watching the moments tick by. Moving her chair slightly to remain in the shade, she noticed a woman with an unusual gait walking in her direction. The woman was tall, gangly, with hair pulled under a bonnet. Although she was well dressed, her arms were swinging along with her legs, making her look a bit like a puppet on a string. Haltingly and in spurts, she made her way to Victoria's makeshift shack. Oh, dear, Victoria realized, a customer. She gathered her skirts back into place and straightened herself at her table.

"Good morning."

"Oh, hello, am I in the right place?" sputtered the woman. She paused to catch her breath. "Fortunes?"

"Yes, dear, have a seat," said Victoria, gesturing to a stool nearby, her bracelets jangling as she moved her arm.

The woman sat on its edge, leaning her lanky body dangerously close to Victoria. The customer thrust her chin into the air and tried to keep her arms from gesturing by clasping her hands in her lap.

Victoria tried to clear her thoughts but the image of this woman's approach kept replaying in her mind. After a minute, she cleared her throat. "How may I help you?"

"Isn't that what you are supposed to know?" Her voice had an irritating rasp in addition to a condescending tone.

Victoria didn't have enough energy or interest to rise to the bait. After a beat, she replied, "What area is of interest to you?"

The woman nearly fell off the stool with her eager answer. "My husband. I want to know about my husband."

Victoria began to get an image of a well-dressed man, also tall with a shank of straight hair plastered over his forehead. She waited.

"Is he—does he—is he seeing—well, has he ever—" the woman could barely put together her words and then it came out with a rush, "Is he seeing another woman?"

Victoria looked at her, nodded and then closed her eyes. She willed herself to forget about the craning woman before her and focus on her view of the man. His image became clearer as he strode down the street. Victoria saw him smile at a beautiful woman with long flowing hair whom he followed into a doorway and up some stairs. Victoria averted her eyes and a few minutes passed before she saw the man again, this time with his arm around a shapely woman, wearing a dress that quite emphasized her buxom nature. He was looking down her bodice and the woman playfully slapped his cheek before he bent to nuzzle her. Victoria again averted her eyes and waited. Finally she saw the man walking down streets at night, looking first in one alley and then another, before stealthily turning down a third, and rapping a series of knocks on a wooden door. When it opened a crack, Victoria could make out a young woman's face with large eyes and blonde hair, who reached out for him and pulled him into the doorway, just as he pressed his lips to hers.

Victoria realized she couldn't possibly pretend that all was fine at home. She slowly opened her eyes, only to see the woman's intent blue eyes peering, fixed, at her.

"Is he true to me?"

Victoria shook her head, afraid to say anything.

The woman rapidly unfolded her lanky legs to stand. "Why, that vile wretch!" she shouted. "Seeing another woman." She paused and then blurted, "There is only one?"

Victoria shook her head.

"What? More than one other?"

"Yes."

"Two, then."

Victoria cast her eyes on the table and shook her head.

"Truly, more than two! Dear God, he will suffer." She threw coins on the table and strode off in her angular, jerky fashion back to town.

Victoria sighed, trying to relax from the interchange. She so hated that type of visit under any circumstances, but the intensity of this woman was overbearing.

The rest of the day passed slowly and still Victoria was alone in camp. She dozed in her chair and was having pleasant visions of times with Prince when she was brought to by a loud crack of a whip.

"Are you the fortune teller?" shouted a man.

She opened her eyes to see the man of her vision standing in front of her. Before she could reply, he pulled back, unleashed the coil, cracked it across her head, and screamed, "How dare you tell my wife about other women?"

Out of the corner of her eye, she saw her *diklo* go flying and felt blood running down her face. In a panic, Victoria placed her hands over her face just as he pulled back the whip and struck her again, this time on the hand, and she started to holler. Her bracelets protected her arms, but her hands took the impact of the whip.

"Oh, so, you think if you scream, I'll stop. You wretch, it only makes me want to hurt you more," he sneered, as he lifted the whip to strike again.

Beyond the stinging pain, she feared that this man's anger would totally consume him to the point of killing her. As he pulled back his arm again, she leaned to the left, ducking under the table to remove herself from his access. On the ground, she spotted a stout stick. She reached down with a fluid movement and grabbed it just as she felt the strength of Prince filling her body. With a start, she rose, brandished the stick, and yelled at the man, "You cheater!" She rushed at him, ousting the whip from his hand with a shove of the stick. She looked, sickened, as the stick, apparently rotten, broke in half from the force.

He stood wide-mouthed, taken aback for just a brief moment. Forming his hands into fists, he took advantage of her proximity to hit her, first on her arms and then on her head and face. She tried to shield herself from his barrage, but he continued to strike her arms as they covered her face. Filled with anger and fear, she shifted her weight onto both legs and began to pummel him, striking left and right at any part of his body that she could find.

Suddenly she heard yelling coming from the river and realized that Daisy and Lottie were on their way. "They are coming to protect me," she yelled. "You better run for your life."

The man looked and then laughed. "It's only two women. I can beat them, also." He turned to face the young women, while Victoria, her strength failing, continued to hit him in the back. When she glanced down the road behind her, she saw her three sons charging towards them. As they reached camp and dismounted, Noah had grabbed a stool and Richard an iron bar, while Belcher was bare-fisted. The three let out cries like wild men, which caused the man to whip around. When he saw them, he jerked and turned to jump on his waiting horse and gallop down the road to town. They gave good chase but he had enough of a head start that he disappeared.

Gasping for breath, the three returned to the *ofisa* where Daisy was trying to help Victoria. "That man, that wretch of a man, how vile he was," Daisy sputtered. "Let me clean you up. Are you badly hurt?"

Victoria shuddered, recalling the impact of the whip and his fists. She felt the world closing in around her and she couldn't breathe. She collapsed to the ground, her mind a swirling mass of arms and hands and whips coming at her from all sides.

The pain of someone touching her face brought her back. "No, stop, you wretch," she yelled. Her fist reached out to stop the cause of the pain and someone caught her wrist and turned her arm away. Her anger grew and she tried to pull herself away, despite the soothing voice whispering in her ear. She thrashed in all directions, making contact at times and not others, until she fell, exhausted, into blackness.

Later, she could barely open her eyes, they were so swollen. She could tell it was dark and smelled a fire. She struggled to sit up, but her arms were too sore to hold her weight. She felt someone come towards her and she cried out in fear.

"It's me, Mammis, I'll help you."

She felt gentle arms lift her into a sitting position and she balanced herself upright. Her head started spinning and she tried to touch her head, but she noticed that her fingers were bandaged. The pain in her head was blinding and she felt nauseated. Someone handed her a cup of something warm and she tried to take a sip. Her lips were split and the liquid stung her mouth. She recognized the taste of willow bark tea and knew she would benefit from drinking, so she struggled to down some of it.

When she next opened her eyes, it was daylight and she saw that she was propped up on pillows near the kettle. She tried to move but winced from the pain, which attracted Daisy's attention.

"Mammis, let me help you."

Together, they were able to shift her position.

"Let me get you some tea."

Victoria nodded and felt her eyes bulge from her head as she did so. She again tried to touch her head, this time with the palms of her hands, and she could feel a series of welts running along her scalp.

Victoria heard steps behind her and she gasped to Daisy, "Help me, someone is coming."

"It's Lottie, Mammis, it's all right. Here's your tea."

"Oh," Victoria inhaled. She had to hold the cup with two hands and managed small sips.

"You're lucky that he didn't break any of your bones," said Daisy.

Victoria didn't agree. She felt violated, no longer safe.

"Richard and Noah went into town to see about your attacker."

"No," shouted Victoria.

Startled, Daisy jumped and Lottie gave a little scream.

"Don't let them get hurt. He's a madman."

Daisy put her arm around Victoria. "It will be fine, Mammis. The police are helping."

Just then, they heard horses returning to camp.

"Quick, hide," whispered Victoria, clawing Daisy's arm. "Help me into the woods."

"Shh, shh, Mammis, it's Noah and Richard. Let's hear what they have to say."

Victoria looked in the direction of the noise but could see only blurred forms coming toward her. She started shaking and calmed only slightly when they called out to her.

"Mammis," said Noah. "He's in jail."

"Yes, they put his bond at two thousand dollars."

She heard Richard say aside to Lottie, "They are waiting to see what her injuries are. Do you think we can get her to the hospital?"

Lottie whispered, "I don't think so. She's terrified of every noise. I think she's suffering from nervous prostration."

"But why would I not be frightened? My camp has been attacked and we are not safe. We must move, go to another place." Victoria was turning her head, speaking in the direction of the various forms she could see, although she truly had no idea which one was Noah or Daisy.

"Mammis, we can leave tomorrow. They won't let him out of jail before that."

"Here, Mammis, have some more tea. It will help your head."

"Let me wash your wounds with this."

"I'll help you."

The voices swam around her and she felt someone unbandage her fingers and gasp. Victoria felt herself slide away.

The *vardo*'s movement hurt her head, even as she was buffered by pillows and comforters in her sleeping area. She groaned and felt herself on fire, the heat radiating from her hands and around her ears.

"Here, drink."

And she did.

TWENTY-TWO

Several weeks passed before Victoria was well enough to sit up while traveling. She perched herself in the sleeping area and was grateful for the caravan's shade, although it grew warm inside. Occasionally, she opened her eyes and looked out the rear window. Their *vardo* wheels raised large clouds of dust as they traveled down the hot, southern roads through Virginia and into North Carolina.

Victoria fanned herself with her skirts and used the corner of her *diklo* to wipe the sweat off her face. Sighing, she traced the welt marks on her hands and along her head. All her wounds had healed and the scabs fallen off but she wondered if the reminders of her attack would ever disappear.

She jumped as someone moved towards her, only to register that it was Daisy offering a cool drink.

"Mammis, do you want to move yet?"

Victoria moved an arm and shifted her weight. "No, daughter, I am still sore."

"All right. Let me know if you need anything."

"Thank you, dear."

Daisy left to sit out on the bench and Victoria turned gingerly on her side to watch out the rear window. She saw Spanish moss hanging down from the great live oaks that shaded the road. Soon they would be heading away from the coastal plain and into the hills. She hoped it would be cooler there and less humid. It wasn't long before she was lulled to a fitful sleep.

A heavy jostle as the caravan hit a rut woke her, and she sputtered from righteous indignation that was developing as a result of the brutal attack by the three-timing man. She thought that was an improvement over fear, but she was determined to remain awake to avoid either. She returned her gaze to the road behind them and was startled. She tried to open her still swollen eyes wider and wiped them with her *diklo* in a vain effort to see more clearly. But certainly, behind the dust of their caravan, she spotted in the distance a team of four large black horses majestically stepping towards them. Her face drained, fingers grew cold, and her heart threatened to explode. Behind them was a large black covered wagon that could mean only one thing.

Heart pounding and mouth dry, Victoria fell back into the corner. She had seen that procession previously, during her brother Samuel's funeral. She shuddered, remembering when her brother Richard had taken sick the year after Samuel's death. Victoria became nauseated as she felt herself swirl into the vortex of those memories.

Five years earlier, that January after Samuel's death, she had been in the kitchen of the old Farmer's Hotel with Daisy, chopping vegetables for the stew and thinking about her family.

"Your uncle Samuel was only sixty," she said aloud to Daisy. "Our father, your grandfather, lived into his seventies, although you never met him."

Daisy nodded. "But I remember stories about him."

"Ah, yes, but your uncles Richard and Samuel were the ones who truly raised me. They took care of me so many times, I don't know what I would have done without them."

"I feel that way about my brothers, also," smiled Daisy.

Victoria gave her a little squeeze on the shoulder. "I'm sure you do, being so much younger. Why, Wash is almost twenty years older than you! Samuel was only eight years older than I am."

She handed Daisy a board filled with chopped onions and carrots to add to the kettle. The image of Samuel's hearse being drawn by four black horses kept trotting across her vision. Victoria shook her head, trying to dispel the vision.

"So hard for Jennie, to be left with so many young children, too," Victoria sighed. "Little Esau is only ten. Too young to be without a father." She moved around the kitchen to the sink. "But what can you do?"

Nothing, she knew, but the disruption of her brother's family upset her sense of order and balance. And Prince wasn't much younger than her brother, which caused her unrest, also.

On cue, Prince came in through the back door and she could hear him taking off his boots and coat.

"Hallo, dear," he said, as he came into the kitchen and nibbled Victoria's ear. "It's cold out there."

"Ooh, your nose is freezing," she laughed. "Let's go sit by the fire together."

They walked across to the living room and sat on the sofa, Prince rubbing his hands together. Victoria saw the four horses out of the corner of her eye. "Prince," she started.

"Yes, dear?"

"Are you feeling well?"

Prince looked sharply at her. "Of course, I am fine. Why?"

"Nothing."

Prince tucked Victoria closer to him. "With you, it's never 'nothing.' Why did you ask?"

"I am feeling unsettled." She hesitated and then blurted out, "I keep seeing Samuel's hearse."

"Oh, my dear," said Prince, caressing her face. "That's what's upsetting you. Well, I am in fine shape, don't you worry." Prince puffed out his chest as he sat next to her and tickled her cheek with his moustache.

"I worry about poor Jennie, left with all those children. If anything happens to us—"

Prince waited, but Victoria didn't or couldn't continue, so he spoke. "Wash is perfectly capable of taking over if something happens to me. He is a genius with the business and gifted with the horses."

"And his brothers adore him."

"Yes, all of them—Richard, Noah, and Belcher—will be willing to follow his lead." He gently cuffed her on the head. "Don't you worry."

She smiled weakly at him, as the horses pawed their way across the room. "Then why am I seeing Samuel's horses?"

Prince's smile faded, his eyes serious. "I certainly can't tell you that. Is there no more message?"

Victoria sat, eyes closed, sheltered and safe in Prince's embrace. They heard the hissing of the fire and clattering from the kitchen where Daisy had continued dinner preparation. Otherwise, all was still. Victoria could hear Prince breathing and they synchronized their intake and out-breath. But still, all she saw was the team of horses.

"Nothing."

"Perhaps it is nothing?"

"It never is."

Prince nodded. "I know. I guess we shall wait to see."

Only a few hours later, the runner knocked on the front door. When Victoria saw him, she felt herself grow weak and had to sit. She knew it would be something serious, a matter that the family wouldn't trust to prying *gadje* eyes of a telegraph operator.

"Your brother Richard has taken ill," he said.

"Oh," gasped Victoria, "now Richard." The four horses snorted in the winter air, puffs of vapor rising from their nostrils.

Prince sat next to her, quickly putting his arm around her for support.

"I must leave right away," she said.

"I can't go with you. There's a shipment of horses arriving shortly from Canada."

"Perhaps Wash can—"

"No, I need him, too. Noah will go with you."

"Noah?"

"Yes. He's eighteen and can take you in the sleigh. I'll go let him know." Prince heaved himself up from the sofa. He lifted Victoria's face with a few fingers under her chin. "I'm sorry, Princess," he said softly, as he wiped tears from her face.

Prince called Daisy, who went upstairs to pack a bag for Victoria sitting numbly on the sofa. She heard Prince go out the back door, presumably to rouse Noah. She couldn't move. She couldn't believe that her other dear brother was on his deathbed, not even a year since Samuel had been on his. She felt as if her very being, the fabric of who she was, was being shredded. She had known she loved her brothers but she didn't realize how central they were to her existence.

Within a short time, Victoria found herself tucked into the sleigh, surrounded by buffalo robes with Noah at the reins.

"Don't forget to stop in Willimantic to switch horses," Prince reminded Noah. "Your brother Richard is at the stable there."

"I remember, Dadrus," sighed the young man.

"God go with you," said Prince, as he kissed Victoria goodbye. "We should be able to join you after the shipment arrives and the horses are settled." He paused. "I hope that won't be too late."

Victoria stifled a sob and nodded.

"Gee," shouted Noah, and they turned right from the driveway onto the main road and set off. Victoria recognized the snow-covered terrain as they headed east. Wide-open fields were dotted with tracks from animals and small slopes had sledding tracks. Several ponds had been cleared of snow and children wearing brightly colored wool caps were skating and warming up at a small pond-side fire. But these pleasant images were lost on Victoria. She saw the scenes but they didn't register as the hours passed by.

"Mammis, are you warm enough?"

She nodded, having no idea if she had lost feeling in her feet and hands due to the temperature or her emotional state. The four black horses kept alongside them as they headed into Willimantic and towards their sale barn. She was terrified that they would move ahead of her sleigh and it would be too late when she reached her brother, but she knew they had to refresh their horse.

"Whoa," shouted Noah, and they coasted to a halt at the barn's entrance. Richard, surprised, came out to meet them.

"Mammis, Noah, what is wrong? Why are you here?"

"It's your uncle Richard. He's taken ill and we are going to Somerville."

"We need to switch out the horse. Which one shall we take?" asked Noah.

Her sons busied themselves with the sleigh while Victoria warmed herself before the fire in the office. She kept wringing her hands but that didn't warm them either. When she saw the four horses waiting for them outside the gates of the sale barn, she felt more confident that her brother would still be alive when they eventually arrived.

One of the grooms came in with several bowls of soup and the three of them sat down once the boys came inside.

"Any idea what's wrong?"

"The runner didn't know."

"Isn't he younger than Uncle Samuel was?"

"No, he was a few years older."

"Will they bury his fiddle with him?"

Noah gave Richard a jab.

"So sorry. I was just wondering."

"Mammis, do you think we should stop here for the night? It's getting dark already."

Victoria looked around and noticed that Noah was right and that the four horses were waiting patiently. "I suppose so. We won't be able to go much farther tonight and it would be safer to stay here."

Richard bustled around to prepare some sleeping areas, while Noah retraced his steps to the barn to unhitch the horse. When he returned, they sat around the fire to stay warm until it was time to sleep.

It was quite early the next morning when they set off. Without the typical harness bells, which Noah had removed before they had left the old Farmer's Hotel the day before, their departure was quiet, almost ghostly. The sun shone weakly in the January sky and the snow on the ground provided the perfect surface for their journey.

Rhythmic movements of the horse and sleigh lulled a worried Victoria into sleep, which had eluded her during much of the night. She startled awake when she heard the trotting of the solemn procession alongside them. She looked but knew she would see nothing real, only the phantom hearse.

It was dark by the time they reached Richard's Somerville home. The yard was filled with *vardos* and horses, campfires, and people. Noah pulled as close to the front door as he could and helped Victoria down. They walked up the trodden snow path and the door opened before they could knock.

"Aunt Victoria," cried Theresa, her brother Samuel's daughter. "We're so glad you are here. My mother is not well and Aunt Margaret is crying all day. We know you will help us."

Victoria felt the heavy uncertainty lift, replaced by her sense of being useful. She could no longer wallow in self-pity about the loss of her brothers; their wives and families needed her. She put her arm around the teenager and gave her a hug. "Can you help Noah bring in our things?"

Theresa nodded and Victoria entered the house. The smell of sickness was pervasive and it took all her willpower to remain inside and not escape outdoors with Theresa and Noah. She walked with determination into the sitting room, where she found Margaret sobbing.

"You poor dear," cried Victoria, as she settled next to her.

"Oh, Princess, you're here." Margaret wiped her red eyes and tried to smile. "Tell me, what do you vision?"

Victoria inhaled sharply. She didn't want to tell Margaret about the horses, at least not yet, but she knew she couldn't lie. "Let me settle in and I'll tell you. May I see Richard?"

"Of course." Margaret glanced around and called to her daughter-in-law, "Brittania, can you take Aunt Victoria upstairs?"

"Certainly," said the woman and she led the way. As she stepped on each stair, Victoria willed herself calmness and strength as she inhaled the growing smell of sickness. When they reached the landing, she felt focused enough to be with her brother. Brittania led her down a short hallway and stood in a doorway on the left. Gesturing to Victoria, she stood to the side and allowed Victoria to enter first. Richard's room was dark and he smelled of sweat. Brittania followed to light a candle and its shadow flickered on Richard's face. He opened his eyes and they focused slowly on Victoria. "Princess, you're here. Am I dying then?"

"I don't know yet, brother. How do you feel?"

There was a long pause, so long that Victoria wondered if Richard had just passed. "Actually, I feel better. I had the fever and now I am more comfortable."

Victoria sat on his bed and pressed the back of her palm across his forehead. Indeed, he felt normal. She took his hand and felt for the beating of his heart, which sounded steady and calm.

"In fact, I may be hungry," he added.

Victoria looked at Brittania, who nodded and went downstairs for some broth. Richard certainly looked wan and had clearly been ill. When Brittania returned with a bowl, Victoria left them and returned downstairs.

"Margaret, he's eating."

"What? Are you quite sure?"

"Yes, I am."

Margaret, letting out a long sigh, said, "Thank you." Victoria made no comment, as she certainly didn't feel responsible for his apparent recovery.

"All it took was for you to come," Margaret continued. "Jennie," she yelled into the other room, "Princess says Richard is better."

Jennie, her face haggard with her own grief, came into the room to join them. "Better?"

"Well, he asked for food," Victoria clarified, still struggling with what to make of her black horse image.

Noah and Theresa returned with their bags and Jennie sent them off to a spare room.

"We are so glad you are here," said Jennie. "I wish you could have come for Samuel. You might have saved him, also."

"Oh, Jennie, I would have if I had been nearby. We had already headed south." Victoria rocked her sister-in-law who shuddered with sobs. When Noah and Theresa returned, Theresa sat next to her mother and patted her back. Eventually, Jennie calmed and they all were quiet.

Victoria settled back in a chair by the fire. It had been a long trip, filled with worry, and Victoria felt herself relax with the relief of finding her brother Richard not only alive but also seemingly recovering. She drifted, hearing the murmur of voices in the background. She felt the heat of the fire warming her, but her hands and feet remained cold. This confused her, but in her half-muddled dream-state, she chose to ignore it.

But she could not ignore the rumbling of the hearse and plodding of the four black horses that returned in her dreams. She must have shouted out, because she awoke with Margaret's hand on her shoulder.

"What is it, Princess?"

Victoria shuddered.

"Not good, I say. Princess, tell me, I need to know. I am strong enough."

Victoria hesitated but Margaret grabbed her hand. "What, you are chilled. You must tell me. You see death, I can tell."

Victoria nodded and then let loose a torrent of words explaining what she'd been seeing.

"Four horses and a carriage like Samuel's. That can't be good," said Margaret.

Victoria shook her head. "But he did seem better when I was upstairs."

Brittania came into the room with an empty bowl. "He just finished his soup."

"Maybe it is just the lull before the storm," Margaret suggested, fearfully. "You know how people sometimes rally before they depart? Perhaps that is what we are witnessing."

"I don't know," said Victoria.

For the next few days, Richard continued to eat and improve. And Victoria continued to see the four horses. "I don't understand," she said to Noah. "I don't want to worry Aunt Margaret but I feel death coming."

"You must trust yourself, Mammis. You are the one with vision."

"Yes, a blessing and a curse," she said, shaking her head as they went to join the family for dinner.

It was while they were eating that Wash's wife, Patience, carrying their two small children, came running into the house. Living separately from Wash for a few years, Patience was in Somerville with her father, one of Victoria's brothers.

"Oh, Aunt Victoria," she gasped. "You have to go home."

Patience fell into a heap on the floor with the children crying around her. Brittania quickly gathered up the children and Theresa tried to help Patience up. Her hands were flying, as if she were trying to grasp something solid that would help provide some sense to what was happening. They were able to move her to the sitting room where everyone joined her.

"What is it, Patience?" asked Noah. He never knew what happened between her and his brother Wash, but she had always been kind to him. He tried to comfort her but Patience started to howl and scream. She gasped and cried and no one could tell what she was saying. Finally, she drew a deep breath and blurted out, "The runner. He came to my house. It's Wash. He's dyyyy-ing." With her final word turning into a wail, she threw herself onto the floor again and started banging her head on the sofa.

Victoria stood, in shock. The four horses grew larger and louder. They headed directly towards her and she could see their nostrils, their tongues working the bit, their hooves rising and lowering in the air. Any second, they would be on top of her and she screamed.

Noise and chaos prevented anyone from hearing the weak voice calling from above. Eventually there was a lull in the outbursts and Britannia cocked her head.

"I'll go see what he wants," she announced to anyone who might be listening. Her movement caught Victoria's attention, and she let go of Noah to sit shakily on her own. Her clan's future rested on their wonder-son's shoulders, which were now facing the four black horses. Wash had always been so special, and Victoria had never seen this coming.

"We must leave right away," she declared. "Patience, do you want to come with us?"

The younger woman shuddered and gasped. "I—I can't. I can't come but I so wish I could see Wash before—" With that she broke into new sobs.

"Mammis, maybe you should take the train?" suggested Noah. "Or we can leave first light, change horses in Willimantic, and be back at the Hotel by nightfall tomorrow."

Victoria felt awash with uncertainty. "You can't travel back alone, even though my taking the train would be faster."

"I'll go with Noah," suggested Theresa.

"But you're only a child. You'll be more harm than help."

"I'm fourteen and I can drive a horse and prepare meals," she said proudly.

Jennie spoke up. "Theresa has been a great help to me. I'm sure she won't be a burden to Noah and can keep him awake."

"One of my grooms can take you to the train station. The first train tomorrow leaves before nine o'clock," added Margaret.

Victoria smelled horse sweat and felt their face bristles brushing her hand. The rumbling of ghostly wheels gyrated through her digestive system and she knew she had to get to Wash quickly. "Yes, the train tomorrow morning. Thank you, Margaret. And Theresa. Yes."

TWENTY-THREE

Victoria sat on the train, her whole body numb and exhausted from lack of sleep. She had hoped that someone in the family would ride with her, so she wouldn't have to think, but she was alone. Alone with four horses and a hearse.

The train sounded its whistle and slowly glided from the station. It gathered speed and the clickity-clack of the wheels on the track was reassuring. It matched her heartbeat and she felt its life-giving force, bringing her to Wash. Perhaps she could save him. She tried to still her thoughts but questions kept arriving: where was Prince, was Wash suffering, could Prince survive if Wash didn't, and on and on it went. She tried breathing deeply and looking out the window. As the train rounded a curve, she could see the engine leading the line of cars and she gasped as she saw, ahead of the engine, four horses and a hearse leading them down the track. The race was on.

She knew she couldn't hurry the train and it infuriated her. Chewing on the inside of her mouth, she tried to calm herself enough to vision what was wrong with Wash but she was unable. All she knew was that she needed to get there before the four horses, and they were in the lead.

Victoria ticked off every second of the trip, but, eventually, the train whistled and began to slow as it crossed the Connecticut River. She looked out the window and could almost see the old Farmer's Hotel. She had thought to disembark here near home, but Wash was at his shanty in Hartford and that was where she was needed. She had sent Prince a telegram and hoped it had arrived and that someone, especially Prince, would be at the Hartford station to meet her. She didn't trust the *gadje* system but she had decided that the

BETH LAPIN

runners would never get from Somerville to East Hartford before her train.

Whistle blowing and engine slowing, the train edged into the Hartford station. Victoria, looking frantically left and right, made her way down the steps, but no one was waiting along the track. She walked briskly into the station and quickly surveyed the waiting room but recognized no one. She went outside and saw no one familiar there, either. She felt the urgent need to get to Wash's and called out to a hack.

"Yes, ma'am?"

"To Westland Street."

The young man helped her into the cab and he gave a crack to his whip and headed north. It was late morning and all the shops along Main Street were open and showing their wares, except the Hebrew stores which were closed for the Sabbath. When they arrived at Westland Street, they turned and she called out for the driver to stop when he reached Mr. Ludlow's stables. Victoria could see Wash's shack behind the buildings as she dismounted and, with hands shaking as she frantically pawed through her clothes for some coins, paid the driver.

"Do you want me to wait?"

Victoria glanced around quickly and noticed her son Richard's favorite horse nearby. "No, thank you."

"I could drive in closer."

Anxious to be on her way, Victoria glanced down the snow-covered path and shook her head. "No, no, I'll walk. Thank you. God go with you." And she turned to face the shack and began to walk, almost run, towards it. As she neared, she could hear the voices of her sons and, as desperately as she wanted to see Wash, she paused to listen.

"Dickie," said Wash, his voice weakened. Victoria almost sobbed when she heard him use Richard's pet name. "I am truly sick and I think I may not recover. If I die, I want all my property to go to my wife, for you and Dadrus already have enough."

She could hear muttering from Richard and then Wash continued, "You will find four thousand dollars sewed in my old vest. You know the one I always wear during horse sales?"

"Of course," said Richard.

"I have another thousand dollars in various clothes that I have, hidden in the usual spots. You'll have to search for that."

"All right," said Richard with eagerness in his voice.

224

"And see that floor board over near the wall? No, not that one, the lighter one?"

Victoria could hear a chair scraping along the floor. After a pause, Wash continued, "Yes, that one. There is about a thousand dollars in gold in a tin cup under there."

She heard someone get up and add more coal to the fire.

"You know, of course, about my *vardo* here and I have ten...no, a dozen horses here. You'll remember all this?"

"Of course, Wash."

"And it all goes to my wife and children."

"Right, Wash."

"And I want a fine funeral, the Gypsy way. Please spare no expense for my coffin and I want my hearse to be pulled by four black horses. If there aren't—"

Victoria heard no more, as she collapsed in the snow, calling, "Wash, Wash, my son!"

Richard threw back the door and emerged from the shanty to lift her from the ground. "Mammis! When did you get here? I thought you were in Somerville. Come inside." He guided her into the shed, closed the door, and led her to a chair. But she made straight for Wash.

"Oh, my son, what is wrong?" she gasped at the sight of him. His cheeks and nose were fire-red and his eyes were sunken into his face. She touched his hand that he offered from under his stained linen cover and it was burning with fever.

"Mammis, oh, Mammis, can you save me? I am dying."

"Wash, what happened?"

"I don't know, Mammis. I slipped while I was clearing snow from my *vardo* and scraped my face on the step. I didn't think it would fester, it was just a small scratch. I started getting the chills and a terrible headache and then this rash and I couldn't move."

Victoria felt a desperate need to do something to help him. She reached for a cloth, tore it into pieces, and looked around the shanty. "Do you have any water?"

Wash nodded to a small bucket in the corner, and she dipped the rag in the cold water and started to wash his arms.

"Are you sure you should touch me? Could you catch this from me?"

Victoria shook her head. "I don't really care," she said.

"Mammis," said Richard, "don't talk like that."

She shot him a foul look and continued to gently stroke her eldest son's arms and hands. She twisted the cloth in the cool water again and touched his face. Wash grimaced when she touched his cheeks, so she just rested the cloth on first one side and then the other of his face. He relaxed a bit and said, "That is soothing, Mammis, although I don't know if it's the cloth or just knowing you are here." He closed his eyes a moment and then looked at her. "I thought you were with Uncle Richard. How is—did he—"

"He seems to have recovered. Or at least he was interested in eating when I left. Patience and the children—" She noticed that Wash winced at the mention of his wife's name. "Richard," she turned to say, "can you fill the bucket with fresh water?"

He nodded and left the shanty. Victoria, calming her breaking heart, started touching Wash's shoulder and arms.

"It hurts here, under my arms," he gestured. She palpated under his armpits and felt the small swollen nodes. Victoria sensed his whole body was trying to fight the festering on Wash's face. She gently rolled aside his covers and pressed through his trousers in the depression where his legs joined his torso to check the status of his other glands. Wash gasped and reflexively reached between his legs.

Startled, Victoria stopped her prodding. "I'm sorry. That hurts?"

"Not exactly there, but my *pele*," he said, gradually releasing his scrotum. "They ache and feel so hot and sore." His face reddened even more and he looked imploringly at her. "That's why I sent Patience away. Her presence, my desire for her, caused my *pele* so much pain that I had to be apart from her." Deep sobs ripped from him as he clutched the covers. "I miss her and the children so."

"Oh, my son, she feels the same, if it's any consolation." Victoria was stricken with sadness by this unnecessary separation. "Why didn't you ask me? I could have helped."

Wash shrugged, tears in the corners of his eyes. "I was embarrassed to bring it up. We decided to live with it, by being without each other."

Victoria sighed, hearing about this second issue separate from Wash's current fever. This would have been something she could have treated, but it didn't matter anymore. Now, something was eating Wash alive and she didn't think she could stop it. She covered him, just as they heard a tapping at the door.

"Come in," she called, wondering why Richard was knocking.

"Hello, Mrs. Williams."

Victoria turned around to see Dr. Jones entering with his little black bag. "Dr. Jones, why, hallo. Have you been helping Wash?

"Trying to. I'm afraid—" he looked at his patient. "Your husband brought in Dr. Storrs and Dr. Peltier, also. I hope you don't mind."

Victoria shook her head, as the doctor settled next to Wash and began his examination. "Why, your temperature seems almost normal," he exclaimed.

Wash smiled slightly. "That's my mother's doing. She just gave me a cool bath."

"Ah," he said, glancing at Victoria. "Good idea." The doctor examined Wash's face and sighed. "No change there."

As Victoria watched the doctor work, she felt her mind grow fuzzy and blank, only to be filled with the image of Wash's heart, beating and beating, almost frantically, as blood swished back and forth but made no progress in his body. Simultaneously, Dr. Jones pulled out his stethoscope, placed it in his ears, and rested the disc on Wash's chest. He listened somberly and then his brow creased, as he listened some more. He moved the disc slightly, adjusted his ears, and tried again.

"It's not smooth, is it?" asked Victoria quietly.

"Ah, ahem, no, perhaps not."

"What does that mean, if my heartbeat isn't smooth?" asked Wash.

"Well, er. Let's see if it's consistent," muttered the doctor.

Victoria looked Wash straight in the eyes. "Your heart is broken," she managed to say, before she burst into sobs. "Oh, Wash, my love, your heart."

Just then, the door swung open and the frame was filled with Prince's body. "Princess, you've returned. Oh, my dear," he cried and rushed to hold her as she cried.

Remembering that Wash was watching helplessly, Victoria tried to pull herself together. She felt Prince shuddering, as he too tried to maintain his self-control. She took a deep breath and noticed both Belcher and Richard standing in the doorway.

"Hallo, Belcher," she called to him, as she and Prince separated. Their two sons stepped into the room and closed the door behind them. It was a tight fit in Wash's little room, with everyone trying to avoid looking at each other.

Dr. Jones rose and shook Prince's hand. "Hello, sir. Let's go outside and give everyone some space." Prince nodded and the two went out into the cold.

Wash's eyes frantically sought Victoria's and she held steady. "Am I going to die?" he whispered.

"I don't know."

He continued to stare.

"Perhaps."

"Oh, Mammis, I'm so sorry. Was it the scrape?"

Before she could swallow back her tears to reply, he interjected, "I guess it really doesn't matter, does it?" His hand shook and he added, "I am only thirty-two. I don't want to die yet."

Victoria collapsed on his bed, gathering her large son in her arms the best she could. "We love you so much, Wash. I don't know what we will do without you." She kept trying to be strong and positive but she spotted the black horses lined up patiently at the stable and she knew she was powerless to change his course. Despite her efforts to portray calmness, she started to shake, just as the door opened and Prince re-entered the room.

"Wash, you look tired. I think we should let you get some rest. Belcher is going to stay with you tonight." He patted his younger son on the back and then turned to put his arm around Victoria. "Let's get settled now. Richard, you have a place to stay?"

"Yes, Dadrus. I'll head out in a minute." Richard placed the bucket of water in the corner on the floor and followed them out the door.

Victoria pulled away from Prince's arm. "I'm not leaving him," she hissed in his ear.

His arm firmly on her shoulder, he said, "We need to let him rest. I brought the *vardo* here so we have a place to sleep. That's what took me so long to get here. Come now."

Victoria knew it was useless to argue. She decided she would sneak out once Prince fell asleep and sit vigil. She turned to give Wash one last smile. "Wash, we love you. We're camped right outside and will see you tomorrow." He nodded and closed his eyes, as Belcher checked the fire.

"What happened with your brother?" Prince asked as they walked towards the *vardo.*

"He seems to have rallied. He was eating when I left."

There was silence as they mounted the steps into the caravan until Victoria glanced by the stable door and blurted out, "Samuel's horses were not for my brother." Her body convulsed with sobs. "What will we do without Wash? Oh, Prince, what will happen to us?"

By then, they were standing inside, warmed by the fire that Prince had left burning. He caressed her face but he said nothing. She glanced up at him and tears were streaming down his face and he looked absolutely hopeless. "Our wonder-boy," he stuttered. "Our pride and joy. He's—he's leaving us, isn't he?"

Victoria nodded. "I wish it were me. I would rather die than lose him. You need him, maybe they will take me instead," she sobbed.

"Can you do nothing?" he asked with the faintest hint of hope.

"It has damaged his heart. Some poison is running so deep inside him that I cannot reach it. Oh, Prince, what shall we do?"

Exhaustion overtook her and she fell against Prince's shoulder. As they leaned into each other, she could only be grateful that they were together. He led her to the sleeping platform where they got under the comforter.

Victoria was surprised to find when she awoke that it was morning. She had doubted that she would be able to sleep at all. She rose from the sleeping platform and her heart sank as she glanced out the window to see the black horses patiently waiting at the stable door. She quickly threw on her shawl and hurried down the steps to the shanty.

As she opened its door, she startled Belcher, sitting on the chair near the bed, but her eyes passed over him. Wash was sleeping, his face still bright red with sweat beaded on his upper lip. She whispered his name and his eyes opened.

"Mammis, you're here," his voice rasped.

She gestured to Belcher to fill a cup of water and tried to give it to Wash. He was unable to lift himself enough to drink, so she added more pillows under his head. He just looked at her with dull eyes and shook his head.

"It's all over, Mammis."

"Wash, don't say that."

"But it's true," he paused, licking his lips. "Isn't it?"

"I—I—I don't know for certain."

"I see the horses, Mammis. They wait—" and he closed his eyes, too weak to say more.

All Victoria could do was to clasp his hand in hers and squeeze as tightly as she could. They sat like that, just waiting.

"My horses," he started to say. "My children—"

"Dadrus and I will take care of your family," she said.

"Thank you, Mammis, I—"

"Shh—don't worry about anything." She sat with him, reminiscing. "Wash, you remember that first sale you made?" She saw him nod slightly. "You were, what, ten, eleven? Standing there so straight and sure of yourself."

Eyes closed, Wash started a small smile that stopped abruptly.

"Not again."

His words brought her back to their current situation. Wash would no longer be buying or selling, or comfort her when Prince was away, or keep peace among the rest of his brothers, or any of the many other tasks that Wash did effortlessly "My son," she whispered, stroking his arm.

A commotion outside caused Victoria to turn to look at Belcher, who rose and went to see what was happening. Victoria remained, her hand still holding Wash's.

Belcher came back inside, followed by Prince. His eyes darted to Wash and then Victoria's hand. He touched her on the shoulder and she turned to look up as he raised a questioning eyebrow. She just shook her head.

"Noah is here with our niece Theresa."

"Oh, he made it back from Somerville," she said, relieved.

"Yes, no problems. They stopped by the Hotel to pick up Daisy."

They heard a shout outside and Prince opened the door to check. "It's Martha."

Victoria inhaled deeply. The family would be gathering here at Wash's shanty.

And so it continued all morning, as her daughters arrived with their families. They came into the shanty in small groups. Sometimes Wash would open his eyes and speak a word or two. Sometimes he would just smile. Other times he didn't respond at all.

Victoria sat, holding his hand until she was so stiff, she had to get up.

"Mammis, here, I'll take over," said Martha. "Go get something warm to drink in my *vardo*. The kettle's on the stove."

At first, she shook her head, but she felt her arms trembling. "Just for a minute." She could barely straighten her legs as she stood and walked tentatively to the door. As she stood there, the door opened and, Prince, looking surprised to see her there, reached for her and guided her to Martha's caravan. They sat side-by-side, holding warm cups and barely sipping their tea.

"Prince, what are we going—"

He stopped her. "We will figure that out when we need to."

"Oh, Prince," she sobbed, "I can't help him." She clawed at his coat. "I can't change his path."

The day of Wash's funeral was cloudy and gray, and the ache in her fingers and knees told Victoria about the potential of snow, but it was nothing compared with the anguish she felt in her heart. She sat outside on the *vardo* seat in Mr. Ludlow's yard, her eyes glued to the four black horses waiting patiently, as Noah attached them to the hearse outside Wash's shack. The black wagon was gilded with gold and silver and its wide windows along both sides provided a clear view of the satin-lined interior. Black velvet mourning curtains with gold fringe and tassels topped the windows. Ostrich plumes pointing up towards heaven adorned each corner and elaborate scrollwork graced the exterior. No need to fill the tank that held the casket with ice in this weather, she registered.

Earlier, there had been great hubbub when the elaborate coffin procured from New York had arrived. Prince had looked all over Connecticut for something suitable for their wonder-son but, in the end, he had to ask his brother in Bridgeport to go to the city and bring one back with him. Victoria had approved of the gleaming coffin with its silver handles and ornate carved moldings, at least with the small part of her that was able to communicate with people in this world. She felt split in two, with the vast majority of her off in the ethers somewhere, not in the real world that now excluded Wash. Just that thought caused her to hiccup and convulse into a small ball where she held herself tightly in hopes that the physical hurt might erase some of the emotional distress. But generally it hadn't worked.

In the distance, although it turned out to be nearby but only dulled by her lack of focus, she heard the arrival of horses. She could not turn herself to see who had arrived and was startled when she felt a hand at her elbow.

"Princess, I'm back from East Hartford."

She looked down to see, somewhat out of focus, Prince looking expectantly at her. She had no recollection of his trip or its purpose. But she could see, as he grew clearer, that his face was deeply lined, like a craggy mountain or an old map. "The grave is dug at the cemetery," he said gently.

She gasped, surprised that she hadn't thought about that requirement. Of course, they would need to bury Wash, that was the reason they had all gathered here. But the concrete image of placing him in the ground was beyond her.

She felt Prince reaching to help her down the *vardo* steps. Wearily, she rose and descended. She glanced down to register that she had dressed in her mourning clothes, the ones she had carried to Somerville for her brother. Aghast that she was wearing them for her son instead, she almost fell headfirst down the stairs, but Prince caught and steadied her. She noticed his hat rimmed with a crepe band and just shook her head, desperately trying to make sense of what was happening.

"The reverend is here, also," Prince added. "He's from North Methodist."

Victoria felt no recognition of the church name but assumed it was one they had known or used. She heard the crunching of snow behind them and, as he rounded the corner, a tall man bowed to her, introducing himself. "Reverend Holmes," he said. "I am so sorry for your loss."

Victoria felt her heart growing larger in her chest and a tide of tears gathering in her hollows, just waiting to gush forward. She tried to keep the flood from surging.

Grooms from the Hotel, attired in funeral garb, who had been standing around the stables, moved purposefully in the shanty, and Victoria saw her family begin a slow surge towards the shack. Prince pushed her forward and they followed the reverend to gather around the casket. Someone handed her a black-edged handkerchief that she tucked in her sleeve. It took a few moments for everyone to settle into place. In a solemn voice, Reverend Holmes began, "We are gathered here today to mourn the loss of George Washington—"

Victoria screamed as she struggled to the center of the group, "No, no, not Wash, take me. I'll go instead, take me, not him." She threw herself on the coffin and started banging on the heavy wood. "Open this up and take him out. I will go instead. Please, help me, get Wash out of here. I belong in there, not him. Ayyee," she wailed, as she continued to pound on the cover. She heard others start keening and their cries filled the air. "Wash, Wash, come back home. You have work to do, I don't. I will be there instead of you." Victoria bashed her head against the coffin and felt arms pulling her off. She struggled, but the arms were stronger and she heard a soft whispering, "Mammis, Mammis, come with us, come now."

"No, no, I won't leave him where it's cold and dark. Oh, Wash, where is your smile, your touch, your skill with the horses? No, it cannot be gone. Oh, help me!" But the arms pulled her off the shiny wood and helped her stand as the reverend continued.

Victoria heard blood pulsing in her ears so loudly that the words were muffled. She could see puffs of air coming from mouths of her other children as they responded to the minister. Out of the corner of her eye, she saw one of the four black horses paw the ground, his black ostrich headdress bobbing as he moved. "You will have him soon enough," she cried in its direction.

Victoria wasn't certain if she had been standing there for minutes or hours, but she felt Prince put pressure on her arm and lead her to one of the hacks lined up behind the hearse with its four black horses. She felt others moving into the cabs behind them and heard voices, as her children and their families organized themselves into the procession. She felt numb but she wasn't certain if it was the cold or the circumstances and she lost herself in the lack of feeling. Suddenly, the cab jolted and they started along the streets of Hartford behind her wonder-son. With every step of the horse, she felt a jab to her heart. "Prince, stop the stabbing," she sobbed. "Stop my heart from bleeding." Although he sat solidly beside her, she felt him shrug and gasp for air and realized he was as helpless and as wounded as she. He grasped her hand and his face was as drenched as hers, the dampness glistening in the craggy lines across his cheeks. "Ayye," she cried, "we are forsaken. We have lost our crown prince. Ayye."

The carriage turned the corner down Main Street and she saw a dozen or more hacks behind them, followed by men on horses. "Those are our horses," she whispered in recognition. "Horses that we sold, that Wash sold, to people all over Hartford. All over the state. Oh, Prince, what a tribute to him. If only he could see how glorious his procession is!"

A light snow began to fall. "Even the angels are crying," Victoria wailed. "Prince, what a sad, horrible day. Will we ever recover?"

Prince, unable to respond, just tightened his grip on her hand and shook his head.

Police officers stood at each corner to stop traffic and allow their procession to pass. Through downtown, they continued and turned left on Morgan Street to cross the river. The plodding sound of the horses' feet echoed, as they slowly made their way across the bridge. On the other side, they continued their steady approach to Wash's resting place, past the old Farmer's Hotel, and turned left on Main Street.

Officer Gimbel stood on the corner, stopping traffic as the procession reached the cemetery entrance. One after another, the hacks arrived and the passengers dismounted until the crowd filled the sidewalks and spilled into the street. The snow was heavier and the day was growing dark, when the grooms reached into the hearse to carry the coffin down the path to the family plot.

Numbly, Victoria followed, with Prince supporting her. She felt the family behind them as they walked the northern lane along the edge of the cemetery. She saw the monument long before they reached the site, with its cantering horse atop the granite obelisk. The last time they had come like this it was to bury little Morris, resting to the side behind the monument. Victoria glanced at the lamb image and sobbed, "Little Morris, our angel, your brother is here to join you," before she collapsed on the path. From there, she saw the raw, gaping hole in the earth in front of their monument so proudly bearing the name "Williams." She never thought she'd be burying another one of her sons. She and Prince were supposed to be the next to go, and she hoped it would be herself before her husband. She didn't think her heart could stand any more pain than it already felt. Someone was trying to help her stand but the new snow made the path slippery and they almost fell atop her.

She must have stood and there must have been a ceremony but Victoria could not recall. The gaping hole was now brown earth and the grooms were standing off to the side of the family. Old Joe was wiping his eyes and she saw his dark face glistening. This was it; it was over. This was how it was to bury her adult son, the wonder-son, the one who was to keep her family going long after she and Prince were gone. She felt fear mixed with the pain, uncertainty, and unreality. Maybe this was just a terrible dream, a vision that would not come true. But the shuddering she felt from Prince's arm as he held hers was real and she could feel spasms shaking her husband's chest. She leaned into him and, together, they walked back along the path to the waiting hacks.

Main Street was filled with carriages that had been blocked more than an hour for the ceremony to conclude, but no one yelled an unkind word or suggested impatience. Prince helped Victoria climb into the cab and hauled himself in behind her. They lowered the mourning curtain partway, still allowing them to see the gathered crowd.

As they left, Victoria glanced out the back window of the hack and saw the four black horses still standing at the cemetery entrance. "Go on, you, git along, leave him in peace. Get on, get on," she screamed, as she clawed at the back of the seat and rapped on the oval window pane. Her voice raw and crackling, she yelled again, "Get out of here, and go home."

TWENTY-FOUR

"Mammis, Mammis," a voice rustled in her ear. "It's all right, no one is bothering you."

"But the horses, the black horses—" she started. When she opened her eyes, she saw a concerned Daisy standing over her in the back of the *vardo* as they ambled down the humid roads of Georgia. "Wash is dead," Victoria sobbed, "and the black horses are right behind us." She twisted to look out the back of the *vardo* window but all she saw were the dust trails and hanging Spanish moss behind them. She turned back to Daisy. "I saw them. Truly I did."

Daisy, nodding, smoothed down Victoria's dress and caressed her hair. "Yes, Mammis, but they are gone now. Would you like some water?" She handed Victoria a cup to drink and steadied her shaking hand as she took a refreshing sip.

They left the Georgia coast and headed upland into the Piedmont where they traveled through low, rolling hills, often following streams cascading down the gentle slopes. Victoria noticed oak and hickory, along with large chestnut trees, and made a mental harvesting note, before remembering that they wouldn't be here for the first frost. At least she hoped that would be true.

Victoria glanced at the scars on her hands and wondered whether her face was marked. Her hair and cleaned *diklo* covered any scars on her scalp, but all mirrors were beyond her reach and she couldn't see the status of her face. She tried using her fingers to sense any disfigurement but they were too rough to know for certain. Generally she stayed inside the caravan, except to toilet herself, although she often walked with Daisy or Lottie when they did washing in the streams.

Several weeks later, she heard her sons talking to Daisy and Lottie around the fire at night.

"Tomorrow, we will be leaving you women alone at camp."

"And we don't want a repeat of what happened in Washington."

Victoria's skin started to prickle.

"So, we were thinking that Daisy could wear Noah's clothes and people will think there's a man here."

Victoria gasped. "It is not allowed, a woman to wear men's clothing," she called out to her family. "It will cause great harm to come to us."

After a moment of silence, she heard, "Mammis, these are unusual times. We three need to leave camp. We must trade horses to get some money. It's our only choice."

Victoria knew that Richard was making a subtle reference to her refusal to *dukker* any longer. When she had started to feel better, the sons had asked, and she had said, "I cannot," and wouldn't budge. Without her income, the men had to work the horses even harder. Although she knew that times and traditions were changing, she was uncomfortable with this idea of modeling as a man. But she had no other suggestions, except to increase her own strength, so she wouldn't be such a liability, and vowed to walk farther the next day. There was silence from the fire and she said no more.

She woke up screaming during the night. Daisy came to her and Victoria focused on her face. "He would have beaten you."

"Shh, Mammis, we are far away from him. It's safe now."

But Victoria could not feel the soft presence of Prince and felt alone.

The next day, Victoria took a short walk up the stream and sat. She could see Daisy and Lottie way downstream and, lulled by the murmur of the water rushing along the rocks, she tried to relax. The noise of the creek filled her head, drowning out the screams and cries from her attack. And then she felt something even worse. It was Prince sitting on a rock nearby, crying, his shoulders shaking. She saw him look at her and whisper, "I couldn't protect you, Princess. I am ashamed."

She threw herself at his feet and cried, "Prince, it's over. You gave me strength to fight back. Come back to me now. I am so alone." She felt a swirling around her as the vision of Prince disappeared. She pulled herself up from the ground and sat, filled with sadness. But she thought she could feel an arm around her, as she painfully rose and walked back to camp.

"Maybe she'll be better once we get home."

Sitting in the caravan, Victoria could hear her sons talking while eating dinner.

"What if she doesn't? It's been two months and she's still jumpy."

She almost felt Noah shrug. "We'll figure it out each day. What else can we do?"

She understood their concern. Sometimes she felt fine and could cook and forage a bit. But other times, hearing a small noise or catching something out of the corner of her eye would send her into a panic. She would tremble and scream and her mind would go blank. Sometimes, she wasn't sure how much time had passed or what happened while she was in that state. Once this had happened at night and, the next time she was aware, it was daylight. She just didn't know how often that happened. Maybe she would be better once they got home. She certainly hoped so. Maybe Prince would be around more often once they got home. She certainly wished that would be true also.

The days were getting shorter, the nights cooler, and they were headed north now, meandering their way through pitch pine and deciduous forests.

"We'll be home in time for the Festival of the Kettles," Daisy said excitedly at breakfast one morning as they skirted past New York. "I love it when we celebrate the harvest all together."

Victoria briefly caught her enthusiasm but then remembered that her brothers were all gone and their families busy with their own, while Martha would still be in Hoosick Falls where her family summered. She wondered who would even come to their Festival.

"Maybe Sonny and Uncle William will be there," said Daisy, almost reading her mind. "And their families."

"Perhaps."

"We can have it behind the old Farmer's Hotel."

Victoria thought about that idea. Usually, they held the festival that heralded the official close of the summer at one of their camps, either in New Haven or Yalesville. But neighbors were less thrilled with their presence and Victoria was not challenged to press the issue. Perhaps Daisy was right. And Victoria noticed herself thinking again about the future, which hadn't happened since her attack.

Perhaps there would be life again.

"Noah, over here," Victoria called. Noah dumped a load of wood in a pile near the kettle pit. Sonny and William had arrived that afternoon, with both their children and their families. Victoria glanced around at the sizable crowd that was growing. Her three daughters, Kitty, Bessie, and Emma, had come with their families and they were bustling around setting up their *vardos* and bringing things to the cooking area. Daisy and Victoria had started a kettle, and now each family was placing their own, each with something different, on the supports surrounding the fire. The smell of cooking food mingled with the aroma of campfire and Victoria felt comforted. The familiar helped her feel that she belonged in this world.

"Mammis, how was your summer?" asked Bessie. Daisy shot her a look but Bessie hadn't heard about the issues yet.

Victoria opened her mouth to reply, but Daisy took Bessie by the arm to guide her to a corner where she could update her sister. Victoria, on the other hand, wasn't quite certain what she would have said. She remembered her nightmares about being attacked and had scars to prove it had happened, but it felt no more real than the whisper and gentle arm of Prince around her when she slept. She was confused about which world she inhabited and whether she was phantom or real. She shook her head, knowing that Daisy and Bessie wouldn't be speaking to her if she were *muló*, so she must be alive.

Later, Victoria was standing by the kettles, stirring the rabbit stew, when she felt a wind blow and stir the embers. The flames danced higher around the pots and she could hear Prince laughing.

"Stop that," she scolded him. "You'll burn the food."

She felt the breeze move on and the trees began dancing wildly.

"Mammis, it's suddenly wild out there," shouted Belcher over the wind, as he brought some benches to the cooking area. "I wonder if there is going to be a hurricane."

"It's just your father."

"Dadrus?"

"Yes, he's kicking up his heels. Wait until we start the fiddles."

Belcher looked at her and then shook his head and walked to join his brothers. Victoria could see them talking and glancing slightly at her. Chut, chut, let them talk. Gusts of wind swirled dust around their feet and the tops of the trees danced, showering red, orange, and yellow leaves upon them.

Daisy set out plates on the eating tarp, which was threatening to sail away. She anchored it with a few tree stumps and the tarp buckled and snapped between its weights. She looked questioningly at her mother, who just smiled and glanced up in the sky.

"Be sure to set a place for Dadrus. Otherwise, who knows what he might do."

Daisy shrugged and placed an extra setting on the tarp. Soon, the sons were standing around the tarp, waiting for their plates to be filled.

"What's this?" asked Noah.

"It's for Dadrus. I was given instructions—"

"What? Who said—" interrupted Richard.

"Mammis is certain that he's here, blowing up the storm."

The sons looked at each other, then lowered their eyes to their plates and ate.

Eventually, they loosened up. "Mammis, good stews here."

"Thanks, dears. I used special herbs because I knew your father would enjoy them."

More silence.

"Mammis, do you think Dadrus is really a *muló*?" asked Belcher.

"Is it because of something we did?" asked Noah. "Maybe we should have burned the chariot."

"Quiet," said Richard sternly. "We did nothing wrong."

She smiled, "Oh, no, dears, he's just waiting for me."

The sons exchanged looks and Noah shrugged, as if to suggest they certainly couldn't change her mind.

"Bessie, doesn't one of your sons play the fiddle?" asked Victoria.

"Yes, we should start the music."

As the wind whistled through the trees, the patter of leaves sounded like applause. Musicians set up their instruments near one of the stumps and began, the sound of their music carrying across the fields and down to the river. The glow of the fire flickered across the faces of Prince's children and grandchildren. Behind the cooking area, Victoria felt the wind caressing her face and tossing her skirts.

"You scamp, you," she laughed. "Always playing with me. Well, I can play back." She lifted her skirts and danced away, her face tilted towards the rising full moon, with a broad smile on her face. Her feet moved quicker and quicker, her skirts swirled and swayed and the ties of her *diklo* sped through the air. Around and around she danced until she could barely breathe and her face was flushed.

"Prince, welcome home," she roared as she fell in an exhausted heap on the ground.

TWENTY-FIVE

She could feel a taste of winter in the air, when she woke and reached for Prince but he was already up. She cracked open one eye to look towards the window and saw that the sun had already risen. Of course Prince was already out and about. He always got up with the sun.

Victoria caught a glimpse of the flowered wallpaper near the window and smiled. Oh, the argument that they had had over that wallpaper. In fact, the argument had been about settling into the old Hotel. Prince was so used to his wandering ways that he couldn't bear the thought of something solid over his head. But she had persisted and he had finally agreed. After all those years on the road, there was no more packing and unpacking.

She slowly swung her feet to the floor and sat at the edge of the bed while her thoughts settled. Her legs poked out from her nightshirt like broomsticks. She had a flashing recollection of making small broomsticks as a child with her *mammis* and *púridaia* so many years ago.

It was when she saw her clothes hanging on the hook that she felt the bottom of her stomach fall and she collapsed into her lap. Prince wasn't up and about. He was gone, she was here alone, and she couldn't bear it. Her body convulsed and contracted, although she shed no tears. She had cried all those out over the past months as life went on around her. She wished she could return to the blissful unaware state of her awakening, but she now remembered all too well the reality of her situation.

Hearing small feet pattering to her door, she roused herself to put on her mourning clothes. As she pulled off her nightshirt, she noticed bruise marks on her arms. They were the size of fingertips, as if someone had grabbed her arm. To catch her from falling? She didn't remember this. She put on her dress and saw that it swam around her body and wondered how it had grown larger. Even with all these new inventions, she didn't think that clothes could get bigger. She shook her head in confusion and concentrated on putting on her stockings and shoes. She sat at the dressing table and coiled her long dark braid, woven with gray, into a neat bun and covered her head with her *diklo*. She remembered days of long ago when she enjoyed dressing and primping and *dukkering*. Now, only her gold hoops suggested any of that former vivacious life. Those she still wore, Prince's favorites, to remind her of their time together, as if she could forget. Her bracelets and bangles were heaped to the side, abandoned with their associated joy and laughter. She glanced at her large, dark eyes in the mirror; she thought she was still inside but, at times, she just wasn't certain if she inhabited her body or not. Victoria walked gingerly towards her door to the hallway. Her legs were steady and she reached out her bony hand to turn the knob and felt a sharp pain run up her arm, which surprised her.

As she opened the door, a small figure darted down the hall. She turned to follow it down the stairs to the dining area. The sun was streaming through the window, which made it harder for her to see, but she held on carefully to the banister and reached the bottom without incident. She thought that hadn't always been the case, but it was only a fleeting thought, and she was uncertain if it was based in reality or just a constant worry, a natural fear of a woman who had raised many children.

"Good morning, Mammis," said her son, who met her at the bottom of the stairs. "How are you today?" His voice was neutral and calm, but his body was hovering near her, as if she might not be fine today. She glanced up at him. A sturdy man, she was certain it was her son, but she wasn't sure if she knew which one. The three of them—Noah, Belcher, and Richard—had been around lately, that she remembered. And Richard, he was oldest, she thought. So this must be either Noah or Belcher. Maybe it didn't matter.

"Good morning, son," she replied. "I am fine today. And you, dear?" she asked. He nodded that he was well, as he slightly raised his right eyebrow and took her arm to walk her to her chair. She sat with the rest of them, gathered around the large table.

The door to the kitchen opened and a woman came in carrying a pot of coffee. "Some coffee for you."

"Thank you, dear," Victoria answered. She wasn't sure who the woman was, maybe Noah or Belcher's wife. Did they live here? Was this the home where she had lived with Prince? She felt confused again and reached to add sugar to her cup. Again, a sharp pain ran up her arm to her shoulder and, this time, she was less surprised, although she didn't understand why the pain was there. She took a sip of her coffee. She liked it strong and dark and it was. She hoped the liquid would help clear her mind and gave it time to do its job. She picked at her food but didn't find it interesting. She felt no appetite, no desire to put anything in her stomach, which had so recently fallen into her body cavity when she had remembered the loss of Prince. It was still not back where it belonged, she was certain.

Maybe if she could get outside, see the sky and the sun, smell the earth and hear the birds, and put the world in its proper place, which she knew was not under a roof, she would feel better. She rose and her son rapidly stood and offered his arm. "May I help you, Mammis?" he inquired. She nodded and they walked towards the front door. She noticed several rocking chairs on the veranda that faced the road and hoped they would do. She felt the crispness in the air as she walked out the door. She turned to one of the rockers and nodded to her son. He helped her settle her body into its cushions and she closed her eyes. She could feel the sun on her skirt and hear the clop of horses as they passed by, and she allowed herself to mold into the shape of the rocker.

She began to relax, hearing murmurs of conversation from inside the dining room. She was inclined to ignore it but she caught a few words that captured her attention. She realized that they were talking about her; they must not realize she could hear them. Or maybe they thought she was too incoherent to understand, but the idea that her sons were scheming about something made her sit up and listen.

"She's really showing signs of nervous prostration," said the deep voice of one son. "Some days she just won't get out of bed. And others, she's a ball of fire."

"I heard her talking to Dadrus again the other day," said the other.

"Does that surprise you?" asked a woman. "We women talk all day to you men and you don't seem to listen, so what difference does it make if he's really here or not." Victoria chuckled at that comment. That must be her daughter, Martha.

"Well, what should we do? I've tried talking to her about the business, but she isn't interested."

"That worries me, too. She was the one who handled all the finances and now we have to figure it out on our own."

Victoria hadn't considered that her abandonment of the family affairs would cause problems for her sons. Certainly their wives would be able to help run the business. But it had always been her job and she hadn't shown anyone else how she had kept track of it all. She felt herself vaguely concerned and somewhat shocked at her lack of foresight. It was true, she never had considered what would happen when she and Prince were gone. Especially after Wash died, she had trouble envisioning what would happen to the family.

The voices continued. "People have been saying that Mammis is getting out of control and we should send her to the Retreat." Victoria sat straight up. Heavens, no, not for her.

Someone answered rapidly, "That is not our way. We will not be shipping her off anywhere. And that's that."

A few voices spoke at once in agreement and she eased back into the rocker. The conversation shifted to some of the grandchildren and their schooling. It seemed the local authorities thought it was important to get them to school and keep them there until the end of the year.

Victoria lost interest in this part of the conversation. She rocked gently and felt her head fall back and her mouth open. She didn't hear the woman peer out at her on the porch. Or her son hush the young children and send them out the back door toward the stables so that Púridaia could rest.

"Púridaia, Púridaia, tell me a story," said the voice. Victoria had been daydreaming in her rocker as she sat in front of the fireplace on this cold, wintry day. She was remembering how they used to break through the ice to get water for washing and cooking, when the small voice brought her back to the present.

She opened her eyes and looked around. The outside light was pale, wavering, as only a December's day can be. Oh, she wished for the days when the children were young and they had camped in their *vardo* throughout the winter. But, as she glanced around the room, she gradually remembered that those days had long passed. Even her Prince was gone and now others in her family surrounded her.

She felt someone pulling at her long skirt and she looked down, squinting in the subtle light. It was a small child, maybe about two, and its mass of dark curly hair made it difficult to tell if it was a boy or girl. But the child raised itself on a small stool and she could see more clearly the rosy cheeks and dark eyes of a handsome grandson. She thought it might be little Richard, Martha's most recent. Although, she reminded herself, Martha is expecting another child and Richard will be the baby no more.

Little Richard, as that was who was peering up at her, repeated his request. "Púridaia, a story, please."

Victoria could not resist, as the boy nestled on the ground between her bony ankles. He hugged himself around her leg and began to suck his thumb. She thought of herself at that age, sitting with her *púridaia* and then her daughter, his mother, doing the same. Martha had had quite a life, admitted Victoria, but hadn't they all. And such a good basket maker she was. Too bad she hadn't done much since the children were born. That reminded her of a story and she settled back to tell it to Richard.

"Once many years ago, there was a Gypsy—" she hesitated and decided to make it about a boy for Richard. "A Gypsy boy. He was a very good basket maker and one day, it turns out that his travels took him to a very distant land where there were only savage men with few clothes. And it also happened that a very rich man was there with him. Only the basket maker and the rich man with all these savages."

Victoria paused to glance down at Richard. She could tell he was still sucking his thumb, which led her to believe he was not asleep, so she continued. "When the rich man saw where he was, he began to wring his hands and cry. But when the basket maker looked around, he noticed that one savage man had adorned his forehead with a decoration. The basket maker saw reeds growing in the marshes nearby and quickly pulled several and braided them into an attractive wreath for the savage man's head. The savage man danced for joy and ran to show all his friends. Soon there was a steady stream of savage men who wanted their reed wreaths. The savage men built a hut for the basket maker and brought him fine foods and drink."

Filling her head with visions of this fine image, Victoria forgot all about Richard. She remembered when her mother had told her this same story, before they got on the boat that would take them to a strange land filled with savage men. Now she was living in that land and it was hers and her mother was gone. And her father. And Prince. And her sons, Wash and Morris, her lamb. The boy between her ankles stirred, probably wondering what happened to the story, so she continued.

"The basket maker was happy and had much to eat. And the rich man? His job was to cut reeds for the basket maker so he could keep making wreaths for the savages." She paused. "Nice reeds make nice baskets," she finished and noticed the gentle breathing from a thumbless Richard.

She could hear her mother's voice saying those last words. When she was very young, it had been Victoria's job to sort the osier branches they made into the brooms they sold. Her mother and grandmother kept telling her to only use the good stems. Otherwise, the brooms would fray and not sweep the earth. Nice reeds made nice baskets, good osiers made good brooms. She had remembered that wisdom and used it during her lifetime and she and Prince had grown wealthy as a result. Quality was important; they had only the best horses, suited to do their work, and that was why their reputation was solid. She hoped her children and grandchildren would keep that tradition. She glanced at Richard, who was too young to understand the moral of the tale. Victoria tried to breathe the thought into Richard's heart and hoped it might matter.

"Mammis, Mammis," the voice called. She swatted it from her and sank deeper into her dream. Prince was riding to her and she didn't want to miss him. He was getting closer and she could see that he was wearing the same handsome clothes as when she last saw him. His face was the same, not older, and his moustache still caused her to laugh with joy. She reached up for him as he rode close but he just smiled and kept riding. She fell to the ground, heartbroken to have seen and then lost him so quickly. Her heart was pounding, as it always did when she would see him after a time apart, but it was also breaking because he had left without her. She lay crumpled on the ground, her skirt swirled around her, her shawl pulled over her head, as she sobbed. Her Prince had passed her by and she couldn't comprehend why he would not grab her by the waist and lift her on his horse with him, as he always did.

"Because he's *muló*," said a voice. She looked around but there was no one.

"*Muló*," she shuddered, and then she pulled herself upright. Of course, that would be true. He's dead and if she can see him, back from the dead, everyone else would think that this was not a good thing, but she didn't care. Why was he coming for her? Or was he not coming for her? Was that why he rode past? Oh, it was confusing and she missed him so much. Her arms ached to hold him and she yearned to caress the coarse hairs of his moustache. Oh, and the other hairs, in his manly places, those, she almost got giddy thinking of them. How they would tickle her belly when they were together, and how she could smell his sweat and seed in them. Evil or not, dead or not, she wanted him. She pounded the ground and sobbed. She threw herself back and forth, side to side in agony.

She heard the voice again, "Mammis. Mammis." She could feel a hand gently restraining her from pitching forward out of her chair. Slowly, the sense of the hand became stronger than the smell of her Prince. She could hear children yelling in the background and the clatter of plates and utensils. Over time, she could feel her arms supported, her feet on the ground and her bottom seated on the chair, not the ground. Her skirt was carefully tucked around her legs and her shawl was over her shoulders.

She hated to do it, but she slowly opened her eyes. Yes, she was sitting in the parlor of the old Hotel where she was now living with her family. And her son, Noah, was standing with her, patiently waiting for her to stop thrashing and moaning and join him in the room. He seemed to know that she had been transported somewhere else, somewhere that he couldn't and didn't want to go. He was gentle with her and gave her the space to return.

"Mammis," he repeated. She nodded. "Mammis, come with me into the dining room. I'll help you up."

Noah carefully placed his hand under his mother's arm and helped her rise from the chair. Her legs buckled a bit at first but then she was able to walk with his support to the dining room.

When she got there, the children became quiet and sat still in their chairs. Noah walked her to the place of honor, the one that Prince had used, and sat her down. Victoria looked up at him, questioning this move.

"Mammis," he said. "Today, it has been a year." He paused.

She tried to think. A year. A year since what? She had no sense of time. She glanced out the window to get some help. The sky was gray and the winds were blowing, there were no leaves on the trees and the ground was brown and barren. Maybe spring was coming. Spring, that would be—. And then she realized. Prince had left in the spring. He had blown out like the lion.

"Mammis, it has been a year since Dadrus has gone."

She nodded. She did understand it had been a year. It felt much longer and it had passed in a second. A year. What did it mean, anyway, time.

"Mammis, it is time for our final *pomana*."

Victoria looked at the table and noticed for the first time that it was piled with food, especially Prince's favorite foods. She inhaled sharply, remembering her vision before Noah had come to get her. She looked around and saw her children and their children all waiting patiently for her to acknowledge this, the end of their mourning. She glanced at the red ribbon, now shredded and tattered, tied around her wrist. Would she take it off today? No, never, she decided fiercely. Prince would always be with her.

One of the younger children started to fidget; his mother tried to hush him, and Victoria saw that it was little Richard. With great effort, she stood alone, holding on to the back of her chair. Slowly, she looked at each person at the table and all was still.

"You may eat, you may sing and dance, you may continue to live." She looked again at each of them. "I will not. But do not let this stop you." She had given what could best be described as her blessing, her acknowledgement that life would go on for them, and released them from their duty as mourners. She sank gratefully into the chair and the meal began.

Soon her children started talking among themselves. One of the sons mentioned a new shipment of horses had arrived and they had sent some to the sale stable in Willimantic and would leave the rest here. Victoria nodded at that; good planning on someone's part, she acknowledged.

"I got you a copy of the paper today," Belcher added. "Someone in a small boat brought it across the river."

"I can't believe that the bridge is gone again. We are isolated on the eastern shore when that happens," added Richard.

Noah nodded. "We should have stables in Hartford, too. Our best customers are on that side."

"The ice was massive. I saw it when I went to see about a newspaper. It ripped out all the ferry landings, too. They say they came down the river from New Hampshire, huge sheets of ice."

"I know the others were upset that they couldn't get over here for today," said Martha, glancing at her mother.

Suddenly Victoria couldn't be in the room with them any longer, listening to them speak of things that didn't matter to her any longer. She could feel anger rising in her, could sense her face was getting red, and realized she had stood up. She moved quickly to the side, flinging her chair as she marched from the room. She could hear the silence behind her.

She really didn't know where she wanted to go. No, she knew that she wanted to be with Prince, but she had no way to get there. Maybe she should go upstairs to their room. Or out on the veranda. Confusion set in and she was stuck there in the foyer at the bottom of the stairs. She could hear one of her sons coming to get her and she knew she had to move quickly. Gathering all her strength, she marched down the hall and toward the back door. Whoever was behind her started walking quickly; she could hear his heavy step on the floor behind her. She could see freedom through the back door window and she reached for a lamp on a small table in the hallway and threw it to the floor behind her as she passed by. She hoped that would stop whomever it was long enough that she could get out the door.

She reached for the knob just as she heard her son's steps crunching in the glass of the fallen lamp. She flung the door open and the wind caught it and blew it wide open away from her. She hadn't realized it was still cold outside and she had no coat or hat. But she kept going. She crossed the back lawn, darting between the large trees and trying to hide herself behind their large trunks. Somehow she hoped that no one would follow. The wind was blowing through the branches of the trees; there were no leaves yet but occasionally a small branch would snap and tumble to the ground as she stood there. The sleeves of her dress were thin and her teeth were starting to chatter.

She could hear her family gathered at the back of the house. Someone was organizing the search party and she doubted that she could escape from the whole group. She was very near the edge of a ditch and decided to get on her hands and knees and crawl to it, hoping to avoid being seen. She went quickly, knowing that her dress was no camouflage and that speed was her only ally.

She slipped into the coarse graveled bed that was still damp from the previous storm. Skunk cabbage was up but everything else was dead stalks and dirt. She pressed her face to the ground, hoping that if she couldn't see her family, they wouldn't notice her. She could hear footsteps approaching and she tried to stop breathing

A short time passed and no one had found her. She thought she heard quiet conversation but she didn't dare look up. Suddenly, she heard a loud noise and the wind blew strongly and she could feel Prince. She raised her head slightly, looking away from the house, and she could see him, striding through the field. He was leaving her and she had to reach him. She rose on her hands and knees and called out to him, "Prince, I am here, please, I am here." He continued toward the stables.

Victoria rose in the ditch and staggered in that direction. She stumbled on the rocks in the ditch but caught herself. No, it was someone else who caught her. She struggled with the fingers pressed into her arm but someone was stronger. She closed her eyes, she tried to scratch at the person, but it had many arms and she was lifted from the ground. She took one last look at the stables but Prince was gone and she felt herself being carried back into the house and up to her room.

Someone placed her gently on the bed, removed her shoes, and covered her with a quilt. They tiptoed out the door, and she heard the click of the key being turned in the lock. She was too exhausted to care.

TWENTY-SIX

She was in that drowsy, dreamy place that happens early in the morning when it was too soon to get up but she wasn't really asleep. Curled on her side, she could feel Prince's warmth wrapped around her. She loved when he cradled her that way, making her feel safe and protected. She could hear his gentle snore; it really was amazing that such a large man had such a sweet snore. She could feel the weight of his arm over her and she dozed.

When she next awoke, the sun was up and she opened her eyes and sensed she was the only one in her room. She tentatively reached next to her and it was empty, as she knew it would be. But she thought that she could still feel the warmth of another body. Or was it just her imagination?

She heard yelling in the kitchen below and at first thought she'd better get up to settle whatever issue it was. She sat up and placed her feet on the floor and was surprised at how sore she was, until images of yesterday's flight came back to her. She rubbed her arms and noticed the same bruise marks she had had earlier in the winter. Had this happened before? Had her son restrained her some other time? She couldn't remember and at first that concerned her. But then she felt it, a whisper of a movement of air, a sense that she was not alone. Although she couldn't see him, she knew that Prince was nearby. That cheered her and she felt willing to get up and see what was happening downstairs.

After dressing, she tested the door and found it unlocked. She decided that she would try to behave outwardly normal because she didn't like the idea of being confined in her room. She could still hear loud voices as she made her way down the stairs. She heard someone talking about William, Prince's son with Mary Defiance Burton. Victoria remembered his arrival after the funeral and her emotions started to rise. But the whisper of air that was moving with her reminded her that William was the firstborn son, and she stilled her anger and frustration.

The voices stopped abruptly when she entered the dining room. She wasn't sure if it was because of the subject they were discussing or her behavior yesterday, but she sat down at her place and smiled slightly at everyone. "Good morning," she said quietly.

She could see the subtle looks passing among everyone at the table. They were probably wondering what she'd do that day, she chuckled. They looked at her, as she made a slight cackling noise and she realized they were keeping a careful watch. Daisy passed around a platter of eggs and several of her sons filled their plates.

After some moments of silence, Noah looked around the group. "The word is that there was a fire at a stable in New York." He paused. "They were covered by insurance." He looked up at Richard.

"No," Richard responded abruptly. "No paper trails, no legal steps. No."

"Yes." The word came from Victoria. "We need to change with the times. Richard, get this house and barn insured." Her voice was firm and clear.

The boys glanced at each other to acknowledge that Mammis was here today, with all her faculties. And they nodded and knew it was the end of that conversation.

Daisy, sitting across from Victoria, seized on the lucid moment to ask, "Mammis, could you teach me how to make tipsy cake?"

Victoria looked surprised. "Of course, dear. I'm certain we have everything we need."

Daisy nodded.

"Well, let's get started after breakfast."

Daisy smiled and Victoria realized it had been some time since she had seen her smile. Poor dear had lost her father and now her mother needed retreat, it was no wonder. Victoria couldn't remember if Daisy ever married poor Richard, but she didn't want to look foolish by asking. She honestly couldn't recall anything beyond her conversations with Prince about the matter, but she didn't see poor Richard around. She did remember that both Noah and Belcher had married and knew that the women sitting here at the table were those wives, although she didn't know which one was which. She decided that was an acceptable luxury for an old woman.

A few minutes later, she put down her cup of coffee. "Ready, Daisy?"

"Yes, Mammis."

They moved into the kitchen where Victoria asked Daisy to gather the necessary ingredients. "Do you have the jam?"

"Here, Mammis, and the whisky and sherry also."

"We will need to whip cream and make some custard."

"I can do that." Daisy began to heat some milk until it steamed. She then added a small amount of the warm milk to some beaten egg yolks and then more, until she could add the yolks to the hot mixture without them curdling. She stirred until the mixture was thick.

Meanwhile, Victoria put crumbled leftover cake into a bowl, covered the pieces with jam, and added the liquor.

"Pour in the custard, Daisy." She handed her the bowl and Daisy melded the ingredients together. She then beat the cream.

"Don't forget, we need to save some for the outside."

Daisy nodded and continued beating for some time, until it held soft peaks and, reserving some, she folded the remainder into the mixture.

"Let this cool outside for awhile and then you can mold it into shape."

"And that's all, Mammis?"

Victoria smiled. "Except for the decorations. That was always your favorite part."

"Yes," Daisy smiled. "I always loved forming the body and head and then adding the almond slivers for quills."

"It always reminds me so much of the hedgehogs my brothers would catch in England. Ah," she sighed, "those were good times."

"But my favorite is adding the cherry for the nose."

Victoria laughed. "And, if I recall, it was your favorite part to eat, also."

TWENTY-SEVEN

As spring blossoms appeared and the red maple flowered, Victoria could feel the throbbing of the earth, as it was reborn. It pulsed through her and she heard the robin's song in her heart. She felt the worms gyrating through the rich soil. She tasted the first greens of the year. And Prince came too.

She caught him next to her on the veranda while she sat out in the rocker in the sun. At first, she thought it was just the nibbling of the spring air around her face and ears. But she realized that it was stronger, more persistent, and more loving. She leaned back into the rocker and closed her eyes and she felt him settle into the chair next to her.

"Spring," he whispered.

"Yes, Prince, it's all starting again."

Startled by the sound of a carriage going by the old Farmer's Hotel, they both looked up to watch as it headed down Connecticut Avenue towards the river. Then peace was restored and they sat quietly together. Out of the corner of her eye, Victoria saw Prince's rocker, which had been moving slightly, come to a halt as he napped.

The door opened and Noah stepped onto the veranda, smiled at Victoria, and started to sit down next to her. The look on her face stopped him mid-air, but then she felt Prince hovering behind her and knew that the chair was now vacant, so she gestured for Noah to sit.

"Mammis, we're starting to plan for our summer travels."

Victoria's heart leapt to her throat, as she remembered the terrifying events of the previous year and the faintness of Prince's presence when they were away. "No, I can't go."

"We thought you might feel that way. We were thinking about some shorter trips." He paused to see her reaction. She waited to feel a message from Prince, but there was none.

"Maybe a few weeks with Sonny and William. Or in Hoosick Falls with Martha and her family."

She still felt nothing from Prince, so she hedged. "I don't know if that will work. Besides, that won't be good for business, will it? Horses are down south, not in Bridgeport or Hoosick Falls."

Noah nodded. "We've considered that. Richard was thinking about working with some of the finer horses along the Hudson."

"Racing," she spat out. "It will come to no good."

Noah sighed and rose from the chair. "We need to come up with something. We can't stay here and we can't leave you here alone."

"Can't leave me here alone," she muttered as Noah returned to the house. "Nonsense. You'll be with me, won't you?"

The rocker began to move slightly again.

Victoria decided to visit the stables later that week. She picked her way slowly across the back of the Hotel and stood, observing, in one of the doorways. She saw a number of horses that would make good sales as either sturdy workhorses or fine carriage animals. She walked inside, peering into stalls and assessing the stock. At first, it was with the eye of a seller. But then, when she saw the gray mare, she realized why she was there. It was the spitting image of Beatrix, who had died shortly after Prince had, and she gasped and simultaneously felt a second heart beat near her.

"It's just like her, isn't it?" Prince whispered.

Victoria could barely speak, so she nodded. She briefly wondered if Prince needed spoken words or if he could read her mind. He draped his arm around her.

"We had fine times with her."

She nodded again.

A clattering in the corner distracted her and old Joe emerged with a shovel and rake to do the daily chores.

"Morning, Princess, I didn't expect to see the likes of you in here."

"Good morning, Joe. I was just looking."

He glanced at the Percheron and back to Victoria before continuing on his business.

A few weeks later, she felt the urging, the clarity that it was the time of year to check the duck eggs, a seasonal force that she couldn't ignore, any more than she could disregard the pulsing in her veins. She had learned that it was best for her to just disappear on her activities instead of mentioning it to any of the family. For they invariably had a reason why she shouldn't do what she wanted to do.

The morning was soft and gentle, as she walked quietly from the old Farmer's Hotel. She stopped to pick up one of Martha's egg baskets, noting her daughter's excellent weaving. She wished that Martha had more time to continue with her work.

Once outside, Victoria veered quickly away from the house so no one would notice her from a window. Before long, she was walking briskly towards the meadows, flooded high with the spring freshet. With each step she felt joy from Prince's increasing presence. She soon reached the edge of the marsh and sat to watch and felt his soft whisper in her ear and a sense of an arm around her.

Before long, a movement caught her eye and she watched the drake circle around until he reached his mate sitting on a nest. Victoria made note of the surrounding grasses and a protruding stump as a landmark. Giving the air next to her a smile, she slowly rose and started her approach. Stepping from hummock to hummock, carrying her egg basket, Victoria made her way to the nest. Pausing about ten feet away, she could clearly see the female duck well hidden in the nest depression. Slowly and gently, she approached until the duck sensed her presence. Giving a squawk, the hen rose and backed away from the looming predator.

"Ten eggs," she said. "I'll take five. You will lay more," she gestured to the duck.

When she was finished gathering the eggs, Victoria made her way back to her resting spot.

"Good work," said Prince. "Too bad I can't eat your eggs once you cook them. I miss that."

Victoria laughed and settled to watch. Soon she saw another male and watched as he unknowingly gave away the location of his mate. She repeated the process and returned with another four eggs.

"I'll try for a few more," she said. "I need enough to feed our brood."

After another hour, Victoria had amassed two dozen eggs and, by then, her feet were drenched. The sun had disappeared behind some clouds, and she started to feel the chill of the snowmelt-fed water. She checked the basket and protected the eggs with rushes from the marsh. When she stood up, the world started to spin and she sat back down in a heap. After a few minutes, she tried again.

"That's better." She looked around and was disoriented. "I thought the road was over here. But I don't see anything." She started in the opposite direction towards the woods surrounding the marsh. Each step dampened her feet even more and, at one point, she slid off the tussock, although she caught herself before falling too far. She kept stumbling towards the woods until she could barely lift her feet. Suddenly, an arm steering her at a different angle and she let Prince direct her to the road. When she finally reached dry land, she collapsed in the brush.

"I wouldn't have made it without you, Prince." She checked the egg basket to be certain that its contents were intact and waited a few more minutes to gather her strength. She felt the chill of her feet moving up her legs and her teeth started to chatter. She was lifted by a gentle hand that directed her home.

"Where have you been? What happened?" cried Daisy when Victoria entered the kitchen.

Wordlessly, Victoria handed her the egg basket and went upstairs for dry clothing. Although she rubbed her feet and legs, there was a chill that wouldn't leave her. If Prince hadn't been with her, she might not have lived. If the family traveled in the summer, she might have to leave Prince behind. She trembled at that thought, being alone, without his guidance. That she would not do.

Victoria could sense that her children were ready to start traveling. She saw signs of it every day. Today, when she looked out the window, she noticed that Belcher was checking the *vardo* wheels and looking for damage to the caravan covering. The day before, she saw one of the women washing all the summer clothes.

The days were getting longer as they moved towards the vernal equinox.

Now, the beauty of nature was painful, tearing her in two, leaving her uncertain as to what to do. Stay or leave? No, she was certain that she wouldn't leave, but her children would hear nothing of it.

"No, Mammis, you cannot stay here," shouted Richard.

"Mammis, we want you to be safe," said Noah patiently.

They had been through this many times in the past month. The river was down, and she knew they would not wait much longer. She herself felt the urge to move, but not without Prince.

"Mammis, we are giving you a week's notice to get ready," announced Richard at breakfast the next morning. "We are leaving the first of June."

Only a week. What could she possibly do in a week? What would change? Her heart beat so quickly she couldn't catch her breath. With difficulty, she went out on the veranda to sit and rock. Prince sat with her but he had no advice or suggestions. He just silently rocked with her.

"Mammis, it's dinner time. Come in and eat."

She just sat there, ignoring the voice. The door opened and a small child, little Richard, toddled out and sat on her lap. She cupped him to her and stroked his curls but she still didn't get up. Martha came to get Richard and looked at her.

"Mammis, it's getting cold. Please come in now."

Victoria felt the chill in her bones and decided she would be more comfortable in bed. Wearily she rose and went upstairs.

The next morning was overcast and Victoria decided that she would stay in bed all day. She didn't see any point at all in getting up, so she curled up on her side and rested.

Mid-morning, there was a knock on the door.

"Mammis, I made you some eggs."

Dear Daisy wouldn't let her go hungry, Victoria knew. "Thank you, dear, but I am not hungry."

"Mammis, even if you don't eat, you know that your sons will carry you to the *vardo* to leave next week. So you may as well have something."

Victoria turned to face her daughter. "I'm fine. Right now, I do not want to eat." Victoria patted her hand. "Don't worry about me."

She heard Daisy's footsteps retreat back downstairs. She settled down under the covers and slept.

TWENTY-EIGHT

She woke suddenly and felt Prince cupped behind her. She could feel him breathing in her ear, kissing the side of her cheek. His hand caressed her face and then moved down her body. She grew warmer with his touch and rose to meet his exploring hand. Behind her, she could feel him poking her and she turned to welcome him.

But he was gone. Not in bed with her. She opened her eyes wide but it was dark. She heard noise at the window, gentle tapping. Was it rain on the panes? The noise grew louder and she could see Prince's hand waving to her, gesturing for her to come outside. He disappeared and she got up from the bed to look. It was dark, there was no moon, but there seemed to be a circle of light heading toward the stables. She heard horses whinnying and a pulse of air whispering, "Come, my love, join me."

Victoria turned from the window and reached for her clothes. Although it was pitch dark, she could sense where they were and dressed herself. She remembered that it was cool and added the silk brocade shawl that had been her grandmother's. She sat on the bed and put on shoes. Suddenly, she remembered that they had been locking her in the room and hoped they had forgotten. She thought it had been days, maybe months, since they had needed to do that.

She moved quietly toward the door and tried the knob. It opened easily and she let out her breath, which she hadn't realized she'd been holding. Prince was knocking at the window again. "I'm coming," she whispered.

Victoria closed the door quietly behind her and stood in the hallway, listening. No one else was stirring. She couldn't believe that they didn't hear Prince and his horse outside, as they were making such a racket. He never was one for patience, she recalled wryly. But she heard no one else and started down the stairs. One step at a time, as Prince rattled the window.

When she finally got downstairs, she went to the back door and let herself out. She faced the stables, which were bathed in a brilliant unnatural light. As she started walking towards them, she heard her window slam closed. Oh, dear, she moaned, surely they would hear that. But she had no time to react, for, from the sky above the house came the magnificent gray Percheron, Beatrix. Mounted on its back was Prince, still wearing his burial suit. He flashed a smile at Victoria and waved with his arm, "Follow me," as he charged toward the stable. She ran quickly after them, watching him avoid getting tangled in the limbs of the large trees in the backyard. She shook her head at his flirting with danger. Always the one trying to get as close to the fire as possible, she remembered, a smile playing on her face. She was running lightly, breathless at the sight of her Prince, and saw he had stopped in front of the stable. She had just about reached him, when he turned and yelled out, "Come quickly!" Several of the horses were snorting and kicking their stalls and Victoria heard the window of her room slam closed again. She glanced back at the house and noticed a flickering light at one of the windows. She realized they had awakened Richard.

But Prince captured her attention again, with his urgent cry, "Come, Princess, up here." She felt the air around her move and lift her up, up, into the air and onto the horse in front of Prince. He grabbed her and held her close and urged the horse forward. It leapt, large prancing steps, and they were airborne.

"My dear, you took so long," he whispered in her ear. The sound of the air rushing past her filled her other ear and her hair, losing its braid, streamed behind her. She pulled her shawl tighter and felt him tuck his head into the crook of her neck and nuzzle her. She leaned back into his large frame and relaxed as she hadn't been able to do in so long, so many months since he had left.

It was dark, pitch black, no moon or stars. They were traveling low to the ground and she could sense shapes below her. Occasionally she could hear the moo of a startled cow or the confused movement of a surprised herd. She wasn't certain if she and Prince were covering much distance. Although she could feel the wind against her cheek, it was as though she and time were standing still.

Suddenly she heard the low "who-whoing" of an owl and she

knew for certain that this was the end and beginning for her. The noise grew louder and she was momentarily confused. Certainly no owl could be that large to make that noise. But from the dark came an enormous bright light with the "who-who" growing louder and louder. The train, the train was running and it was at the crossing, she realized.

Prince was tapping her on the shoulder. "Think we can jump this train?" he asked. His eyes sparkled with the thrill of a challenge. Victoria nodded, although she had no idea about the capabilities of her husband or his horse in their current state. She could envision them traveling on the train, starting life anew at some western outpost across this immense country. Prince smiled and leaned forward, cupping his body around hers.

"Here we go," he yelled, as he urged the horse directly into the window of the passenger car. She heard it shatter from their impact; it turned dark for a brief moment and then quite light. She felt Prince inside her, she inside him, and all was well.

EPILOGUE

Noah, startled by a small sound, awoke in his chair. He had thought he'd been awake all night in the sitting room with the solid white oak casket that held his mother, but apparently not. For a brief second, he feared that it was her *muló*, but he then saw a curly dark head peeking around the door that was slightly ajar. He recognized Martha's little Richard and waved him away.

The brothers had been taking turns during the night, while the girls were covering the daytime hours. Noah half-closed his eyes, as the coffin's shiny silver trim sparkled in the sunlight. The undertaker had done an outstanding job of reassembling her body within her clothing, but the damage was still evident and her memory was protected by the lid's closure. Flowers cascaded around her and Noah thought how much they would have pleased his mother. He was having a difficult time thinking of her as gone, no longer with them. He kept wanting to tell her things, like, "Look, Mammis, the coffin is lined with the same material as your grandmother's shawl that you loved. I had to argue with Richard about it, but I knew you'd like it."

For the past three days, family had been arriving: his uncles' families from Somerville, his sisters from Massachusetts and Rhode Island, New York and Pennsylvania. Even Prince's two sons with Mary Defiance had come from Ohio, out of respect, they claimed. The old Farmer's Hotel was packed and the yard was covered with *vardos*. As was the custom, life was at a standstill, waiting for everyone to arrive. Just as people had swarmed to their house when Prince had died, they came again.

Noah heard people stirring and the front door open. Within minutes, there was a gentle tap on the sitting room door and Reverend McVey entered. He bowed his head, hat in hand, and stood silently for several minutes. After sighing, he looked at Noah and said, "It sorrows me to be here again so soon. Is everything ready for the funeral?"

"I believe so," replied Noah. "Richard and Belcher were checking with the cemetery."

"We will begin at two o'clock then."

Noah nodded as Martha joined them. Glancing at the flowers overflowing around the casket, she wailed, "Oh, Mammis, they are so pretty!" After a few sobs, she caught her breath and faced them. "Hallo, Reverend." He nodded at her.

"Go stretch your legs," she suggested to her brother.

Noah excused himself and threaded his way through throngs of family assembled in the house. He finally reached the back door and started towards the stable. Even the yard was filled with family and he noticed that members of the community were standing in the front of the Hotel on this fine May day. "Mammis," he whispered, "we have a crowd for you." In fact, there were so many people that, for a few moments, he was overwhelmed and could barely see or breathe.

Escaping, he continued to the barn to check on the hearse and be certain that his wishes had been followed. He wanted two white horses, while Richard kept pushing for black. "Richard," he had said, "you know how Mammis was haunted by those black horses from Wash's funeral. We must use white."

Noah relaxed when he saw the two white horses and noticed that, with their silver bridles, they matched perfectly. He thought of her and Prince, the way they harmonized, even if they didn't look that much alike, and thought it was fitting.

He watched the grooms from the stable bringing around a full dozen hacks that would be part of the procession to the cemetery. They lined them up near the hearse and tried to calm the horses. One gray mare kept bucking and pulling forward to the front of the group.

By now, the wailing and moaning of the relatives reached such a level that Noah could hear them from the stable and he hurried back to the Hotel.

The tall monument in the Center Cemetery was all too familiar. The words of Reverend McVey droned on, as Noah fingered the small pouch in his pocket. Earlier, he had gone to his mother's room and had noticed her collection of shells. He didn't know why his mother had them, but he remembered her touching the pouch during times of trouble and wanted to send them off with her.

When the minister finished, before they covered her casket with dirt, Noah leaned down and placed the pouch on the mass of flowers almost filling the grave to the top. He noticed Richard raise an eyebrow but he chose not to look directly at his brother.

"Mammis," he whispered under his breath, "whatever this means to you, wherever they came from, may they comfort you."

The family returned home after the burial. Noah began to arrange wood in the cooking area outside, while Martha went upstairs to gather their mother's clothing. Richard, coming from the stables, sauntered over to the fire that Noah had started.

"Burning her things?"

"Of course."

"We didn't do that with Dadrus. We kept the chariot."

"Maybe that's why Mammis lost her senses. Maybe his *muló* wouldn't have haunted her if we had burned everything."

"You don't truly believe that, do you?"

Noah looked briefly at his brother, censored his response, and continued making the fire. Martha and her sisters returned outside, each holding a bundle of her mother's possessions.

"Is that everything?" asked Noah.

"I think so," said Martha. "Although I couldn't find her Princess coin."

"The one she got on her second trip to America?" asked Belcher, who had joined them.

Martha nodded.

"Her Princess coin," repeated Noah. There was a long pause.

"Oh, her Princess coin," said Richard. "I put it in the coffin this morning."

Noah tightened his grip on the bag of clothing he was holding. He silently begged his mother to keep him from striking his brother on the day of her funeral. He asked for a sign. Was Richard telling the truth?

Noah looked up at the blue sky filled with puffy clouds moving slowly across the horizon. Meanwhile the flames grew higher as the others placed clothing on the fire. Ashes floated in the air and then he saw it: there above them, above the ashes of his mother's clothes, he saw a cloud in the shape of a horseshoe. Like his father's diamond pin that was the harbinger of good luck. It wasn't upside-down, but he hoped that would do.

AUTHOR'S NOTE

Caravan of Dreams was inspired by a snippet in the *Today in History* section of my local paper included at the start of this book. Unaware of gypsies in my native state, I began my research to find cultural details about Roma (gypsies in general) and Romanichal (gypsies from England, Scotland, and Wales). I was fortunate to connect with Victoria's great-granddaughter, who shared historical research and family lore she had been gathering for many years. The core of my novel was based on her factual information (birth and death certificates), newspaper articles, and genealogical records. A great-great granddaughter, who had been raised in the Gypsy tradition, later corroborated my cultural content.

As can be imagined, these factual data only went so far in developing a complete picture of the Williams family in Connecticut in the 1800s. I have taken creative liberties to add color and richness to their story. For example, Morris's death certificate provided the date, location, and cause of his death. A newspaper article reported other members of the family were also sick. Chapter Fourteen demonstrates my artistic license in portraying what may have happened, the community response, and its impact on Victoria.

Likewise, I used Emma's elopement with the Squires boy to expand on the issue of marrying outsiders. Although the couple did run away to wed, the Squires were a prominent Romanichal family and no disrespect was intended to portray them as otherwise.

Any representations of Williams family members' personalities, interactions, or conversations are completely based on my imagination. My intention is to provide a glimpse into a little known and misunderstood culture and sometimes maligned people who helped shape the history of our country. Follow me back to those times to gain a better appreciation and understanding of the Romanichal (who, by the way, are still present in twenty-first century Connecticut) and, of course, to enjoy a good story.

I thank Rosa Roman for her encouragement; early readers (The Novel Group, JC, and EG) for editing and critiques; Kay Lapin Hammerson for the title; Curt and Ruth (Smith-Worthington Saddlery Co.), Judy Hunt (Shelburne Museum), and Marcy Klattenberg (mushrooms) for technical details; GP (Golden Lamb Buttery, Shelburne Museum, and Mystic Seaport) and Joe Diedrich (Hoosick, NY) for field work assistance; and Alan White for continuing to be my beta reader.

I am grateful to Lisa Wells for finding me and offering insight into family historical events and cultural context. My biggest and warmest thanks goes to Ruth "Marty" Lambert Speed, without whom this book would have been a shadow of what it is now. Her support and trust in my telling of her family story has been a true gift of friendship.

ABOUT THE AUTHOR

BETH LAPIN has been writing and publishing since elementary school. She has two previously published novels, *To Say Goodbye* (a Wings ePress best seller) and its sequel, *The Light Gets In*.

Born and raised in Connecticut, Beth has lived in Puerto Rico, Massachusetts, Maryland, and all the states that begin with "C." She enjoys kayaking, hiking, contradancing, and family genealogy. She currently lives in her home state.

www.BethLapin.com